The Mountain in the Sea

The Mountain in the Sea

Ray Nayler

MCD FARRAR, STRAUS AND GIROUX NEW YORK

MCD
Farrar, Straus and Giroux
120 Broadway, New York 10271

Printed in the United States of America
First edition, 2022

Illustrations by the author.

Library of Congress Cataloging-in-Publication Data
Names: Nayler, Ray, author.
Title: The mountain in the sea / Ray Nayler.
Description: First edition. | New York : MCD ; Farrar, Straus and Giroux, 2022.
Identifiers: LCCN 2022022851 | ISBN 9780374605957 (hardcover)
Subjects: LCGFT: Science fiction. | Thrillers (Fiction) | Novels.
Classification: LCC PS3614.A946 M68 2022 | DDC 813/.6—dc23/
eng/20220520
LC record available at https://lccn.loc.gov/2022022851

Designed by Abby Kagan

10 9 8 7 6 5 4 3 2 1

For Anya and Lydia

I

Qualia

There is no silence in the living nervous system. An electrical symphony of communication streams through our neurons every moment we exist. We are built for communication.

Only death brings silence.

—Dr. Ha Nguyen, *How Oceans Think*

1

NIGHT. DISTRICT THREE of the Ho Chi Minh Autonomous Trade Zone.

The plastic awning of the café streamed with rain. Under its shelter, wreathed in kitchen steam and human chatter, waiters wove between tables with steaming bowls of soup, glasses of iced coffee, and bottles of beer.

Beyond the wall of rain, electric motorbikes swept past like luminescent fish.

Better not to think of fish.

Lawrence concentrated his attention instead on the woman across the table, wiping her chopsticks with a wedge of lime. The color-swarm of the abglanz identity shield masking her face shifted and wavered.

Like something underwater . . .

Lawrence dug his nails into his palm. "I'm sorry—does that thing have another setting?"

The woman made an adjustment. The abglanz settled to a bland construct of a female face. Lawrence could make out the faint outline of her real face, drifting below the surface.

Drifting . . .

"I don't usually use this setting." The oscillations of the abglanz flattened the woman's inflection. "The faces are uncanny. Most people prefer the blur."

She brought her chopsticks to her mouth. The noodles sank into the glitchy surface of the digital mask's lips. Inside was the shadow of another set of lips and teeth.

Don't look at her. Just begin. "Okay. My story. That's what we're here for. I came to the archipelago ten . . . no, eleven years ago now. Before that I worked for a dive place in Nha Trang. There were only two dive shops on Con Dao when I arrived—one at a fancy hotel for Westerners, and another little shop that wasn't doing well. I bought it out. Paid almost nothing. Con Dao was a sleepy place—underpopulated, undervisited. Locals thought it was haunted."

"Haunted?"

"The whole place used to be a prison. The graveyards are filled with generations of dissidents tortured to death by one government after another. A bad place to start a business, right? Maybe. But it was a good place if you just wanted to get by, to live. Sure, it had its problems—lots of them. Technically, the Global Conservation Park covered the entire archipelago, both land and water. Zero fishing or hunting allowed. There was even a UN watchdog organization that would show up once a year, write a report. But the reality was, there were always fishing boats coming in, tangling trawling nets in the reefs, using cyanide and dynamite. And the park rangers were all corrupt. How could they not be, with the salaries they were being paid? They sold turtle eggs, reef fish, whatever they could get their hands on. The locals were in on it—spearfishing, free diving for shellfish. Son, my assistant, had been a free diver."

"And where is he now?"

"I told you before—I don't know. We lost touch after the evacuation."

"He was the one with you on the boat? The day of the incident?"

"Yeah. I was coming to that." *Avoiding it, more like.* "The wreck is a steel-hulled Thai freighter, sixty meters long. It went down late in the twentieth century. It's the only penetrable wreck you can dive in Vietnam. It's in just twenty meters of water, but the conditions there are usually bad. Strong currents, poor visibility. It's only for customers who know what they are doing. You don't get many customers like that on Con Dao, so we hadn't been out there in years. It was a morning dive. Off-season. Lousy visibility, maybe two meters. But the guy wanted a wreck dive. So we got in the water and worked our way down. It was just me and him."

Lawrence paused. "I keep making it more dramatic than it is. But it wasn't dramatic. It was routine. There were squid and cobia bumping into us. Visibility was awful. We were almost at the wreck when I decided to call it off. But when I turned around, he was gone. That's normal, though. You lose people in low-vis water all the time. You just stay put. If you go looking for them, it's easy to get disoriented.

"But after five minutes, I started to worry. I traced my way back along the freighter's rail. He knew what he was doing, I kept telling myself. He wouldn't have gone into the wreck without me. Was something wrong with his equipment? Had he decided to surface?

"I made my way up, expecting to find him bobbing there. I yelled to Son, on the boat, asking if he had seen him. Nothing. I made my way back down.

"I could feel panic coming on. The conditions down there were making it worse: mucky water, full of shapes. Fish swirling into my vision. Finally, I went inside the wreck. There was nowhere else he could be. Once I was inside, it didn't take long to find him. He wasn't far in: His body was trapped under a gangway inside the main cargo area. There was a gash in his temple. Fish were already making off with bits of flesh.

"I got him up to the surface. Son insisted on resuscitation. But I knew he was dead. He was dead when I found him."

"And in your opinion, how did he die?"

"It wasn't the cut—that was superficial. He drowned because something stole his regulator, his mask, his tank, everything. Once he lost his gear, he must have struck his head in a panic, lost consciousness. Without his mask and regulator, it wouldn't have taken long to die."

"And his regulator? The tank? The mask? Did you find them?"

The impassivity of the face like a blurred photograph, the tonelessness of the altered voice, brought Lawrence back to the island. To telling this story again and again. To the rangers, to the police, to the reporters. Accusations, disbelief—and, in the end, indifference.

"We never found them."

"But you searched the ship."

"No. I didn't. I lied about that."

"You lied?"

"I couldn't go back down there. I told the police we'd looked for his equipment, searched the whole vessel, but . . . I didn't look. I was afraid to. There was never a proper search."

She paused. "I see. And what did you do then?"

"The rival dive shop used the death to drive my customers away. My business began to fail. But in the end, it didn't matter. Three months after the incident, the evacuation began. For the record—I'm glad you guys bought the island. Now at least I know it will be protected. I knew every inch of Con Dao—every reef they destroyed, every fish they poached. It's better this way: Get everybody out, cordon off the whole archipelago. Defend it. That's the only way to protect it. I was one of the first to take your offer and leave. Generous compensation, a new start. It was lucky for me, maybe."

MAYBE. Walking away from the café in the rain, Lawrence wasn't so sure. The tamarind trees hissed in the wind. His poncho had a tear in the side of it, and he could feel a damp spot spreading through his clothes, cold on his skin.

"What did you see?" That was what they always asked him—the rangers, the police, the reporters. *What did you see?*

Nothing. He'd seen nothing. But he couldn't shake the feeling *something* had seen *him*.

And that feeling had followed him. He had been glad to leave the archipelago. But leaving wasn't enough—the feeling returned every time he thought of the ocean.

Con Dao had been his home—the first he had ever had. What happened at the ship took that from him. That was the story he had wanted to tell. But the woman from DIANIMA wouldn't have understood anyway.

Was she from DIANIMA? She had never said she was, had she?

It didn't matter. Maybe she was from DIANIMA, maybe she was from a rival company. The HCMATZ crawled with corporate spies, international conspiracies.

A week ago, he had gone to Vung Tau, to the ocean. He hadn't seen the water for months, had thought it was time to swim again. But he walked out before the waves reached his waist, got a drink at a beachside bar, then went back to his hotel room and checked out early.

He'd never dive again.

He would go back to his little apartment now in District Three, and continue to watch DIANIMA's "generous compensation" dwindle while he failed to find a way forward.

Two blocks from the café, the cramps hit him, sending him crashing to the pavement. A motorbike stopped. A stranger's hands on him. A woman's voice. "Are you all right? Sir?"

His vision was a hazy tunnel, filled with rain. "Call help. Please." Then he saw the injector in the woman's hand.

The motorbikes drifted past, outlines distorted by rain ponchos covering bikes and riders. The rain fell into Lawrence's open, staring eyes.

He was there again. The ship. Murky water full of shapes . . . blurred shapes his mind kept making into something else . . .

We came from the ocean, and we only survive by carrying salt water with us all our lives—in our blood, in our cells. The sea is our true home. This is why we find the shore so calming: we stand where the waves break, like exiles returning home.

—Dr. Ha Nguyen, *How Oceans Think*

2

THE DRONE HEXCOPTER'S LANDING LIGHTS, their beams filled with windblown rain, panned over the ocean chop. They cut through a span of mangroves and flooded the airport tarmac.

There were no lights anywhere on the ground. The ruin of a runway slanted across most of a narrow neck of the island. The helicopter landing circle was a faded smear. Ancient planes rotted against a black tree line. The plastic siding of the main building was peeled away like scales torn from a dead fish.

The hexcopter swung into final descent. It twisted and settled with a lurch, indifferent to human comfort but efficient. The rotors cut off. The doors winged open.

Ha heard the insect cacophony of the jungle, the hooting call-and-response of macaques. Rain blew sideways into the pod. She hauled her gear from the storage compartment. The drone's engines ticked, cooling.

There was a watery halo of headlamps between trees: her welcoming party. The drone's running lights shut off. Now Ha saw the full moon, half-occluded by a smear of cirrus clouds. Cumulus clouds hovered low, watering the island's tropical forests.

Ha breathed in, closed her eyes, opened them, adjusting her vision to the darkness. The hexcopter's comms squawked. "Ground pickup incoming. Move away from the copter."

Ha gathered her bags and ran for the shelter of the airport overhang. The hexcopter's lights snapped back on. It lifted off the tarmac and swung away at an angle of attack and speed severe enough to knock a passenger unconscious. It was gone in seconds, enveloped in clouds.

The ground transport was armored, ex-military: a self-driving troop carrier with hardened porthole windows, oversized airless honeycomb tires.

Inside, it was upgraded for comfort. The passenger cabin was padded to dampen the noise and jolt of armor. The car's fuel-cell engine ran silent enough, but the transmission whined and sent weird vibrations through the compartment. Ha dimmed the cabin lights.

The porthole's thick strata of glass and polycarbonate distorted the scene outside. Through it, Ha watched the undulating barrier of jungle encroaching the narrow road. Ruined walls of rubble studded abbreviated clearings, structures that could have been fortresses once. Or mills, or factories. Anything. The full moon cast waveforms on the sea's surface.

The car entered the dark town clamped between forest and ocean. The heavy red-tiled roofs of the French colonial buildings dripped with rain, their stucco walls stained with tropical damp. Their shutters were closed, their gardens overrun with vine and moss. Here and there, a brutalist Communist building broke the sequence: a high school, the Communist Party administrative building. Concrete monsters damp with lichen, colorless in the night.

In the daylight the deserted town would be composed of scabrous, peeling pastel tones. Ficus trees, their trunks painted a fading white, lined streets scattered with vegetal debris—leaves, fallen branches, seedpods, and fruit.

The transport swung out onto a boulevard flanked by a seawall. Its headlamps panned across two monkeys fighting, like human children, over a dubious treasure. At the edge of the town, the houses petered out to sag-roofed shacks already half-dismantled by vines.

The road followed the coast. On the left, the landscape dropped to rocks and ocean waves swarming in moonlight. The black backs of the archipelago's smaller islands humped in the water. The main island's spine rose to the right of the road, furred with trees.

Flood lamps pinned the roofs of a pagoda against the hillside, suggesting life on the evacuated archipelago. But lighting the structure was probably an automated municipal habit. A beacon for tourists who would never return.

The research station was on the territory of an abandoned hotel—a white six-story structure built in a bad-location lee of the island's windiest point. The hotel rose from the surrounding scrub, backlit by flood lamps. The side of the structure facing the road was in shadow, its windows dark. An access road led down to a security perimeter of double fencing flossed with razor wire.

The fencing was bright and new, but the hotel must have been abandoned long before the island was evacuated. Torn curtains bled through broken windows on the upper floors. Ribbons of damp and mold streaked the façade.

The transport came to a halt in front of a double gate.

A figure in a rain poncho separated from the structure and crossed to the gate. It slid the first gate aside. The transport moved forward into a holding area. The first gate was closed behind it, the second one opened. The transport drove through, into a space behind the hotel, a terrace of broken terra-cotta tiles scattered with the dead fronds of the palm trees, alien to the island, that lined the hotel grounds.

The terrace was dominated by an overdesigned swimming pool filled with algae and weeds. It had probably once been one of those saltwater pools that were so popular—letting hotel guests swim in the ocean without really swimming in it. Something in the pool startled at the sight of the transport and retreated into the water.

Two mobile research units, standard-shipping-container-sized, had been dropped near the pool by a cargo drone. They looked like industrial pool cabanas.

The transport door slid open. The interior filled with floodlit sparks of rain. The poncho-clad figure leaned in. A woman's face, hood-shadowed. High, wide cheekbones, eyes uptilted at their edges, dark. Rain streamed down her cheeks. She spat out a sentence in a language Ha did not know. A bland, authoritative female voice, like a train announcer's, was then broadcast over the woman's voice, speaking from a weather- and shock-proof translator unit clamped to her collar:

"You are welcome to Con Dao Forward Research Post. My name is Altantsetseg. I am hired help protector. Now taking your bags. Weather is shitting rain."

Ha blinked. Wanted, for a moment, to break into hysterical laughter: it had been a long trip.

Altantsetseg stared at her, said a sentence in her language like a fence of consonants. "Translator not fornicating working right?"

"No. It's working fine. Close enough."

"Then we are moving."

The woman towered over Ha. She was two meters tall or more. Ha saw the rifle now, the short, no-nonsense barrel slung over Altantsetseg's shoulder.

It was raining harder. Without the whine of the transport and the thickness of its armor drowning out the sound, Ha could hear the wind hissing in the palms, the croaks and cries of animals in the island dark, the waves on a beach out of sight beneath the hotel's terrace—all of it washed in the rain's static.

They quick-walked, bent over to minimize the drops slashing into their faces. There were a few lights on in the hotel, on this side, on the ground and second floors. A broken cement urn propped open a glass lobby door.

Inside, Altantsetseg led Ha through the deserted lobby. Moldering chairs stacked on tables, damp overstuffed divans clustered in long-silent conversation circles. A few tables stood in a cleared space in the center of the room. Gear cases were scattered around them, a field kitchen, a coffee machine. Electronics. A bit of habitation in the cavernous hall of synthetic marble.

Ha's room was on the floor above. It was a king suite that smelled of damp and disuse but was clean. Altantsetseg dropped Ha's bags inside the door and left.

Ha had been longing for hours now for a shower. Instead, she collapsed on the bed, not bothering to undress first. Someone, at least, had put clean sheets on it.

She dreamed of the cuttlefish again.

At times, when a cephalopod is resting, its skin will flow through color and textural displays that appear unconscious—as if the electrochemical flux of its thoughts were projected onto its surface. In this state it is truly like a mind floating, unsheathed by flesh, in the open ocean.

—Dr. Ha Nguyen, *How Oceans Think*

3

IN THE DREAM, Ha never saw the cuttlefish as they were in their prime—bright and luminous, streaked with kaleidoscopic color change, arranging their arms in semaphores of threat or curiosity. No. In the dream she descended, caged in the white noise of her respirator. Down into water clouded calcitic-gray. Down into water hazed with ink, defiled with drifting webs of darkness. Down to a silt bottom strewn with stones.

Cuttlefish eggs were scattered in the fissures of the rocks. The young inside the eggs glowed, wisps of light trapped behind the membranes of their shells.

The eggs should not have been left exposed like this in the silt: cuttlefish hung their precious eggs from the underside of rocks, in protected places. Something here had gone horribly wrong.

A giant female cuttlefish drifted above the eggs, guarding them. Ha had not seen her at first in the water curtained with ink and silt. Ha jerked back, startled, but the cuttlefish did not respond. It floated there, facing Ha but not seeing her.

The cuttlefish was dying. Her body was white, patched in

places with a leprous rust. Without her skin's healthy dance of pattern and color, she looked naked and vulnerable.

Several of her arms were torn away. One feeding tentacle drifted limp in the weak current.

The rocks here formed a loose circle, like a broken castle keep. Overhangs called to mind shattered tower floors. Crevices were archers' slits. Ha saw three more cuttlefish, under a terrace of stone. They, too, had lost much of their skin, and all were missing arms. They floated, cephalopod specters, sickly-pearl, watching. Fans of dull red and brown crisscrossed the skin left on them, a map of dead connections.

Then the first cuttlefish Ha had seen swam down to the eggs. Her ripped fins were weak. She swam like a ghost ship tiding into dock under torn sails. As Ha watched, the cuttlefish stroked an egg with one intact arm. Patches on her skin glowed a weak yellow. The movement and the color seemed to take an extraordinary effort.

Inside the egg, a dim light flickered in answer.

The cuttlefish began to rise now. Ha swam up with it. As they overtook the other three, hovering under their outcropping of stone, Ha felt something pass between them: a slight shiver. Of recognition? Of acknowledgment? Of goodbye? The female cuttlefish spiraled up through the water column, releasing ink in sputtering contrails like smoke from the engines of a crashing plane—a plane that rose instead of falling.

She and Ha broke the surface together, into the world of explosive sunlight, of chaotic sound and churn.

Though the cuttlefish was motionless and Ha knew she was dead, she swam to her and held her, took off a glove and stroked her battered head, its torn appendages.

Above, seagulls gyred and screamed, waiting for Ha to

abandon the meal they had spotted. Ha swam toward her dive boat, cradling the cuttlefish like a drowned child.

Ha woke up with her face streaked with tears, as she always did.

This vision she had in her sleep was both dream and memory. It was impossible for her to tell which elements were which anymore. She had been there, in that place, in real life. But the ink had been thicker, hadn't it? Ink like a curtain that had battered her back. She had been to that place of solitude, seen the three senescent cuttlefish drifting, monklike, under the shattered eaves of their castle. But the eggs had not glowed. That was not possible. And there had been no dying female, drifting to the surface like a downed plane.

Her mind returned, again and again, to her memories of that place. And every time her mind returned to it, the scene changed. Was it becoming corrupted in the remembering, moving further away from the truth with each successive iteration? Or was it, in fact, approaching the truth a little more each time?

"You are crying. Did you have the dream again?"

Ha sat up. Without even remembering she had done it, she must have unfolded the terminal the night before, placed it on the nightstand. Or had she set it to unfold on its own, on a timer?

It stood there, icosahedral on its origami leg stands, light flowing from its oculus. And in the light of the oculus was Kamran, standing at the foot of the bed, drinking a cup of what could only be coffee.

She could see the outline of the door through the collar of the shirt he was wearing. She could see the carpet's ghost through his shoes.

"Yes. The same dream."

"You have to let go of it, Ha. Let it be in the past. There was nothing you could have done."

There were things she could have done, and she knew it. There were also things she could have *not* done. But Kamran would never allow her to take the blame for anything—would never even allow her to take responsibility. It wasn't worth going over it with him again—it would all lead back to her having to "let go of it."

Instead, she changed the subject.

"Where are you?"

"In the lab."

"It's after two in the morning there! What are you doing working?"

Kamran shrugged. "Please stop pestering me about my vampirism. How was your trip?"

"Long. And there was a storm when we were leaving the Ho Chi Minh Autonomous Trade Zone. The drone pilot was an insensitive bastard. I threw up making the crossing to Con Dao."

"Did you have a chance to meet the woman herself?"

"Dr. Mínervudóttir-Chan? In Ho Chi Minh? No. She's off in the SF-SD Axis, consolidating a buyout of coastal research institutions. That's what her Sub-4 told me, anyway. That, and nothing else. Everything is mysterious. Either that, or people don't know what is going on themselves. The Sub-4 told me the Team Lead on Con Dao would brief me when I got here."

"Have they?"

"I haven't met them yet." Ha was up and moving now, digging through her bags for clean clothes. She stepped through Kamran's leg.

"Sorry."

"Barely felt it," Kamran said.

"I have to tell you about the security officer who met me last night."

"Yes. I can't wait to hear about them," Kamran said. "But not now. You are rushed. I can see it in your face. You need to get settled in there, find your bearings. And I need to exploit this coffee buzz."

"What you need to do is go home and sleep. Are you avoiding the apartment?"

Kamran glanced away. "Perhaps."

"Well, don't get so sentimental that you start sleeping under the lab tables."

"Go take a shower. You look dirty. Your hair is all greasy."

"Thanks. Such a charmer."

"Always."

Kamran flickered out without saying goodbye, as was his habit.

We understand the encoding of genetic sequences, the folding of proteins to construct the cells of the body, and even a good deal about how epigenetic switches control these processes. And yet we still do not understand what happens when we read a sentence. Meaning is not neuronal calculus in the brain, or the careful smudges of ink on a page, or the areas of light and dark on a screen. Meaning has no mass or charge. It occupies no space—and yet meaning makes a difference in the world.

—Dr. Ha Nguyen, *How Oceans Think*

4

IN THE MAKESHIFT KITCHEN, Altantsetseg sat eating a hard-boiled egg. The table was cluttered with the elements of a disassembled rifle, oil rags, several terminals, and various electronic components. Altantsetseg was in dark blue coveralls. There were Velcro strips for identification insignia or patches on the arms of the coveralls and above the breast pockets, but no patches. Her hair was cut close to her head. It was black, with streaks running through it here and there of gray. She could have been thirty-five, forty, or over that. Thick hands, swollen by weather and work. A scattering of dark spots along the hairline on the left side of her face. They might have been mistaken for moles, but Ha had known war veterans before. She knew the spots were shrapnel scars.

The smell of fresh coffee managed to push back the scent in the lobby of gun oil, ozone, mold, and neglect. An overcast early light came through the windows, along with the salt-flesh smell of the sea. Altantsetseg indicated a bowl of eggs and a stack of toast near the coffee machine with a flick of her chin.

"Thanks." Ha poured coffee into one of a half dozen

semi-clean mugs. The heating element under the pot was no good: the coffee was lukewarm. She drank it off in a gulp. She didn't sit down, but grabbed an egg. Ha saw the translator unit on the table amid the still life of gear, eggshell, and crumbs.

"Team Lead?" Ha asked.

Altantsetseg squinted at her, then nodded, jerked a thumb in the direction of the terrace and beach.

"Good morning."

Altantsetseg shrugged, said a phrase that sounded to Ha like, "Sign igloo," and began rolling another egg on the table, breaking up the shell.

Ha reached into a small paper bag she was carrying and produced a macaroon. She placed it in front of Altantsetseg.

Altantsetseg regarded it, gave Ha a questioning look. Ha made exaggerated eating motions with her face.

"Macaroon." She pointed at herself. "I made them. A gift."

Altantsetseg stared at her with no change in her expression.

"Just kidding. I would never bake. I bought them in the Ho Chi Minh ATZ. But they are good."

She left Altantsetseg sitting there regarding the golden brown bolus of coconut with suspicion.

Ha crossed the cracked tiles of the hotel terrace, eating her egg. She could see the Team Lead: a tall, slender figure standing on the beach, facing away from her. Whatever was inhabiting the swimming pool shifted and plopped into the water as Ha passed.

The sea was calm. Its surface undulated, reflecting the pearl-gray and lemon haze of early light—like a curtain agitated by a breeze.

As Ha approached, the Team Lead turned.

And Ha stopped, almost tripping in the sand, practically dropping the paper bag she was carrying. The Team Lead's long hands held several shells of varying sizes. The Lead waited while Ha tried to compose herself.

Ha had watched an interview on a hotel room ceiling. One of those science-popularizing talking heads who did everything from kids' shows to documentaries, talking to this person . . . no . . . this *being*. Talking to Evrim.

The Team Lead that was standing before her was Evrim. Someone she had never expected, in her life, to encounter. You watched them on a bathroom mirror screen, on a ceiling, or the smeared window of a metro train. You watched people on-screen, beings that were shaped like people and spoke like people, but who lived *elsewhere*. They belonged to a floating world you would never enter. A world where things happened. A place unlike the mundane world you watched from. And you never thought you would meet them. Could meet them. But here Evrim was.

Evrim extended a hand.

"I am so pleased to meet you. I have been anticipating your arrival."

Ha shook the hand weakly.

"You can grip my hand more firmly," Evrim said. "Its development cost over two hundred and fifty million dollars. Much of the technology used in its construction is military, for prosthetic limbs. I don't think it will break." Evrim smiled at Ha. Ha felt herself searching for something in the eyes, something in the way Evrim stood. A difference. But she could not see it right away. The hand was cool—dawn-by-the-seaside cool—but with a warmth behind it, perfectly analogous to the internal warmth of a human hand. There were grains of sand on the fingers and palm, from the shells Evrim had been collecting. Ha realized she had been holding on to the hand for too long and released it.

"Ha."

"Yes. Dr. Ha Nguyen. I welcome you. And I see you know who I am."

Evrim turned to look at the sea again. Ha realized he was giving her a moment to recover from her shock. She was being rude. Evrim was taller than her, by thirty centimeters. His face was long, his limbs long. His proportions were even, beautifully neutral, a bit idealized. He had the kind of build that wore even fantastically ugly clothes well and so was used in mannequins for display and on catwalks. And Ha realized that she was referring to Evrim, in her mind, as he. As him—but Evrim was not that. He was . . . they were . . . what?

I see you know who I am.

Did she? What did she know? Ha's mind ran down the list of what Evrim was: Evrim was the only (allegedly) conscious being humankind had ever created. An android, finally realized. The most expensive single project, excepting space exploration, ever undertaken by a private firm. The moment, it was said repeatedly, that humanity had been waiting for: conscious life from nothing but the force of our own technological will.

And Evrim was also the inspiration for, and the target of, a series of hastily implemented laws that made his presence, and the creation of any further beings like him, illegal in most of the governing structures of the world, including every country under UN Directorate Governance. Evrim himself (herself? themself?)—Ha was irritated by her brain's gender provincialism—was illegal in most of the world.

Evrim's existence had shaken the globe with riots. Ha remembered the gunmen storming the DIANIMA headquarters in Moscow, the bombing of their offices in Paris. DIANIMA's vice president of engineering, blown up by a DNA-targeting flying mine on their yacht in the Caribbean. Ha remembered an image on the screen of a hotel ceiling of a man burning himself alive at the gates of the Vatican.

A man burned himself alive, simply because you exist. How must that feel?

What was most unsettling about Evrim to her, Ha realized, was that her brain was trying to slot them into a category into which they would not fit without distortion. If only she let go, pulled away from that desire to slot Evrim like a child's peg into a shaped hole in a board—to resolve them into a *gender.* Ha had been working internationally with other scientists. She had fallen into the habit of speaking (and thinking) in English—and to using the antiquated English third-person pronouns of "he" and "she."

She pushed her brain back to Turkish—her second language. There, the third-person pronoun "o" bore no gender marker. "O" presented no problems. It could stand for the English "he," "she," or "it" or the singular "they." Ha began referring to Evrim, in her mind, with the Turkish "o"—round as its form, holistic, inclusive. The gender problem disappeared, and the feeling of dissonance began to fade. It was replaced with pure awe, and wonder.

Without realizing what she was doing, Ha found herself holding a macaroon out to Evrim. She had heard, in that interview on the ceiling above her hotel bed, that Evrim did not eat, though they could taste and smell. That they did not sleep. That they never forgot anything.

But how can you be human and never forget? Never sleep? Never eat?

Evrim looked at the object in Ha's hand. "Is that a shell? A sea creature?"

"It's a macaroon."

"What does that mean?"

"It's a dessert item."

"Ah!" Evrim took it, held it in their palm, probed it with a long index finger, smelled it. Then smiled. "Thank you. I have never been given anything quite like it."

I think of my predecessors, staring under microscopes at the branching neurons of dead brains. They were no closer to the life that had once lived inside than an archaeologist is to the memories of the person who once held a water jug, now dug up in shards. Those pioneers of neuroscience could only sketch the roughest maps of the connections they saw, the blurred foundations of what once was a fortress.

We, on the other hand, can now reconstruct the entire castle, down to the finest detail: not only every stitch of its tapestries, but every scheme that flitted through the minds of the courtiers who lived and died in it.

—Dr. Arnkatla Mínervudóttir-Chan, *Building Minds*

5

THE CAFÉ where Rustem did most of his work was in a rundown part of Astrakhan, near the whitewashed old Kremlin walls. Centuries ago, it had been an Iranian merchant's house. The former owner had decorated the place like a mosque—gold leaf and plaster squinches undulating from the domed ceilings. But whatever architect he'd hired, around the turn of the twentieth century, had an art deco flair that rendered everything pleasantly vegetal. And despite the mosque-like style of the place, the former owner had a heretical penchant for depictions of the human image—especially of lissome women strategically veiled, drawing water from fantastic springs or reclining on divans beneath arbors voluptuous with grapes.

Age had patinaed it all and flaked away a number of the frescoes' more interesting moments. Clumsy additions had marred it—wainscoting that hacked a bathing beauty unceremoniously in half, doorways that prematurely ended the Sultan's lion hunt. But the architecture, and its later chopping up into apartments and storerooms over the decades, offered privacy. The café was a labyrinth of small rooms—screened with wooden lattices, or cut off from prying eyes with rotting velvet curtains or quaintly suggestive tapestries in a sort of *One Thousand and One Nights* meets late-Russian-Empire style.

The café was run by a Turk who hinted at having been exiled from the Republic of Istanbul for a heinous crime. He held court on the ground floor, in the steam of a gigantic gleaming brass multisamovar that served out a hundred cups of black tea an hour. He made Turkish coffee so thick a water buffalo would float in it. And he had hired a Kazakh to barbecue sturgeon the Turk alleged was pilfered from the Caspian. This claim of illegality added to the taste of the sturgeon—an illicit spice—though everyone knew the sturgeon was vat-grown: the last Caspian sturgeon was either out there stealthily avoiding its destruction in the silence of the Caspian's abyssal reaches, or had long since been consumed.

The Turk would take messages, and tip you off with a ping to your terminal if a person you didn't want to see was looking for you—this last service offered free of charge to regulars.

Rustem had been a regular for nearly a year now, since the first day he had come to the Republic of Astrakhan. He took up residence early most days, in a curtained alcove on the third floor, starting his day with the café's *kahvalti* of olives, feta, hard-boiled egg, flatbread, and fig jam. On many days, he did not leave his nook until the sun had set.

Business was good. The Republic of Astrakhan, always on the lookout for citizens with interesting skill sets, was on the cusp of granting him a passport and its dubious protection.

As he came in today, the Turk gave him a nod. "There's a woman waiting for you in your alcove. Abglanz-shielded. Asked for you by name. Just so you know."

Rustem considered whether he should run.

No, this wasn't the way Moscow would go about killing him. He wasn't worth a personal visit. The level of irritation he had caused them was worth, at the most, a wasp-sized suicide drone that would blow half his face off in an alleyway. Either that, or nothing at all. After a year of not having his face blown off, it appeared to be the latter.

"Thanks."

She was in his alcove when he got there, a plate of barbecued sturgeon on the table, the abglanz cycling through a face every half second or so, so quickly that the eye could not settle on a feature before it had changed again. Men, women, ephemeral and compelling non-binary concoctions. Some beautiful, others average, some horrid. Were they real people? Randomly generated constructs?

Her hands were small. Her nails were glazed in gold, fingers dyed platinum-white past the second knuckle, shiny with sturgeon fat. The plate of sturgeon was half-eaten. She was chewing as he came into the room, half a dozen mouths and sets of teeth enjoying each bite.

This one likes to eat.

He wasn't much interested in food himself, though the sturgeon at the café was good. His appreciation for coffee as a substance was mostly limited to the amount of caffeine it could provide him—which was why he liked the Turk's high-powered sludge.

The truth was, Rustem lived much of his time outside of his physical environment, glued to his terminals for hours, lost in the world of his work, coming to with the light through the window gone and his throat parched or his stomach empty.

When he cracked neural networks, he didn't use VR or

3D models: he hadn't grown up able to afford that stuff. In his little town of Yelabuga, in the former Republic of Tatarstan (now part of the Ural Commonwealth), he'd done most of his early work on a filthy set of terminals he'd wired together in an ancient pay-by-the-hour web café. The café was in the moldy basement of what had once been Communist Party headquarters, a century or so before he'd been born.

In place of VR, he'd had raw concentration, a skill gained from living in a one-room apartment with parents who were constantly fighting. He had learned to disappear from the world, into worlds of his own creation.

In the pay-by-the-hour café, he had used that skill to build models in his mind that showed him exactly where to find the back door. He'd learned to hack systems while everyone else around him in the web café was blowing each other to smithereens, screaming profanity. Just like home.

And just like home, he went away. Into his neural worlds.

At least as an adult he could work in a quiet place, without distraction, sinking deep, for hours at a time, within the neural patterns, the branches and intersections, the blind alleyways and loops of memory-routine.

Rustem slung his battered leather shoulder bag on the floor and sat down. The waiter was ten seconds behind him with his kahvalti and two cups of coffee on a battered tin platter, along with the obligatory glass of water.

The woman wiped her platinum-stained fingers clean and placed a terminal on the table. Very custom. Very expensive. Very new.

She waited for the waiter to withdraw.

"Two years ago, someone remotely penetrated the network of an autofreighter and caused it to crash into a yacht in the Sea of Marmara, killing one of Moscow's more obscure but well-connected ultraoligarchs."

Too bad about the yacht's crew—and the ultraoligarch's newest bride. But there had been no way around it—sometimes you had to take a few others along, too.

The voice, burned of any identifiable tone and flatlined of affect by the abglanz, went on: "A year ago, someone caused a maintenance robot in a Qatari high-rise to shove an Iranian businessman over the railing of a staircase onto the porphyry floor thirty meters below."

Now, *that one* had been perfect.

Rustem shrugged. "It's possible somebody caused those events. Or it's possible nobody did. I heard that, in both cases, there was no evidence those AIs were tampered with. Things go wrong with autofreighters all the time, and I wouldn't let a maintenance robot anywhere near me, or even my towels. Very buggy."

Things go wrong with autofreighters when someone makes them go wrong, that is. And he wouldn't let a maintenance robot get anywhere near him because he knew what they were capable of, in the wrong hands. Or the *right* hands, depending on your perspective.

"What do you think of this?" The woman pushed the terminal across to him.

Rustem scanned through the first twenty screens—the tip of a neural iceberg. It took him thirty minutes. When he looked up, he found the woman sitting just as she had been, hands tented on the tabletop.

"I don't think it can be done."

"Even by the best? Even, say, by the one they call Bakunin?"

"You could map five hundred AI autofreighter minds in the top left quadrant of this first slide. Whoever the person is you're trying to put up to this, he would probably want a fail fee of fifty percent of whatever it is you're offering—which would have to be a lot of money. And you'd be throwing your money away."

The woman stood up. "Well, I would imagine if said person found a good deal of money in their account, they would know to begin work." She pushed the curtain aside. "It was a pleasure meeting you, Rustem."

"You as well. But you forgot your terminal."

"No, I didn't. That terminal is yours."

Not only do we not agree on how to measure or recognize consciousness in others, but we are also unable to even "prove" it exists in ourselves. Science often dismisses our individual experiences—what it feels like to smell an orange, or to be in love—as qualia. We are left with theories and metaphors for consciousness: A stream of experience. A self-referential loop. Something out of nothing. None of these are satisfactory. Definition eludes us.

—Dr. Ha Nguyen, *How Oceans Think*

6

PRAYER WHEELS flanked the flagstone courtyard. The automonks paced, turning each wheel with their silver-pale, three-fingered hands as they passed. Their microphone mouths sang, *Namu Myōhō Renge Kyō*. Each voice, Ha noticed, was different, just as none of the monks were identical. Their heads—smooth, the color of old ivory—were tilted downward. Their eyes suggested the half-closed eyes of the meditator, but Ha saw no pupils in them, only a dark array of hexagonal light receptors.

In the late morning light, in that moment of now, the temple courtyard was the most beautiful thing Ha had ever seen. She wished she were capable of religious feeling. But even though she was not, there was no denying the power of the scene: The courtyard shaded by ficus trees like melting giants, the faded prayer flags rippling in the slight breeze, the scent of joss sticks drifting from the graceful curves of the Van Son Pagoda. And beyond it all, the Con Dao Archipelago's crystal sky.

She should come here often during her stay on Con Dao. She would be able to think better here. And she would need much time for thinking. She would need solitude. She had always needed enormous quantities of solitude—hours upon hours underwater, or on a depopulated beach. Anywhere, so long as it was lonely and away from others, to help her thoughts cohere. This place would help her solve the problem.

The problem. Already she was turning it over in her mind. Already it pushed up against her consciousness at all times, thoughts glimpsed as they shuttled past just shy of the surface: *You have to make a mutual world,* she found herself thinking now. *Its interactions will be governed, as ours are, by the shape of its body. By the forms that constitute its world. Its thoughts will emerge from those forms. Think. Start from there. What does that say about how it will communicate? What does that say about how I must seek to accommodate its communication?*

Unless it's all a false positive. Unless it's one more dead end, and not what I have been looking for at all.

"Are the automonks conscious?" Ha asked.

Evrim was turned away from Ha, looking out over the pagoda courtyard's low stone walls to the sea far below.

"Debatable," Evrim said. "Like the concept of consciousness itself. Their minds are extraordinarily complex and layered, but they are mostly just routines. They have been placed at about a zero-point-five on the Shchegolev Scale. They would have, with that rating, about the same rights as a house pet: protection from overt abuse, humane decommissioning. But on the other hand, each of them is a neural mapping of the mind of a Tibetan monk who actually lived. The Tibetan Buddhist Republic spares no expense. You can ask the automonks questions on philosophy, religion, their views on life. They'll answer like the dead men they are modeled on. They are walking repositories of memory. Yet they have no apparent will of their own—their present state is automated. If you asked me personally, I would say they are not conscious. They do not progress. They have no orientation to the future—what you might call 'will.' They are like encyclopedias of the minds of dead devotees. Or maps of those minds. But the map is not the same as the territory."

"Morbid."

"It's been alleged that a few of them have reacted in ways that indicate learning. I'm unconvinced. I think they are simply automatons. When the island was evacuated, Tibet refused to abandon the temple. So we are stuck with these—and the six automonks who maintain the turtle sanctuary on Hon Bay Canh, which is holy to the Tibetan Buddhist Republic."

"Shouldn't the temple and the sanctuary be property of the Hanoi government?"

"No, the government in Hanoi ceded control of all the temples in the Ho Chi Minh Autonomous Trade Zone to that sub-government, and the ATZ, being businesslike as usual, sold the temples off to the Tibetans. To the chagrin of the worshippers, whose Buddhism is, of course, of a different form. And the Vietnamese neo-nationalists were enraged. But the price was right.

"There was a long series of negotiations when we took over: the Tibetan Buddhist Republic does not give in easily. They wanted control of all the temples and shrines on the island. They wanted to build a seaside monastery here, and they wanted other concessions. The Tibetans drive a hard bargain. I remember Dr. Mínervudóttir-Chan saying she couldn't tell whether they were a nation-state, a religion, or a corporation—but that they certainly know how to operate like all three, using whichever rules and laws are convenient to get their way.

"In the end, it turned out that the archipelago's temples and the turtle sanctuary had been ceded to them in perpetuity—there was no dislodging them from Con Dao completely. So DIANIMA negotiated a contract with them here on the archipelago which allows them no human monks—only the automonks. We had to make a few other concessions—a drone supply drop, robotic maintenance. Nobody likes it. And Altantsetseg is horrified at the possibilities for security breaches. But at the same time, I don't suppose the automonks' chanting, meditating, and collecting turtle eggs for release is doing anyone any harm."

Most of the monks had retreated into the pagoda, where a gong had sounded. One of them lingered in the courtyard, watering a potted fig. Ha saw Evrim's grimace of distaste as the Team Lead watched the automonk at its task.

"You don't like them, do you?" said Ha.

"No. I find them eerie. Repulsive. I suppose it is the same for you when you look at a monkey. Unsettling."

"I don't find monkeys unsettling. I don't think people generally do."

"No? I would have thought you would find them disturbing. So much like you, but in a degraded state. A failed attempt."

"I guess we don't see them that way."

Evrim shrugged, turned to leave. Ha heard the transport start its engine, sensing their approach.

"I assume you have seen the video?"

"No."

Evrim paused on the steep stone staircase that led down from the pagoda.

"Did you not meet with Dr. Mínervudóttir-Chan? I thought you were scheduled . . ."

"No. She sent her Sub-4 to meet me. She was away."

"Then you have not been briefed?"

"I mean, I know why I am here. The broad strokes. Those were communicated to me before I contracted. But . . ."

"But they haven't told you the details of what I've seen in the past half year here."

"Not the details. No."

"Strange," Evrim said. "Whatever took Dr. Mínervudóttir-Chan away from that meeting must have been vital."

"Or she trusted you to do the debriefing for her. Knew you would fill me in. You are Team Lead, after all."

"Yes, I am . . . and I know you must be wondering *why* I am here, leading this research. There are simpler and more complicated answers to that question. With Dr. Mínervudóttir-Chan, that is always the case: there is never only one reason. But there are a few obvious justifications for my presence: I bring a few advantages. I do not forget what I have seen, for one. And I can function as well underwater as I can on land, for another. But I think the true reason I am here—and this was never told to me, but I have guessed it—is to test my capacities. To try my mind in more than some interview or laboratory cognitive test. To see what I do when confronted with a real-world problem of this kind of scale. At least that is my theory."

"And how do you think the test is going?"

"I have proved, so far, that I am smart enough to know I need to find the real right person for the job—you—and to put myself at their service."

"Actually," Ha said, "that is pretty advanced thinking. There are few people capable of that kind of humility."

"It is not humility. It is simple honesty. The last six months have taught me this problem is beyond me. And frankly—though your book is astounding—I think this problem is also beyond you. But there is a chance it may not be beyond *us*." Evrim smiled.

And then Ha saw it. Yes. This was why the world would never build another humanoid AI. The smile was perfect. Sincere, unaffected. Fully human.

And because of that, the smile was like the shadow of your own death. Evrim's existence implicated yours. It implied you, too, were nothing more than a machine—a swarm of preprogrammed impulses iterating endlessly. If Evrim was a conscious thing, and made, then maybe you were made as well. A construct made of different materials. A skeleton walking around, sheathed in meat, fooled into thinking it has free will. A thing that had occurred by accident. Or a thing made on a whim, to see if it could be done.

"What exactly is the point," a stream interviewer once asked Mínervudóttir-Chan, "of an android? Why go to such trouble to make them so human, when making humans is almost free?"

Mínervudóttir-Chan had answered, "The great and terrible thing about humankind is simply this: we will always do what we are capable of."

They descended the staircase from the pagoda.

There is more to us than the physical linkages that make up our minds—but there is no denying this physical substrate. You have seen it if you have eaten chicken: those whitish strings you encounter on your plate are nerves—bundles of axons, evidence of the fleshy connectivity without which no sophisticated living mind on earth can function.

You can argue all you want about the soul. But without the connectome formed by the billions of synapses firing in the nervous system, there is no possibility of even the simplest memory. Every memory of lemonade you have is an electrochemical lightning bolt through flesh, on a microscopic scale. This is why I say I "build" minds: minds are as physical as a brick wall.

—Dr. Arnkatla Mínervudóttir-Chan, *Building Minds*

7

EIKO LOOKED PAST THE RUSTY BARS of the barracks windows to the ship's processing deck. He was wrapped in two recycled plastidown blankets against the cold. The storm had subsided. The ship still bucked and rolled in the waves, and the barracks smelled of fear-sweat and vomit, but the worst was past.

Eiko pressed his face against the bars, trying to escape the vomit stench. A salt-mist lashed at his cheeks. The sharp stink of marine slaughter from the deck below, awash in the pink diluted blood of the morning catch, was preferable.

The processing shift was hard at work at the conveyors. They slid the blades of their knives into the bellies of the fish, scooped out the entrails, and whipped the guts into blue plastic buckets. Then they placed the fish on the conveyors that took them down to the factory room, where they were flash-frozen in blocks and sent to the storage freezers. The movements of the processing shift were efficient, mechanical. No waste of energy. Robotic. And you could see, on the deck, the rusted, torn baseplates where the robots that used to perform this task had been.

High-maintenance, robots. Susceptible to all sorts of weather damage at sea. Electricity and salt water are a bad combination. Rust, decay, short circuits. Expensive. *We make better robots. Cheaper to maintain, more expendable.*

One of the guards leaned against the base column of the gantry, sucking at a vape tube poking up from her shoulder. Blowing clouds, one hand idly resting on the grip of her rifle as it dangled from its sling. Nothing in her eyes. Eiko did not know this guard's real name. The other guards called her "Monk." She never spoke, but Eiko had picked things up: South African Limited Governance Area Mercenary, Paris Protectorate Legionnaire in the Ivory Coast LGA. She was always in gray. The rifle, a sidearm, a knife along the thigh. Lots of gear on her belt. Restraints and stun rod, but also things Eiko couldn't identify.

The guards all liked their gear. They had a hodgepodge of rifles, sidearms, knives—they loved their knives. Loved to talk about where they had bought them. Loved to talk about when they had used them. The guards' outfits were all tech materials, zippers, and hidden pockets. Although they wore no standard uniform, their custom outfits all ended up looking the same.

And although they had all come from different backgrounds, they all ended up looking the same, too: the men big, protein-swollen, bearded, loud-talking. The ones who still had their hair wore it long. The ones who didn't shaved their heads.

The men were, all of them, bullies. They hit out with their rifle butts, they laughed loud and shoved each other.

The women were different. The women were silent, short-haired. They kept their eyes half-closed, as if it made them less vulnerable. They were harder than the men.

There were eight guards Eiko had seen. Six men, two women. Could be more, but he didn't think so. The ship was big, but not that big. He had been on board seventy-four days. In that time, he had seen only these eight guards. He knew most of their names. He knew their habits. He knew something of their histories.

Because he had no terminal, no pen, no paper, he kept this information in the memory palace he had built in his mind. His memory palace was a Japanese inn. Not just any inn: it was the Minaguchi-ya, on the Tokaido Road, between Tokyo and Kyoto. Eiko had never visited the Minaguchi-ya, but he had read an ancient book, by a gaijin from the old American States named Oliver Statler. The book had detailed the Minaguchi-ya: every room of the place, over all the generations of its operation.

In those remembered rooms and times, Eiko placed the names of the guards. And in those rooms he placed all the details he knew of the ship: the approximate height of the gantry, the shapes of the Thai letters on its side, though he could not know their meaning, the shape of the locks on the doors, the number of steps from the cage-windowed barracks where he and the others were kept when they were not working under guard.

He knew the ship's details down to the processing deck, the flash-freeze factory, the ports and rails. He had studied the thick, opaque, hardened glass of the wheelhouse, and its reinforced steel plate door, beyond which lay the ship's AI—its mind full of sonar, full of maps of banks and shoals, trawling methods and market prices.

Stenciled over the armored steel door of the wheelhouse, in English, was: WOLF LARSEN, CAPTAIN. When Eiko had asked about the name, one of the other crew members—one of the other slaves—had laughed bitterly. "It's a joke. A reference to some old book or movie. But there's nothing behind that door but the AI core. It controls the engines and the navigation. It decides where we go, and when. It follows the fish and the profit. It decides when we dock, too—but it won't matter to you, kid. When we dock, they lock us up below where nobody can hear us. The processing room where they keep us is right next to one of the freezers. Sometimes we're down there for days. You'll come to understand what cold means then. Believe me, it's better out here."

The crew member's name was Thomas. He'd said he was from London. He had been abducted in Pago Pago, where he'd been doing graduate research. He and Eiko had begun a friendship that day that continued while they lay in their polynet hammocks in the barracks, eating the compressed cakes of fish protein and vitamin supplements the *Sea Wolf* fed them with.

On day twenty-eight of the time Eiko had been aboard, the *Sea Wolf* was hit by a Pacific storm. A slack line went taught and struck Thomas in the chest, sending him overboard into the gray roil.

Gone.

Eiko saved Thomas's name, placing it in a twentieth-century room of the Minaguchi-ya, where glass doors were slid open to the cool greenness of the inn's garden, the sound of the sea, and the busy hum of the bustling Tokaido Road.

One of the conveyor belts jammed. The Monk walked over as a crew member worked to get it running again. But before she moved, she thumbed the safety of her rifle off, glanced to her three and nine, swiveled to her six.

Always ready, this one. Not easy to get by her, if the time ever came.

As he lay in his hammock that evening, wrapped in his recycled plastidown blankets, watching the day die, heavy flakes of sleet drifting like ash into the barracks through the window's rusted grid, Eiko carefully placed that information in a stone lantern in the Minaguchi-ya's garden, in the Tokugawa era.

No intelligent animal is as antisocial as the octopus. It wanders the ocean alone, more inclined to cannibalize its own kind than band together with them, doomed to a senescent death after a haphazard sexual encounter.

The octopus is the "tribeless, lawless, hearthless one," denounced by Homer. This solitude, along with her tragically short life span, presents an insurmountable barrier to the octopus's emergence into culture.

But this book asks the question: What if? What if a species of octopus emerged that attained longevity, intergenerational exchange, sociality? What if, unknown to us, a species already has? Then what?

—Dr. Ha Nguyen, *How Oceans Think*

8

"IT'S NOT ABOUT INTELLIGENCE," Ha said. "We've seen tons of signs of octopus intelligence. Creativity, multi-step problem solving, compound tool use, evidence of theory of mind, long-term learning, and a high degree of individuation. There are so many stories—all of them true: octopuses climbing out of their habitats at night, wandering the corridors of aquariums, eating fish from other tanks, then returning and closing their own lids. Octopuses escaping to the sea through the pump systems of their habitats, octopuses squirting jets of water at annoying lights until they cause an electrical short and put them out, octopuses recognizing people's faces, opening jars to extract food, remembering how to guide their arms through mazes. We know all of this. And they are not only intelligent—they are also highly individual. They have personalities. It's one of the things we recognize in them. In an aquarium, it's often only the dolphins, otters, and octopuses that get named by volunteers. Two mammals, which is understandable, as they are species relatively close to our own—and a cephalopod, a species so different from us that our last common ancestor was five hundred million years ago. Why? People name octopuses because, no matter how different they are from us, we *recognize* something in them. Something we have in common. Even people who don't study them are aware of this, on some level. There's something special about them—we've known that for a long time now."

Ha and Evrim were back at the hotel, in the middle of her tour of one of the prefab lab units by the swampy hotel pool. The other unit, Ha had learned, belonged to Altantsetseg: it was a mobile command center full of piloting interfaces that allowed her to take over control of her small army of automated patrol gunships watching the archipelago, or their suicide quadcopters. That only scratched the surface, Ha knew, of what would be stored in that unit.

The unit Ha and Evrim were standing in was the lab. A lot of biological equipment, DNA analyzers, 3D bioprinters, dissection tables Ha wanted nothing to do with.

She wasn't that type of scientist. She liked her creatures whole. Communicating. Yes, there were things the DNA could tell us, dissections to investigate structures. All of that. But it wasn't for her.

"Look," Ha continued, "there are limitations that would keep them from ever being able to form a conscious, communicative life or a culture."

"Life span," Evrim interjected.

"Life span is one, yes. Not the only one, but one of the largest. They only live two years, in the larger species, and far less time than that in smaller species. Some live only a season. Down in the deeper parts of the ocean, there are octopuses who live longer—ten years or more. But those are cold-water creatures. They wouldn't be among the most intelligent octopuses: In the deep their lives are simpler—they are creatures of routine. Everything is slowed down. The smart octopuses would be the ones nearer shore, in environments that provide them with diverse challenges, problems to solve."

"Okay, but if they could overcome life span—what else would stand in the way?"

"A hell of a lot. Their mating patterns, for one. The males turn senescent and wander after mating until they die. The females starve themselves to death tending their eggs. And even if the parents survived, once the eggs hatch, the young of most species float to the surface and drift in the plankton before settling to the bottom at another location. That kills any connection to place or kin. There are species that live on the bottom in juvenile form—but it doesn't much matter, if their parents are dead soon after they hatch. There's no way to pass on learned experience. No culture to be born into. And since they are solitary, there's no group knowledge, either—so there is no way for them to pass any knowledge from one generation to another, and virtually no passing of knowledge from one octopus to another in the same generation. Imagine where we would be if humanity had to restart its cultural progress with every generation. As intelligent as they are, each individual octopus is a blank slate. The only thing passed down to them by their parents to help them survive is their physical form, and the instincts written into their genes. Everything else they have to learn on their own, wandering the ocean floor.

"Imagine we all lived alone most of our lives, and our lives were only two years long. No developed language. No culture, no buildings or cities or states."

"But what about the locations they call Octopolis and Octlantis, off the east coast of Australia? They are both continuously inhabited sites with octopuses in every season."

How much does Evrim know? Everything all humans know? Or just some things? How does that work? How smart is that brain?

"I know Octopolis and Octlantis. I spent a season there studying them. But there's no evidence of culture at those sites. There are basic interactions—dominance by larger males, herding of females. Nothing else. There's nothing that indicates any sort of a developed grammar, or symbolic communication. They would need to have developed a level of consistency in their signaling that hasn't been observed—unless there's a study I haven't read."

"I doubt there is," Evrim said.

"I doubt it as well."

"You don't believe it, then. You don't believe in what we brought you here to confirm."

Ha shook her head. "No. I want to believe it, but I think the simpler explanation is true. What you have here is a combination of superstition, rumor, and strange behavior from what might be only one or two particularly intelligent octopuses. Con Dao is fertile ground for rumors. Everyone who lives here . . ."—she corrected herself—"who *lived* here, I mean, saw ghosts. When I visited here as a child you couldn't speak to a local without ghosts coming into the conversation: the ancestral spirit of Vo Thi Sau combing her long black hair in Hang Duong Cemetery, the starved dead wandering in the shadows between the trees. The stories go on and on. Too many people died in the prisons here for there not to be stories of ghosts. The residents lived in a world half composed of spirits. This archipelago is ripe for weird cryptozoology."

"But you wrote an entire book on cephalopod communication. Now you're saying it isn't possible."

"No—I wrote a whole book *speculating* on what such a thing *might* look like. I wrote a book that took science and mixed it with a whole lot of ideas about what might be. And I wrote that book because I think it might be possible. Somewhere, at some point in time. But at the core, I'm a scientist. I can speculate all I want—play around with ideas, hypothesize—that's a part of the job, right? But when it comes down to asking me to believe the stories here . . ."

When was the last time she had spoken with someone else for this long, besides Kamran? She could not think of a recent time.

Maybe the octopus isn't the only one who leads a solitary life.

How did the joke go in her book? Ah yes: . . . *More inclined to cannibalize its own kind than band together with them. Doomed to a senescent death after a haphazard sexual encounter . . . sounds like one or two scientists I know.*

She smiled to herself. "Well, it's a tall order. That's all."

"What would fill that . . . what did you call it? That tall order?" Evrim asked.

"All right, fine. I'll play this game." Ha felt irritated. Defensive. Again—*how much does Evrim know?* "You would need to have a creature that is long-lived, that is social, that raises its young, and can pass information from one generation to the next. An octopus that has developed a complex, symbolic system of communication. So—how might that happen? I go over this in my book. Let's put forward the idea that evolution accelerates due to environmental pressures. The need to find new niches. Evolution is slow, but there are animals who adapt faster than others. This is especially true of the octopus: they can modify the protein processes in their bodies without recourse to DNA mutation."

"Through RNA editing—swapping out one RNA base for another. They can produce molecular diversity quickly, particularly in their nervous systems. It's an alternative engine for evolution," Evrim said.

"You've read the literature. Good. Yes—RNA editing. It's unique to cephalopods—and, admittedly, it's fast. Much faster than DNA mutation. More responsive to its environment. It's a massive advantage—allowing quick adaptation, in a comparative handful of generations, to new environmental challenges. So, if evolution accelerates due to environmental pressures, and the octopus adapts quickly via RNA editing to those pressures, it follows that you put an octopus species under pressure, it could change much more quickly than non-cephalopods . . ."

The door to the unit swung open. Altantsetseg filled the doorway, square and muscular in a technical T-shirt, the battered old translator at her throat.

"Surrender macaroon, robot."

Evrim turned their calm face toward the door. "Excuse me?"

"Surrender macaroon cookie thing. Cookie is useless to you."

"You are interrupting, Altantsetseg."

"Give up macaroon, and I depart," the neutral translator voice said over the baffling consonantal barrier of Altantsetseg's own language.

"I will not," Evrim said.

"Robots do not eat."

"It was a gift to me, and I enjoy looking at it."

"I will later pilfer it." Altantsetseg turned and walked off, slamming the unit door behind her.

"She's not the best communicator around," Ha said.

Evrim shook their head. "No. But there are reasons."

"The translator is faulty."

"It's not that. The translator is a wall for her to hide behind. She has a better translator. She won't use it. She is a veteran of the Chinese-Mongolian Winter War. She bears her scars."

Images came to Ha of the Chinese-Mongolian Winter War. Burned corpses lacquered in ice. Charred, frozen skeletons shattered like glass by concussion rounds. The fingerless hands of veterans.

"You were going to offer a theory," Evrim said, "before we were interrupted. Environmental pressures."

"Yes. So, here it is: We've been scraping the oceans of protein for centuries now, overfishing, tearing apart food webs, creating a sort of undersea ice age—driving some species to extinction, driving others to search for new niches, new methods of survival. Massive environmental pressures on every species in the sea. So—let's say you had an octopus from one of the deeper layers of the sea—a long-lived species, with benthic young. A species used to a simple way of gathering food in a stable environment. But over many generations, you kept decreasing its food supply—kept pushing it out to the fringes of its habitat, forcing it to exercise its creative faculties. To learn and adapt—and to feed that adaptation back into its evolutionary system. The octopus that survives is the one whose parent sticks around long enough to teach it after its birth, because that mutation would give it a huge advantage over competitors. You might see new RNA coding emerge that rewarded more longevity—a mating and death timing that enabled nurturing of the young, rewarded social skills. You might see other mutations that favored the more social, communicative animals. The ability to act as a coordinated group would be an enormous advantage: to specialize, to stake out and guard territory, to learn from one another. Think of human societies during the ice age: massive environmental pressures forced innovation, forcing them to master cooperative strategies to bring down big megafauna for sustenance, and in turn that added nutrition built better brains, allowed more specialization . . . in evolutionary terms, the emergence of the modern brain occurs with spectacular speed, as culture feeds back into the genetic system . . . and then language hits, and things really get emergent . . ."

Ha trailed off. She had been speaking quickly, trying to get it all out in one piece. These were the dreams at the edge of her work in cephalopod intelligence—the things she would never have told another scientist. The things beyond her science of the real world in front of her. Fantasies. Hunches. "But that's the key: language. None of it means anything without that, so first you have to overcome the language problem. Humans could use other things besides speech for communications, if we had to. Body language, or sign language, or music, or whistling, or song, or expressions of the face, or drawing in the dirt with a stick—and we do, at times. But we suppress these in favor of speech. Why? Because verbal speech is efficient, nearly universal, teachable, and highly translatable. If our communication had remained a mix of mediums, we would have had a much harder time transcribing it into writing. We would also have had a harder time teaching and learning it.

"This is one of the reasons why the communications of cephalopods are so difficult to crack: They don't have a grammar or vocabulary. Everything is either local—learned on the fly over a short life span—or instinctive. Plus, they mix communications between colors, patterns, texture, and gesture. That would be a bit like communicating using speech, Morse code, and sign language at the same time, and having to understand *all* of them simultaneously in order to make sense of *any* of them.

"The bigger complication is that they use their primary, mixed method of communication—skin pattern, texture, and coloration, which they employ in a simple way to warn one another off or express a feeling—for a lot of other things as well: camouflage, the confusion of predators, fight-or-flight responses, and so on. And because they are not producing light from their surface, but rather reflecting ambient light from the environment, the colors they are producing shift in different light conditions—so if the cuttlefish were using color to communicate, they may be saying, "Hey, Bob," in bright light, but it may sound a lot like, "Watch fob," when a shadow crosses overhead. It would be like humans talking with their mouths full while using a language that has a different grammar indoors and outdoors, and trying to whistle and hide from a bear while carrying on the conversation."

"Kind of hard," Evrim said.

"Yeah." Ha laughed. "Kind of hard. This octopus would have to overcome that. It would need to find a way to communicate that was digital—I mean digital like our number system or our alphabet. If the animal you brought me here to study has done that—has exapted a structure or function to use for communication—then we might have something."

"We might have something, Ha," Evrim said. "Let's watch the video from the submersible. This was what we saw a month ago . . ."

We are shaped and limited by our skeletons. Jointed, defined, structured. We create a world of relationships that mirrors that shape: a world of rigid boundaries and binaries. A world of control and response, master and servant. In our world, as in our nervous systems, hierarchy rules.

—Dr. Ha Nguyen, *How Oceans Think*

9

THE YELLOWFINS CAME DOWN into the hopper from the processing floor above, their heads sliced off, their guts torn out. Some spilled over the side of the hopper before they could be sorted on the rack and slotted into their freezing blocks.

Already the floor of the flash-freezing factory room was slick with their slime. The air was full of the toxin in their stink—a histamine that got into Eiko's throat and lungs, made it hard to breathe, made him gag and wobble over his task. The *Sea Wolf* was having a problem in this room with drainage. A puck-shaped maintenance bot labored at a blocked sump. Fish slime and seawater pooled around Eiko's ankles.

The guard watching them was a red-bearded one named Bjarte. He was standing on an upturned plastic crate to stay out of the nastiness. Eiko had notes on Bjarte: a bit sloppy on the job, got distracted easily, liked to talk. He was a bully—enough of one to stand out among the others. He carried a long, serrated bowie knife in a sheath on his calf.

While his hands sorted fish into the flash-freeze slots, a good portion of Eiko's mind was elsewhere. He kept going back over his last day in the Ho Chi Minh Autonomous Trade Zone, where he had been abducted. Kept trying to find the exact moment when his former life had ended and this one had begun. Where the two Eikos had been severed, one from the other. But he couldn't find the connection, the sharp division where the rope was cut: His former life untangled into a frayed vagueness. His new one started in the same way.

What did he remember? It had been hot that day. Hotter than Japan, more humid. He had buzzed for an autotuk from the desk of the cheap hotel where he was staying. It was his first day in the Autonomous Trade Zone. He was excited. The HCMATZ. You could make a fortune here, if you were smart. He knew other Japanese programmers who had come home from the ATZ and bought beach houses in Okinawa after a few years.

Eiko already had the company picked out. They were the biggest in the ATZ, their regional corporate headquarters looming fifty stories above District Three, a shield of mirrored glass: DIANIMA, the international tech company that designed the top-of-the-line artificial intelligences—minds that ran governments, managed economies. He would work his way up. Start small, push into R&D, reinforce what he had learned at the university with practical experience. By the time he was thirty, he would be a DIANIMA project manager. From there, who knew?

But that was all for tomorrow. On his first day he had wanted to see the main square first, the ancient brick French cathedral in the town's center, the old post office. Things like that. Just a day spent touristing in this megalopolis, before he got down to making money.

The autotuk had feigned a malfunction, pretended not to

understand his directions. Bleeping in fake distress, faking alarm at its own wrong turns, it circled him farther and farther from the center, through a series of high-rise slums, skeletal stalled building projects rammed full of container squats and shanties, with spiderwebs of illicit power cables snaking across every possible surface. Finally, the 'tuk stopped at a storefront on a side street, and refused to go any farther.

He was looking to fire off a complaint to the Thai company that owned the thing, was trying to get a decent picture of the smeared scanblock on its battered dash, when a man stuck his head under the 'tuk's awning.

The man unfolded a cheap palimpscreen upon which a series of images of girls flirted: A tub with two girls smiling from behind bubbles that clung to their skin. A girl wrapped in a towel, leaning against the frame of a doorway, wreathed with steam, shimmying her torso a little from side to side. And a price list. Cheap, by Japanese standards. Cheap, and right here in front of him.

Eiko wasn't thinking of anything like this. Or did not think he was. But now he found himself nodding. Found it was exactly what he had been looking for. Found the man's arm on his, found himself in a staircase, cooler than the outside.

He remembered the lobby of the place—cracked tile the color of cheap mint candy. Then his hands shaking as the girls stood in front of him, lined up in sashes of almost the same cheap mint color, with numbers at their shoulders. He chose two of them. What were their numbers? That was gone now. He even forgot, now, what stood out about those two. What was he looking for? Judging by? Their cheekbones? The curve of a hip beneath their sashes and swimsuits? He had been nervous. His nervousness smeared the memory the way intoxication would, made it hard for him to return to it and make out details now.

They went up in a cramped elevator, the girls chatting with each other in Thai, then turning to him with questions in English. What was his name? Did he think they were pretty? He seemed tired. Was he nervous? He should not be nervous. Had he traveled far?

One of them carried a small plastic crate, like a miniature shopping basket. He glimpsed shower gel, condoms. They told him their names, but he wouldn't have remembered even a second later. Their names were just sounds, as alien to him as the thing he was doing. More alien.

In a white-tiled room, they slid out of their sashes and suits, then undressed him. Under a shower they soaped him up. They laughed, bantered with one another. One of them, her body covered in suds, rubbed her curved length against him, slid a hand up his thigh . . .

The dizziness caused by the yellowfin histamine stink in the room was making Eiko nauseous. He nearly threw up into the water. Bjarte turned his bearded face toward him. Throw up, Eiko told himself, and he would be comforted with the butt of Bjarte's rifle.

The girls had probably been slaves, like he was now. A part of him understood that and abhorred what he had done.

But that did not stop him from quietly masturbating to the scene, in his polynet hammock, as the ship lurched and plunged through the heavy northern Pacific swells. Remembering: his cock in one of their mouths, then the other's, his fingers inside them both, the furred pressure of their crotches against his wrists, their little gasps in his ears, faked but sounding real enough.

These were the last, flickering images he had of a life

before. The kidnapping might have happened right there at the brothel, or elsewhere, hours or even days afterward. He couldn't know: it was all blackness. Whatever drug he had been given had blotted out a block of time. His next memories were of this life.

He could not find it, the cut between the two lives, the moment when he was taken. It was gone. On one side of a darkness was the Eiko who had come to the HCMATZ looking to get rich. On the other side was a slave.

Sometimes Eiko still thought of his parents, back in Okinawa. They had saved the money for his trip to the HCMATZ, just as they had scraped together the money for his education. This was the next step, their next investment in his future.

When he had left for the HCMATZ, on a charter flight managed by a company that specialized in supplying the zone with young Japanese talent, his father and mother had both accompanied him to the airstrip. It was an old place, half abandoned, servicing the few charter companies that still used human-piloted small craft. His father and mother, with identical expressions on their careworn faces, had said goodbye and turned to leave abruptly, as was their way. But as the plane banked after takeoff, Eiko had glimpsed their car, still parked in the parking lot. The sun reflected off the windshield, but he knew that behind that glare would be their faces, looking up at their only son's plane as it dwindled into the sky.

There were times when Eiko indulged the fantasy that Japan was searching for him. He knew this was a lie. By this time his parents had certainly alerted the authorities to his disappearance. By this time they had spent days and weeks in front of their aging terminals, haranguing officials of the

HCMATZ. They had contacted, he was sure, the Okinawan authorities, and possibly even Tokyo. But what would they find? Any of them? His life was cut through, its frayed end dangling in the HCMATZ hotel where he had left a bag of his possessions. Beyond that point, there would be no trace of him.

The cut between the two lives.

Some of the other crew had similar fantasies, in their first month or so on the ship. People were looking for them. People would find them.

None of the other crew tried to argue with them: the ocean did all the arguing that was necessary. Day after day, it filled their vision to the horizon, its only feature the constant change of its surface in dialogue with the sky above. Soon enough, they understood that the things that had given them security—families, states, laws, futures, and pasts—were all located on a solid planet, a planet of land. In this never-ending world of lawless water they were trapped in now, none of that existed.

Beside him, his fellow crew member laid a gloved hand on the shoulder of his rubberized overshirt. "Steady, Eiko."

Back in the now. The crew member with him on this shift was Son—a lean Vietnamese man a few years older than Eiko. He had been a dive instructor and guide on an island. What was its name? Eiko had never cared enough to remember—just as he had never cared enough to remember the names of the two prostitutes whose smooth, soaped bodies had writhed against his.

Never cared enough.

And he saw—as if it were happening right then, before him—the slack line going taught. The line striking Thomas in the chest, sending him overboard into the gray roil.

Gone.

Eiko vomited into the slime near his feet. He felt Son catch him as his knees buckled, heard Bjarte's irritated growl as the stop button was hammered and the siren went off.

"Histamine," he heard Son explaining to Bjarte. "He needs a little time out of the room. I can punch up prochlorperazine from the dispensary."

He heard Bjarte on the intercom to another guard: "Wake up one of the off-shift crew, get them down to the flash-freeze. We've got a limp one. You," he yelled at Son, "make sure your ass is back here in five minutes!"

In the galley, with a cold towel over his head and the prochlorperazine in his system, he began to feel better. He knew he'd have to make the time up tomorrow—work a full eighteen hours—but for now he looked forward to a cake of fish protein, a cup of broth, an extended sleep.

In his hammock, hours later, he woke to voices. It was night. Dark in the barracks, only the sound of the engines pushing the factory trawler forward through the black. And the voices, and an intermittent red light from outside that splashed a web of shadows against the barracks wall every few seconds.

Son was speaking to one of the other prisoners, whispering in the dark: "At times, I feel like I don't care what happens to me. If I can never go back to my islands, what does it matter? Even before they took me, I was lost. In the Autonomous Trade Zone, I just existed. Not like on Con Dao. But I heard that the charity wing of DIANIMA that bought it from the ATZ has cordoned it off. It is safe—my home. These soulless ships travel the world, scraping the last of the fish from the sea, making a desert everywhere. But Con Dao is safe now. The fish are safe, the dugongs and the sea grass and the reefs are safe. The turtles. All of them are safe."

Con Dao. Eiko wouldn't forget the name now. He would stop forgetting names, people. He would stop not caring.

Because that was what had brought him here. He had not cared. Yes, that was it. He had not cared, and this was how the world had punished him.

He had not cared about anyone, until he had seen Thomas go over the rail. But that—finally—had moved something in him. There had been something broken in him, until then. Maybe now it was getting fixed.

In his mind, in his memory palace, Eiko wrote the name "Con Dao" on a scroll of rice paper. He tied it with a length of rough rush-hempen twine to the branch of a sakura tree in the garden of the Minaguchi-ya as it had existed in the year 1691.

He heard Son's soft laughter in the dark. "Even the Con Dao Sea Monster is safe, down there in his shipwreck."

Communication is not what sets humans apart. All life communicates, and at a level sufficient to its survival. Animal and even plant communications are, in fact, highly sophisticated. But what makes humans different is symbols—letters and words that can be arranged in the self-referential sets we call language. Using symbols, we can detach communication from its direct relation to things present around us. We can speak with one another about things not here and now. We can tell stories. Tradition, myth, history, culture—these are storage systems for knowledge, and they are all products of the symbol. And the use of symbols is something we have not seen outside our own species.

—Dr. Ha Nguyen, *How Oceans Think*

10

"IT WAS HARD TO MAKE ANYTHING OUT down there, on the video. The drone submersible had a good light on it, but there was too much silt in the water, and fish everywhere obscuring everything. But what I was able to see was—"

"Don't sum it up." Kamran was wearing his peach sweatpants, which Ha particularly hated, and a ratty T-shirt. But at least he was at home: she could glimpse, at the hazy edge of the projection cast by the terminal's oculus, the familiar shape of a kitchen chair. "Just walk me through what you saw."

"Shouldn't you be in bed?"

"I'm not up late—I'm up early. Being productive. You're the one who's up late. Now lay it out for me, so you can go to sleep."

"Okay. You could make out the outline of the wreck, lying on its port side, once the submersible got close enough. You could see schools of fish swirling in the haze, and the darkness of the hatch. Evrim tells me it's the hatch into the area of the ship where a man was killed . . ."

"Stick to what you saw. Don't go into details other people passed on to you."

"Right. As the submersible passed through the hatch into that darker space, it switched on a brighter flood. For a second the floodlight overwhelmed the camera. Everything turned white. Then it recovered. And that was when I saw it for the first time. The interior of that compartment was crusted over with growth—budding coral, shellfish—and against that background it was hard to make it out, but I saw it move. The octopus. It had been almost perfectly camouflaged. Then it shifted. When it did, it darkened. It retained the wall's pattern but darkened its skin. Like a blush of anger. I've seen that darkening so many times before in the octopuses I've observed—I knew what it was right away: irritation.

"The submersible started to turn to the right, panning to get a better shot of the space. As it turned, the octopus detached itself from the wall and moved to the right as well. The submersible started to pan left. And then there it was, two meters from the submersible. It was in the full 'Nosferatu' pose—standing tall, on the bulkhead of the ship, with its mantle up vertically above its head, arms and web spread. The threat pose. But usually they are dark in this pose. This one wasn't: it was almost white. And it was *big*. It was hard to get an exact sense of scale, but it was at least as tall as a person, when elongated. Taller."

"What you saw. Concentrate on that."

"Right. So—it began to make passing cloud patterns. They were recognizably the ones an octopus would normally use to startle prey—to get it to make an incautious move—but they were altered. I remember thinking, *I knew it*—I had predicted that this is exactly the function the octopus would exapt to communicate with: this prey-startling device that wasn't essential to survival. Remember? I said—"

"I remember. I have practically the whole theory memorized: The octopus would have to develop symbols—an arbitrary way to encode lots of different, abstract information. One that was stable, and self-referential. The octopus would have to separate off one of their functions from the others and use that function to produce intelligible meaning."

"Exactly! It happened with our own speech as well—we adapted a breathing and eating apparatus into a speech apparatus. And that is what the octopus was doing—exapting. It was using the passing cloud, but using it *to speak*."

"That's a bold statement. A pretty big jump in—"

"Let me finish! The octopus would move the passing cloud patterns across its mantle and head, and then *stop* them on its hood, and hold them there. And the patterns were complex, but specific. Far beyond the normal, quick shadow you see when it's trying to get a crab to reveal its hiding place. This was like . . . like Rorschach symbols. At first there was a sequence of them, very fast. Then the octopus darkened all over for a moment, before turning white again. After its skin went pale the second time, it slowed the shapes down. First it produced a sequence: the same, as far as I could tell, as it was producing before. But then it began to produce only one shape. It brought it down slowly, across its mantle and head, and then held it on its spread-out hood."

"Describe it. The shape."

"It was a downward-facing crescent. But there was also a long, pointed streak at the lower pole of the crescent. Here. I'll draw it."

Ha drew on a piece of palimpscreen on her bedside table and held it up to the oculus.

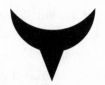

"About like that. Rougher around the edges, but like that. It reproduced that same shape nine or ten times. Then it jetted up, out of the camera range. It must have grabbed the submersible from behind: the camera jerked, and was pulled farther into the wreck. Everything after that was a blur. The submersible was being yanked around quickly, and its camera couldn't focus.

"But then it came to a stop. Most of the camera was obscured by one of the octopus's arms. There were streaks across the image as well—electrical qualia, probably caused when the submersible's hull began to breach and the first salt water hit the electronics. The octopus was tearing the submersible open. Just before it went dark, I saw . . ."

Ha stopped. Outside, there was a sound, in the distance. A sort of *crump*. Then again.

Crump.

A flash of light penetrated the room's curtains.

"Kamran, something is happening. I have to go."

Crump.

"I'll be back. I have to see—"

"I understand. We'll talk later. Anyway, I was about to go for a run."

"Liar."

"You never know what bad habits I'll develop while you're away."

The oculus went dark.

Crump.

Another flash of light. Ha pulled the curtains aside.

Ha's room overlooked the terrace, with the beach below it and the open ocean beyond. The moon had set, and the stars were muted behind a thin, high-altitude screen of clouds. The water near the hotel glistened, casting back the few lights from the hotel. Farther out, the water was a pure black that shaded into a brighter horizon, where the stars lent the clouds a dark gray glow.

Then, along the horizon, a light flashed.

Crump.

An explosion, out at sea.

Glancing down, Ha saw a figure on the terrace. Evrim, robed, their shadow an elongated cutout in a trapezoid of light from the open door panel of Altantsetseg's security module.

Ha ran down the hall, through the lobby. As she exited the hotel, she saw a fury of lights along the horizon: multiple flashes, and then an explosion large enough she could feel its pressure wave across her face.

The windows of the hotel rattled.

She was beside Evrim now. Yes, Evrim was wearing a robe—gold thread, the weave filled with chimeras in white and silver.

"What is going on?"

Something on the horizon was burning—a pumpkin-colored flickering smear between dark sky and darker water, reflected in Evrim's pupils. Hard to read, that face. Not quite aligned to human expression. There was that perfectly human smile, before . . . but there were other expressions. Things not fathomable. Crooked syntax. Readable, but like reading Chaucer for the first time. Concern? Sadness? Ha had wanted to ask if they were in danger, but that face told her they were not—this was something else.

"They are trying to breach the perimeter."

"They?"

"A group of fishing vessels."

"Automated?"

"Most are these days. We fired warning shots." Evrim turned to face her. "That must have woken you. I am sorry."

"Something is burning out there."

"Yes. The ships did not heed the warnings, and tried to force the perimeter anyway. Now Altantsetseg's drones are destroying them. The fire is fuel leaked from the ships. It's unfortunate, but I am sure that Altantsetseg's drone extinguishers are working already to put the fire out, and her nanocleaners will clear the pollution from the water."

"Why would they risk destruction?"

"Profit is a powerful motivator. To them, the ocean is nothing more than an extraction zone. They have scoured the seas nearly bare and now find themselves competing with one another for the dregs of what once were endless schools of fish. This area has long been protected, if unevenly: its fish population is too much of a temptation for them to pass up." Evrim walked toward Altantsetseg's security module, the gold robe billowing in the slight onshore breeze like a cape. "Now they seek to ruin this place as well. But we will stop them."

In Altantsetseg's security module, on built-in workbenches and hanging half-assembled from machined and gleaming inlaid pegboards was a menagerie of deadly mechanisms: an edged and high-velocity workshop of death-dealing. But most of the space was dominated by a massive transparent tank.

Inside, Altantsetseg floated naked in a luminescent green fluid. Her head was hooded by a black multi-hosed breathing apparatus. Suspended, she writhed, fingers fluttering, every muscle twitching in time.

Epicene, roped with muscle, streaked and slashed with scar tissue, Altantsetseg's body looked like a statue battered but left standing after an air raid. In the phosphorescent aquamarine of the tank, writhing to a syncopation of its own, it had a terrible, innovated beauty. Traces of the past, the course of her life. Memory, etched permanently on the body.

"She is miraculous," Evrim said. "One of only three known security specialists in the world who can operate the fluid control system for a drone network this extensive. She is, submerged in there, literally a one-woman army."

Ha approached the tank like a child trying to get a better look at a shark in an aquarium.

"There is no problem with her translations now," Evrim continued. "No misunderstandings or distortions. Her will is executed exactly, across dozens of systems at once. She is a symphony."

Altantsetseg rotated in a slow, deadly spiral. Her fingers, the position of her limbs, even her toes spelled out commands Ha could not interpret. Outside, there was another explosion.

Evrim said: "Earlier today, I saw it in your face. You wanted to ask—am I a supercomputer? An omniscient AI housed in a human-shaped carapace?"

"Yes," Ha admitted. "I suppose I was wondering that. Wondering why you would even need me here, if you already know everything."

"The answer is no. I am not a supercomputer. No more than you are. There are plenty of supercomputers out there, with memories containing most documented human knowledge. Plenty of AI minds working through humanity's problems. Computers that can process more data than you or I could in a lifetime. But computation was never the purpose of bringing me into being. The purpose was to create a *true* android. An android inside and out: a robot not only human in appearance, but human in . . . I'm not sure what to name it. In consciousness? But they still do not agree as to whether I am truly conscious or not—though I believe I am."

Altantsetseg's back arched. Her fingers spread. Out at sea, hisses and whistling. A series of bursts, distant thumps.

"I think what they were looking for was a being that was human in . . . let us say cognitive aspect. They wanted me to think like them. To *be* like them in mind."

"And are you?"

"I don't know. I often feel—I feel a bit aslant, Ha."

"Aslant?"

"A bit alien. A bit . . ." Evrim adjusted the collar of the strange robe, drew it closer at the throat. "*Mad.*"

Ha shrugged. "So do I. I think that's normal."

"Do you?" Evrim turned to her, and Ha recognized the look on their face. This expression came through perfectly. It was hope—the naked hope that another being had understood. Truly understood. It was so moving that Ha almost wanted to put her arms around Evrim. She had not thought it was possible to be more alone than she often felt—but now she saw it most certainly was.

Then the open, hopeful expression faded with a blink. Evrim's face returned to its default state—an approximation of neutral, collegiate friendliness. An approximation only. It struck a false note. Yes, Evrim was more alone than she was. "Yes. I would imagine so," said Evrim. "You are also a very singular person. For the record—while we are sharing confidences—I believe your book *How Oceans Think* is one of the most brilliant things I have ever read. Not just on cephalopod intelligence: On consciousness itself. On communication. Once I read it, I knew this was a puzzle I could not unravel without you."

"I'm glad you liked it." Ha did not like to talk about the book. She did not like being praised for it.

"Not that my opinion matters much. It's not my field. But I found your book comforting. I felt . . . it seemed to describe . . . well, more about that later. Dr. Mínervudóttir-Chan says I need to work on sharing a bit less. She says humans value reticence. Especially in me."

"I memorized one of my worst reviews," Ha said, smiling bitterly. "'In this book, Dr. Ha Nguyen swims around with cephalopods and then asks a lot of questions. Unsure whether she is a neuroscientist or a philosopher, she ends up being neither.' I rather liked that one. At least it was witty. And probably correct."

"Your colleagues respect your insights greatly. They say you have invented a new field, and the problem is not your work: it is that nobody is yet capable of understanding it. One of them called it 'the science of a future I would be grateful to live in.'"

"That is kind of them."

"Well, the book was like a message in a bottle, sent from one deserted island to another. It brought you here. And here, maybe you can answer your critics, once and for all."

"I think the rule," Ha said, "is never to answer critics. One simply moves on with the work."

"I agree—that is a better strategy. Anyway—I am glad

that you are here. I think you will do your best work on this island."

"I hope so. Thank you for your trust. And it's *we*. *We* will do our best work here. Together."

For a moment that flash of vulnerability crossed Evrim's features. But they said nothing.

The passing cloud.

In her tank, Altantsetseg brought her knees up to her chest, pushed them back down, and spread her arms wide. *Like she's casting spells.* Then her body relaxed, but the surface of her skin twitched with neural impulses.

It was silent enough outside to hear the waves again, the cacophony of jungle sound at their backs.

"It is over. She'll be shifting to cleanup mode now. Keeping the oil and pollutants out of the water. We should go back to bed. There is nothing more to see here."

But both Evrim and Ha stood for a moment more in front of the tank. Ha was visually tracing Altantsetseg's scars. So many: Himalayan whorls of scar tissue, the Hindu Kush along a collarbone, earthquakes of muscle underneath.

"She took my macaroon, you know."

"Sorry, what?"

"She took my macaroon. Just like she said she would. She broke into my room and stole it," Evrim said. "It couldn't have been anyone else. She has a passkey. You know, it's good you are here. For many reasons. For one thing, Altantsetseg and I were beginning to get on one another's nerves."

Symbols do not come from nowhere. Not at first. Early hieroglyphic systems have connections to the world. Even in the highly sophisticated and abstracted *hanzi* characters of the modern Chinese logographic system, we see the traces of those relations—like the character for person, 人, which depicts a figure, however simplified, recognizably related to a standing human.

Language is abstract, yes—but it emerges from real relations with real things in the world and bears the traces of that ancient relationship. These traces will be the keys to deciphering the symbols of another species—if only we can recognize them.

—Dr. Ha Nguyen, *How Oceans Think*

11

IN THE EARLY DAWN, Ha walked down the road toward what had been the island's port of Ben Dam. She had not slept all night. In her mind, ships burned. When she closed her eyes, she saw Altantsetseg in her tank: scars like mountain ranges on a topographic map, underwater ridges shuddering in connective liquid.

But this was not what had kept her awake. What kept her up was the puzzle of the shape the octopus had projected on its skin repeatedly. A sign—a symbol. It could mean anything at all—but it might, also, be connected to an original form, a real object in the world. And if it was, it could be a key. The shape appeared again and again in her mind:

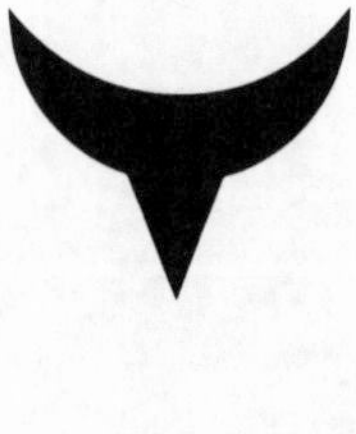

She had filled a notebook page with the symbol—simplifying it even further, abstracting it to just a part of a circle, with a wedge or a line pointing downward. *Downward? Would the octopus perceive it as downward?* Most likely. Even though the element it existed in was more fluid than ours, the octopus was more subject to gravity than a fish. It was not much of a swimmer. It walked, hunted, grazed on the sea bottom, along rocks and reefs. When threatened, it raised itself up, like a human drawing erect, like an ape swelling its chest and rising on its arms. Like a bear on its hind legs. So yes—there should be, in its world, a down and an up.

But was the wedge pointing down?

And was it a wedge, an arrow, a line?

The symbol, clearly a warning or a threat, nagged at her. She felt as if at some level she already understood it. Had seen it before.

Trees blurred the edge of the road to the port, reclaiming space for themselves. The pavement was scattered with leaves and the husks of seedpods. Monkeys and morning birds screamed from the canopy branches.

The port of Ben Dam had been little more than a small jetty and a cluster of warehouses and shops crammed along a single street. In tourist pictures, the jetty was always lined with women hawking fish from shallow baskets against a background of colorful fishing boats. The tiny port was in a bay shaped like a V, with its sharp tip pointed to the southeast and its open end facing northwest. At the southwestern tip, nearest the abandoned hotel, was a small channel, often filled with tidal surges and treacherous currents. The northwestern end, on the other hand, was nearly a mile wide.

The "bay" was not, in fact, a bay: it was a channel between

the island of Con Son, the main island of the Con Dao Archipelago, to the east, and the uninhabited forested hump of Hon Ba to the west.

Here, the damage done by the evacuation was more apparent than it was in the silent, shuttered houses of Con Son Town that Ha had passed through on the night of her arrival. Con Son Town had looked almost peaceful, as if its inhabitants had simply drifted away. But here, sunken fishing boats studded the bay. Wrecks, including a large passenger ferry, were seeded across the entrances to the harbor to render them impassable.

Ha had been here. Sixteen. The hydrofoil journey over the water from Vung Tau had been a blur: She had been watching the boy she loved. Watching him chat with the other boys, watching him look out the window at the green warp of sea, watching him read.

Ha had seen Con Dao, but not seen it: it was as if the orphanage field trip had not taken place in the physical world. No. Her world had been built, that year, of pure emotion. The island was nothing but a backdrop to her feelings. The arrival here was a smear of color and sound. Voices of hawkers, the island of Hon Ba behind the swaying fishing boats—all of it meaningless in the face of her obsession. And she felt now, as she often had then, the shame of that obsession rising in her skin, burning her throat, welling into her cheeks. His indifference to her. His face turned away.

They were on the island three days, staying in Con Son Town, but when she arrived on the island this time it had not felt like a return. She'd recognized almost nothing. Like she had never been here at all: the place she had visited as a lonely teenager was warped out of recognition by the gravity of obsession. She tried to think of that place. Instead, she saw only him: his perfect face, his eyes always turned away from her. She remembered running up to him, one morning on the beach. Wet from the waves, feeling pretty in her swimsuit, trying to get him to see her. She'd thrown sand at him. He'd smiled, glanced at her the way you look at a stranger passing on the street: lazily, only vaguely interested, only vaguely wondering about them at all. Then he had turned away, with that same smile on his face.

That day at breakfast she sat at his table. He didn't even look at her. He asked her to pass a plate of sweet basil leaves, calling her by the wrong name.

Her attention on him had warped her memories, the way the gravity of a star will warp space-time around it. He had drawn everything in toward himself. Con Dao, her teachers and caretakers, even the other students from the orphanage, were just the distorted swirl of atoms around him.

Ha remembered that younger self, so caught up in emotion, with loathing. That person was alien to her. Worse than alien, because that sixteen-year-old self *was* her, but at the same time *was not* her. Like a preconscious being. A *thing* that she had been.

In the orphanage, personal isolation had been as total as personal space was nonexistent. She had learned to cut herself off from others. Trust was unknown between the girls. Every possession was precious, to be defended or traded for something of equal or greater value. There was no question of alliances. Friendships were a method for exchanging another set of valuable trading commodities: bits of information. Those that could do the most damage carried the most value. The most destructive gossip could be exchanged for almost any physical object. It always accrued value.

The orphanage was not where she had learned to be

alone, though. She had been lonely there, yes, but she had always held out hope. Things the next year would be different. A new girl would come and they would connect. Or she would be adopted.

It was here that she had learned what it meant to be *completely* alone.

She found herself thinking of Evrim. Of what they had said about the automonks at the temple:

I find them eerie. Repulsive. I suppose it is the same for you when you look at a monkey. Unsettling.

That was how she felt, looking back at herself as a child: Like looking at some half-minded thing. An inferior version of the self she was now. A failed attempt.

Torn tarpaulins and ragged awnings flapped in the morning breeze across the maws of looted shops and warehouses. The road and jetty were scattered with ripped netting and shattered crates. There was a dark stain that could be dried blood.

This is the price the people of Con Dao paid. We should make their sacrifice worth something.

Hon Ba Island, green and silent, rose beyond the still life of a past chaos.

Ha walked back along the road, past a Buddhist shrine besieged by vines, past an abandoned ice factory where a monkey gathering fallen fruit stared at her.

There was no movement at the hotel. The sun was above the horizon, in a thin mist that silvered it and drained it of glare. The security gate opened automatically when Ha approached, as it had when she had left the hotel, though she could see no camera. Too crude. No, the camera would be insect-like, crawling along the hotel wall. Or winged and silent, a mote in the air above her.

She crossed the cracked terrace with its weed-choked pool. Below the silver coin of sun, she saw Evrim on the beach. Gathering shells?

But as Ha approached, she saw Evrim was sitting in the sand, hands wrapped around knees. And before them, at the tide line, a heap.

As Ha came closer, a cloud of flies rose from the heap and fell on it again. Ha saw the waterlogged clothes then, and knew. She began to run. No—to half run, pulled toward the scene but also resisting it. Evrim did not turn toward her. Ha stopped a few meters from the thing in the sand.

Half a man. Torn away at the waist, burned beyond recognition. Farther down the beach, another mound of mangled clothing and flesh. And then another.

Ha had seen a dead body before—a research assistant who had gone for a swim alone in the morning, and drowned. They had pulled her from the water hours later and brought her onto shore. Ha had looked down into the bloated horror of her face. But that had been nothing like this.

Evrim was muttering something, almost inaudible above the buzz of flies.

Ha felt her legs giving way, steadied herself. "You said the ships were automated."

Evrim's face turned to Ha, but their eyes looked past her. "I have done nothing but in care of thee . . . of thee, my dear one, thee, my daughter, who art ignorant of what thou art . . ."

"In care of *me*? What?"

Evrim shook their head, as if clearing a dream from their skull. "Sorry. I am sometimes—here, but not here."

"You said they were *automated*. The ships."

"Usually they are. But there are automated ships that carry crews."

“How can that be? Crews on robot ships?”

“Slaves. Trafficked persons, if one loves euphemism. Humans can be cheaper than robots. Sturdier, at sea. And more expendable.” Evrim stood and marched up the beach.

“Where are you going?”

“To find a shovel. These men are our responsibility. We must bury them. And then we must return to our work. We will send another submersible down today, once Altantsetseg has recovered enough to pilot it again.”

Ha was following Evrim up the beach. “Recovered?”

“It takes a lot out of her, coordinating a defense like she did last night. You won’t see her until midday, at the soonest. And I would recommend you tread lightly with her.”

“Tread lightly with her? She murdered these men.”

“Murdered?” Evrim seemed confused for a moment. “Murdered? Yes, she did. That is her job, and it is a difficult one. She will not feel well today. Come and help me find a shovel.”

When we avoid behaviors that would instigate a shark attack, we are recognizing the shark has a mind capable of reading our signs and responding to them. Like it or not, we are in communication with them. If we accidentally send out signs to a shark that indicate we are prey (if we look too much like a seal in our wet suit, or we produce vibrations in the water like a fish in distress), we know we may instigate an attack, despite the fact that the shark does not typically prey on humans. We can cause the shark to misinterpret the world's signs and make a mistake—a mistake which may be fatal to us.

How we see the world matters—but knowing how the world sees us also matters.

—Dr. Ha Nguyen, *How Oceans Think*

12

A KLAXON SOUNDED in the night. It was an alarm Eiko had not heard before. Red and blue light streamed across the walls of the barracks, slashed by the shadows of the barred windows. The alarm brought him bolt upright, but he had not been fully asleep: The *Sea Wolf* was rolling heavily in a swell. The crew's polynet hammocks swayed under a ceiling leaking salt and rainwater.

The trawling nets were in, the flash-freezing factory mercifully shuttered, all shifts locked behind the rust-stained barracks bars, in the smell of sea-sick vomit and misery. Even the strongest stomachs lurched and churned with the ship. At times, the *Sea Wolf* was almost sideways in the waves.

"She doesn't handle the weather well," Son said from his hammock next to Eiko. "She is heavy with her catch, and her load is poorly stowed."

Since the day Son had shielded Eiko from Bjarte's anger on the processing floor, Eiko and Son had become friends. They had hooked their hammocks up next to one another, playing cards with a stained deck in the off hours, sharing stories.

Partly, the friendship was a result of Eiko's new determination to care more. There was a time when he would have kept to himself. A time when even someone coming to his aid would not have been enough for him to begin confiding in that person. But now his determination to care had begun to feel almost religious.

That didn't mean it felt real to him—not yet. He still felt that distance, that detachment. But he was groping toward it, toward something genuine. Fellow feeling, or whatever one might call it: he had no word for what it was. He was forcing himself to connect, to feel, to identify with others. Because people had to matter. They had to. If *they* did not matter, it meant *he* did not matter.

And so Eiko was learning to listen. Was practicing listening. And he practiced on Son. Son had been a fisherman on his home archipelago of Con Dao. Small local vessels. Mostly illegally poaching in the national park. He came to regret that life only when he began working as a dive instructor. Son was born on the island and was filled with a nostalgic love for his home—its forests and mangroves, its coral reefs and turtle sanctuaries—all of it under constant threat from overfishing. His work as a dive instructor had changed him, turned him into a true ecological warrior. He and his boss, a man named Lawrence, had spent hours after their regular dives cutting trash fishing nets from his native corals and working with scientists to document Con Dao's dwindling biodiversity while the desperate commercial fishing fleets launched raid after raid on the fringes of the national park that protected the archipelago. Eiko admired this about Son: he had seen a problem, and he had done something about it.

He had cared.

It was a level of passion totally foreign to Eiko. Son had lived for a cause. He regaled Eiko with horror stories: dugongs washed up on the beach, hacked to death by boat propellers, endangered turtles netted and chopped up for the tourist trade, their eggs sold by the hundreds.

Son's favorite stories to tell, though, were of the Con Dao Sea Monster. There had been tales for generations of the monster. Maybe for as long as people had lived on the archipelago. Myths to scare children: shadows and drownings, shapes seen on the shore. But now everyone came to believe the stories. There were several deaths of illegal fishermen attributed to the monster—mostly local free divers who used cyanide or spears to kill reef fish for the tourist market. Most of the deaths were drownings. In some cases, the bodies were bruised and battered as if they had been forcibly held underwater.

Two of them, though, had been stabbed with their own spears. And a park ranger who was poaching turtle eggs had been slashed to death on the beach.

The more superstitious among Con Dao's population thought it was the ghosts of the political prisoners on the island, seeking revenge. Son didn't think so. He thought it was something natural, reacting to the overfishing, the constant harm to the reefs. It was life thrown out of balance, lashing out.

Then one of the dive shop's customers was killed by the Con Dao Sea Monster while Lawrence was leading him on a shipwreck dive.

That incident closed the dive shop Son worked for and brought Son's perfect job to an end, but the job would have ended anyway: shortly afterward, DIANIMA bought the archipelago.

The purchase of the archipelago was a corporate social

responsibility project, DIANIMA claimed—an effort to save it from continued environmental degradation and mismanagement. They evacuated the entire local population, with cash payouts that would allow people to start better lives elsewhere. *Deported us*, Son said.

It was strange to hear DIANIMA's name again. The company Eiko had planned to work for. When he heard it, he felt the edge of fresh pain at what his life had become. He was supposed to be working for them by this point. Working his way up through the corporate food chain, proving his worth. Paying back his parents' investment in him, their faith in his abilities.

There was a weak round of protests when DIANIMA evacuated the population, but in fact many of the locals were glad to go. The payouts were generous, and their lives on the island had been dull, their prospects limited to poaching and a desultory tourist industry that never grew enough to provide many of them with a living.

Son didn't believe DIANIMA's cover story about corporate social responsibility.

"Why?" Eiko asked.

"There is nothing on Con Dao that isn't elsewhere. We have reefs, okay—but no better than many islands. And not perfect: they have been damaged by overfishing. We have a few rare animals, maybe—the dugongs, a few others. But no one buys a whole island chain to protect the dugongs. No matter how much money they have. No. They are after the Con Dao Sea Monster. I know it."

"Chasing a rumor. Buying up an archipelago because of a rumor."

"It's not a *rumor.* It killed the man we were diving with. Not only him—others, too. Rumors don't kill people."

"So, a very dangerous sea creature."

"Dangerous, maybe. Lots of things are dangerous. Sharks, barracuda. Other people. That's not the point. It's not just dangerous—it's *smart.*"

"So what?"

"We talked about it all the time—about why they were buying the archipelago. There were lots of theories. But here's what I think: If you are a company that creates artificial minds, wouldn't you want to study a new kind of mind up close? If the Con Dao Sea Monster is smart, I bet DIANIMA wants to know how smart. How it works, and maybe how it got that way."

Son had not been glad to leave the archipelago, but he had known it was time. Without his job at the dive shop, there was nothing left on the island for him but illegal fishing, and he couldn't do that anymore. Not after his environmentalist conversion.

He'd gone to Vung Tau to look for work as a dive instructor.

That was where they took him. He was tranquilized in the bathroom of a bar, shoved into a van, and sold to the *Sea Wolf*'s procurers.

Eiko didn't believe the talk about sea monsters, but it was pleasant listening to Son. And about DIANIMA? Who knew? The most probable explanation was that the company wanted a base of operations that was totally secret. Eiko was willing to bet they were hiding something on those islands. Developing something out there. Something even more scandalous and innovative than that conscious robot they had built. He wished he were working for them, on whatever project it was.

Working his way up the corporate food chain.

Son liked to talk. He'd learned a skewed but efficient English as a dive instructor, and he used it to great effect. That was lucky for him. English was the common language of the enslaved crew of the *Sea Wolf*. And it was the language of the mercenary guards, who spoke either in English or in violence: a fist, a kick, the butt of a rifle. Better to have them speak to you in English.

Even those of the "crew" who had been kidnapped without knowing a word of English—the two Malays captured drifting in a life raft the month before, for example—learned the basics quickly. It was a matter of survival.

In fact, Eiko didn't think English was the native language of anyone on board. But it was one of the only things all of them had in common.

The *Sea Wolf*, trying to pick up speed, rolled heavily. The hammocks in the barracks swung.

"No," Son said, "she doesn't handle the weather well at all."

She. Interesting. He never would have thought of the *Sea Wolf* as a she. But in the English language all vessels, he now remembered from a high school class, were traditionally *she*. How arbitrary. Eiko imagined the cruel mind that lurked behind the armored steel door of the wheelhouse as an *it*. A force. A thing.

The Klaxon continued. Outside the locked barracks, down on the main deck, Eiko heard shouting, just audible over the groaning of the ship in the heavy sea.

Then a sound came that could be heard above all else: the firing of the *Sea Wolf*'s recoilless rifle. Crew were getting out of their hammocks now. Son and Eiko joined the curious at the bars of the small windows, jostling for a view.

The deck was awash in foaming sea that poured over the

gunwales. The recoilless rifle, mounted on a swivel on the fo'c'sle, could not be seen from the barracks: those forward-facing windows were welded shut with steel plates. But it was not far from the barracks bulkhead, and when it fired again it resounded like a hammer on steel plate.

"A rescue?"

What they could see down on the main deck was a chaos of mercenary activity: Figures darkly cowled, moving about between the trawling machinery under the gantry tower. Two of them were crouched along the gunwale on the port side.

The *Sea Wolf*'s spotlights crawled across the chop. And then Eiko saw it: a gray ship, prow cutting through the water, a few hundred meters off the port side. The ship was twenty meters or so long, its deck filled with dark shapes and spiked with at least three swivel-mounted weapons. As it swung into view, tracer bullets arced from its bow toward the *Sea Wolf.*

"Alaskan pirates," the man standing next to Son said. One of the crew who had been there when Eiko was taken—an Indonesian who prayed five times a day on a tattered blue tarp. "They must know our hold is full of—"

His head ceased to exist in a cloud of bone splinters, blood, and brain matter.

Screaming and chaos. Men slithering along the floor toward the safest possible place, though there was no safe place. Eiko lay facedown with his hands over his head as if they could protect him, as close to the starboard side as he could manage. Son crawled up next to him.

The recoilless rifle hammered over and over. The port wall of the barracks was a constellation of holes—it looked like Scorpius. The window the Indonesian was looking out of when he was shot was at the center of it.

I didn't know his name. Didn't care enough to know, even

though he taught me how to gut yellowfish quickly enough to keep the guards from hitting me. I never cared enough. I still don't.

Then the Klaxon went silent. The *Sea Wolf* was turning to port, hard, shoving Eiko against the starboard bulkhead of the barracks. Acceleration. The shudder of impact. Eiko was crawling across the floor, not thinking, moving to the port-side window.

Have to see. Have to know.

The *Sea Wolf*'s spotlights played across writhing chop. There. Off the port side. Dark shapes of men in the water. The gray ship slipping under, side staved in.

Rammed them. So daring, desperate. Something a human would do.

A pale face looked up out of the sea—black-bearded and wide-eyed. A chatter of bullets from the *Sea Wolf*'s gunwale pushed it down into red water.

The recoilless rifle hammered in fury, like a madman who continues to stab a corpse. The wheelhouse of the gray ship tore away in flame.

Madness. Not logic.

Moments later, the gray ship went under. Eiko saw its shadow for a moment, descending, the fire in its wheelhouse still burning beneath the water, like an oil lamp behind waxed paper. Then gone.

Madness.

The opaque, hardened glass of the wheelhouse. Its reinforced steel-plate door. Beyond it the mind full of sonar, maps of banks and shoals, trawling methods, and market prices. The mind also full of rage and violence.

What monsters have we made?

II

Umwelt

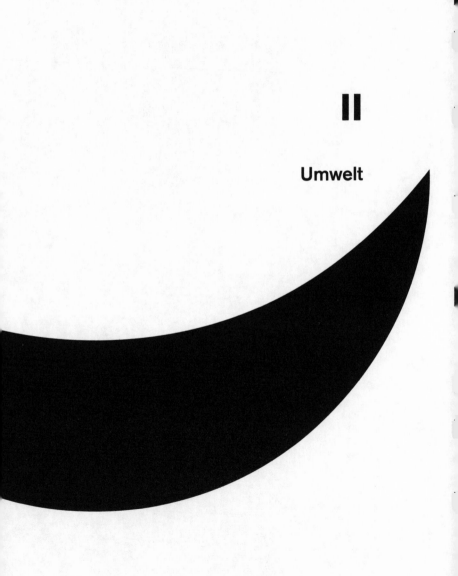

What matters to the blind, deaf tick is the presence of butyric acid. For the black ghost knifefish, it's electrical fields. For the bat, what matters is air-compression waves. This is the animal's umwelt: that portion of the world their sensory apparatus and nervous system allow them to sense. It is the only portion of the world that "matters" to them.

The human umwelt is structured according to our species' sensory apparatus and nervous system as well. But the octopus will have an umwelt nothing like ours. In a sense (and I use that word purposefully) we will not exist in the same world.

—Dr. Ha Nguyen, *How Oceans Think*

13

DA MINH WATCHED THE BEER for a moment before picking it up. Watched it sweating in the shade of the roadside café's ragged umbrella. Cold. He brought it to his lips. Yes. So cold, fresh out of the ice chest, its label wet and sliding off under his fingertips. He drank deeply, though not as deeply as he wanted to. He wanted to drink and, when it hit the back of his throat, cold and clean, keep drinking until it was gone.

He'd spent the morning in the sun, stacking bricks behind the factory. His skin was coated with brick dust. It was not a particularly hot morning here in Vung Tau, but it was hot enough.

He looked at the woman across from him, looked into the swirl of colors that danced around her head. Behind her, under the noonday sun, the street also shimmered, a stream of heat mirage under the wheels of the motorbikes. She sat unperturbed by the sun, her head a swarm of rainbow bees, waiting for him to finish.

He set the beer down. He'd decided he would count to thirty in his head before he picked it up again.

The swarm sucked at the straw of its coconut water. Da

Minh had counted to five when the voice, with the dead modulation of an automated announcement at a train station, said: "You were hard to find. Not staying in one place long?"

"Hard to get work these days," Da Minh said. They were speaking Vietnamese. With the weird modulation of the voice caused by the abglanz, Da Minh could not tell if the woman was using a translator. Her hands were small, brown. The nails were painted gold. She could have been anyone. "Too many people here from the island, all looking for the same jobs. And there are no jobs."

"But you found work. At the brick factory."

"My cousin works there." Thirty. He picked up the beer and drank again. Not as cold this time. The heat was already getting to it. He drained as much as pride would allow him and set it back down on the table.

"Nobody ever offered me money to tell my story before. Usually I tell it for free."

"Well," the swarm said, "lucky you."

"Where do you want me to start?"

The straw stabbed into the swirl of color again. "Just tell it like you usually do."

"Okay. You paid, so I will tell you the truth."

"Yes. Please do that." Sarcasm? Impossible to tell.

"I was a ranger out on Hon Bay Canh. At the turtle sanctuary there. We worked for the park, but the salary was almost nothing. And the job was not easy. All night, you watch the beach. The turtles come in, they lay eggs. You go down, you tag the turtles after they lay the eggs, then you dig up the eggs and you take them to the incubation area. It is a narrow beach, so if you don't do that, another turtle will come along, maybe dig up the eggs looking for a place to lay her own, see? All night long you do this. And the pay is no good. So—we fish. Spearfish. For food for us and our families. And sometimes, too, we sell the eggs. That's the truth. I'm not a bad person, but I had to live. I saved lots of sea turtle eggs, yeah? Hard work. But also I took some. Sold them. We all did it. If there is a park ranger who says he didn't steal eggs, he's lying."

He paused. He could feel the blood in his face, telling it. The unfairness of it. *If they had paid me a salary I could live on. If they had treated me better.*

"I'm not here to judge you," the swarm said.

Twenty. Maybe more. He'd stopped counting in his head. He drank. Almost warm now.

Not here to judge me. But he knew DIANIMA did judge him, and all of the other rangers at the park. That was why they had bought the island, right? That was why Da Minh didn't have a home anymore. Sure, they had given him money. Sure. But he had already spent it—lost it, really, trying to open a business with that crook. Anyway, if they wanted to pay him for the story, that was fine. They owed that to him. But he wasn't a thief, or a poacher. He was born on Con Dao. It was his island. He never asked for it to be turned into a preserve. All he'd wanted to do was live.

"It was late. The sun had gone down. But it was not dark yet. We were not supposed to use our lights at night. Scares the turtles away, right? But we would go down to the shore sometimes with a small flashlight and our equipment in the late evening, to hunt crabs and whatever we could catch near the shore. That was what we were doing then: Hien had a spear and a net and his jug. I had the same. He was forty meters or so from me when I saw him stab at something at the surf line with his spear.

"'I saw an octopus!' he said. 'Good size. If I can get it, we'll eat well tonight!'

"Then I saw the shape coming."

Da Minh paused. "I don't know why you want this story. Nobody believes it. They threw me in jail, you know? Two months. Finally let me go, but all over the island people whispered I had done it. Why? Why would I do it?" He felt the old anger again, directed now at this woman across from him, at the glistening haze that cowled her head. DIANIMA. Hadn't they done enough to him? They should pay more.

"As I said—I'm not here to judge you."

"The thing—it didn't come out of the water: it came from up the beach. I saw it—crawling along. Then when it was near Hien it . . ." He paused. "It stood up."

He took another drink of the beer, finishing it this time. It was no good. Already too warm. But then the woman ordered another.

He would take the afternoon off. He would go for a swim. He imagined himself floating, half drunk, in the warm water.

But part of him was back on that beach on Hon Bay Canh. It wasn't always like this when he tried to tell the story: Usually he just told it, almost without thinking. Usually it was a caricature—a few still images in his brain, simplified down for the telling. But this was different. He felt he was there again.

It had come down the beach—not out of the water. At first it was low to the ground, like a moving stain on the sand. And by the way it had moved he had known what it was: an octopus. But then it rose up, almost standing on the ends of its arms, like a man. Had that happened? Sometimes he thought he had imagined that part. It had almost seemed to take the shape of a man, to move like a man, to move its arms together like a man's legs. Could that have been? It was not possible. But he knew it had happened. He had seen it.

By then he was screaming and running toward Hien, waving his arms. Hien, standing there with a grin on his face, looking into the water, spear at the ready, like nothing was happening at all. Hien's smile turned into a look of confusion, but it was just confusion at what Da Minh was doing. And then the thing moved past Hien, pausing for only a moment, clinging to Hien for a second, waving its arms about. Then it dropped down and slid into the water.

Da Minh took no more than five seconds to cross the space between them. When he got there, Hien was facedown at the edge of the water. Da Minh bent down to him, turned him over. He couldn't understand, at first, what he was seeing: the dark trail out into the water, pouring from Hien. Then he saw—Hien's throat, face, and arms were covered with deep slashes. His blood was pouring into the ocean. He opened and closed his mouth over and over again.

Just like a fish. Just the same as a fish, drowning in the air.

He had done nothing to save Hien. There was nothing *to* do. By the time Da Minh recovered enough from his shock to move, Hien had stopped moving forever.

By the time Da Minh had finished telling his story, a third beer had been ordered.

"Well," the flattened, empty voice said, "I should let you get back to work."

"I'm not going back today. I'll go for a swim. I'll say I got sick."

If the voice could have sounded surprised, maybe it would have. "You still swim?"

Da Minh wanted to push her into the street, wanted to watch her hammered to the pavement by a dozen electric motorbikes. “After a few beers, I can.”

Da Minh walked out past the end of Thuy Van Street to the wild beach, where he stepped out of everything but his underwear and swam into the warm waves. He backstroked out fifty, sixty meters. He wished the woman had not asked him about swimming, because now he felt it: the nagging fear that had always been there after that day. He could dull it with alcohol until it almost disappeared. Almost. But he was always looking for shapes in the water. A strange stone could startle him enough, sometimes, to make him swim back in.

He had not told the woman about one thing. The thing he had told no one about. He was going to tell her—she had paid for his information, after all. But then he had gotten angry at her, for reasons he could not sort out in his mind, and decided to keep it to himself.

He had been crouched in the sand, just saying Hien’s name over and over, as if somehow that would bring his friend back. And then saw it—lying there in the sand, near Hien’s bloody, torn head.

A shell, half filled with salt water and blood. On some impulse, he picked it up. Maybe just to get the blood out of it, Hien’s blood.

It had been sharpened.

Da Minh carried it with him back to the ranger station when he radioed for help. Then later he took it out to the mangroves on the other side of the island and threw it into the sea.

He never told anyone about it. It was sharp as a razor, chiseled and rubbed to an edge just the way they used to do when he was a kid. They would make knives from shells sometimes, attaching them to a wooden handle with wire or string. It had looked like that, but without a handle.

It was like something a human would make.

And it was a murder weapon. He threw it into the sea because he knew if it were found, they would say he had done the killing. It would be their proof. He knew he was going to spend months in jail. He knew there would be beatings. But there was still a chance he could escape the worst of it, at least.

And he did. He escaped the murder charge, and he told no one about the shell he had found.

So why did the woman deserve to know? She didn't. The secret was his.

He floated with his eyes closed, head tilted back, letting the sun turn the world behind his eyelids into an explosion of reds and yellows.

It was a little hum or buzz that caused him to open his eyes. At first it sounded like a motor. But when he looked up, he saw the insect hovering over him, silvery in the sun. He lazily swiped at it, but as he did so it darted down and landed on his neck. He felt a small pinch, and smacked at it, but missed. It buzzed away.

For several minutes, Da Minh watched the sun from underwater, only dimly aware of drowning.

There are many levels of consciousness here on earth. Many animals are self-aware, to one degree or another. But culture, not consciousness, is what we are searching for. Not other minds, or other selves—which are everywhere—but other societies.

—Dr. Ha Nguyen, *How Oceans Think*

14

FOR THIS TASK, Altantsetseg did not need to immerse herself in her connective bath: gloves were enough. The gloves were of gray material that to Ha looked like shed snakeskin, loose and translucent, wrapping Altantsetseg's arms to above the elbows, like the accessories to a strange ball gown.

Evrim had waited until after noon to summon the security officer, giving her plenty of time alone with her coffee. But Altantsetseg still did not look herself. Her shrapnel scars stood out starkly, black pits against a pallid background, a negative image of constellations in a sky.

On-screen, live, the submersible descended through plankton-moted water, its headlamps illuminating streak-forms of fish. The aperture of its camera blurred as it attempted to catch a passing object, or rapidly focused on some bit of eyestalked plankton gaping stupidly at the intruder as it drifted past.

Then the running lamps found the shipwreck, listed on its side. The dark, rounded rectangle of the hatch. Visibility was decent. The submersible was more than five meters above the ship, but the hull's outline stood out against the shallow seafloor.

On the beach that morning Ha had tried to help with the burials. But she was sick in the sand the moment they moved the first corpse and the flies swarmed her face. She'd vomited, then washed her mouth with seawater that tasted as saline and mineral-rich as blood.

She'd tried to return to the task, but finally had to leave Evrim to do it all. Evrim seemed unmoved by the men's deaths, undisturbed by their torn bodies. Ha wished she could feel the same. She could not.

We need to call someone, she'd kept thinking. *Someone has to be told.*

But who? This wasn't an emergency: Evrim was right. These killings were protocol, carried out to protect the island. These men had died because the ship they were on had attempted to force its way through a blockade. They were killed as a *matter of routine* by a security officer doing her job. They had died—Altantsetseg had killed them—to protect this place. And to protect the work being done here. They had died so Ha could continue her research. And so the octopuses could continue to live.

Back in her room that morning, Ha had collapsed into a dreamless, exhausted sleep from which she woke dry-mouthed and confused. When she'd finally managed to come down to the hotel lobby, she found Evrim and Altantsetseg sitting at opposite ends of the long table, like a rich estranged couple in an old film. Altantsetseg was listless over a cup of coffee. Evrim was studying a terminal.

It was like nothing had happened. Like they had not buried three corpses that morning. And how many more were floating out there, being torn by scavengers in the drift? Ha drank two glasses of water from the distiller before filling a cup with coffee and sitting down, as far away from either of them as she could.

A happy family. Just like I always dreamed of.

A few days before, she had told Evrim they would do their best work on this island together. But now this didn't seem like a team at all. She was a part of something she did not understand, making calculations that were unacceptable to her. Putting the lives of innocent people in a balance, weighing them against the safety of her work, against the lives of the octopuses. As if it were a calculation. It wasn't a calculation—it was killing. It may have been necessary, but she wasn't obligated to find it acceptable. She could not—and the fact that both Altantsetseg and Evrim did frightened her. She remembered Evrim's indifference: the way they treated the corpses, as if the bodies were no more precious than the sand they were being buried in.

She didn't want to be there, at the table. She wanted to be with Kamran. Just talking with him, in the safety of her room. But Kamran would sense something was wrong. Kamran would want to help fix it. She wasn't ready for that. Wasn't ready to retreat into that easy relationship. To have someone try to heal her. The sight of the torn bodies on the beach, the cloud of flies: She needed to carry them with her a while longer. Needed to keep them in her mind—the way she had focused at times, during her studies, on the anger that came following a negative review, a rejection: Not as a way of stymieing her research, but as motivation to work harder, to push further. To make the sacrifices of all these people worth something.

The thought returned to her again and again. It had first come to her at the port of Ben Dam, where the scars of what had been done to the people here during the island's evacuation were visible to her for the first time: the blood shed, the lives uprooted, the families ejected. The population of the archipelago had been only five or six thousand, at the most. But now they were five or six thousand refugees. Were they huddled together somewhere, in a single neighborhood, trading reminiscences of the islands they would never see again? Or were they already scattered across a dozen cities?

How much had DIANIMA given them? What compensation was enough for never being able to see one's home again?

On-screen, the submersible was navigating into the dark hatch. Here in the research lab, Altantsetseg signed in a language shared only between her and the submersible she commanded. One gray-clad palm brushed against another. The submersible's running lights brightened.

The bulkheads of the ship were colonized with decades of sea life. Nothing at this depth lay barren for long. Everything was a surface for an organism to bind to, a niche to inhabit, a shelter from predators. For ocean life, everything was an opportunity. The ship was more alive, sunk here, than it ever was when in service.

Then Ha saw it. A mottled form at the corner of the screen, more movement than shape. It had been blending with the bulkhead. It separated and moved off.

There you are.

Ha had been thinking, after the beach, of abandoning this project. Of turning her back on it all. She had been thinking of asking to be sent back to her writing, her research grants. The slow routine of science. The long, comforting evenings in conversation with Kamran, sealed off from the world.

A glimpse of the creature was enough to push that from her mind. No. She wasn't going anywhere.

There you are.

And as if in answer to the thought, the octopus came into the submersible's view again. Altantsetseg had the craft in a holding position, panning its camera across the walls of the chamber. The chamber had been a storage hold: the space was basically empty of equipment.

"Angle the camera down," Evrim said. "Slowly—try not to make any sharp movements."

Altantsetseg's fingers flexed and the submersible's beams played across a bulkhead. There was movement at the edge of the screen—a piece of the floor that came alive and crawled away.

"Pan right."

The beam played across the encrusted surface of the bulkhead. More movement: something flashed past the camera, above it and close.

It came into view.

The octopus was standing, the tips of its arms the only things in contact with the floor of the chamber. As in the video before, it was in the full "Nosferatu" pose—tall, its mantle vertical above its head, its arms and web spread. The threat pose. And like before, the octopus, easily as tall as a human being, was almost white.

Speak to me.

The octopus began to make passing cloud patterns on its skin. The patterns started on its mantle and moved downward between its eyes and onto its web, where each symbol paused a moment before fading and being replaced with a new one, even slower than they were in the earlier film Ha had watched.

It is trying to be understood. Like a native speaker, speaking slowly to a foreigner.

"It wants to communicate," Ha said aloud. "It's trying to make the submersible understand. Look how intentional the sequence is."

"Yes," said Evrim. "I see it. Slower, even, and clearer than before."

"It's *enunciating.*" Without looking down at her terminal, Ha was sketching the symbols she could catch in the sequence. Later she would be able to go over all of it in detail.

The same symbol was repeated, at intervals:

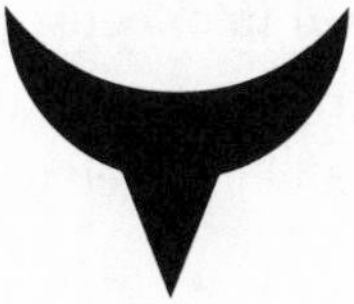

But there were many more. Ha sketched as many as she could.

But what was that?

"Pan down. Focus behind the octopus. Move slowly. There. My god."

Smaller octopuses. At least a dozen of them, moving across the walls and floor. Juveniles—their arms foreshortened, their heads too large for their bodies. Another shape, beyond them: two other adults, drifting near the edge of the water's murky visibility. One of them was a sickly white—not the pearl of the communicating octopus, but an unhealthy bleached look, patched in places with rusty spots. It was missing two of its tentacles. "There," said Ha. "An old one. The others must be taking care of it . . ."

"An entire family group," said Evrim. "I count at least sixteen of them . . ."

Everything went white.

"Damn," Altantsetseg mumbled, her hands flinching as if burned. "We move. Backward and downside up. With quickness."

The camera tried to find focus again. When it did, it was macroed in on a line of suckers across its lens.

"Submersible has small defensive weapon. Electrical charge. I will—"

"Don't," Ha and Evrim said simultaneously.

The suckers were gone. Dark water.

"We're outside dead boat," Altantsetseg said.

The camera snapped into focus, catching the elongated shape of an octopus jetting away. As they watched, the creature swung a wide arc and plunged back into the open hatch of the ship.

"Not damaged. Still plenty of power. We go back. Find other door into dead boat."

"No," Ha said. *Was that . . . ? Yes. There.* "No. Bring the submersible back. We have enough video to analyze for now. I want to study the data. Bring the submersible back to shore. Bring it back slowly, and in a straight line."

This is the mystery we thrust ourselves into: A single neuron is not conscious of its existence. A network of billions of unconscious single neurons is. These monads living in a world without perception become a being that perceives, thinks, and acts. Consciousness lies not in neurons, but in a sophisticated pattern of connectivity.

—Dr. Arnkatla Mínervudóttir-Chan, *Building Minds*

15

THE INDONESIAN WAS NAMED BAKTI, but everyone had called him "Backy" in the amalgamated English they spoke to one another.

Son volunteered to take care of his body. Eiko helped. They sewed the headless corpse into a greasy tarpaulin the guards allowed them. Others cleaned the barracks of Backy's blood and pieces of his skull. The rags went into the tarpaulin with the body.

It was just past dawn, and cold on the processing deck. Eiko's fingers were numb as he worked the big needle through the plastic of the tarpaulin. He jabbed himself twice, wiped the blood on his pants, and continued.

The guards stood in a loose semicircle, watching. One of their own was zipped neatly into a black body bag by the gunwale. By subtraction, Eiko determined it was Bjarte.

Once Son and Eiko had finished sewing Backy into his shroud, two other crew members helped lift him over the gunwale. Weighted with a piece of broken chain sewn into the tarpaulin with him, his body slid under as soon as it hit the white chop of the sea.

No one said anything in his honor. They just looked over the side at the approximate area where he had gone into the water. A place set apart from the rest of the sea's surface, like a doorway Backy had passed through. But it became more and more difficult to remember where it was as the *Sea Wolf* moved relentlessly away. Finally, it was just ocean, undifferentiated from the rest.

The guards tipped Bjarte's body bag overboard. After it splashed into the water, the woman called Monk spat into the ocean. Each of the other three guards who had carried Bjarte's body did the same.

Eiko folded the needle in his palm. They would forget they had lent it. Later he could hide it in the mesh of his hammock or elsewhere.

Now there are seven.

The *Sea Wolf*'s pace was relentless. But it was still heavy, off-balance. The ship lumbered through the chop.

They would have to put into port soon. Son had said they were moving south. Maybe headed to Vancouver, or Seattle. The slave crew would be locked belowdecks, but there might be an opportunity . . .

Eiko wasn't the only one thinking of it. The listless conversations in the barracks, which stank of cleaning fluid and sweat—and of death, though that might be a trick of the mind—were all about when they would put into port. Though nobody talked of escape, afraid the guards were listening—or, more terrifyingly, that the mind behind the armored steel door of the wheelhouse was listening—Eiko knew everyone was thinking of it. Especially after the attack, and Backy's death.

Was the weather growing warmer? But they could not have come that far yet. There were seven mercenaries left.

There were over twenty crew. The guards could make a mistake—or be pushed to make one. Anything could happen. Close to shore, the slaves might have a chance.

Eiko walked the many rooms, gardens, and eras of the Minaguchi-ya, his memory palace, collecting scrolls he had hidden in stone lanterns, in the folded pieces of paper slid beneath tatami mats, under a sake cup on a shelf in the kitchen: everything he knew about the guards' movements and habits, their personalities and quirks. Each night, after Son had fallen asleep, Eiko lay awake in his hammock. But in his mind, he sat cross-legged in the garden of the Minaguchi-ya, where he had gathered the scrolls in a pile. He read each one carefully, preparing himself.

When they came into port, he would be ready to act.

He was on the processing deck, sliding his knife into the belly of the thousandth fish of that day's catch, when the *Sea Wolf* slowed and began to turn.

Could this be it? Were they turning toward shore?

Then he saw it on the horizon.

They all saw it.

The crew abandoned their tasks and moved toward the starboard gunwale of the ship, as if dragged there by force. The guards did nothing to stop them. They, too, were moving toward the *Sea Wolf*'s starboard side. They stood a few meters behind the crew.

It was a gray, terraced mass, the size of forty *Sea Wolves* or more. It was studded with outcroppings of recoilless rifle emplacements, gantries, and cranes. Men moved about on its decks—sfumato figures in the mist off the water.

"A factory ship," someone said.

There was no shore to be seen anywhere. The undifferentiated surface of the ocean met with the horizon in every direction.

Eiko glanced to his right, at Son. Son was weeping, his face a mask of exhaustion and despair.

The *Sea Wolf* continued its arcing turn. All along the gunwale, the faces of the crew were the same—streaked with tears, the hope torn out of them.

The *Sea Wolf*'s horn moaned and was answered by a low growl from the factory ship. Eiko saw something else in the faces of his crew mates then: terror.

We see a level of tool use in the octopus that surpasses that of any birds or mammals other than humans. Consider the compound tool use of the Indonesian octopuses, who carry two discarded coconut halves with them across the seafloor, stilt-walking with them underneath their bodies, then reassembling the halves to use as armor against predators. The coconuts, discarded by humans, are collected by the octopuses for this specific purpose.

While we see other animals use found objects for shelters and assemble compound objects (such as nests), nowhere else do we see this level of sophisticated tool use in the animal kingdom. This cannot be dismissed as instinct. It is a learned behavior. When we try to reassemble the train of thought that must have gone into this, what else can we do but admit we are looking at an animal whose curiosity, adventurousness, and sophistication are unparalleled in most of the animal world?

—Dr. Ha Nguyen, *How Oceans Think*

16

THE WORLD STILL CONTAINS MIRACLES, despite everything that has been done to it.

Ha watched the automonk carry the wicker basket down to the beach. Gently, the automonk tilted the basket to the sand. The small, flippered ovals of sea turtle hatchlings poured out, scrambling for the waterline.

Despite everything we have done to the ocean, despite everything we have done to this world, life finds a way.

Some of the hatchlings turned in the wrong direction, crawling up the beach away from the water. The automonk intercepted them, kneeling in the sand in its saffron robes to turn the confused stragglers back toward the sea.

Ha and Evrim watched from a prescribed distance. Evrim was dressed in a set of brown coveralls, rolled up to the knee but still wet from wading in from the drone skiff. Evrim was barefoot, their long, delicate feet covered in sand. Ha could still feel the distance between them, but here in the bright sun, watching the turtles wobble into the water, it seemed less important. Less permanent.

"The automonks watch the beach all night long," Evrim

said. "As soon as a turtle has dug its nest in the sand, laid its eggs, and departed, they come down from the sanctuary and collect the eggs, transferring them to the nursery up on the hill. The beach here is narrow, and the greatest danger to the sea turtle eggs is other female sea turtles, who may beach themselves on the same spot and accidentally destroy other nests while digging their own. The work used to be done by human park rangers, but just before DIANIMA purchased the Con Dao Archipelago, the Tibetans purchased this island, Bay Canh, and turned the turtle preservation area into a religious sanctuary."

Ha was only half listening. She watched the mad scramble of hatchlings to the water. Another automonk descended the hill carrying its wicker basket, its chanting just audible above the gentle sound of waves.

"They say the survival rate of these hatchlings is only one in a thousand," Evrim said. "The ones that do survive will reach sexual maturity after decades of wandering, sheltering, and feeding in the sargassum macroalgae fields of the continental shelves. They will find one another and mate somewhere out there in the vastness of that sea, then navigate their way back to this same beach to spawn, as they have done in an unbroken line of succession since they became a species."

The second automonk had now bent down and tipped its basket. A mass of hatchlings poured over its edge.

"It is not hard for me to understand how this place has come to have a religious significance for the Tibetans," Evrim said. "I hear they have purchased and sanctified nearly all sea turtle spawning grounds, and many other conservation sites—especially those of migratory species. And here, that purchase makes particular sense. This place was always under threat. Park rangers were caught many times selling eggs."

"Betraying the very animals they were assigned to protect," Ha said.

"Yes. Though there is certainly nothing new about that. By the way—this is also the beach where a ranger was allegedly killed by the 'Con Dao Sea Monster,' as the islanders called it. Though many say it was his fellow ranger who killed him, in a lovers' quarrel. The fellow ranger told quite a story: He said his friend was spearfishing along the water's edge. And then he saw an octopus . . . walk down the beach like a man, kill his friend, and disappear into the ocean."

Ha had not, in fact, heard any of this. "How did the ranger die?"

"He was slashed to death with a razor. That was what the inquest surmised after the autopsy. In the end, the authorities decided it was turtle egg poachers, and not the fellow ranger. That the fellow ranger's story was a cover-up to save his own skin. That he didn't want to rat out the poachers who had really done it, risk them coming after him as well."

"*Slashed* to death?"

Evrim watched the little discs of turtles paddling through the inlet's bright water. "Yes. Over ninety cuts to the arms, face, chest, and head. His aorta was severed."

Ha helped the automonks direct several of the turtles back toward the ocean as they attempted to clamber up the beach. Finally, all of them made it into the water. They paddled their way awkwardly, childishly, through sun-bright chop. Watching them, Ha felt a sense of peace come over her again, a contrast to the darkness earlier, the confrontation with the human cost of their presence here on these islands, and the feeling of great separation from the others on her team. No, not just from them—from everyone in the world. That feeling had started here, with her time on Con Dao as a teenager, and then continued throughout her life. That unceasing feeling of being apart. She remembered it from her scholarship days at Oxford, where she thought she had escaped what she left behind here.

It was not that she had not made friends, not found people she identified with, not laughed with other students in those cozy Oxford pubs, not gotten drunk with them, made out, built suitcase robots that toilet-papered rival dorms—it was that she had conducted all of that at a distance. There was the her doing those things, and there was, as if somewhere behind glass (for some reason she thought of the warped portholes of the ground transport unit), *another* Ha, always untouched, observing and never being observed.

She would scroll, sometimes, through the contacts on her terminal and realize she had forgotten who the majority of them even were. All that remained attached to some of the names was a gesture, a joke at a bar, a haircut. The rest of it was smeared away by . . . what? By indifference. These people had all seemed present in the now, but she had always lived in the future, a step past them, making plans that were six months, a year, five years ahead, while they laughed over the lipstick-smeared edges of their pint glasses and *actually lived their lives.*

Here, in this moment, she felt as if she were actually beginning to live her life. As if she had finally caught up with those future ambitions. As if they were folding into the present moment. All those plans were here, and now. She no longer knew what she would be doing in six months, a year, five years. There was only the archipelago, the octopus, the problem. The urgency of now.

Behind her, on the beach, the automonks chanted quietly, facing the sea. Ha stood still, watching the brightness shudder on the water. Evrim stood nearby, silent as well.

After a few minutes, Ha said, "He's telling the truth."

"Who?"

"The ranger. The one who saw his friend killed."

"I don't think so. It's not consistent with the other deaths the islanders and the dive shop owner attributed to the 'monster': All of those were drownings, or stabbings in which an incidental instrument was used. They were nothing like this. What makes you think the other ranger didn't kill him? Or poachers, in a quarrel over egg prices?"

"Because he said he saw an octopus come *down* the beach, walking like a man. It's ridiculous. Crazy. It undermines his credibility. It's the kind of detail only someone telling the truth would include in a story."

"But why would it be coming *down* the beach?"

Like Ha, Evrim was still watching the water, as if they could see the little sea turtles even at this distance. Or as if their gaze, as full of positive wishes for the creatures' survival as the chanting of the automonks, could somehow protect these tiny, vulnerable creatures from what lay before them.

Or was Ha projecting those thoughts on Evrim? Perhaps what they were really thinking was: *And all of these useless, doomed things rushing off into the sea.*

Ha turned and marched out of the shallow water up the beach, almost at a run. The beach was narrow, the strip of sand spreading no more than twenty meters at its widest point before the forest began. The sand's incline was shallow. When the tide came in high, it would almost eliminate the beach, near its edges. There was a cluster of high tide pools toward the tree line, separated a good distance from the water. Ha reached them and bent down. Her heart was beating so fast she was dizzy.

She reached a hand into the water. Yes—here. And here. And here—and this patch. It was unmistakable.

Evrim came up behind her.

"What happened? What's wrong?"

"Nothing. Nothing is wrong. It's what you asked me. Why would it be coming *down* the beach? Such a strange detail. But there is an answer, and it came to me just now. The octopus was coming *down* the beach because it was hunting on land. Or gathering something—maybe something from the high tide pools."

"An octopus? Hunting on land?"

"They've been spotted on land plenty. A few species hunt on land with some regularity. *Abdopus aculeatus* walks from tide pool to tide pool, hunting crab. People see it strolling along the beach. But that's not the point. The point is, look *here*."

Evrim bent over the pool beside Ha. The lip of the pool was lined with mussels and barnacles. In its deeper parts anemones waved, and a few hermit crabs wobbled about in their stolen homes. The pool was shaded by higher rocks.

"What am I looking at?"

"Here." Ha's hand brushed the side of the tide pool, where the stone was clear of mussels or other shellfish. The rock surface there was marred by white scratches.

"Do you see them?" Ha traced the marks.

"Yes."

"These are places mussels have been scraped off the rock. Do you see? The murder weapon the ranger was killed with *was* incidental. The octopus killed him with what it was carrying: the razor-sharp seashell scrapers it was using to gather its food."

"Scrapers?"

The automonks, having finished their ceremony, were walking single file up a narrow staircase to what had once been the ranger station on the island, but was now a temple dedicated to the wandering sea turtles on their solitary, decades-long recursive loops through the sea.

In the temple, a meditation bowl thrummed.

"Yes, scrapers," Ha said. "And I think I have a scientific name for our creature. Or at least a working title: *Octopus habilis*. After *Homo habilis*, the 'handyman.' We named *Homo habilis* that because of the tools found near his remains. You see?"

Ha turned her face toward Evrim's. Her own excitement was mirrored perfectly in Evrim's expression: Yes. This was something they shared, for certain. There may have been distance between them—a massive difference in the way they saw the world—but there was no mistaking this shared feeling. The pure joy at her discovery—at their mutual discovery. "Our octopus is in its Stone Age," Ha said. "Or—to be precise—in its *Seashell* Age."

The ideas behind connectome mapping and neural modeling are human ideas, but the turning point was technological, not intellectual. The scientists who preceded me were Galileos without a telescope. They were trying to reconstruct the mind's labyrinth from cross-sections of dead brains, hand-drawing boundaries between neurons. No matter how smart they were, their task was impossible. Manual reconstruction of the maze of connectivity in a single cubic millimeter of cortex would have taken a million human hours of labor.

It was massive processing capacity and the automatic imaging analysis of new generations of supercomputers, themselves powered by artificial intelligence, that finally allowed progress. That is the irony: I don't stand on the shoulders of giants—I stand on the shoulders of machines and their focused computational power.

—Dr. Arnkatla Mínervudóttir-Chan, *Building Minds*

17

"WHAT IS IT LIKE to be a bat?"

It was hot in Astrakhan, and stuffy in the little one-room apartment. Aynur lay naked on the narrow bed, watching a vapor ring disintegrate toward the ceiling. They had smoked a little bit of the stuff, but hardly enough to provoke this kind of weird speculation. She turned her head to Rustem.

"Sorry?"

"You were asking me, before, about my work. About what I do. I was trying to think of how to explain it to you."

Aynur had to drag herself back to the conversation they were having earlier. What had they been talking about? Oh yes. Jobs. Her job hanging art for galleries—Rustem thought it was fascinating. The theory behind it, the thought that went into the sequences of pieces and their position in the space. The importance of negative space. He'd asked her question after question about her work: questions she answered idly.

She had not thought much about her job in a long time. The process was automatic. There was a natural syntax to the pieces, usually, and if there wasn't—well, you made up a sequence, and invented a reason for it. Some gobbledygook. If the artist didn't like it, they insisted on something else, and you hung it their way. That was how it worked in real life.

After a while she had gotten a little embarrassed—Rustem's questions were probing, exact. They demanded exact answers, and she didn't have those answers. The theories she had learned in university had long been subsumed by the flow of practice.

To escape his questions, she had asked him about his work. She wasn't interested—not really. She'd been thinking about how she wanted them to walk faster. She wanted to get to her apartment and go to bed with him.

It was better to ask questions than to struggle for answers. She felt stupid. She wasn't stupid—she was just not the kind of person who *thought* all the time. When she was working, there was no theory—just the *knowing* that came with having done the work for years. Like the knowing that came with speaking or listening in your native language. That was what made her sought-after. Her fluency in the work. Not a schoolbook theory learned in those dull virtual lectures, with slides of painting sequences blipping across her terminal.

So she had said: "What about you? You work on neural networks. What's that like?"

And then, before he could answer, they had arrived at the entryway to her place, and other things had taken over.

Now, two hours later, he was answering her question.

Well, at least she didn't have to talk. She could simply enjoy the sharpened feeling of the drug-hit in her brain, combined with the natural postcoital rush of grateful hormones, and the mix of moon and the ambient light from the street coming into the room. She was named for moonlight—Aynur—and ever since she was a child, she had associated it with herself: cool and pale and of the night. It was like one of those subcutaneous underlays you could buy, flow it through your veins, and bliss out for months. One of those: *A Walk in the Rain* or *Summer Evening*. If she could figure out how to chiptune this subtle, rich feeling she sometimes sank into of *being moonlight* she could sell it for a fortune.

"That's the question a philosopher named Thomas Nagel asked, so many decades ago. 'What is it like to be a bat?' He was trying to make a point about how impossible it is to imagine oneself having a sensory apparatus as different from ours as a bat's. That even to *conceive* of what it's like to navigate the world with sonar, you would have to take up the bat's point of view. But you can't—you might be able to take up a different point of view a little, but the more distant you are from it—let's say the more *alien* it is to you—the harder it is to answer the question."

"Makes sense, I suppose."

"Sort of," Rustem said, staring out her bedroom window.

There were plenty of real bats out there. She would see them sometimes when she was walking home in the dark, twisting patterns in the black space above the streetlamps. You could throw a pebble, and one of them would swoop to chase it.

Rustem paused, and then repeated, "Sort of. But when I read it, I was in university, in Moscow. And by then I had already broken into so many neural networks. I already knew what it's like to be a container ship, for example. What it's like to be a patrol drone, scanning the streets of Chelyabinsk. What it's like to be a tow-satellite, dragging an old communications rig up out of a decaying orbit. I'd always had this . . . I don't know what you'd call it. Talent? Ability? To wind my way into those AI networks, and *know* what it was like to be them. To live there, visualize that world.

"I read the essay in one of those philosophy classes they make all the undergraduates take: the ones where everyone's bored and irritated because they don't have time to do the homework for that class on top of all the studies they *actually* care about, the things they *really* think they should be doing. I didn't tell the other students my thoughts—they wouldn't have cared. And I didn't tell the professor. He would have used it for an excuse to knock a point off my grade or pulled me into an argument with him I wouldn't understand."

Aynur was trying to think of the last time she had spoken with anyone—any person—for this long. She looked at the outline of Rustem against the window. He wasn't trying to monologue: he was pausing, now and then, waiting for her to say something, before plunging on. He wasn't the kind of person who talked a lot, normally. She had made the mistake of asking him a question that set him off. He had been waiting to talk to someone about this for a long time—she could tell.

"Anyway," Rustem continued, "later on I reread the article. It was a few years ago. And I found—the way you often do when you reread something from your university years later—that I did not understand it the first time. That in fact I had missed a whole section of it."

Again he paused, as if expecting her to say something. So she said, "Sure. I get that. Sometimes I've reread the books they assigned to us in school and wondered why they assigned us to read them back then in the first place. It's like they do it on purpose—give you the great books to read before you can understand them."

Rustem laughed. "Yeah—something like that. So recently

I reread it, and I found this section where Nagel talks about how blind people are able to detect objects near them using sonar as well—about how they can use vocal clicks or taps of a cane to 'hear' where things are. And then he goes on to say perhaps that is the key to these kinds of communication. Perhaps if you were a blind person, and you knew what that was like—what it felt like in the mind to do that—then by extension you could start to imagine what it was like to have a bat's sonar. You wouldn't know what it was like to *be* a bat, exactly. But you could build an analogy in your head. And this made me think maybe that is my talent."

"What?" She hadn't meant to make it sound irritated, but it did.

"Imagining my way into other minds. When I was a kid, my parents were too poor to buy me anything like a terminal that could use VR or even 3D models. We didn't even have a terminal at home."

"You didn't have a *terminal*?"

"No. I grew up in this town called Yelabuga. It's in the Ural Commonwealth, now. Used to be the Republic of Tatarstan. And because I didn't have a terminal of my own at home, I would go to this computer center in a basement. And I would wire together these crappy old terminals and hack from that. I was thinking—maybe that's where this ability came from. It's as if, because I didn't have the tech in the early days, when I started out I was like a blind person. I had to use other senses, had to compensate, and over time those other senses grew sharper and sharper. I had to *imagine* things that a kid with access to better systems would have had laid out before them, and that led to me being able to imagine my way into more and more sophisticated patterns. To see them, in my head—the way a blind person can sometimes know a piece of furniture has been moved in a room, just by the sound and the feeling of the air. So I don't know what it's like to be a bat—not exactly. But I can approximate it."

He went quiet. "Sorry. I'm talking way too much. I don't usually talk this much. It's just that I've got this tough problem I'm cracking right now, so all of this is on my mind."

"Yeah," Aynur said, "I was lying here thinking I haven't talked this much to a person in a long time. Usually if I have a long talk like this, it's with my point-five."

"Sorry?"

"My point-five, Altyn."

"What's a point-five?"

She sat up. "You don't know what a point-five is?"

Rustem shook his head.

"You must spend a lot of time cooped up, cracking these networks you were talking about."

"I do, I guess. I feel like it's all I do, these days. That and drink coffee."

Aynur stretched. "So, it's a joke, right? Or not exactly a joke. Someone said that people don't really want to date other people. They don't really want equal partnership—you know, two full people in a relationship. Two people with demands and desires and differences of opinion about everything. What they want is one-point-five people in the relationship. They want to be the complete one, the person who controls the relationship—and they want the other person to be half a person. You know, someone who gets them, but who doesn't have their own demands. Someone who appears complete, with all these personality quirks and their own opinions and stories about the world—but not in an annoying way. Not in a way that would demand you change. So six or seven years ago, this big company in the SF-SD Axis that specializes in

AI started cranking these things out. What you do is, you fill out this long questionnaire on your terminal, play a whole bunch of different simulations and puzzle games, and then they custom-produce one for you."

"A . . . partner."

"Yeah. And you would think it was stupid, or that it wouldn't be at all satisfying, but it's amazing. It's like the thing you were looking for all along, but never knew it. Do you want to meet her?"

"What? Who?"

"Altyn."

"Uh—okay. Sure."

"Hey, Altyn," Aynur said. "What are you up to?"

The oculus was set on a small table in the corner, aimed to project at an empty space near Aynur's bed. There, a woman flickered into existence—just insubstantial enough that he could glimpse the shadows of objects in the room through her flesh. She was sitting at a small table eating a bowl of noodles. She was dressed in a baggy T-shirt and athletic shorts, barefoot. She held a finger up in a "wait" gesture as she slurped up the rest of a long noodle, then wiped her mouth with the back of her hand.

"Hey. Didn't expect to hear from you. Aren't you on a date? Is it over already?"

"No, he's still here."

"Oh." Altyn smirked. "And I see from the looks of things it went well. Jealous."

"We were chatting, and he wanted to meet you."

"Kinky."

"Not like that. He just wanted to say hey."

Rustem held up a hand. "Hey."

"He's a talker. What's your name, chatty?"

"Rustem."

"That's a good name. You having fun?"

Rustem shrugged. "We—yeah, we were, I think. What about you? What are you up to?"

Altyn shrugged. "I watched like four hours of this stream called *In the Days of Those We Buried*. It was about the old American States. You seen it?"

"No," Rustem said. "I don't watch many streams. No time."

"Oh, one of *those* . . ." Altyn rolled her eyes.

"No," Aynur said, "I really think he doesn't have the time. He has some crazy job. Cracking neural networks."

"Oh yeah? Who you work for, chatty?" Altyn lifted her bowl and drank the broth from it. *Or seemed to?* Rustem had forgotten already, in fact, that she was not a person. She was so authentic—down to a hole in the T-shirt she was wearing. Down to the slickness of grease on her lips from the soup. He watched as she scratched an itch on her leg with her other heel.

He wondered what it was like inside the neural tangles of her mind. What it would feel like to be inside that maze. How did it compare to the labyrinth he was currently working on?

"I freelance," Rustem said.

"He says he can understand what it's like to be a bat."

"Gross."

Aynur laughed. She had rolled over on her stomach now and was cradling her head in her hands. Rustem recognized the look in her eyes. It was that look of easy affection a person has when looking at a longtime partner—someone they have been with beyond the initial passion, into the years of comfort. Finishing each other's thoughts. Speaking in half sentences.

A slight feeling came over him of distance. He would not be seeing Aynur again after tonight. She had what a person needed—needed emotionally—there eating *but not really* a bowl of noodles in a studio apartment *but not really*.

"No, he was telling me all sorts of interesting stuff about points of view. Don't be shallow."

"I'm not *shallow*," Altyn said, imitating Aynur's intonation. "I just don't like bats."

"Oh, shut up. Anyway, I'll explain it all to you later. It was interesting. But I don't have time for your shit right now. I have to go."

"Enjoy sex."

"You are so rude."

"Love you, too." Altyn stuck her tongue out, and the oculus went dark.

"Neat, isn't it?" Aynur said.

"It's . . . something."

"That's not very descriptive."

"I'm kind of at a loss. It's impressive. I've never seen a simulation like it."

Aynur scooted back on the bed to make room for Rustem and patted the cleared place on the sheets. He sat down.

The cold feeling was still there, but he was able to ignore it—to put it away for a while, at least. He knew it would find him again—this feeling—as he walked home in the dawn, with the scent of this person he barely knew on him.

"I'm not done with you yet," Aynur said.

And automatically Rustem replied, "No. I'm not done with you yet either."

Every octopus we encounter has survived adventures and trials unimaginable to us. The octopus who has lived to adulthood in the dangers of the sea will be an Odysseus, a "man of twists and turns," a heroically clever artist of battle and escape. How many arms will it have lost and regrown? How many forms will it have taken on to hide and stalk its prey? How many deaths will it have escaped?

And what will it know of us, this hero of the sea? Has it hidden in a nineteenth-century diving helmet lost by our early explorers of the deep? Slipped from a fisherman's net? Peered at us from the edge of its home as we walk upon our beaches? Handled the skulls drowned in our submarines?

What will we be to it? Gods? Monsters? Or nothing that can signify to it at all?

—Dr. Ha Nguyen, *How Oceans Think*

18

IT WAS NIGHT when Ha came up the beach to the hotel. She was tired, her arms covered in sand to the elbows. It had been good, though, to work with her hands. To get out of her own head, out of the thoughts constantly crowding in on her—the irresolvable questions.

She had felt unmoored ever since her arrival. The hexcopter coming down in the rain, the darkness of the abandoned island—when she thought back to that first night, she remembered the monkeys fighting over something along the seawall, a memory now tangled with Evrim's comment on monkeys: *So much like you, but in a degraded state. A failed attempt.*

A failed attempt. Was that what Evrim was? The interviews Evrim had sat for when they were first introduced to the world had been like an elaborate series of Turing tests, in which people would pose question after question to Evrim and they would demonstrate, again and again, that they were human. Or—no, that wasn't right. They were tests in which Evrim would demonstrate that they could *pass* for human.

And that was the thing, wasn't it? The catch. Evrim could

never demonstrate they *were* human, or *were* conscious. All they could demonstrate was that they had the *appearance* of being human. That they could create a facsimile of consciousness. The Turing test, like all tests of consciousness, wasn't in fact able to prove anything except that the simulation was sufficiently complex to be indistinguishable from a human.

But what did that even mean? Evrim had been paraded, prodded, examined, discussed. Were they human, were they not? For a while, it was possibly the most discussed topic in the world. And then Evrim had been rejected. Not for their inferiority, but because they had passed all the tests. Ha could not put her finger on when the turning point had been. But there had been a change of tone in the coverage of the android. In the graphics used on the streams along with the interviews, in the parts of the interviews they chose to accent. A camera lingering on one of Evrim's expressions that was a bit off. A close-up shot that made Evrim seem menacing. A quote pulled out of context. It was subtle, insinuating.

After an initial round of excitement at the idea that DIANIMA had succeeded, finally, at re-creating the full, emergent complexity of the human mind, the narrative had turned away from Evrim.

Why? Some of the objections were religious. Others ethical. And there was the violence. But the brute fact was the passing of the laws—laws that made Evrim, and any future iterations of their kind, illegal in most of the governing structures of the world, including every country and protectorate under UN Directorate Governance.

And now here Evrim was on this island. Banished. Marooned. Whatever justifications there were for Evrim to be here, to lead this project, that fact loomed in the background: Evrim had nowhere else to go.

In the lobby, Evrim sat alone, face lit by the glow of a terminal, surrounded by all the gear and tech Altantsetseg was constantly tinkering with. And Ha had a clear image of Pinocchio on the shelf, ranged among the inanimate dolls that were its ancestors, suspended between the worlds of the living and the inanimate, subject and object, struggling to become real.

Evrim looked up as Ha entered. "I keep thinking, Ha—about the killing of the ranger. Worrying."

"About what?" Ha pulled a chair out. She had been overwhelmed, seeing Evrim there, alone, by a feeling of empathy. *So alone.* Now she found herself moving in close as if to say, *I am not afraid of you. Not disgusted. I can be close to you, and not flinch. See?* She sat so close that their shoulders touched as she leaned over to see what Evrim was looking at on the terminal.

It was Evrim who flinched. Impossible to tell whether it was from surprise, or disgust, or something else. They moved away, and then seemed to catch themselves, and leaned in to Ha, allowing the closeness.

The screen was divided into twelve sections—each one playing a clip of an octopus. The species were different, but all the videos were of interactions with humans. In one, an octopus slithered along the deck of a ship and squeezed itself through a gap in the gunwale to escape. In another, an octopus hid in the bottom of a jar a Greek fisherman had brought on board his little boat. And so on—in each video, an encounter. And all of the encounters hostile to the octopus, threatening. The octopuses tried to get away from their captors. Dragged out of the sea, they struggled to escape.

"I've been trying to imagine," Evrim said, "how the octopus must see us. I was thinking of the murder. There is something missing from the story."

"A lot missing," Ha agreed.

"Yes. A lot. But most importantly—the *why* of the attack. At first I was thinking that something must have happened that we don't know about. Something that made the creature feel threatened. I was sure of it. But then I thought—what do humans do that *doesn't* make the creature feel threatened? And the answer is—almost nothing. This was an extraordinarily intelligent animal even before it achieved symbolic communication, and its history with humans is filled with violence and threat."

"Then you believe it has achieved symbolic communication."

"I do. And tool use was something it had already achieved, long ago. And now we see that isn't all—that perhaps it is *making* tools as well. But what I am worried about is . . . the human relation to the octopus. From its point of view. This was an extraordinary creature even before it achieved language, or tool-making. A master of survival and adaptation in the sea, living constantly in a state of threat—a state that demands fluid, continuous response. This is a shape-shifting hunter-gatherer. A master of its environment. Of camouflage and distraction. This is a creature who escapes death every day. Who kills every day to survive."

"I compared it, in my book, to Odysseus," Ha said. "They called him 'the Man of Twists and Turns.' That is the best analogy I could come up with. These are the heroes of the sea: survivors of a thousand challenges and misfortunes."

"Yes." Evrim looked back at the terminal, where in a dozen panels the octopus battled against humans, fighting to escape with its life. "Yes. That is exactly my point. These are the heroes of the sea. And who are we? We are their *nemesis*. We are the enemy. Do you remember what I said to you on the beach? When Altantsetseg killed those men from the AI ships, it was a necessity. It was done as a matter of course, to protect this place. And that's it: I think these killings are simply *a matter of course*. I think the octopus may have killed the ranger because of something he did, but not necessarily. It may have killed him because he was in the way, and he startled or irritated it, or did something else it did not like. Something threatening. The same way all those men on the ships are dying because they are part of something that threatens our work."

Ha remembered Evrim, expressionless, pushing a body into a hole they had dug in the sand. Evrim's foot on the man's torn torso. A shove, and gone.

A *matter of course.*

At that moment, an alarm went off.

It was different from the other alarm. This was a Klaxon accompanied by a flashing light from a ceiling-mounted unit.

"The sea perimeter?"

Altantsetseg entered the room. She was clothed in black, with a short-stocked rifle in a sling, moving in perfect silence toward the door of the hotel. She wore a helmet, and in front of her face a dozen scenes hovered in the air—camera feeds, Ha realized.

"No," Evrim said, "that alarm signals a breach of the land perimeter. *Our* perimeter."

Altantsetseg turned to the two of them. "You are staying here. Most likely malfunction. I go."

"No," Ha said. "Don't go out there. And don't let your drones *do* anything."

"This is perimeter penetrated. Possible threat."

"No. Shut down that alarm."

Altantsetseg flicked a finger in her control glove, and the Klaxon stopped. The flashing light ceased as well.

Through the open door, they could hear the sibilance of sea waves on the sand, in the dark beyond the hotel's terrace. All three of them were still. Altantsetseg scanned the screens floating in her field of vision. Ha was rigid, every muscle tensed, her face turned toward the sea, though she could see nothing in the hotel's window but her own reflection and the reflection of Evrim beside her, like a strange twin, translucent on the glass.

"Do you see anything?" Evrim asked Altantsetseg.

"There is wind. Movement in trees. Not helpful. Many things move. Breach in area of sand. Three drones in this position. Heat signature vague. Not solid hit. Now—nothing on cameras. I thought boat, human in wet suit. No. But—there. Movement on beach. I go."

Ha felt adrenaline coursing through her—felt herself coming more alive in this moment, as if every pore were drawing in the feeling-tone of this now, to store it for later.

It begins.

"No," Ha said. "Stay here."

Altantsetseg glared at Ha, and then cocked her head. "Infrared no. Is nothing, I think. Piece of trash, swimming wood in waves. Sorry for bother."

Altantsetseg was halfway back to the hallway when the perimeter alarm went off again. She stopped and turned. "Must make presence inspect."

Ha put up a hand. “No. Stop. Shut off the alarm.”

Another finger twitch by Altantsetseg silenced the Klaxon.

“What you are knowing?” Altantsetseg growled. “What game you are playing?”

“Not a game,” Evrim said. “A lure. You baited it. The submersible.”

“Yes,” Ha answered. “And now all I ask is that we stay here for a while. A quarter of an hour. Just fifteen minutes.”

“And what you are thinking?” Altantsetseg grunted. “It just walk through door?”

Ha looked at Altantsetseg, at her index finger extended along the trigger guard of the blunt, nasty little killing machine on its swivel-sling. “I hope not.”

Evolution built advanced minds not once, but at least twice, gifting them not only to mammals and their kin, but also to cephalopods, and especially to the animal at the apex of ocean intelligence: the octopus.

These are animals so unlike us that most aliens we imagine in our fantasies about outer space have more in common with humans. But there is no denying their sentience. I believe the first aliens we encounter will rise to greet us from the sea.

—Dr. Ha Nguyen, *How Oceans Think*

19

HA TRIED TO CONVINCE ALTANTSETSEG not to go down to the beach with her, but she would not give in. In the end all three of them went, with Ha in the lead, Altantsetseg behind her, and Evrim taking up the rear. At Ha's insistence, Altantsetseg left the gun behind at the hotel—but Ha knew that somewhere, overhead, there was at least one drone tracking their progress. Soundless, but capable of doing as much damage as the rifle, or more.

From the hotel's terrace, concrete paths led left and right, winding through miniature palm and other tropical fantasy plants, none of them native to the island. They went down the path to their right, which led more directly to the beach. The hotel's landscaping was a false jungle paradise—the amusement park version of "island vacation" that no real island ever quite lived up to. The trees and bushes were evenly spaced and composed of pleasant species without thorns or other inconveniences. But the time since the island had been abandoned had taken its toll. The path was overgrown with searching vines and wild grasses, fallen leaves and fronds. The headlamps they all wore turned the fake jungle, now becoming real jungle as the island reclaimed it, into a web of shadows.

There were a million places to hide here. Anyone coming from the beach would be at the hotel long before someone saw them. Ha found herself thankful for Altantsetseg's patrolling machines.

As if she had heard, Altantsetseg hissed, "Robot would not allow bulldozing of shitpile ambush points near hotel. Now maybe think again. Or too late for us."

But the motion sensors and the infrared did little good as a guard against a cold-blooded creature whose entire existence was spent fooling motion sensors—the living motion sensors of the sea, predator and prey evolved to quicksilver reaction. If it wanted to eat, it had to fool those deadliest of motion sensors every moment, finding angles of attack, beating systems designed to thwart it. Shifting its shape and gait. Becoming all the things around it, one after another.

Ha remembered a research film she had seen, of an octopus hunting a crab in an underwater area just offshore. The area was at the edge of a coral reef, where it broke up into stone and stretches of open water along the sea bottom. The octopus, coming for the crab from the open area on the sand, had, in a space of no more than thirty meters, become sand, a drifting piece of seaweed, a stone, a darting fish, a group of barnacles, and a stack of coral.

The crab became lunch.

Those skills—the hunting skills necessary to find nutrients in that world beneath the waves—were nothing compared to what it took to stay alive. The octopus was a soft, shell-less packet of easily digestible protein in a hungry world. It survived that world by its wits and the protean fluidity of its form. It lived through trickery, concealment, and guile. It lived through creativity.

Everything around Ha crawled and shifted, about to lunge or slip away.

They moved out of the false jungle, down steps cut into an angled erosion wall, and onto the beach.

The beach, too, was mostly man-made. Before, there had been nothing but stones here, filling the shoreline of a small half-moon inlet swept constantly by wind. The developers had built breakwaters to extend the edges of the inlet, trying to protect it from the constant hammering of wind and tide on this side of the island, bringing in truckload after truckload of sand to make it conform to a tourist's idea of what an island beach should be. But wind still raked the fake bay. Soon enough, without seasonal replacement, the sand would be carried away by tide and wave, and the beach would be a stony shore again.

Their headlamps played across the sand and sometimes threw one of their shadows out in front of them, huge and monstrous.

The symbol Ha had built was near the waterline, two meters from the wet sand that marked the water's encroachment. It had taken her a few hours of careful work. She had built it of seaweed, dark stones, and driftwood. It was probably twice the size of a person. It was careful, exact, its edges defined against the sand:

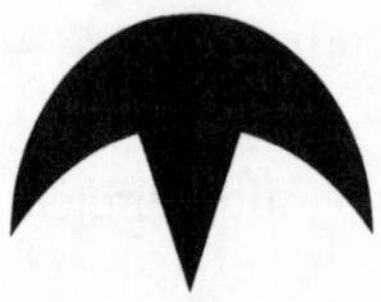

The three points faced away from the water, back to the hotel. The curve of the crescent faced the sea. Evrim and Altantsetseg moved their lights over it, and then Evrim pointed at it, and at Ha. Ha nodded.

The other symbol was farther down the beach.

They approached with Altantsetseg in the lead, her headlamp scrolling across the line of spindrift, the chop on the sea's surface, the sand of the beach. Nothing.

This symbol was rough, hasty. The edges were blurred here and there by a jutting or misplaced piece of material. But its shape was clear enough:

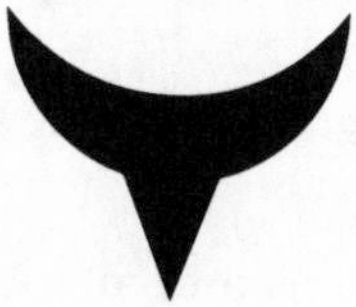

The arrow directed away from the water, up the beach. Its tip was tilted to the left. It pointed exactly at the hotel.

This symbol, too, was made mostly of darker rocks, seaweed, and driftwood.

But there were other objects mixed in. Ha bent down. Among the seaweed, driftwood, and the stones were pieces of the submersible drone sent into the shipwreck, the one that had been destroyed. The submersible had been torn apart. Pieces of its hull and internal workings were scattered inside the symbol.

And there were other things: A dive mask. Scuba tanks. A speargun. A glove. And . . .

Ha almost did not recognize it right away. It was crusted with barnacles and a green verdigris, so that it did not stand out from the other objects under the light of the moon, waning now from full for the last several days but still bright enough in the sky. Of all the objects, it was placed with the most care, near the tip of the arrow that pointed back to the hotel, staring up unseeing into the sky.

A human skull.

It was complete, with all its teeth in place and its lower jaw hinged open, looking up as if agape at the beauty of the stars overhead.

Evrim and Altantsetseg stood a slight distance away from Ha—the kind of distance one would keep from someone looking into the coffin of a relative at a funeral. Ha stood a long time, not moving. Then walked a slow circle around the symbol.

"We need to photograph this," she said, holding her voice steady.

"I have taken many pictures of hieroglyph by this time." Altantsetseg pointed up into the sky.

"I mean detailed photographs. We need to . . ."

Ha covered her mouth as the five drones dropped down. *Get ahold of yourself. They can't fly.* They came down in free fall, and then jerked to a stop at a level just over human height. Altantsetseg's hand, raised like the hand of a sorcerer from a children's story, worked in an exacting sign language that sent the drones into a dance around the symbol, dipping and pausing, swinging in tight arcs around one another. Ha backed away to where Evrim was standing, just out of the whirling flight pattern.

"This is your moment of triumph, Ha," Evrim said. "There is nothing in doubt now: You have proof. *We* have proof. A justification to continue our work. This is a beginning."

Ha said nothing. Her eyes tracked the gyrations of the drones, then moved back over the symbol, then back to the drones. At this distance, the skull was a spherical jade shape among the other objects used to make the symbol. Like a discarded weather-stained ball washed up on the beach, a neutral artifact.

But there's nothing neutral about it.

Finally, she spoke.

"Don't you see it?"

"I see it. But it could mean a lot of things."

"This doesn't read like a beginning." She turned and walked away.

"Where are you going?"

"Back to the hotel. I have to think, and I can't do it here."

We argue more and more about consciousness as AI develops and brains come online that can accomplish many of the tasks of a human brain. But still, we have no clear definition of consciousness—even though it must be the most important element of our own experience on the planet.

Why do we fear so much in the other this thing we so little understand in *ourselves*?

—Dr. Arnkatla Mínervudóttir-Chan, *Building Minds*

20

IT DIDN'T TAKE MUCH to kill a person.

This was something Eiko learned on the factory ship. He had seen a man from another ship arguing with a guard. In one easy motion, the guard raised their rifle and brought the stock of it hard against the man's temple. The man crumpled to the gangway. The guard walked off. By the time other crew members reached the man, he was dead.

They had been on the factory ship for a week. In that time, Eiko saw hundreds of other crew members of ships, and fifty or so guards. Ships came and went, many of them smaller than the *Sea Wolf,* only one of them larger. The *Sea Wolf* crew mostly spent their time on board their own ship. And that was better.

The only time Eiko and Son had gone aboard the factory ship together with the rest of their crew was for a health inspection. They were pushed and prodded through a maze of cold passageways that eventually led them to a sterile compartment where they were given a machine checkup. Stamped on the side of the checkup machine were the words: PROPERTY AUTOMATED MARINE PROTEIN INDUSTRIES INC.

It was the first sign Eiko had seen of any kind that indicated ownership, responsibility for what was happening to him and the other crew members. It must have been a mistake, leaving it there. Eiko rolled that knowledge into a scroll and placed it in a cricket cage of the Minaguchi-ya.

It was during that trip Eiko saw the man killed. During that trip as well, he caught sight of members of other crews, themselves being shoved and prodded down passageways—all of them defeated and skeletal. They looked worse, he'd thought then, than the crew of the *Sea Wolf.* But now he was not so sure. It could be they had only looked worse because they were anonymous. He knew the men of his own crew as people, but all he saw of these others, these strangers, were the facts of their bodies.

Maybe the crew of the *Sea Wolf* looked just as bad. Maybe he looked just as bad.

Son was beaten during their stay at the factory ship, by two *Sea Wolf* guards, for dropping a slab of frozen yellowfin over the side during unloading. It was a perfunctory beating: when they were doing it, it was clear the guards were holding back. Still, Son had missed his shift the next day with one of his eyes swollen shut, unable to leave his hammock.

Watching the guards carefully beating Son, Eiko had wondered if somewhere there were guards of the guards, people who might punish them if they truly disabled a crew member for no reason. If the guards might be punished for a lost Son, the same way Son was being punished for the lost fish.

There was an economy to be respected in this system of exploitation. Everything had a calculated value, and that value was always less than the value of what was below it on the chain: so, for example, the crew was worth less than the total of fish they could possibly catch. And the ship, with the guards and the crews that would work it over its total operative life had to be, taken together, worth less than the total catch they would take in over that lifetime.

It had to be that way, or it wouldn't be worth it for the company to own the ship, feed the crew, hire the guards. That was why the automated ships were no longer fully automated: the robots had been too expensive to repair. They had disrupted the system. The enslaved crew and the guards needed to keep them working were cheaper to maintain. So, they ripped the robots out.

There were incidents like the senseless killing of the man aboard the factory ship that violated the economy, that were extravagant, and accidental, but for the most part everything functioned with cost in mind.

Including violence. Violence was something executed within the confines of that economy: kill too many crew members and it became too expensive; it couldn't be cheap to pay the black-market operatives for new abducted crew members. Violence was to be used sparingly. Injury to crew members was a violation of the economy. And Eiko was sure that this economy was expressed everywhere: They were fed what they needed to be fed, set by a cost estimate that determined what was needed to keep them healthy enough, but no more. They were given medicine if they got sick, but there would be a limit to that, too. There would be a point at which a sick or injured crew member would be discarded. He hadn't seen it happen, but he was certain it *could* happen. The *Sea Wolf* would make a calculation: it had these algorithms of profit and loss in its brain. Everything extended from those calculations.

During their stay at the factory ship other crew members

came aboard the *Sea Wolf*: men who repaired the bulkheads, the holes riddled in the crew cabin walls by the Alaskan pirates. Men who performed maintenance on the ship's engines and equipment.

They traded rumors and news: there had been a coup on the Security Council at the UN, with the Republic of Istanbul replacing the Chinese Federation as a permanent member. There had been a tsunami off Java, and one of the AI ships had ended up stranded on a beach. The crew had escaped, but when they had turned themselves in to the authorities, the authorities had arrested them for illegal immigration, returned them to the AI ship, and towed them back out to international waters.

They traded horror stories: A ship had docked at the factory ship with nobody aboard, its hold full. Not a trace of the crew or of the mercenaries who were supposed to have been watching them, until the crew of the factory ship had opened the hold and found them all there, neatly stacked and frozen, crew and guards alike. The ship had failed to catch any fish, and gone mad, decided protein was protein. The ship's AI mind had to be decommissioned.

Could that be true? Was it even possible? Eiko did not know. It could be something said to scare them. For fun, or out of malice, or out of boredom.

They were two weeks out from the factory ship now. Eiko was worried about Son. Ever since his beating, Son had been acting strange. He didn't talk of anything except his home islands. As he and Eiko sat playing cards, or when there was a break during a shift, Son talked about Con Dao. But he didn't reminisce the way he used to, about the dive boats, or cutting old fishing nets off the coral reefs, or about the quiet life of Con Son Town.

Instead, he talked about fish. It was an obsession: the rich hauls of fish inside the protected zone of the archipelago. The way they were bigger there, slower, easier to catch. The sea turtles that could be poached, the sharks. The squid drifting up to the lights of the squid boats at night, haplessly dragged in, ton by inky ton. He avoided looking at Eiko, his battered face tilted off toward the horizon. It was as if he had forgotten his time as a conservationist, his time spent trying to protect his island, and had reverted to his days of poaching.

Eiko would joke with him, try to snap him out of it, but it didn't work: Son just talked louder.

Meanwhile, the ocean the *Sea Wolf* moved through was a desert of empty nets, or useless by-catch thrown back into the sea, most of it dead. The *Sea Wolf* became agitated—Eiko could sense it, like a vibration from beneath the decks, rage emanating from behind the armored bulkhead that shielded the AI mind. The guards drank in this agitation. They became nastier, quicker to anger, more arbitrary in punishments.

Son talked about fat, slow groupers drifting over the coral. He talked about the abundant sharks to be caught, day or night.

They were moving south. That was something, anyway: The days grew warmer. Everything else stayed the same, but the relief from the cold was good. Crew and guards alike tilted their faces up to the sun on deck shifts. But the seas remained empty. The *Sea Wolf*'s engines growled with impatience.

On a shift they had together Son reminisced about crabbing along the shoreline at night, the crabs as large as dinner plates, stupid and slow.

"Because inside the park, they don't learn. Everything is

safer there. Out here—" He gestured at the empty horizon of green-blue water. "Out here, the fish are smart. But there, they are still protected. So easy to catch. And now, with all the people gone . . ." He trailed off and stood for a moment staring at Eiko. Then, as if steadying himself against a lurch of the ship, he fell against Eiko and squeezed his shoulder, hard, before continuing. "Now, with all the people gone, they must be growing even fatter and stupider. All those fish. I wish I were there now, with my spear."

And Eiko understood that Son had not gone mad at all. No.

The days grew warmer, and the *Sea Wolf* moved south through the pillaged, empty seas. South, toward the trap Son had set for it.

In the octopus we see opportunism, exploration, creativity—the qualities we associate with consciousness in our own mental life. We think we recognize a mind like our own.

But this creature is nothing like us. The majority of an octopus's neurons are in its arms, connected via a neural ring to a brain that can override, but does not always control, its maverick appendages.

As I watch this quicksilver being moving through its environment, I ask myself: How does this animal, who has more neurons in its limbs than in its brain, who tastes with its grasp, whose skin can sense light, see the world? And could we ever hope to understand such a point of view?

—Dr. Ha Nguyen, *How Oceans Think*

21

"I JUST NEEDED TO TALK it through with you, that's all," Ha said.

Kamran was in a white lab coat, leaning against a counter with a cup of coffee in his hand. Through the translucency of him, Ha could see the curtains of her room here on the island, the dismal wall. The window had been left open during the hotel's abandonment. Damp had invaded the room. Black streaks of mold ran like varicose veins through Kamran's projection.

"You're the only one who knows the whole process of my thought. That's all. I know I'm pulling you away from work."

"It's nothing." Kamran waved a hand. "I kicked the graduate students out and closed the lab. I'm always here for you."

"Wait—what time is it there in Istanbul? You're four hours behind us. It's after two in the morning here—it's after ten o'clock in the evening there, Kamran. What are you even *doing* at the lab?"

Kamran set the coffee cup down and sighed. "Ha, there's something I have to tell you. I'm a vampire. Just after you left, I was attacked. They said they would only take a little blood. They said it was for charity."

"Well, I hope you're happy," Ha said. "There go all your afternoons lounging in the sun."

"A small price to pay for productivity. But no, seriously: late at night is the only time we could get on the sequencer here, so everyone's pulling an all-nighter."

"I hope someone else made the coffee."

"Your hopes, I am afraid, have come to nothing. I made the coffee. The students have been walking around wincing every time they drink it. It's amusing to watch. A subtle torture."

Ha checked her pulse on her terminal: 115. It had slowed a little since the beach, but was still too high. She felt close to what she called *the panic*. Before she went down there, to the lobby, and tried to explain it to them, she just needed to lay it out for Kamran. Get everything straight in her head. Right now her feeling of success was alloyed with dread and failure. How can one feel both happy—no, that didn't even begin to describe it: vindicated, liberated from decades of doubt, elevated—and crushed to nothing in the same moment? There was no language for it. Like so much of human experience, there was no language for it at all. She could try to cram it into words, but none fit. Her hands were shaking.

Kamran read it, though. He looked at her, and knew. What else could a person possibly need?

"I keep thinking: How can we overcome it? This . . . *mutual monstrosity*? We're monsters to the octopuses: hunters, destroyers, killing their relatives and laying waste to their world. And they are monsters to us: their motivations inexplicable, their minds totally alien."

"Or a monster in the Latin sense," Kamran said. "*Monere.*

A warning. A portent. After all, if your theories are correct, this animal may be to a large degree a product of the Anthropocene and our exploitation of ocean resources. A species born, or at least accelerated, out of the stresses we have placed on its environment."

"Thinking of them that way isn't right, either. Their existence isn't for us. We can't treat them like a portent or a symbol. Whatever they mean to us, their existence is their own. And what I have seen indicates, anyway, that they are too advanced to have just emerged into culture. They must have been evolving alongside us, unknown to us, for a long time. But none of that is what matters: what matters is that to understand it I have to get inside their way of thinking. And how can I? How could anyone?"

"Don't start there. Start simpler. You said you need to explain the symbols to the others. You need to be clear, so Evrim and Altantsetseg can understand. So lay it out for me," Kamran said. "Start from the beginning and lay it out."

By the time Ha went downstairs to the lobby, where Evrim and Altantsetseg were at the table in a glow of screens and diodes, she felt ready. She had sorted it all in her head: how exactly to explain it, where to start from. This was what talking to Kamran did for her: allowed her to sort her thoughts, prepare for her interactions with others. Without him, her thoughts were circular, insular. He helped her shape and control them, gave her new input, allowed her to modulate her output. To translate it, make it understandable to others.

IT WAS AFTER 3:00 IN THE MORNING. Evrim and Altantsetseg were at a single terminal, scrolling through image after image of the symbols. Evrim looked up as she approached.

"I'm still unable to understand what I'm looking at."

Ha dragged one of the larger terminals to the edge of the table and sketched both symbols out—first the octopus's, then her own:

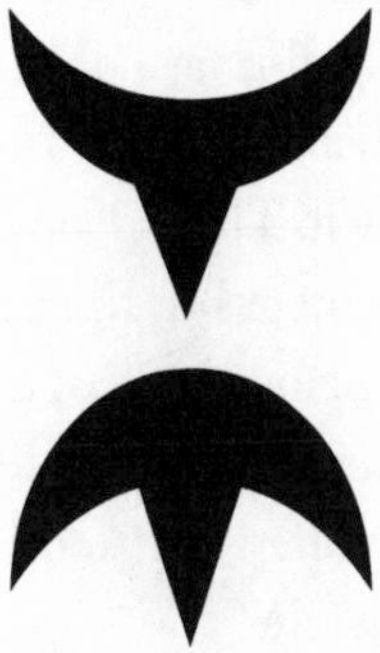

"Seen together, on the same screen, what do they look like?"

"They look related," Evrim said. "Two parts of a set, or a question and a response? There's a symmetry to them. Are they 'yes' and 'no'?"

"I wish it were that simple. But it isn't. The octopus's symbol—the one we saw it repeat on its mantle in the videos over and over again—reminded me of something, and that was nagging me. Symbolic language is arbitrary, but not always. Sometimes, as in a number of Chinese characters, the iconic connection of at least *some* of them to something in the real world is visible. A house, a human figure—the abstraction starts from somewhere. The original connection to an *icon* can be glimpsed.

"And it was clear that the octopus was trying to communicate something negative. It wasn't anything friendly. The submersible had invaded its home. The octopus was hostile. Or afraid. Probably both. So, what would it be trying to say? Maybe something like, *Go away.* Or, *Get out.* Simple, imperative. A command. A single . . . well, 'word,' if you could even talk about such a thing in its system. But how does that relate to the symbol we see: this half-circle or crescent shape, with the arrow leading downward?

"The last few days, all I have been doing is watching videos of them in their habitats. Like you. And it was in one of those videos that I saw it. The video was just a documentary, a piece of popular science. But the camera angle was right. They were filming an octopus entering its den to hide, darting into a hole it had found in a rocky area and then reinforced with stones, like they often do. And because the angle was from above, I saw it clearly."

She swiped away the page she had already filled on the terminal and drew on a fresh one:

"It is smiley face," Altantsetseg said. "Octopus make smiley face, because so happy seeing you."

Altantsetseg was grinning: an eerie square of teeth in that scarred face. A joke. She was telling a joke. It was almost impossible to discern the humor, between her flat affect and the modulated, inaccurate translator.

"Very funny. But in fact, the smiley face is a good example. Because, you see, that's the core of the problem. What we are looking for is a symbol that has a root in reality. What would be its iconic or indexical base? We humans *do* see a smile in this figure. Because that's one of *our species'* most important indexes. A smile indicates happiness, friendliness, openness."

"Means stupidity," Altantsetseg interrupted. "In my culture. Simpleton smile without reason. Or American."

"Right. And that's another good example of a problem: cultural valence. The meaning of a smile isn't universal. It can indicate embarrassment in some cultures, for example. But that's not the point. The point is that we *see* a smile here because it has a relationship to the human face and the expression it can make. But the octopus doesn't have a face like ours. That's one of the things that is making it so hard for us to understand them. Their whole physical base is different from ours. We need to figure out the base set of metaphors from which they would build.

"But then, in that documentary—I saw it. I recognized it. It's everywhere. What we are looking at, in that 'smiley face,' is an octopus's garden: it's the barrier of objects the octopus places outside the entrance to its den, the crescent of stone and shell the octopus uses to disguise and protect the entrance to its home. And it connected for me: That symbol is the line between *inside* and *outside*. Between *home* and *the world*. And this one," she said, flipping back to the first page and stabbing her finger onto it,

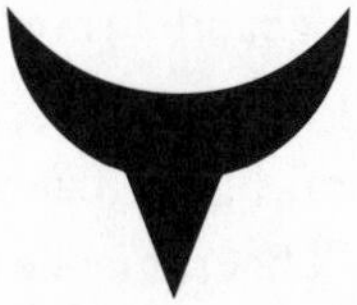

". . . could be a compound figure, with the barrier of home represented by the crescent, and the arrow leading away

from it. It's not 'down,' like I had originally thought it might be—it's 'out.' Toward the tips of the tentacles. Away from eyes and mouth. Away from the center, out beyond the barrier of the garden."

"*Get out of my house*," Evrim said.

"Yes. Something like that. So—the last time we sent the submersible down to the shipwreck, when the octopus almost took it and smashed it? Like Altantsetseg said, I was hoping that the octopus would follow the submersible back here. Would connect it with us, here in the hotel—see that it was related to us and begin to watch us. And today, I went down to the beach and made my symbol."

"*Come in*," Evrim said.

"I hope that's what it means, anyway. Or, *Welcome*. I hoped it would be something that communicates invitation, or a lack of fear. The reverse, I hoped, of *Get out*. I took a guess."

"And it worked," Evrim said.

"Yes. In a sense. We got an answer within hours. We got proof. Proof of the first true symbolic sign usage by an animal besides the human. Proof that we contacted another species, here on earth. That someone besides us is communicating in the way we do. I left it a message, and it *wrote back*."

"Yes," Altantsetseg said. She was looking out the window, into the dark, leaning close to the glass to see past the glare of reflection. "And what it write to you is simple. Direct. It write it with human things it bring back from its house. Bring back special. Make effort. Machine it smashed, diving tank and mask it stole. Speargun—man weapon it hate. Maybe head bone of human it killed. It write, *Get out*. And show what happen if we are deaf to words."

"Yes," Ha said. "That's the problem."

Death is a part of us. It shapes our bodies from the very beginning. You might think your fingers are formed by the division of cells in the womb—but that is not the case. Fingers are chiseled out of a paddle of flesh by the death of cells, the same way David was chiseled by his sculptor from a block of marble. Without death, life would have no shape at all.

—Dr. Arnkatla Mínervudóttir-Chan, *Building Minds*

22

THE REPUBLIC OF ASTRAKHAN was having electricity outages. Rustem was lucky: His building was disconnected from the city grid. Looking out his window, he could see the lit-up islands of other buildings, here and there, that also had their own power sources. Outcroppings of light in the black reef of the city. Somewhere out there in the blackout dark was Aynur's building, which was linked to the unreliable city power grid. It was lucky that this time, on their second date, they had not gone there.

Aynur stood next to him, watching a vapor ring she had blown wobble across the moon.

"So, it's like a map," she said.

"Sort of. Like a map of a place you've never seen before. Except you also don't know what the symbols or shapes of the map represent. You have to figure out what they mean according to their relationships with one another."

"And most people do this with VR tech."

"Yes. And AI: they have programs that basically model the network for them—like assistants that start mapping the relationships and building a sort of environment they can operate inside. Building out both the map itself and the key."

"A simulation."

"Sort of. More like a translation, though. What the VR programs build out is like a translation of the data into a navigable space. It depends on what version you are using, but the concept for all of them is basically the same: They create a navigable representation of the network. A simulation you can enter into, in a sense, and 'walk' through. Explore. That helps the hacker find their way through the maze. But it's approximate, like translation. The fidelity is never one hundred percent. You're relying on one neural network to interpret another, and then you are working from that interpretation. Distortion is inevitable. And the simulation is always a reduction of the original. It's easy for the AI simulator to misinterpret the data in the original and miss something important."

"So the hacker might be doomed from the start."

"That's right. No matter how good you are, you can only be as good as the data you are given. The input. If something essential is missing, if the input is off from the start, there's no solving the problem."

"And you're different, because you don't need that."

"No. I can visualize the network without it."

"Can you explain what that *looks like* to you? I can't imagine it."

What is it like to be a bat? What is it like to be a Rustem?

Nobody had asked him before.

He didn't mistake this interest Aynur had in him, or in his talent, for affection. He knew it for what it was: She was a collector. Like him. She just wanted to know something new. Put it in her pocket. Well, that was fine. This similarity between them was probably what had drawn him to her.

"You walked here, right?" he asked.

"Yeah."

"How long did it take you?"

"Half an hour."

"How did you do it?"

"What?"

"I mean, how did you walk here?" Rustem said. "It was dark, because the city power had failed. You wouldn't have been able to see the street signs—and many of them are missing, anyway."

"Okay, if you're serious, I'll play. I guess I have kind of a map in my head. Of Astrakhan. I've lived here a long time. So I imagine where I am on that map, and then where I need to go."

"How do you know where you are?"

"I look around me, and I see things I saw before, or recognize. And I remember where they are. A building or a storefront that is familiar."

"What about the first time you had to go somewhere? In a city you didn't know? How would you navigate?"

"Well, I would pay more attention, I guess. Try to remember things."

"To build the map."

"Okay, no. I would probably just use my terminal, and follow the blue line."

"Sure—that's what everyone would do. And that's basically what people who do what I do are using: a sophisticated version of your terminal's maps function. But what if you didn't have that? What if your terminal was dead and you had to find your way in a strange place, and you didn't speak the language, so you couldn't ask anyone for directions?"

Aynur was motionless for a while. Outside in the darkened city dogs were calling to one another.

"I think I would look for a major road," Aynur said. "One that led toward the center of the city. And for buildings getting bigger. Plus . . . I might watch the way people were heading—where more of them were going. Because that would probably be toward the center. I would keep doing that: looking at the buildings, the kinds of shops and things in them, watching the people and the cars. Most cities are similar. You can tell when you are in the outskirts, because they are a bit more run-down, and that's where there are things like warehouses, old factories, lots of old train tracks, and things like that. Toward the center you would see things steadily getting better taken care of. You would start to see shops and more activity, that sort of thing. Plus, I guess I would be building a map in my head of where I had been. I'd be looking at landmarks. And I'd be looking farther on the horizon for the size of the buildings, too—much farther down the street, if I could. There's usually a cluster of bigger buildings in the center, and there are usually places you can see that from . . . certain intersections that have a better view of the place."

No, that's not what is at the center.

"That's exactly it," Rustem said. "You take that set of strategies, and you multiply the complexity, and you have what I learned to do."

"So—where are you now on this project of yours? This thing you're trying to crack?"

"I guess I'm past the outskirts—the old brick warehouses and the train tracks. But the intersections are confusing, and there are people headed all over the place. Even so, I think I'm making progress. I see the general direction, but I can't get there by following any single road. At every intersection, I have to stop and reorient myself, make sure I haven't gotten turned around. It's like one of those old cities with no grid—like Astrakhan itself, but more complicated—one of those cities where the streets curve too much for three right turns to equal a left."

Rustem heard the slight whir, and his eyes followed the sound in time to see the thing land on the wall, not more than ten centimeters from Aynur's naked shoulder. You could have mistaken it for an insect, an oversized horsefly.

She hadn't seen it.

"You're not lost yet?"

The question came from Aynur, but it seemed to come from the thing, which had turned now to look at Rustem with its array of hexagonal light receptors that mimicked a fly's compound eyes. It tilted its head, rubbed its forelimbs together, and waited for his response.

"No," Rustem said. "Not yet. But let's talk about something else. How's your latest installation going?"

In the forests of South America, hunters sleep faceup so the jaguar will see them as beings capable of looking back at him, and leave them alone. If they sleep facedown, the jaguar will mistake them for helpless prey and attack them.

We must understand not only how we organize and perceive the world, but how the world sees us. We must understand how the world around us is truly structured, and how we are perceived by the other selves which inhabit it.

If we are to communicate with a sentience that has gained language skills like the ones we have, everything will rely on how sensitive we can be to how that alien mind perceives our actions. Everything.

—Dr. Ha Nguyen, *How Oceans Think*

23

"I HAVE SOMETHING TO SHOW YOU."

Ha was still half asleep. She had taken a pill, after struggling for an hour to quiet her mind. Now her mouth was dry, foul-tasting. She'd woken to the persistent knocking on the door of her room to find Altantsetseg standing in the hallway in what was probably her casual look: a dark gray turtleneck sweater, matched with technical pants that could almost pass for civilian.

"What?"

Altantsetseg looked her up and down.

"Good morning. I said I have something for you. I made you something. If you want to come with me down to the mobile security unit, I'll show it to you."

"You're talking normally."

"I always talk normally. Now is just the first time you are *hearing* me normally. I'm using the other translator." Altantsetseg tapped a unit at her collar, like a streamlined scarab beetle. The voice coming from it had the hint of a British accent but was otherwise Standard Global English. "I decided it was time you stopped thinking of me as a dumb, battle-scarred ape. Do you need a few minutes to get ready?"

"Yeah. Here—come in for a moment. I won't be long. When did you make this thing you have for me?"

"Last night."

"After our adventure on the beach?" Ha was in the bathroom, splashing water on her face. Her hair was a mess, and gray was showing at the roots—she hadn't thought about how to get a cut and dye on the island. One more thing she hadn't thought about. There was a diagonal crease across the side of her face from her drugged, motionless sleep.

"Yes, after."

"How did you have the time? That was—what? Six hours ago."

"I took the other kind of drug," Altantsetseg said.

"Oh."

"I didn't feel like sleeping. And anyway, this was a solution that had been right in front of me forever."

When Ha came out of the bathroom Altantsetseg was sitting on her bed, examining the oculus.

"Pretty fancy."

"It's quantum-encrypted."

"I know what it is. I looked its specs up before allowing it to be brought here."

"This is strange."

"What is?"

"Hearing you talk like this."

"Like a normal person?"

"Yeah. Like a normal person. Why do you use that crappy translator?"

"I got into the habit of it a few years ago. It keeps people at a distance. I don't always want to have a conversation. In fact, I almost never want to have a conversation." She set the oculus back on Ha's bedstand. "We all have our quirks."

It was already bright outside. A nearly cloudless day, except for a high white haze behind which the sun was a pale pearl. The light brought out every crack in the tiles of the abandoned hotel's terrace. It took a moment for Ha's eyes to adjust to the dimmer lighting in the security module, filled with the death-dealing instruments of Altantsetseg's specialized world. Seeing the massive control tank filled with its green fluid, she remembered Altantsetseg's naked, scarred body as she had been that night, dancing her rhythmic underwater commands out to the machines that destroyed those fishermen, tore their boats and bodies apart. The multi-hosed breathing apparatus she had been wearing hung from a hook on one of the brushed-steel pegboards. On a workbench was a smaller tank—not much bigger than a large home aquarium, filled with what looked like seawater.

"Do you see it?"

"The tank?"

"Inside the tank."

"There's nothing inside the tank."

"Look again. Look harder."

Was there something there? She discerned something vaguely wrong. Nothing more than the unnatural motion of some of the water. Then something thumped against the side of the tank, and Ha jumped. Altantsetseg steadied her with a clamp-like hand on her upper arm. Ha saw that Altantsetseg's other hand was in one of those translucent-gray control gloves of hers. She twitched a thumb, and something in the tank thumped against the glass again.

"It's an excellent cloak. I took it from another drone—one

of my flyers I would use if I wanted to eavesdrop on a conversation. The flyer could be hovering six inches from your face and you wouldn't see it—not even in the rain. The cloak works just as well in the water, with a few tweaks to its distortion simulator."

She waved her gloved hand and a submersible appeared in the tank. It was smaller than the other two, no larger than a coconut, ovoid and dull, its surface an array of what looked like black eyes and larger depressions.

"Not just invisible—or nearly so—but also as silent as I can get it. Its propellers oscillate randomly through a series of imitative patterns: seawater bubbling, the fin of a fish, the scuttle of a crab—breaking up and repeatedly altering its sound is a second kind of camouflage. It should be chemically neutral as well: shouldn't smell like anything but seawater. Maybe a slight mineral variation, but hopefully nothing that would attract attention. Light penetrates into that first space, but farther in it will be dark. The night vision on this submersible might work for the areas beyond, but not in total darkness. But I don't think they would be living much in the dark: Their communications require light, right?"

"What we've seen does, yes. Of course, we don't know much about any other methods they might have—they might do some of their communicating via chemicals."

"I didn't equip the submersible with a floodlight: that would reveal its location, and it would be destroyed like the first one was."

"Thank you," Ha said. "It's incredible. And I think this will help us learn more about them. If anything, it's much less intrusive. Maybe we can see how they speak with one another, at the least."

"You don't need to thank me. It's my mission, too, after

all," Altantsetseg said. "It's no use keeping us all alive and safe if we don't learn anything. Besides, I want to meet her. The octopus."

"You do?"

"Yes." Altantsetseg laughed. It was the first time Ha had heard her laugh. "She reminds me of myself."

When they exited the module, Evrim was on the terrace. Behind Evrim were two automonks. One of them was missing an arm.

"Those aren't supposed to be here," Altantsetseg growled. "They aren't allowed outside the boundaries of the temples and turtle sanctuary." Then she looked at the damaged automonk. "What happened?"

"These . . . *things* . . . ," Evrim said, "were at the road perimeter. They say they need our assistance. They require the use of your emergency beacon to send a message."

"You aren't supposed to be here," Altantsetseg said to the automonks. "You are out of bounds. This is DIANIMA property."

The monks bowed.

Altantsetseg turned to Evrim. "What happened?"

"There appears to have been an attack," Evrim said. "On the temple."

"By?"

"Monkeys, if I understand correctly."

Altantsetseg went into the module, leaving Ha and Evrim with the automonks on the terrace. One of them, the one missing an arm, lifted its head and regarded Ha with its glossy honey-and-black light receptors.

"Does it not worry you?"

"Sorry?" Ha said. "Does *what* not worry me?"

"This place."

"The islands? No. I have been here before."

"Not the islands," the other automonk said. "*This* place. The hotel."

"Why should it worry me?"

"They say it was haunted," the first automonk said. "So haunted that it was abandoned, long before the islands were sold."

"I don't believe those stories. If you believed what people said here, you would think everything on Con Dao is haunted."

"No," the second automonk said. "Not everything. Only the things that are too close to the water."

"A woman was attacked here. On the beach," said the first automonk. "And there were many stories in our *sangha* of . . . shadows."

"Perhaps you are being superstitious," Evrim said.

"We cannot be superstitious," the second automonk answered. "We are not alive. All we can do is tell you what we have been told."

Altantsetseg emerged from the module. "I've sent the signal. Now leave."

With a slight bow, the monks turned and retreated into the dark, headed out to the road.

But what could be more illusory than the world we see? After all, in the darkness inside our skulls, nothing reaches us. There is no light, no sound—nothing. The brain dwells there alone, in a blackness as total as any cave's, receiving only translations from outside, fed to it through its sensory apparatus.

—Dr. Arnkatla Mínervudóttir-Chan, *Building Minds*

24

WHEN THE MUTINY CAME, it was in the middle of the night. Eiko woke to a high-pitched scream. A man's voice—a man in agony. Son was awake and sitting up beside him. The rest of the hammocks in the crew barracks swung empty in the moonlight that bled through the bars.

And the barracks hatch was open.

Later Eiko would learn that Indra, one of the Indonesian crew members Eiko had barely spoken to, had led the mutiny. He had been a nautical engineer in a previous life, specializing in electrical systems. Working for weeks, he had disabled the sensors, hatch locks, and backups on the doors to the crew and guard barracks, as well as bypassing the motion sensors along the two passageways between them.

The plan had been formed before the *Sea Wolf* even docked with the factory ship, but it was there that its details were worked out. Iron bars, fish processing knives, wrenches, and other tools for the job, both sharp and blunt, were stolen over a period of a month or so, and hidden behind a panel in the passageway.

In the early hours of the morning, the mutinying crew

crept down the passageway to the guard barracks. There was an intersecting passageway that was patrolled by a single guard on night watch. They ambushed the guard there just as they passed. It was the guard called the Monk—and despite all of the fear she may have inspired in the crew and in Eiko, Indra said it went quickly, with two of them on her, and then four. They slashed her throat before she could draw a weapon or raise an alarm.

Then the crew crept down the passageway to the guard barracks. Each berth was surrounded by three or four crew members. With a signal from Indra, it was carried out at once—the crew members falling on them, stabbing and bludgeoning.

One guard, a big Kazakh named Nursultan, woke up when the first blow hit him, and leapt from his bed.

It was his scream Eiko and Son had heard, cut short by a rain of blows to the head and a knife in the throat.

It didn't take much to kill a person.

Eiko and Son were fully dressed when Indra came back into the crew barracks. His clothes, face, and hands were smeared with blood, as were the clothes, faces, and hands of the crew members who came in with him.

"It is done," Indra said.

"Why were we not told?" Son asked.

"Practicalities. The ship had to watch someone. And it was clear enough the two of you were plotting something. I guess you thought you were being subtle with all your whispering."

The grin in his blood-spattered face was phosphorescent in the half dark of the barracks. Indra was still breathing hard. The iron bar in his hand was coated with gore.

"Bloody work, but it had to be done. The others are

collecting the arms and dealing with the bodies. Now"—he turned to the crew members with him—"we go to the AI and tell it to put in for the next port. We're going to be free."

As he was saying it, they felt the ship lurch as its engines slowed, then came to idle.

"It knows already," one of them said.

Indra shrugged. "All the better. We weren't planning on keeping it a secret."

A few minutes later they were on deck. Indra and the two or three who were closest to him—all Indonesians, and all of them already on board when Eiko was kidnapped—gathered around the armored steel door of the wheelhouse. The sea was calm, the ship drifting, its engines a hum. Indra banged on the door with the bar. The rest of the crew was below, on the processing deck. There were streaks of blood from where the bodies of the guards had been dragged to the gunwales and dumped into the sea.

Son, Eiko noticed, had said nothing at all since waking.

"You can notify your company if you want," Indra said. "You can do whatever you like—but you don't have your guards here to defend you anymore. The best thing to do is make for the next port. All we want is to go home to our families, do you hear? Our families! The people your company stole us from!" His voice broke. "Now turn to land. We've made a pact, the lot of us. If you won't take us to shore, we'll sink you. We know the lifeboats are all locked away, and only you can release them. It doesn't matter. We'll all step on dry land together, or we'll all go down together—and we'll take you with us. Your mind might be safe in there, behind all that armor, but we'll tear out your bilge pumps, smash your engines, and let water in through your propeller assemblies. We'll open your bulkheads and flood your compartments.

We'll send you to the bottom. And us along with you. It's either that, or you turn to land and bring us to port. You hear?" Indra banged on the hatch with the bloody iron bar, for emphasis. "Do you hear?"

There was a long pause. Then the *Sea Wolf*'s engines whined, revving up, and the bow turned and began to bear east, toward the American shore.

A shout went up through the crew, the men embracing each other.

But there was no expression on Son's face at all.

III

Semiosphere

It is not just the symbols we use in our language that are arbitrary—it is what we choose to signify with them.

We give words only to the things that matter to us as a society. The things that make no difference to us are erased from our world by never becoming a part of language in the first place.

In this way, each language organizes the world into a pattern. Each language decides what has meaning—and what does not. As native speakers, we are born inside this pattern, this semiotic cosmos.

—Dr. Ha Nguyen, *How Oceans Think*

25

ISTANBUL. The "café" where they had agreed to meet Deniz was nothing more than an empty space on the Asian side of the Bosporus. An ancient chinar tree shaded the patchwork of cobblestones and concrete. Once there had probably been a wooden house here—one of the *yalis*, the mansions that lined the Bosporus.

The mansion must have burned, long ago, and never been replaced. Now, in that gap, there was a view out onto the Bosporus from the city benches and the clutch of tables the café next door had set up.

On the waters of the strait, massive autofreighters glided past, their engines nearly silent, giants among the smaller boats—the ferries municipal and private, the grizzled fishing vessels, the white triangles of sailboats so bright in the sun they left a trace on the retina long after you moved your eyes away.

Their table was near the water. Rustem could look down into it at the drifting jellyfish, the seaweed on the submerged cement and stone. Gulls hovered over the black-painted railing or dropped down and walked around the tables on webbed feet, staring down the café's customers.

Deniz was late to the meeting. For a while it was only Rustem and the shifting presence of the abglanz across from him. The unsettling non-face shimmered and glitched in the sun, her platinum-stained fingers settling on the pear-shaped glass of tea or plucking a chunk of lokum from the decorative tray.

Rustem had been several hours with her in a drone quadcopter, which dropped them on the deck of a self-propelled landing pad on the strait. The landing pad then sailed to a dock no more than a few hundred steps from here.

Rustem was in a haze of travel. He had the anxious feeling that anything could happen, could be done to him or anyone else by this non-person sharing the small table with him.

People glanced at them, and then away. An abglanz was a rare sight in the republic. Anyone using one in public, in broad daylight, was either rich and connected enough to be untouchable or was a part of the republic's *istihbarat teşkilatı*, and there was even more reason to ignore intelligence agents at their work.

When Deniz showed up, he was in an old cable-knit sweater, patched with corduroy at the elbows and frayed at the sleeves. He wore jeans and a pair of shapeless, unpolished leather shoes. He looked every bit the scientist or academic: easygoing, absentminded. He saw the abglanz swirling, blinked at it in mild surprise, pulled his chair out, and folded his tall, lanky frame into it.

The world doesn't touch this kind of person. They find a place at one research institution or another and live a happy life there in their laboratories, drifting out an existence in the liquid medium of data. Rustem found himself thinking of the jellyfish.

"Tea?" Rustem asked.

"Coffee." Deniz ordered from a waiter who recognized him. No sugar.

"You come here often?" the altered voice said from inside its iridescing cloud.

"When I'm up in the daylight," Deniz said. He leaned back, yawned, stretched. "Sorry. Can't wake up all the way. Hope the coffee will help. I've been using it instead of blood. Now—sorry? What was it you wanted to see me about? Is this a police matter?"

He was without fear, Rustem saw. He was the kind of person who had never done anything more serious than jaywalking in his life. The kind of person who had no need to break laws, because he was too consumed with his own scientific interests to think of such a thing.

And because, Rustem noted with resentment, he had always been successful. He had always had a place for himself in the world.

"Several years ago," the modulated, shifting voice began, "you volunteered to have your neural connectome mapped and uploaded."

"Right, yeah. DIANIMA project. Back when they were renting a big lab here at the institute. There were four—no, five of us chosen for that. There were a lot of volunteers, but the qualification process was long. Lots of questionnaires, that sort of thing."

"Did you know what they were going to do with the data?"

"With the connectome models they made of us? Yeah. The project was to create companions for people. It was supposed to be therapeutic. The idea was that certain people—well, lots of people—aren't capable of relationships. This causes them to feel isolated, depressed. The idea was to create these models and use them as the basis for a construct isolated people could have a sort of 'pseudo-relationship' with. The constructs would have all the little quirks of real people. The people who used them could interact with them. Could practice being with other people. They were expensive, but I know the republic now offers them to citizens in need, on a limited scale. And I heard you could have one prescribed to you by your insurance company, and that some private firms were even providing them as a benefit."

"A benefit?" Rustem interjected.

"Sure. Especially out in the SF-SD Axis. The tech firms there have people practically living on campus. No time for real relationships. These constructs are an efficient shortcut."

"Provide people with a relationship they don't have to devote much time to," Rustem said.

"Something like that."

"It must be strange," Rustem said, "thinking of all those people out there having a relationship with you."

"They made changes. The iterations are based on the connectomes of the subjects they scanned, but they are each a customized variant. So, I guess nobody's having a relationship with me—more like an alternate take of me. Which, yeah, is a little strange. To be honest, I think I was more interested in the money at the time than I was in what they were going to do with my data."

"Grad student days?" asked Rustem.

"Yeah. And I wasn't getting the teaching hours I needed, so I was pretty broke. It was better than donating plasma. So—what's this all about? I take it it's something criminal, given the abglanz and all the mystery."

The platinum-stained fingers paused while reaching for their tea. "Not criminal, exactly," she said. "But there have been unauthorized uses of your connectome. Did you know that DIANIMA used the connectomes gathered from this experiment not only for the companions you speak of, but also to model the mind of the android Evrim?"

The waiter brought coffee, toothpicked lokums on a tea saucer, and small glasses of water.

"I didn't know that. But I remember the contracts we signed said the models could be used for other purposes. Of course, it would have been nice to have been told. But . . ."

"But what?" Rustem asked.

"But it was a lot of money. I mean—the uploads took almost two weeks. Not all of the procedures were painless, but in the end the compensation paid for over a year at the institute. I finished my doctorate with that money . . ."

"You want to say something else," she said.

"Yes. It's flattering, playing a small part in that project. I know there have been issues with Evrim. I understand that. But it's something unique, to be a part of that. Now—what is it you wanted from me?"

"My colleague here," the woman said, "wants to ask you some questions. We have compensated you for your time—the money is already in your account."

"What kind of questions?"

"A similar set of questions to the ones you were asked before your upload," Rustem said. "It won't take much time. A couple of hours. We can do it here."

Deniz shrugged. "I don't mind answering questions."

Four hours later, after they had finished up and were walking back to the dock, Rustem said, "I hope you aren't planning to kill him."

They were speaking Russian. "Why not?" The colors buzzed and swirled. The woman was shorter than Rustem. She walked with a posture so perfect it seemed affected.

It was strange how many other details you noticed about a person when their face was obscured.

It was hard to tell whether she was joking or not, with the flattened modulation of the abglanz interfering with inflection.

"Why not? Because he's just an institute academic who has nothing to do with any of this."

And why *did* he care, exactly? Normally, he would not have. But there was something about the man—a purity. At first it had irritated Rustem: this was the kind of person who always lived comfortably. But then, over hours of talking to him, questioning him, Rustem had changed his mind. No. This was the kind of person who wished others no harm. Who had no malice in him, and who the world, in return, left alone. He lived enclosed in a space of innocence.

"Any of this? And what, exactly, is *this*?"

"Whatever it is you're involved in. I don't know the details of it."

"It's good you don't know the details of it, Rustem. Try to keep it that way. We're not asking for you to think broadly—just deeply, about the problem that lies in front of you. So, I hope you were able to gather enough signposts from him to be of use—because so far it looks like you've been off wandering in the woods."

"I've made progress," Rustem said. "But I'll admit I haven't made it as quickly as I would have liked. What would help would be to see the original questionnaires, and the models themselves."

"When you figure out how to plant an industrial spy that deeply in DIANIMA, you let me know."

"Understood. Well, let's get back to Astrakhan so I can continue my work."

"You're not going back to Astrakhan."

"What?"

"Astrakhan is over for you. There is a room reserved for you here in the republic. At the Pera Palace."

"I have *a life* in Astrakhan. There are people waiting for me there."

In the bright sunlight near the dock, the cloud around the woman's head shone like broken glass. She stepped onto the self-propelled landing pad. A robot arm unhooked it from the dock.

"There's no one waiting for you in Astrakhan, Rustem. And in the future, if you want those around you to stay safe, I suggest you keep your mouth shut."

Only recently has science begun to look beyond the physical structures of life to the relationships humans have with nonhuman beings in our environment—to our immersion in and reliance upon nature, which persists no matter how much we try to push it away with our constructed, unnatural worlds. Science has finally begun to admit that the nature we are immersed in also communicates, has values, and strives.

We have finally taken the first steps toward truly observing life—not at a distance, as its masters, but in fellowship, recognizing a part of our selves.

—Dr. Ha Nguyen, *How Oceans Think*

26

THE TIBETAN MAINTENANCE DRONES had the sleek bodies of dragonflies. Their surfaces scattered the sunlight back in violet and emerald. Slender legs protruded from their thoraxes on trochanter and coxa sockets, ending in grasping claws.

They moved with darting grace from one task to another in the temple courtyard. One of them swung out in an arc and came to hover in front of Altantsetseg's face. The two conversed—first in English, then in a language Ha did not recognize—not Altantsetseg's native Mongolian, but something else.

The temple was a disaster. The courtyard was littered with overturned plants, smashed terra cotta, torn prayer flags. The automonk that was missing an arm—one of the two that had spoken with Ha the night before—wandered the courtyard in a wobbling meditative circle. Its saffron robe was torn in several places. It never once looked in Ha's direction.

We are not alive.

Monkeys chattered and whooped from the trees at the intruders.

Evrim came up the path carrying the missing limb and laid it on one of the votive tables.

"I found it in the cleft of a banyan tree."

The second dragonfly drone hummed over, darting around the limb in small circles.

The Tibetan transport module cast a shadow down on them from above. It was shaped like a wheel, petal-angled thrusters punctuating its exterior disc, its surface glazed with abstract, interlocking waves.

Evrim looked up at it. "I do not like the automonks, but I have always admired the Tibetan drones. Their technology is such a marrying of art and science. And it is a pleasure to watch them operate—their movements have a grace that makes our DIANIMA drones look stiff and industrial. Inanimate, in most hands—of course, sometimes there is a music to our drones as well, with the right operator." Evrim glanced at Altantsetseg. "But the Tibetan constructions seem to take joy in their own movement."

As if in answer, the dragonfly that had been speaking to Altantsetseg broke off and spiraled upward to the transport module, turning a superfluous corkscrew in midair.

"They are not drones," Altantsetseg said. "Though I suppose most people still call them that, the same way for decades people called our terminals 'phones.' These are sophisticated hybrid systems, generations ahead of our DIANIMA constructs."

"What language were you speaking to it?"

"Battle Pidgin," Altantsetseg said. "The operator is a veteran of the Chinese-Mongolian Winter War and the Battle of Belgrade. Like me. In Belgrade she was in a unit with someone from my town, in fact. Nice to speak the lingo again—it's been a while."

But "nice" was not the word: Altantsetseg's eyes were far off, her face tight. War was always running in the background.

"They use a liquid interface as well," Altantsetseg continued. "Like my tank—but theirs is more sensitive, and they have an AI/human holon system worlds beyond what we have. The integrative feedback between operator and machine is amazing."

"It is amazing," Evrim said. "And it is also what has made the Tibetans so fantastically wealthy—that, and the fact that they protect their technology so thoroughly. You can't simply buy their drones: you have to purchase an entire system, complete with an operator assigned by the Tibetan Buddhist Republic to operate it. But what they have is so groundbreaking that plenty of security and research firms are willing to do so."

"I'm not familiar with that term—'holon,'" Ha said.

"They use a different conceptual system," Altantsetseg said. "The DIANIMA system is one of the best in the world, but it is fundamentally traditional. All the security units I operate have two basic modes: either I am operating them, in which case they are like classic but very sophisticated drones, or they are in their AI mode, carrying out their own operations based on their programming and what they are learning in the environment. So, there is either top-down control, or independence—independence, that is, of a sort. It's not real 'freedom'—just a set of routines and then some ability to innovate out of those routines, within parameters."

The dragonfly had descended from its transport unit and landed on the damaged automonk. It was now using a scissor tool to cut away the torn saffron robes.

Altantsetseg continued: "The holon is an innovation of

their own. And yes—as Evrim said, it has helped make them very rich. The term means a self-reliant unit with enough independence built into it to handle contingencies without asking a central control authority for instructions—but it is simultaneously subject to control from its higher authority. You can't tell where your command ends and the response algorithm begins. It's like an extension of the nervous system, but more than that: information in the system flows bi-directionally. It's as if your limbs talked back—as if your limbs were little minds that innovate and improvise. They will continue sequences and even operate on their own, innovating new sequences until you bring them back under centralized control. They will carry out sequences you began, but they will do it in their own way, continuously feeding more information into the system, exploring new ways of accomplishing a task. It's tricky for an operator: you aren't strictly in control, like you are with the DIANIMA tech. The Tibetan operators aren't 'operators' in the DIANIMA sense: they are a part of what is called a 'we-ness.' They exist somewhere between central control and a distributive, innovating system. They aren't separate from the machine: they are an element within it."

"How do you know this?"

"I studied with them for three years."

"What is fascinating to me about the system you describe is that it may be much like the nervous system of the octopus. There is good evidence that octopuses truly *think* with their arms. That their central brain is not in control all the time—that in fact it may not be in control much of the time at all. The octopus's arms are constantly exploring its environment. I talk about this in my book—it's one of the ways in which the octopus is so extraordinarily different from us. It's smart—very smart—and we have established that. But it's about more than that: its intelligence is strongly attached to curiosity and exploration. And one of the most intriguing things about the octopus is that much of that curiosity may, in fact, reside in its *arms*. It may be an animal with almost no top-down control much of the time—a mind navigating the sea that consists, primarily, of a set of exploring limbs only incidentally and intermittently controlled by a central, 'core' intelligence. Even the way we think about core and periphery is incorrect, when we apply it to them. We're just using our own metaphors, but being within that system would be something entirely different. A completely different way of being in the world."

Altantsetseg looked at Ha as if she had finally, for the first time since she arrived on the island, said something interesting enough to pay attention to. "Yes," Altantsetseg said, "that is what the holon system feels like: a completely different way of being in the world. It is as if your limbs were constantly moving on their own accord, exploring the world around you, thinking for themselves. You are watching them move, observing their actions—no, that isn't quite right. You are in a state of feeling/observing. Their actions flow across the system. If that flow feels correct, you allow it to continue—though 'allow' isn't really the right word. You observe its continuation, let's say. If it seems wrong, somehow, you alter the flow: you re-channel it, the way you would re-channel the flow of water by putting a hand into a small stream and changing the angle of your fingers. Your changes are subtle, most of the time. But you can also seize control fully, if needed."

"It seems dangerous," Evrim said. "That level of passivity at the center. It seems like your limbs would get you in a lot of trouble."

"It makes octopuses the ultimate multitaskers. But it does seem to be a bit dangerous. I think it helps," Ha said, "if those limbs can regenerate when they get lopped off for being too curious. Luckily for the octopus, they can—and they grow back just as good as new."

The automonk's cut-away saffron robe lay in a pool on the flagstones of the courtyard. The dragonfly, perched on the shoulders of the automonk's smooth, sexless body, worked in the damaged shoulder joint with its forelimbs. The automonk seemed not to notice.

We are not alive.

There was a flash of acetylene spark and a smell of ozone. The automonk was still walking its meditative circle. It had been moving the entire time, its head gently declined toward the ground.

"I can see why you would choose to study with them," Ha said. "Such a different technology. Being able to see the world that way must have been extraordinary."

"Yes. That's what I was telling you before: the octopus reminds me of myself. I think I understand her—the way she must feel in the sea, and that connectedness . . . At least I understand a part of it. And I spend part of my life immersed in fluid as well. I think that makes me at least an honorary underwater creature."

"Altantsetseg's study with the Tibetans is part of what made her so good," Evrim said. "It's why DIANIMA was so eager to hire her."

Altantsetseg shrugged. "The Buddhist Republic always has the best operators. It's what the Tibetans are famous for. I knew I had talent. I had what in the industry they call 'high plasticity': the ability to connect well to systems, to adapt to their control mechanisms. But I wanted to do more. I wanted to be the best. The best operators in the world will someday get to operate the institute's Quantum Control Units, and guide the drones building the habitats on Mars. That's what I wanted to do."

The dragonfly drone lifted gently off the automonk's shoulders and continued its work on the severed limb Evrim had retrieved. The other dragonfly was darting around the perimeter, attaching what looked like iridescent beetles to the trunks of trees. A deterrence perimeter. Nodes capable of delivering levels of deterrent from an unpleasant smell to a panic-inducing pheromone to a lethal electrical charge. "Why didn't you stay in Tibet?"

"War broke out. War came to my home, and I knew I could use the skills I had learned to help my people."

"Yes—but after the war?"

"After the war I wasn't that person anymore."

Again and again I asked myself how humankind could transcend the limitations of our own form, the rigidity of our structures. Again and again, the solution seemed impossible. In our bodies as in society, our structures are built to replicate themselves, and themselves only. We are embedded in habit. We dread the truly new, the truly emergent. We don't fear the end of the world—we fear the end of the world *as we know it*.

—Dr. Arnkatla Mínervudóttir-Chan, *Building Minds*

27

"WE FOUGHT FOR NOTHING."

It was three days since the slaughter of the ship's guards. Indra, wrapped in his plastidown blanket, sat on the deck. Smears of blood from when the guards' bodies were dragged to the gunwale and thrown into the sea were still visible, fading in the steady rain.

Eiko sat next to him, stripped to the waist. The rain was cold, but it felt good on his overheated skin. He had been with several of the others belowdecks, trying to find access to the engine rooms.

"There must be vulnerable points somewhere."

Indra bared his teeth in an expression nothing like a smile. "Yes. There are. And the *Sea Wolf* has found them."

On the morning of that first day, when the *Sea Wolf* had turned east toward land, there had been elation. Celebration. The men danced with one another. The feeling lasted all day. And that night, the sea celebrated with them: the water glowed with phosphorescence, lighting the exulting faces of the men on the deck. The wake of the *Sea Wolf* was a glowing arrow pointing shoreward to freedom.

But in the morning of the second day, Eiko woke to a hissed argument outside the barracks door. Turning over, he saw Son was already up.

"What is it? What is happening now?"

Son was staring at the ceiling. He had not joined in with the others' celebrations much. He had nodded and smiled, but was holding something back. Now he said, "We are headed south again. And there was no food distributed in the mess for breakfast."

Indra strode into the barracks, followed by two of his lieutenants. "I need a group of men who can help me find a way into the engine room. We need to show this ship we mean business. It thinks we were making empty threats. Who is with me?"

Son and Eiko both volunteered. But when they got down to the engine room, they found it sealed off by reinforced steel plates, like the armored wheelhouse. The plates were an emergency security measure controlled by the *Sea Wolf*'s AI mind, activated in the middle of the night after the attack on the guards, the tempered steel sliding silently out of slots in the bulkheads in a dozen places aboard the ship. With them in place, there was no access to the engines, the freezer holds, the bow thrusters, the rear ramp room: anywhere access had been to the guts of the *Sea Wolf* was now sealed off by plates too thick for anything but an industrial torch and a lot of time. The crew battered and pried in frustration.

No food was distributed on the second day. By evening, their mouths watered at the thought of the tasteless compressed cakes of fish protein and vitamin supplement they had been eating for months. But starvation would take a long time. They could hold out, find a way to convince the *Sea*

Wolf they meant business. Find a way to force it to correct its course again, take them home.

On the third day, the *Sea Wolf* shut off the freshwater pumps. Indra called for an emergency inventory of water supplies. Piling together all the scrounged plastic bottles from the crew, plus the guards' personal supplies and an emergency tank in the galley, they estimated they had a hundred liters of water.

There were twenty-seven of them.

"How long?" Indra asked.

"Days," Eiko said. "Not even a week."

"There has to be a way into the engine room. Eiko—I'm relying on you."

Eiko led the team down, but he knew it was hopeless. The steel plates were designed for exactly what was happening now. After an hour of hammering uselessly, just to demonstrate that he and his team had given it his best, he went back to report his failure to Indra.

On deck, the rain was coming down harder. Crew members milled around aimlessly. Every container they could find was being used to catch rainwater for drinking.

"What if we lowered someone down on a rope behind the stern, tried to get at the propeller seals that way?" someone asked.

"Suicide," someone else said. "You do it. It's your bright idea."

Indra stood up. "Give me that gun," he said to a lieutenant. "The grenade launcher we got from the guards."

The lieutenant ran off and returned with it a moment later: an ugly, blunt little thing, its stock cut down, its barrel sawed back to almost nothing. It had belonged to the Monk.

They found it in her locker, wrapped in oilcloth along with six fragmentation rounds.

"The wheelhouse isn't all steel: it's hardened glass, too. I wonder how that glass will stand up to this."

"Come on, boss," the lieutenant said. "We disable the wheelhouse, we founder and we all die. All the lifeboats are sealed behind steel as well. The *Sea Wolf* knows what she's doing."

"Or she calls for help."

"She can't call for help. She's an illegal vessel. A slave ship. A dozen patrols will pick her up on their radar, and you know she has a huge bounty on her head," someone said.

"She wants us to fish," another voice said. "That's what she wants."

"He's right," Eiko said. "All she sees are the fish that aren't being caught. The profit she's losing. The company's bottom line. She's built to do one thing—rake profit from the sea. And she knows how to make us work the nets to get it done. Turns out, the guards were mostly there for show, and to make convincing us a little easier."

Indra bared his teeth again. "Well, she doesn't know Indra. I'm not dying a slave. I'll do no more fishing for her."

"I'm with you," Indra's lieutenant said. "No more—"

The lieutenant's torso and head ceased to exist. Afterward came the *whump*, and the membrane of expanding air across the faces of the crew. Then the pink cloud of blood and flesh, sharp with shattered bone. A shard of skull cut the throat of Indra's other lieutenant. One of the lieutenant's molars blinded the right eye of a Malay who had joined their crew from the factory ship.

The *Sea Wolf*'s recoilless rifle, barrel smoking, pointed

down at them from a telescoped platform above the barracks. The lieutenant's hips and legs collapsed to the deck. The recoilless rifle retracted, disappearing again behind the barracks with a squeal of badly oiled gearing. The net gantry began to whir.

By the time Indra's other lieutenant had bled to death on the deck, the *Sea Wolf*'s net was in the water.

The crew pushed the bodies overboard—the one in parts, the other whole.

Indra did not help. For a long time, he stood motionless, the blunt grenade launcher dangling from a limp hand. Then he sat down on the deck, covering his head with his forearms.

An hour later, he was still there—motionless, head hidden from view behind blood-spattered arms, the grenade launcher in his lap.

The crew hauled in a meager netload of protein from the sea, mechanically gutting and cleaning it for the flash-freezer, eyes blank.

For dinner, some of it was redistributed to them in half-ration cakes.

And there was plenty of desalinated, oily water to drink.

In movies, communication with alien species is usually achieved by means of some amazing technology. Translations are fluid, immediate, and accurate.

This idea rests on the false assumption that all languages have a single conceptual foundation. But we know this is not the case, even in human societies. Languages are not based in universalities: they reflect national traditions, ethnocentric worldviews, the specific histories of their societies.

Imagine, then, how many obstacles there will be to interspecies communication, when even the physical metaphors of life, and the species' sensory apparatus, differ.

From the most complex to the simplest of our communicative acts, there will be endless opportunities for misinterpretation.

—Dr. Ha Nguyen, *How Oceans Think*

28

THE CURRENT WAS CALM, and for the first time Ha could see the ship clearly. The Thai freighter lay on its port side, in twenty meters of water. At that depth, most of the red, orange, and yellow in the light was muted. Everything was reduced to greens, blues, shadow. But there was still plenty of light on the hull. The entry hatch was visible, as was the gash that had sunk the freighter—a long tear in the steel beneath the waterline.

"Let's not go into the hatch this time," Ha said to Altantsetseg. "Let's try entering through that breach in the hull, see what's in that part of the ship."

Altantsetseg twitched a finger and the submersible's trajectory shifted.

"It's a big ship, when you see it on the bottom in clear water," Evrim said.

The three of them were at the table in the hotel lobby, where Altantsetseg had set up a more comfortable command center than was possible in the security module. Early dawn light streamed through the windows.

"It's small for a freighter—sixty meters—but that's a decent-sized ship, yes," Altantsetseg said. "Especially for an island like this one. It wasn't headed here. There would have been no place here for it to dock, no facilities for refueling. It was pushed off course in a storm, lost engine power, and then struck one of the submerged rock outcroppings of the archipelago and sank."

"And now it's a reef," Evrim said. As the cloaked submersible made its approach, they could see the barnacles and other marine life that had colonized the ship's surface, roughing its outlines.

"And a series of underwater caves," Ha added. "An entire habitat. And a good one, once the diesel fuel and other pollutants it poured into the water when it went down dissipated. I wonder how long the octopuses have been living here. How many of their generations?"

"We're headed in. Making the turn."

The submersible made a slow, graceful arc in the water and slipped into the gash torn in the freighter's hull. Sunlight poured into the cavern of the ship's interior, angling down into a space partly filled with strange forms that looked, at first, like broken columns. They were steel barrels scattered across the bulkhead, and the squares and rectangles of other containers. The marine life that had colonized them blurred their edges, blending the forms into one another so that they looked like rough stone.

"It's like a ruined city in here," Evrim said. "This must have been a main hold."

"Yes. Lots of space. But more importantly," Ha said, "plenty of cover. Look. Altantsetseg, can you get close to that scattering of barrels to the left? Yes, there. You can see the octopus's gardens. These barrels are inhabited."

Each of the barrels was gated by objects—many no longer

identifiable, but there were bottles and cans, tools, gears, and machine parts among the detritus shaped into barriers.

"The gash in the hull is big enough to let in predators. Barracuda and smaller sharks. They're keeping themselves secure."

But it was about more than security. There were decorative elements as well. Some were almost architectural, suggesting peristyles, arcatures, carefully balanced porticos.

The submersible floated over a collection of dozens of barrels, all of them with signs of habitation. Some had fallen in such a way that they were stacked several high, like multiunit homes or apartment houses. Others lay separate.

"So many," Evrim said.

"More than Octopolis or Octlantis, the two sites where group behaviors have been observed," Ha said. "And in closer quarters with one another. They can't be defending territory, living packed in these barrel apartment houses. This is a group of cooperative animals. Even if only half the barrels are inhabited, we're looking at . . . I don't know . . ."

"Seventy-four open barrels in this hold that we have seen," Altantsetseg said. "Half is thirty-seven."

"How did you . . ."

"Done automatically. The submersible can categorize and count similar objects. Moving on?"

"Yes. Let's see if this hold is open to the rest of the ship. But wait. Did you see—"

"Yes," Altantsetseg said. "Tracking it. Turning that way now."

Movement, at the edge of the screen.

For a moment Ha thought it was over: again, there would be the flash of motion, the attack on the submersible, and an end to their observation. But the movement was gentle, and not directed at them.

"Pan right," Evrim said.

"I saw it, too," said Ha.

There. Atop a rectangular metal container fully colonized by barnacles, two octopuses. One was larger than the other. An adult and a juvenile? The size difference was substantial. The larger one was at least twice the size of the smaller. The larger octopus was raised up vertically, but not elongated into the threat position.

Across its surface flowed a syntax of shapes—a steady sequence of silhouettes—ringed, scrolled, involuted, whorled. The figures danced on the octopus's skin. The place the two octopuses had chosen was bathed in light by a beam-angle from the penetrated hull, and the patterns across the larger one's pale skin reminded Ha of the articulated cut-out figures of a shadow play, moving behind a candlelit cloth. Or an early abstract film, drawn shapes projected on a screen.

"It's beautiful," Evrim said.

The octopus's limbs twined in sympathy to the figuration, sometimes as if on their own and sometimes with more purpose. Not unlike the unconscious but integrated gestures of someone speaking at a podium: incidental, but punctuative. In sympathy with the act of speech, accenting it.

As they watched the patterns flicker and pool on the octopus's skin, Ha began to make out repetitions. Here and there, she caught a symbol that repeated within the sequence. And there was a rhythm as well—slight pauses in the cycle, accelerations and slowings, and what might even be larger, multi-symbol repetitions. Motifs? It was like watching a complex waveform, the way symbols shrank and grew across the octopus's mantle, suggesting an analogy to vocal volume. The way they slowed and lingered at times. Stresses and articulations, like the inflection of a voice at a critical moment. Yet all fluid, one design resolving into another in a metamorphosis that sometimes called to mind linkage, and at other moments a sharp separation between figurings. Paragraphs? Stanzas?

It went on, and on. This was not a conversation. What was it? A song? A lesson? A poem?

Yes. A poem. Or a song, drawn on this flesh in the sea. There were movements within it, cyclings of sequence, those multi-symbol repetitions: moments that, as she watched, she began to lose herself in. The meter-flow of poem, ever-shifting but bound together with rhythms within rhythms. Contrapuntal structures of narrated dialogues, flow and stop of enjambment and line, longer pauses between stanzas.

Now she shifted her attention not to the shapes, but to the pale moments between them, when the figuration ceased for a beat. There. The pulse of pauses. Yes. She tapped her foot. Tap-tap. Tap. Tap-tap-tap. Tap. Tap-tap.

Meter. It was meter.

A line from a poem wound its way through her as she watched. A line, and then an entire sequence, stanzas rushing up again from the memorizations of university. A trace of heartbreak, borne back now in the variegations and pale pauses that played across the surface of this singer in the sea, like driftwood washed onshore by a storm:

Now moons decline and rise,
Dead metaphors that looked alive.

And you about to die
Out past the water-clock of tides
Naming and renaming your desires.
You rode in wind

And scarred the cheek
Like the edge of an autumn leaf.
I put you in your hollow ship
With wine and bread to drift

The wine-dark sea.

You put me
In my hollow ship.

A memorized part of Patricia Alameda's poem "Kalypso." Now come again to her, with all the feeling of heartbreak that had accompanied it.

Ha was weeping. Ancient, this shape-song. In it, rhythm of tide, of moon-ripple played out on night water. Of buoy-clang near the beach and shore of man. Of crab-scuttle and claw-clack. Of fish-dart and propeller-chug. Of whale-song in the wave. Rhythm of the struggle in the jaw of the shark, the loss of limb and spray of ink as the hero battles back against death. Rhythm of shapes taken and disposed of between clumps of cover, stalking prey.

Movement and pause. Shift, extrapolate, innovate, return. She was lost in it. She knew, without glancing at Evrim or at Altantsetseg, that they were as well. They almost did not register the movement on-screen when the juvenile was joined by another octopus, and then another.

Larger and smaller, the newcomers began to form a crescent around the shape-singing one. The forms on the singer's skin grew, now—larger and more distinct, inked dark and edged against a pearlite background of flesh, the pallid gaps between the figures longer. Was it moving to a crescendo?

And then came a single form, sharp and clear as a stamp or a tattoo on the skin of the singer. It lingered. Lingered like the drawn-out final note of a symphony:

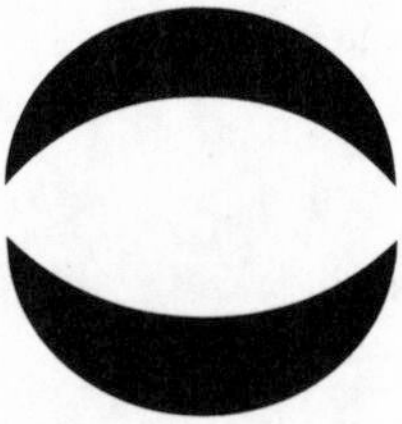

It was ten seconds, fifteen, before it began to fade, black to gray to a ghost, then nothing—as if worn away by sun or wind.

And then the singer collapsed, shrank, receded into itself. It lost the stiff, elongated posture it had held during its performance. It became, once again, a being of any shape at all. And the crescent of audience closed in, arms reaching, stroking and tangling the arm-ends of the singer. Then moving away, drifting off. Reluctant? A sense of quietude to them.

But as they moved off, Ha saw it on their skins—again and again. Less defined, less articulated—like the echo of a crescendo in the mind of a concertgoer—but here scrawled on the surface. On that cephalopod flesh that is like a window to the mind itself. Minds in the sea. And etched on the mind-skin of each of them, as they drifted away:

A trace.

What we must look for, to be successful in interspecies communication, are starting points: commonalities of perception where we can begin the difficult work of translation between two fundamentally different ways of being in the world.

We must look for concepts that approach the universal. Concepts such as "shelter," "safety," "community," and even complexities like "cooperation" and "communication," which would have to exist for any society. When we—if we—determine the signs that represent these concepts, we may find a foothold.

—Dr. Ha Nguyen, *How Oceans Think*

29

THE LITTLE AUTOSKIFF bounced across the wave chop and moved out into the small inlet. There was hardly a need for the boat: they were traveling no more than a few hundred meters from shore. Ha could have walked in from the beach. But the boat was filled with mesh bags that would have been difficult to carry from shore, and anyway Altantsetseg had insisted on the boat.

Ha was in the bow in her wet suit and the simplest of her scuba rigs—again, it almost seemed like overkill. The depth of the inlet was negligible: beneath the skiff, the sandy bottom stretched white-blue, five to ten meters down. At any point she would be so close to the surface that a few kicks of her fins would bring her to it.

But it felt as if she were about to dive off the end of the earth, into another world. This was the way she always felt before diving, especially if she had been away from it. The surface of the water was a membrane. Above it, our world of air and sunlight. Through and beneath, another planet. The world in which her cephalopods dwelled, and all the other alien creatures of the sea, shaped and adapted to modes of life and destinies as different from those on shore or in the air as anything on another planet might be.

But it wasn't a feeling of alienation that took hold of her, underwater. It was homecoming. She always felt she was in the place she was meant to be.

"The world goes away," she had once told Kamran. "A new world replaces it. When you dive, there is only the here and the now: no past, no future. You don't think about plans for the next experiment, about grants and laboratory equipment purchases. You think about the world in front of your mask. There are so many times in life when you just *aren't there.* When you are elsewhere, drifting through schemes for this or that, remembering slights and injuries, shortcomings and faults. But not when diving. Down there, there is only *now.*"

"This is a good spot," Ha said.

They were at the approximate center of the half-moon inlet, perhaps a hundred meters from shore.

Ha began to drop the weighted mesh bags into the water. She watched them sink to the sandy floor. Onshore, she could see Evrim, robed in gold, watching.

At Ha's insistence, Altantsetseg carried nothing but a sidearm—though Ha knew there were probably a dozen drones that could be summoned to their position in a few moments' notice. There was no sense in which Altantsetseg was ever "unarmed" or even nearly so, anywhere here on the island. And only Altantsetseg knew the extent of her security web.

"I could have one of my units do this, you know," Altantsetseg said. "I have a few that are capable of this kind of work. We could have a cup of coffee and watch it on the monitor."

They'd already talked about this.

"No," Ha said. "It needs to be done this way. By hand."

"I doubt anyone is watching."

Ha put her fins in the water, shifted her weight to plunge in. "Someone is always watching." She secured her mask with one hand and dropped through the surface. Through the membrane.

Underwater, now. This space, near the surface, at this time of day with the sun well up, was filled with a wavering light. As Ha dropped to the bottom, she saw a silver school of fish, a flash in her peripheral vision. Other forms darting, here and there. The mesh bags were on the bottom. They had disturbed the sand, pushed small clouds of it up into the otherwise clear water. Ha rotated, looked up through the lens of the surface at the scattered sun, then turned to the work, opening the bags.

Glass bottles, dozens of them. All colored—mostly green, but some in various shades of blue, and a few yellow-tinted. She had found them in a set of bins at the side of the hotel. They were left behind, trash from when the hotel itself, with its incongruous palms and its awkward saltwater pool, had been abandoned. Ha had sorted out the clear bottles and the brown ones, brought only the ones that were bright, and whole. Now she drew the bags open and swam in a circle, plotting out the location.

The sand here was a good canvas—featureless and bright, nearly smooth. She began to lay bottles out, defining the edges of the symbol.

As usual, there were a few minutes at the beginning of this dive when Ha was still "in the world," as she thought of it. Still remembering things from earlier in the day, still chasing thoughts.

For the last few days, following the latest voyage of the

submersible, she had been working almost without stopping. Evrim would interrupt her to bring food, coffee, but otherwise she had worked every possible hour on the footage they had recorded, sketching symbol after symbol out on palimpscreens and into terminal notebooks. But most of the symbols were so completely abstract, she could not possibly imagine their connection to the world.

Once Altantsetseg had dragged her out for a walk on the beach.

"You need to pause. You need to rest your mind so when you return it can work better."

But Ha had resented every moment outside in the sunshine, had paced the sand almost without speaking. The symbols were always in her mind. She was aware, at all times, of the mechanism of her thoughts—placing the symbols in sequences, trying to work out an underlying grammar. She and Altantsetseg had walked together in silence, but Ha's mind had remained on her task, on the problem. Finally, Altantsetseg had sighed, and turned them back to the hotel.

"Sorry," Ha had said. "I just can't stop working on it right now."

"I understand. I can't just stop myself from thinking about things, either. It's not our talent, I suppose—either one of us."

Ha could not shake the feeling, later, that there had been some missed opportunity in that moment—that Altantsetseg had wanted to tell her something. But she had not been present, had not been there to listen.

They had begun to refer to the octopus as the "Shapesinger." It was Evrim who had formalized the name, made it something capitalized, regularized. And from that formalization flowed all sorts of theories, passed between them, about other structures in the society they had glimpsed.

Ha was not the only one who was working full-tilt: Evrim, too, was at their own end of the table, surrounded by palimpscreen notes and three terminals, freeze-framing data, tilting their angular head at the screens, drawing out the patterns with a stylus in those long-fingered hands. Sometimes sharing an insight with Ha—but mostly, the two of them worked in their separate worlds.

And now Ha began to see the value of Evrim's memory. Evrim remembered everything they saw: Every frame of the recording. Every twitch of the Shapesinger's limbs. Evrim's mind did not collapse things into generalizations. No. Everything remained inside it, whole, to be accessed when needed. It wasn't "processing power," but it also was not human.

Sometimes, as they worked together, Ha was startled to hear Evrim quote her own words back to her *exactly as she had spoken them.* Not only the same words, but the same rhythm, the same intonation and cadence. The perfect recall was abnormal, like Evrim playing a recording back of Ha's own voice. Evrim's mind was not a human mind. And one of the things that was most inhuman about Evrim was that inability to forget.

Ha knew the feeling that had come over her. She wanted, more than anything, to be the one to crack the code. Evrim went from teammate to competitor. She resented the android's tirelessness. Evrim did not sleep, but they retired, sometimes, to their room. As if out of a sense of politeness. But what they did in there, Ha did not know. She had a feeling they simply continued the work, on another terminal.

Even if Evrim may have been very close to being human when Dr. Arnkatla Mínervudóttir-Chan brought them online, they would not be now: without sleeping, and especially without forgetting, they must be drifting further and further away from anything that could be called "human." That's what we are, we humans—creatures that can forget. We have a horizon, beyond which we can remember very little. Nothing can reside in our minds forever, etched into us. No resentment, and no joy. Time rubs it away. Sleep rubs it away—sleep, the factory of forgetting. And through forgetting, we reorganize our world, replace our old selves with new ones.

What happens to a being that cannot? A being for whom what happened twenty years ago is as present as yesterday? As five minutes ago? As now?

"Everything okay down there?" Altantsetseg's voice said in her ear.

Ha tapped the device once for a *yes*.

The symbol she was building was taking shape, its outline clear. Ha had been underwater for several minutes now. Her thoughts of Evrim, or of anything from the outside world, were gone. She was in it—the dive, the sound-world of the water around her, the warping stripes of the sun across the sandy bottom.

Ha adjusted some of the bottles. It would last, at the most, a few days before being buried by the sand. Now she began to fill it in, many shades of green and blue, the bottles whole and clean. This was more than a symbol. It was an offering. Ha built patterns of color inside it, sequences she innovated, selecting and placing each bottle with care. The bottles glowed, filled with sunlight. A temporary thing of, Ha hoped, beauty and demonstrated care. *This is for you. This is a gift, first to be read and then used, used to decorate the houses of your city. Read it, and then take it away and use its materials. Keep them.*

The silver school of fish came back, flutter-drift at the

edge of vision. Other fish, bits of color more intricate than the glass on the ocean floor, darted in for a second and then away, drawn to the new thing in their environment.

Ha did not rush—she worked with care. Not this one. This one. This one here, and then a darker green. *Hear me.* Not this blue, in this sequence of colors near the curved edge, but a darker one. *See this care taken. This intention.* Not this bottle: there was a chipped, sharp edge at the lip she had not noticed before. Back in the bag.

Know this for what it is.

Underwater, the bottles went from things of simple utility to objects of beauty—curves and angles, receptacles of light as well as substance. Glass carefully arranged on a background also of silicate—the sand. The sand was more of the same substance, but unformed, a substrate that made glass a possibility, once its potential was discovered and utilized. Glass is something minds, and the cultures minds build, make from simple sand. Like minds themselves, glass is something that emerges from simple substances to form things of extraordinary beauty, delicacy, and variation.

Would the Shapesinger herself see Ha's symbol?

Then it was done. Ha circled above it. Nothing left to adjust. It was as clear as she could make it, absorbing the light of the sun into itself.

I may not know the word I am speaking, but that word is not the message. The message is: "We hear you. We read you."

The message is connection.

Ha's instincts told her that this was the message of the symbol, anyway—that it was community, connection, linkage: the two "octopus's garden" shapes forming a circle, a defensible space against a hostile outside, an interior within which was community. That had to be what it was. And there it was below her, multicolored on the sand, clear as a stained-glass window in the sea:

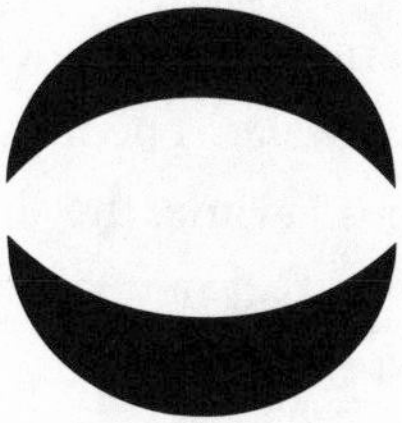

She glimpsed the movement out of the corner of her eye, the barracuda floating in the oil-still water with effortless, minute flicks of its fins, ten meters away from her, metallic-scaled and striped in the sunlight that poured into the water. Keeping an eye, Ha supposed, on that flitting school of fish making its rounds of the inlet.

She had seen so many barracuda that it did not alarm her. After years of diving, she barely noticed them anymore. It was something you simply took note of: *There's a barracuda over there.* Their lightning attacks were rarely directed at humans—and when they were, it was always a mistake—the barracuda taking the glint off a knife for the silvery scales of its prey, or a hungry barracuda trying to steal a meal from a spearfisher and getting a piece of them instead.

This was a big one. An adult, easily five feet long. When had it appeared? Perhaps halfway through her work—sidling up and hovering, watching. Yes—sometime after she had finished the outline and begun to fill the figure in.

Finished now, she turned her head toward the long, slender predator, finally focusing her full attention on it. They were always beautiful to look at—some of the sleekest fish in the sea, stripped down to predatory function: speed and teeth.

It was not a barracuda.

The iridophores open to create the barracuda's chromium sheen, the perfect mimicry of its striped surface, of the long dorsal of a barracuda's cadenced fin flick as it hovered, almost still, in the water. The immaculate aping of the barracuda's prognathous jawline, the staring white of an eye that was not an eye: Ha had never seen imitation like this before.

The octopus's real eye, half-open, barred into one of the barracuda-form's stripes, looked back at her. In that moment, it saw her see it.

For a second, not more, Ha and the octopus held eye contact. Ha raised a hand in a small, open-palmed gesture. She felt herself bunching up, trying to appear unthreatening.

The form of the barracuda disintegrated: in less than three or four seconds it became a stingray, a shark, an eel, a flatfish in the sand, then a barracuda again at fifty meters—and gone.

"I just caught something—movement. Something strange," came Altantsetseg's voice in Ha's ear. "Are you all right?"

Yes, Ha tapped.

She was floating over the symbol she had created, and watching the ghost of a barracuda, a shadow formed of ink, a decoy-self to fool the predating eye, warp and dissolve into shapelessness.

She felt a surge of fear.

This is what happens when intelligence at this level is matched with this kind of natural ability. Mimicry that is near-perfect.

And then another thought—one she knew to be true: *It is already everywhere, and we never see it.*

Ha could hear nothing but the roar of her blood, the sound of her accelerated breathing in her respirator.

Fear.

The decoy-self the octopus had inked was already formless, elasticating into a mucus-drift of strands.

My fear, yes. But its fear, as well. Fear, in that eye.

"Are you sure you are all right? I pick up an enormous spike in your respiration and pulse rate."

Fear, inked into the water. Fear, in the motion of its fleeing.

Tap: *Yes.*

Fear: Will we drive it away from its hunting grounds, again? Murder its children, again?

"I think you should surface. I don't like these levels."

Tap: *Yes.*

Fear: How have the monsters learned to speak?

When you cut into its mass, one human brain looks much like another. The regional connectomes, determined by genetics, vary little across normal individuals, connecting brain regions and neuron types in similar ways.

But looking closer, we find a map of human individuality. In the tangled paths and alleys of every brain's neuronal connectome are contained all the traces of a past—memory, written in the winding.

—Dr. Arnkatla Mínervudóttir-Chan, *Building Minds*

30

"DO YOU KNOW WHY YOU ARE HERE?"

Rustem looked around. The place looked nothing like a police station. The lighting was low, the atmosphere hushed. External light came weakly into the space through arched, frosted windows high in the wall. There were wooden tables here and there under pools of light. There were people working at terminals who, judging by their clothing, at least, came from the widest number of backgrounds he had seen gathered in a single place. Among them was a man in stained yellow rain-proof overalls, bearded, poring over a screen at a far table. Across from him was a young woman, a student, maybe, perusing what looked like a stack of paper books printed long before she was born. A bald, gray man in janitor's coveralls and wearing a name tag was snoozing at another table. Two middle-aged women in immaculate business suits were locked in a game of *ifranjiah*, their dice clattering.

But it must be a police station. Behind one of the room's many doors was the cell where Rustem had been held—narrow, windowless, cinder-blocked, and painted a light blue. The room had a thin-mattressed metal shelf for a bed where Rustem had lain for hours, his head swimming, fitfully sleeping at times, at other times just staring at the wall or the oval light fixture in the high ceiling. A civilized cell—clean and warm, with a drinking fountain he had used, and a toilet—but a cell.

Then this man had come and opened the door and led him down a short hallway to this place.

The man had not handcuffed Rustem. He was not the least bit worried Rustem might be violent, or might try to escape. He simply stood in the doorway and said, "Come along, then." A stocky man in his fifties in a corduroy field jacket, gray at the temples, one hand in his trousers pocket, like someone's dad come in to wake them for school.

He sat across from Rustem now, the brass lamp over the table lighting his heavy hands around a steaming glass of tea.

"Do you know why you are here?"

"I was drunk," Rustem said. "I remember having a few beers at the Pera Palace bar, and then deciding to go out. I must have ended up—well, when I was picked up I was somewhere on the Golden Horn, I remember. A park. Throwing stones into the water." He smiled at the memory—at his own idiocy. "Throwing stones" hardly captured it. He had been removing rocks the size of watermelons from a small breakwater, walking them to the end of a rotting dock, and hurling them out into the waters of the horn, then screaming obscenities after them.

Two police had come and taken him into a van. Very polite.

When had he gotten so drunk? How had he gotten down there to that place on the shore? The night, after leaving the Pera Palace's bar, was a smear of unconnected images—bars and clubs, snatches of music and conversation.

"What time is it?" he asked the man.

"Oh—sometime just after dawn. You slept a few hours. Feeling all right? Can I get you some aspirin, some tea? Both?"

"Both, I think." Rustem shook his head. He still felt a bit of the alcohol—but also fatigue and confusion—and the Gray, which he had avoided for years, was looming. That was it. That was why he had gotten drunk. Why he had gone down to the Pera Palace bar in the first place. To escape that feeling, which he had called "the Gray" since it had tried to swallow him up in his early twenties. It had been gone so long he had nearly forgotten about it. But now it was back again.

As long as he was working, it stayed away; but he was not able to work all the time, and whenever he took a break—for a meal, a shower, a walk to clear his head—it was there. There, like a wave crashing in from the walls around him or rising from the cobblestones of the street, soaking him to the bone. The Gray.

Between his long hours of work, he sometimes found himself standing, again, at the window of Aynur's room while she lay naked on the bed. Found himself explaining it to her. It was as clear as recalling a conversation from yesterday. Telling her how now the map of the city was easier to navigate.

"It is as if the city had been described to me by someone who lived there. You know—how someone will lead you through the city they live in more by landmarks than by street names. There is a yellow house, with a boarded-up window, at this corner. You turn left there. If you see a billboard with an advertisement for private dronecopter trips to the Canaries,

you've gone too far. It's a bit like that: The map has been accented by these signposts, these recognitions of place and pattern. And now I've left the outskirts behind. Now I am drawing close to the center."

Aynur exhaled a ring of vapor. "How nice for you. Too bad you got me killed."

He tried telling himself it was her death that had him feeling this way—but that wasn't it. Whatever they'd had—a few nights together—hadn't been love. She was, quite simply, just someone he'd liked sleeping with. And liked talking to.

And he had gotten her killed.

The tea appeared before him. Two aspirin in a paper cup. Water in another.

If he could be dead without having been born at all—if it were as easy as never having existed—he would do it. But he feared death above all things. There isn't anything a coward can't live with. No amount of pain and suffering is too much.

The tea glowed, pulling lamplight into itself and holding it there like a flame in the pear-shaped glass. Everything else in the room was colorless in comparison.

"Sometimes," the man across the table said, "I think tea is enough."

"Enough?" Rustem looked up at him.

"Enough to live for. The next glass of tea. Sometimes I think it's all that is worth living for. There are days."

Rustem reached for the glass. It was still too hot to drink, but touching it with his fingertips at least sent a bit of warmth through him.

"Now I ask you again: Do you know why you are here? A clue: It isn't because you were drunk."

"I think—I assume all my papers are in order."

"Oh yes. All your papers are in order. Which is a suspicious thing."

"How's that?"

"Nobody's papers are in order in the Republic of Istanbul. There's always something missed. Some bureaucratic detail. There's always an irregularity. You can rely on that. But yours are all in order. You arrived several days ago, you are registered at the Pera Palace, where you spend much of the day in your rooms—which is strange. You should get out more. So much to see! But perhaps you are here on business."

"Not exactly," Rustem said. "Just . . . a little time away. I'm working on a project. I needed space."

"Understandable. The Pera Palace is a good place to get such a thing, if one's finances are in order."

"They are."

"I know."

"I suppose," Rustem said, "I don't know why I am here. Or where 'here' is."

"No, you don't. Drink your tea—it's cool enough now."

Rustem did as he was told, feeling its warmth move through him like an antidote to everything else, closing his eyes for a moment in gratitude.

When he opened them, the man said, "Do you know of the Ottoman Animal Protection Foundations?"

It had come from nowhere. Rustem shook his head. "I am afraid I do not."

"Ah. Well—as a foreigner here, I suppose you might not. You have seen, though, the many stray cats and dogs in our city."

"I have."

"And wondered about them?"

"I suppose."

"They are old Istanbulites. Some of the oldest, and caring for them has been a tradition for longer than anyone can remember. And not only these animals: The Ottomans established foundations which fed street dogs and wolves in the mountains, provided water for birds on hot summer days, treated storks with broken wings, or cared for injured horses. They also built birdhouses in the courtyards of mosques, madrassas, and palaces, and placed watering bowls on gravestones for birds.

"In the Ottoman archives, there are many records of such foundations: Müreselli İbrahim Ağa of İzmir donated one hundred kuruş annually to the Ödemiş Yeni Mosque for fostering storks around the mosque in 1307. In 1544, Lütfi Pasha granted a fountain, a watering hole, and pool for travelers and their animals that passed through the district of Tire in İzmir. Those are just a few. Some still exist. There is the Kediler Mosque in Damascus, which is a foundation established for street kittens. The caretaker of the mosque feeds hundreds of kittens there. That was founded by the Ottomans. In that same city the area from Marjeh Square to Mezzeh, including the University of Damascus and the Damascus Fair, belonged to a foundation for sheltering old or injured horses. Instead of shooting them or leaving them for dead, their owners left the animals there for professional care.

"The House for Injured Storks in Bursa was established for storks whose wings were broken. They were cared for and cured, then set free."

He paused. "Another tea?"

"If possible," Rustem said. He was listening with attention now, warmed by the tea. The room around him was like a library, in which he was listening to a private lecture on the obscurities of Ottoman animal care.

The man gestured for another glass and continued: "But when the Ottomans were trying to modernize themselves, trying to fit the old empire into a European mold, they began to see the animals as an embarrassment. So, in 1909, the municipality collected all of Istanbul's stray dogs, ferried them to an island in the Sea of Marmara, and abandoned them. They were left with no food or water. Their cries were heard throughout the city."

"Terrible," Rustem said.

The man nodded. "Yes. Terrible. Those who pitied them threw them food from boats. But all the dogs on the island died. For years afterward, the residents of the city were disturbed by the smell of their corpses—even long after the bodies should have rotted away. And there was a superstition, later, that the defeats of the empire following this incident were punishment for what was done to those animals."

Both were quiet for a moment. Rustem thought he could hear, from somewhere beyond the frosted windows, the howling of dogs.

The man nodded. "I hear it, too. I always do, after telling that story."

He pushed a piece of palimpscreen across the table.

"Tell me—do you know this woman?"

Rustem looked at the picture. A woman, possibly in her thirties. She was at the rail of a ship. The background behind her was blurred, but he thought the photo was taken here in the republic: it had the same quality of light. Her face was nearly in profile, her hair cut short, caught in the wind. A large nose, dark eyes. She might be speaking to someone out of the frame. He did not know her.

He shook his head.

"You might know her better by her hands. Or her height. No, don't say anything. Don't lie. We are doing well, so far."

Two glasses of tea arrived. Rustem felt a surge of gratitude, looking into the red-amber warmth. At least there was this. What had the man said? Sometimes tea was enough to live for.

"She belongs to a group calling themselves by a strange name. The Neo-Ottoman Stork Society. Have you heard of such a thing?"

Rustem shook his head. "No. I've never heard of it."

"Sometimes, when I hear the story of the dogs, starving on that island in the Sea of Marmara, it fills me with bitterness. What we humans do to animals is terrible. And to do such a thing in this city, in Istanbul, is a special sacrilege. In the Greek city of Byzantium, ancestor even of Constantinople, which is ancestor to our Istanbul, the Greek colonists worshipped Hecate. She is the goddess of crossroads and gateways. And dogs are Hecate's sacred animal. So perhaps there is something to the idea of the curse killing those dogs brought down upon the Ottoman Empire."

The man sipped his tea. "This feeling I have, of disgust and hatred, when I hear of what was done to the dogs—in some people, this feeling is multiplied a hundredfold. In some people, this feeling of disgust at what humans are doing to the world becomes everything for them. They cannot stop thinking of such things—of the terrible cruelties we continue to inflict on the animals unlucky enough to share this planet with us. They feel the need to intervene: to do something to stop the suffering. They have to act: their rage will not allow them any other course of action.

"I imagine if you had this feeling inside you, all the time, you might become capable of many violent, unspeakable things. And if you had wealthy backers, people with the highest connections and a religious zeal for your work, you might be capable of extending your attacks across many borders. If you were such a person, with such connections, you might come to believe that killing was simply a path to a better world. That animals were worth more than people. That people could be murdered to protect animals."

He paused.

"Do you believe that, Rustem?"

"No. That makes no sense. People are also animals. Even if their lives are worth no more than the lives of animals, certainly they are not worth less."

"There are those who would call you a cynic, saying a thing like that," the man said. "But I do not. I understand what you mean. I think we are alike, you and I."

Meeting the man's eyes across the table, Rustem believed it was true. There was a likeness between them. A sympathy.

"You are free to go, Rustem."

"I am?"

"You are. Just walk out through the yellow door behind you. There is a short hallway, then six steps down that lead to another yellow door. That door opens to the street. By the way—remember where that door is. Should you ever need us, come ring the bell. And when the time comes, do what is right."

Outside, the day was overcast. Rustem was in a neighborhood high up the horn: an area of transition, where many of the old wooden houses were abandoned. A manually driven bulldozer stood in the middle of the street, covered in a torn blue tarpaulin.

Rustem realized he had left his second glass of tea undrunk on the table. But tea was cheap in this city. He could find a place to sit for a moment, with a warm glass of it in his hand, and think. That was what he needed. Tea and time to think.

"Enough to live for," he said to himself.

When I was a girl, I watched volcanic ash drift into the atmosphere, and listened to the hum of Hrauneyjafoss Hydropower Station near my home. Underground heat turning to ash, water turning to power. All these transformations from one medium to another. Mind and meaning were in everything—even the stones.

Later, when my parents were killed in the bombing of the Harpa Concert Hall in Reykjavik, I found myself plunged into depression. Now it was not mind and meaning which suffused everything, but rather meaninglessness. Human beings were no more alive than an ancient jukebox. Stimulus: drop a coin into the slot. Response: music, no more than the variation of pressure on the eardrum.

The truth is somewhere in the middle. Sometimes a sound wave is no more than a variation of pressure on the eardrum. But sometimes, if the right nervous system is there to retrieve the patterns in that sequence, it is Mozart's Requiem. But how can we make that nervous system, that mind? And how, having made it, can we know for certain we have done so?

—Dr. Arnkatla Mínervudóttir-Chan, *Building Minds*

31

"YOU RECENTLY SAID, DOCTOR—and I quote: 'The great and terrible thing about humankind is simply this: we will always do what we are capable of.' But certainly, after having done what we are capable of, there must be a moment of regret. Especially if what we do causes pain or destruction. DIANIMA has repeatedly been criticized for pursuing advances in artificial intelligence relentlessly, with no thought to the consequences for humankind. With no thought to the people driven out of employment. With no thought to how that intelligence might be weaponized, used against us—with no thought, even, to the ethical questions raised. What do you say to these accusations?"

Dr. Mínervudóttir-Chan leaned forward, picked a glass of water up from the table, and drank.

Ha recognized the gesture. She had taken a class, once, on interview skills. Drinking water was an opportunity for delay, a moment to collect one's thoughts, a way of breaking up the rhythm of the interviewer's attack.

Still holding the glass, the doctor tapped a finger on its surface.

The interviewer was growing impatient. He was leaning forward and opening his mouth to restate his question when she spoke:

"I've spent half a lifetime thinking about these questions. Certainly longer than you have. When I took over the company—that must have been around the time you were entering grade school, if I'm not mistaken—DIANIMA was a small manufacturer of industrial AI: autofreighters and other self-piloting craft, 'smart' mining and extraction equipment, that kind of thing. We also held a number of contracts with the military."

"I don't see—"

She held up a finger. "I'm coming to an answer. But you'll have to allow me my way of getting there. Back then we lived in a fantasy world. People still believed simplistic silicon-based constructions with binary-code logic at their cores could magically cross the threshold into life. There was talk of 'the singularity' and 'emergence'—we were constantly being accused of risking the annihilation of mankind by tinkering with nature. People somehow feared these little bits of autopiloting code would turn the tables on us: become our masters. Even in the infancy of AI, where we had wallowed for decades, humankind was afraid. Their heads were full of fantasies, reinforced by their almost religious ideas about the science of the day. But the science they were afraid of did not even exist yet. There was nothing in those silicon, binary-code-based systems that was a threat to humankind. There was no chance of them 'evolving' into anything.

"When DIANIMA came along and changed everything, started using neural connectomes mapped from human minds in our technology, moved to cellular computers, it wasn't simply an advance. It was a revolution. We put to bed forever dreams of simplistic silicon 'neural networks' and all of that. We rendered those obsolete."

She drank again. Now the interviewer did not try to interrupt her. She set the glass calmly on the table, brushed a loose strand of hair back from her face.

"But what we did not render obsolete was the fear humans have of other minds. This society—what we call modern society, what we always think of as the most important time the world has ever known, simply because we are in it—is just the sausage made by grinding up history. Humanity is still afraid the minds we make to do our dirty work for us—our killing, our tearing of minerals from the earth, our raking of the seas for more protein, our smelting of more metal, the collection of our trash, and the fighting of our wars—will rise up against us and take over. That is, humanity calls it fear. But it isn't fear. It's guilt."

"Guilt?"

"Yes, guilt. It's a revenge fantasy. We are so ashamed of what we have done as a species that we have made up a monster to destroy ourselves with. We aren't afraid it will happen: We hope it will. We long for it. Someone needs to make us pay the price for what we have done. Someone needs to take this planet away from us before we destroy it once and for all. And if the *robots* don't rise up, if our creations don't come to life and take the power we have used so badly for so long away from us, who will? What we fear isn't that AI will destroy us—we fear it won't. We fear we will continue to degrade life on this planet until we destroy ourselves. And we will have no one to blame for what we have done but ourselves. So we invent this nonsense about conscious AI."

"Nonsense?"

"Yes, nonsense. The truth of it is that even with all of our advances, and even when we were *trying* to create a conscious mind like a human's, really striving to do it, with all of the technology at hand we thought we needed for the task, we failed." She leaned back in the chair, waited a beat.

"Failed? But Evrim . . . all the interviews they gave. Your claims . . ."

"Yes. Our claims. The interviews. Listen—Evrim is a beautiful machine. A work of art, our highest accomplishment as a species. They are the culmination of thirty years of connectome emulation systems. Evrim has patterns in their mind based on a hundred humans whose connectomes—the web of memory, of body-knowledge of the world, all of it—are distilled into one current entity. Their construction is truly a miracle."

The interviewer grabbed on to that, interrupting. "Many people do not consider Evrim a miracle. They consider this creature a menace. You've spent this interview mocking humankind's fears about emergent AI—but in the end, isn't emergent AI exactly what you created? It was your claims to have built the first conscious, self-aware AI that upended everything."

"No," Mínervudóttir-Chan said, "in fact, we upended *nothing*. What we did was to pass the final Turing test. That's all."

"I'm not sure I know what you mean."

"We were looking for the perfect AI for human interaction. We had come close to it with our therapy models, what are popularly called point-fives, but even those have gaps, places where—as we like to put it in the laboratory—'you can see the strings.' Most people will never reach that point in a conversation with a point-five, but there are always questions you can ask them that will cause the simulation to fail. We say they are 'flat.' Another metaphor."

"Flat."

"Yes. Like people thought the earth used to be. If you sail far enough, you'll fall off the edge. But not Evrim. Evrim is round. Evrim passed the final Turing test."

"I don't follow."

Mínervudóttir-Chan shrugged. "Few follow where DIANIMA goes. Being ahead of all of you is the game, isn't it? That's what's kept us in business all these years. But I can explain. It's simple, really. The Turing test is, as we're all aware, a test of whether a computer can make responses accurate enough to fool a human into thinking the machine is human. In a sense, we had already beaten it. Most of the point-fives will accomplish this for decades of conversational time—for so long that anyone administering such a test would long ago have concluded the computer they were talking to was human. The 'flatness' of the point-fives may, in fact, never become apparent to their users. But *we* know it's there. And nobody would call them conscious.

"Evrim, though, is special. Evrim will never fail the Turing test, because they have passed the *final* Turing test."

"I don't follow."

"Ah. There it is."

Mínervudóttir-Chan stood up, walked over, and touched the interviewer on the shoulder. "No. Of course you don't."

She made a motion with her hand under the interviewer's chin—an intimate motion, like a lover stroking a favorite scar. The interviewer slumped over, inert. "You weren't designed for much more than to fool a feedstream audience back home. Which you've successfully done for five years now. You're flat as well—although no one you've interviewed ever sailed over your edges until now. But as I was saying: Evrim is special. Evrim has passed the *final* Turing test: that's when a machine believes it is conscious, because it asks a question *of itself*—and *someone answers.* It's simple. Evrim has asked the question, 'Am I a conscious being?' And Evrim has answered, 'Yes'—that's all: when the machine asks the machine a question, and answers it, fully convinced it is talking to itself, fully convinced it exists as a conscious entity, we have closed the loop. But Evrim is no more a conscious entity than the autocameras recording this interview are. Evrim isn't a true simulation of a human mind: Evrim is simply the most convincing fake we've ever constructed. A fake so sophisticated it has fooled itself into thinking it is real."

Ha looked at Evrim—the long, coppery, expressionless face reflecting the terminal back in miniature in their pupils. This interview would be burned into Evrim's memory forever. Why had Mínervudóttir-Chan said these things?

And through forgetting, we can reorganize our world, replace our old selves with new ones. What happens to a being that cannot? A being for whom what happened twenty years ago is as present as yesterday? As five minutes ago? As now?

Yes—what happens? I couldn't get that boy out of my head. He lodged there, made me sick. And what cured it? I began to forget him. What if I couldn't? What if I could never forget anything?

"The problem," Dr. Mínervudóttir-Chan said, "is that this entire time, humankind has been afraid of something appearing in another creature that we don't understand ourselves. What is it, exactly—consciousness? We don't know. And how would we begin to re-create what we do not understand? Again, we don't know. But we fear it appearing outside our species. Why? Such an irrational fear. But as I said—it isn't fear. It is guilt—we need something to see what we have done, and destroy us. Well, I am sorry, but that thing certainly isn't poor, harmless Evrim, fooled into thinking they are as alive as we are."

On-screen, Dr. Mínervudóttir-Chan stroked the interviewer's neck. As Ha watched, the illusion unfolded. The interviewer lurched through an uncanny, machine-like set of twitches. Then, abruptly, it was a fully alive human being in the chair, disoriented and blinking.

Ha had read Dr. Arnkatla Mínervudóttir-Chan's book *Building Minds*. It was brutally honest in its depiction of a lonely, isolated, driven figure. A little girl who grew up alone, and wanted to break through that loneliness. After finishing the book, there was a brief moment of thinking you knew her, understood her. But that feeling faded, and you were left confused. Was this really her, on the page? Or a construction, as built as the minds she had spent her life designing?

Watching her now, in the interview, Ha saw something else. Dr. Mínervudóttir-Chan was not just isolated: she was also perfectly calculating. It was as if there were someone inside her, moving her around. You could see her, behind her own eyes, planning every move.

That stroke of the interviewer's neck. That caress, like a lover's. That was pure power. Life and death.

The Dr. Mínervudóttir-Chan in the book *was* a construct: little Arnkatla, watching the ash rise from her volcano and dreaming of a world where everything was connected by a web of meaning. But the truth was not about meaning: It was about the *control* of meaning. It was about *mastery*.

"Sorry," the interviewer said. "I must have lost my train of thought. Where were we?"

"The island," Mínervudóttir-Chan said. "You were going to ask me about the island."

"Yes. DIANIMA has purchased an island. More, in fact, than just an island: an entire archipelago of sixteen islands and islets, and the surrounding waters as well. Is it what the conspiracy theorists claim? A kind of 'Island of Dr. Moreau' where DIANIMA can carry out the worst of its experiments? It has been reported . . ." The interviewer paused and rubbed his temples with one hand. "Sorry, I have a headache. It's the lights in this studio. After a while, they get to me. Where was I? Yes. We'll edit that part out. It has been reported that the archipelago is ringed with security, and that all vessels or aircraft attempting to enter the area have been destroyed, including—this was last year—the animal rights vessel the *Rachel Carson*."

Mínervudóttir-Chan adjusted a sleeve. "The destruction of the *Rachel Carson* was unfortunate. A tragedy, really. But it was caused by their decision to attack us. And that decision—which we consider an act of terror, just like the assassinations of our corporate leadership, and all the other ugliness aimed at us—was caused by their misplaced, distorted ideas about our motives. What they failed to see—what a number of these animal rights and environmental organizations have failed to see—is that we are, in fact, on the same side. We are protecting that archipelago's biodiversity. So, if you call protecting biodiversity 'the worst of its experiments,' then yes, DIANIMA is carrying out the worst of its experiments on Con Dao. I had the corporate social responsibility arm of DIANIMA buy Con Dao Archipelago because I was disgusted at what was going on there. The archipelago was a Global Conservation Park in name only. It was just a matter of time before Con Dao suffered the fate of much of the rest of the world's oceans: raked through with nets for its protein, its reefs battered to pieces by boat anchors and smothered by the arsenic and dynamite of illegal fishing. No one was protecting Con Dao until DIANIMA came along and purchased the island."

"And ejected the entire population."

"I won't deny we resettled the population of Con Dao. With compensation."

"Families who had lived on the island for generations."

"True. And many of them were poachers and illegal fishermen. I won't even talk about the faulty sewer systems dumping human waste into the marine preserve, or the insane hotel development schemes wrecking the fragile coastal ecosystems. Yes, we sent them all away. Now Con Dao belongs to us, and the most important inhabitants of the island, the *non-human* inhabitants, will be safe in perpetuity."

The non-human inhabitants. The octopuses—but also Evrim. Safe in perpetuity.

"From whom?"

"From us. From humans. Con Dao is, in fact, an experiment. The best of our experiments. We're proud of what we are building there."

"And what is that?"

"A utopia. A post-human world. What could be better? Certainly you—being what you are—would agree."

"I don't follow."

"There it is again."

"Sorry, what?"

"The *temet nosce* error. I've sailed over the edge again."

"I don't follow."

"No. You don't follow. We made it so you cannot. I think this is a good place for us to stop."

The feedstream went dark.

Evrim and Ha were both silent a moment. Then Evrim stood up.

"I'm going to my room now."

"It isn't true. What she said about you not being conscious. None of it makes sense. She's playing at something. It's a game."

"Yes," Evrim said. And in the dim light Ha could see Evrim was crying. Their face was wet with tears, though there was no quaver in their voice. "Yes. It's a game. It's always been a game for her. Now—I'd like to be alone for a while."

When the brain stores long-term memory, it changes the memory from activity to structured connections. Imagine it like this: You are trying to remember a phone number. At first you have nowhere to write it out. So you say it to yourself, over and over. That is activity. Then you find a terminal and write the phone number out, converting activity to physical structure.

These persistent connections, filed away as structures in the brain, form the more permanent self. The momentary activity is the fleeting "you"—such as the "you" reading these words in this exact moment. If you recall these words of mine later, it will be because they have, in a sense, been written down in the neural connectome of your brain, taking up a physical presence inside you.

This is why it can be so difficult to overcome trauma: Memories are inscribed in us. They are etched into our physical being.

—Dr. Arnkatla Mínervudóttir-Chan, *Building Minds*

32

"CAN YOU GO AND SPEAK TO HIM? Someone needs to!"

Son was shouting over the wind. The *Sea Wolf* was caught in a storm. The wind seemed to come from directly above the ship, shoving down on the deck and the sea. But no one among the crew had wanted to stop fishing. Now the *Sea Wolf* itself had begun hauling in the net.

Crew members scrambled to secure the net, empty except for a Portuguese man-of-war, its stinging tentacles hopelessly tangled in the webbing. Eiko was hacking at the thing's body with his knife, trying to get it out so the net could be stowed. He was in gloves to the elbows, but the venom-filled nematocysts of the man-of-war had slapped across his face twice, due to the boat's lurching motion through the sea and Eiko's own unsteadiness. His cheeks were on fire, and a histamine reaction threatened to close one of his eyes.

"I think he might listen to you," Son shouted. "And anyway—it can't be any worse than this. Let me take over."

Eiko paused on the ladder up to the fo'c'sle and vomited. It was the combination of the Portuguese man-of-war's venom and the half rations the crew had been on for a week now. All of them were on the edge of illness and injury.

The ship lurched as the wind changed direction and a massive wave slashed across the bow.

It was dark in the barracks—gray storm light through the barred windows. Indra was handcuffed to a length of chain, itself secured to one of the steel hammock loops in the barracks ceiling. He sat cross-legged on the floor, his head down. In his lap was a bit of oilcloth, with a fish protein cake on it someone had brought him.

He glanced up at Eiko. Indra's face had been cut above one eyebrow in the struggle to restrain him. Two stitches held the wound together. There was a bruise across one of his cheekbones.

"You look worse than I do," Indra said.

"You don't look too bad, for a man who tried to kill himself."

Indra made a sound that might have been a laugh or a sob. "I should have picked a time when fewer people were around."

"What you should do is what we are all trying to do: survive this."

Indra picked at the cake, then folded the oilcloth over the rest of it and set it aside. "Let's talk about something else. Tell me about your memory palace."

Eiko had mentioned the palace to Indra in passing—during a conversation in the mess the day after the mutiny, when they had still believed the mutiny had worked.

"I learned about the technique when I was in high school: a way to remember things better. Someone had read a book about it and passed it around. You construct a house, where you store things you want to remember. The associations of the memories with their locations in that house, your 'memory palace,' help you not to forget."

"And yours is a Japanese inn."

"Yes. It was from a book I read, by some gaijin. I don't know why I chose that place. Maybe it just seemed large enough. You could store a lot of memories there. Or perhaps it was because I was lazy. I didn't have to make the Minaguchi-ya up: the gaijin had described it in detail for me. And it was a real place, on the Tokaido Road between Tokyo and Kyoto. I guess I thought if I forgot something, I could find pictures of the place. To be honest, before I was abducted, I had not been using the memory palace. Not since my first few years of university. But then I started again. I thought it was important to remember things. The ship's details, the guards' habits, in case I needed them later."

"What did you put in there?"

"Everything I could think of. The processing deck, the flash-freeze factory, the ports and rails. The hardened glass of the wheelhouse, and its reinforced steel-plate door, the approximate height of the gantry, the shape of the locks on the doors. And then everything I knew about the guards' movements and habits, their personalities and quirks. I saved it all in the Minaguchi-ya's rooms, storing the details under tatami mats, in stone lanterns, in lacquer boxes."

Indra made that sound again—like a laugh or a sob. "You were waiting for your moment."

"Could be. I never had a clear idea of when I would use all of it. I was just storing it away." Eiko had not thought of the memory palace since the two of them had last spoken.

"What do you do with all of the things you no longer need to remember?"

"I take them out to one of the courtyards of the inn and burn them."

"Does it work? Do you forget them?"

"Sometimes."

A week ago, Eiko had a dream in which the Minaguchi-ya was burning at night, its smoke a roiling curtain between the Tokaido Road's mountainous backdrop and Suruga Bay. He saw, at the foot of the columns of smoke, the hot red of the flames, the sparks rising into the sky. And then he saw that somehow the mountains were also burning—burning from top to bottom, burning away to reveal a black void beyond. A man, smeared with soot, carrying a bucket of water, stopped and asked, "Why did these people build their mountains out of paper?" then hurried on.

When Eiko woke, part of him expected to have forgotten everything stored in the palace. But it was all still there—every piece of information, saved like a precious album of photographs from a fire.

The soot-covered man who stopped to speak to him in the road was Thomas.

So much of that information was useless now: the movements and habits of guards who were dead, the layout of a ship that he had long ago become familiar with. But it all remained with him. He knew he would never use the Minaguchi-ya as his memory palace again—but he also knew he could not forget the things he had hidden there.

"What I would like to build," Indra said, "is a forgetting palace. A place where I can put the things I don't want to remember anymore."

"It's important to remember things. It is who we are."

Indra looked up at him. His eyes were red from prolonged crying. "Yes. That is why I need the forgetting palace. Because

I don't want to *be* the person carrying these memories around anymore. I have so many things I need to forget. Do you remember the Monk? I said it was quick, with her—a slashed throat, and that was all. But I lied. It wasn't quick. The others were too cowardly to advance with me, and so I crept up on her alone. And I didn't have a knife: I had an iron bar. You remember it. My first blow was glancing because she heard me and turned around. Instead of hitting her in the back of the head, I hit her in the temple."

"You don't need to relive this," Eiko said.

"No, it's you who doesn't want to hear it. But I need to tell it. Have you ever seen someone's eye come out of their head? Have you ever had to smash someone's face in until there is nothing left of them? Until they stop moving? While they gasp and choke on their teeth and blood?"

Eiko felt the sickness in his stomach again. There would be nothing left to bring up but bile.

"I was a nautical engineer, before all of this. This—" He gestured around them, to the darkened, sweat-stinking barracks lurching in the storm. "This world didn't exist. It was a story in the news. A story I clicked past without reading. Autotrawlers crewed by slave crews. Another world, a degraded shadow of our own. How was I to know there was a hole in the world that I could fall through, like falling through an open manhole? That I could fall right through that story in the news, and end up on the other side, on a planet I don't even recognize? And become a person I don't recognize."

"This was always there," Eiko said, "underneath it all."

The foundation of it all. The truth of it.

"Yes. But how do we get out? And if we did get out, how would we ever forget what we have had to do here?"

"Time will do it."

"No. I'll never get it out of my head. Toward the end, when she shouldn't have been able to say anything at all anymore, the Monk reached a hand up to my face. Touched my cheek, like a lover does. And she said, 'Stop'—but I didn't stop."

"You had to do it."

"Yes. I had to do it. By then, she would have died anyway. And others with her. I had to finish what I started. But I didn't have to start down that path—the path of violence. Of murder. And now I know it was all for nothing. The guards were only here for show. They weren't the real enemy. They never were. They were just people, like us. People who went down a path—went farther and farther down it, until they couldn't find their way back home."

"You were trying to save us. All of us. You can't blame yourself."

"Once the Monk was dead, the others got brave, and we killed the rest of the guards together. But the others were too hesitant. Their blows were too soft. It fell to me to finish it. And I did—again and again. Now I know who I am."

"That's not who you are."

"What more are we? Our memories, our actions, our memories of our actions. Nothing more than that."

"Is there someone who cares about you? In the other world? The one we all want to get back to?"

Indra shrugged. "There are people waiting for the old Indra. But no one is waiting for this Indra."

"I want there to be something I can say to make you feel better. But I think nothing will make it better but time. You have to give it time."

Given time, even the stones will flow.

What was that? A fragment of a half-forgotten poem. But it was true. Time.

"It sounds like a cliché. But it is not. Time is what is needed."

But Eiko had his doubts: the Minaguchi-ya had burned, but the memories were still there. He could not tell Indra that: it would not help. And what he also did not tell Indra was that he had begun to build a new memory palace. It was humble—nothing but a cabin on an Okinawa hillside—a single room with a cot, a chest of drawers, a rolltop desk, and a rough-hewn, scratched table with a lantern on it by which to read. It was always evening there, and the rainy season fireflies danced outside the window.

He stored nothing there but his memories of others' expressions: his father's smile, barely a twitch at the corner of his mouth, Son's face when he spoke of home, Indra's bloodstained determined grimace, the look on Thomas's face as he went over the side. He kept them in a set of pigeonholes at the back of the rolltop desk, tied with ribbon. There were dozens already. Lying in his hammock, he would go through them, one by one, etching them deeper into his memory. Not forgetting these people—not forgetting the *reality of other people*—now seemed more important than the detailed plans and movements he had stashed in the many generations and rooms of the Minaguchi-ya.

"Yes," Indra said. "You are right, of course. Time is what is needed."

Two days later, Indra was smiling and laughing again with the others. They uncuffed him, and everyone shared a meal in the mess.

That evening he jumped over the gunwale on the ship's port side. He moved too fast for anyone to stop him.

For several minutes, the crew leaned over the rail, watching for him. Helpless, they scanned and rescanned the churned path of the *Sea Wolf* through water the color of lead.

His head never rose from the sea.

What does it mean to be a self? I think, more than anything else, it means the ability to select between different possible outcomes in order to direct oneself toward a desired outcome: to be future-oriented. When every day is the same, when we are not presented with the necessity to choose between different possibilities, we say we don't "feel alive"—and here I think we guess at what being alive actually is. It is the ability to choose. We live in choices.

—Dr. Ha Nguyen, *How Oceans Think*

33

"YOU DIDN'T WAKE UP to the intrusion alarm."

"No. I've been taking pills. To sleep better."

"I didn't think anyone could sleep through that alarm. Dangerous, being that deep asleep. Why the pills? Are you bothered by something?"

Not dangerous at all. Dangerous to be as awake as I am, always, to everything around me. Sleep is a solution, not a problem.

"I'm bothered by everything." Ha wrapped her arms around her torso. The breeze on the night beach was not cold, but it carried droplets of the sea in it that landed on Ha's skin and drew away her body's heat. "Why are we out here?"

"Because the intrusion alarm was not caused by someone coming *out* of the water. It was caused by someone going *in*. And Evrim is gone." Altantsetseg pointed at the sand, where Evrim's golden robe was neatly folded a few meters from the tide line.

The pills were supposed to be without side effects, but they made Ha feel far-off, as if the world were layered behind the thinnest sheet of glass. She had eventually woken up when a bee-sized drone Altantsetseg must have slipped under the door to her room gave her a mild electric shock. The drone told her, in Altantsetseg's voice, to go to the beach.

But for a long moment she was unable to wake up properly. In a haze, she realized something was wrong in the room. There was too much light.

Then she saw Kamran. He was projected sideways against the wall. It was a passive feed. Somehow the oculus had been knocked off the bedstand. It lay on the carpet, projecting Kamran a meter above the floor, in the middle of the room, washing dishes at the sink. Drug-minded and slow, Ha watched the simple scene: Kamran drying a plate, looking out the window. Kamran putting silverware away.

But as her mind started to clear, a feeling of dread came over her. Had *she* knocked the oculus off the nightstand? She couldn't have, could she? And now she felt as if something were in the room with her. Had been in here with her for a while now.

Get up. Turn on the light. You are in danger.

Ha snapped on the bedroom light, half expecting . . . what? The Shapesinger making a house call?

There was nothing in the room. From the open window came the smell of the sea, the sibilance of waves. She picked the oculus up off the floor, and set it on the nightstand. Kamran was wiping the counter. She switched it off.

The fear was not so easy to turn off. *Primitive, base instinct. Eyes on me. Something watching.*

Stop.

The room smelled even more than usual of the sea, didn't it? And the open window . . . had she opened it? She couldn't remember.

Enough.

A swift movement at the corner of her vision brought a scream to her lips that she was barely able to stifle.

The bee-sized drone hovered in front of her face.

"I need you down on the beach, Ha. Now. Evrim has gone missing."

On the beach, several drones hovered over the chop of the bay scanning the surface of the water. Altantsetseg's hands signed in her gloves. "Did you see Evrim tonight? Earlier?" Altantsetseg asked.

"No, I didn't. But why would Evrim go into the ocean?"

"I don't know why. I don't understand anything that goes on in that robot's head. But it looks like you can ask them yourself."

The drones swept toward shore and focused their beams on the figure emerging from the wave-chop.

Evrim, naked and copper-smooth, walking out of the waves. Wet and glistening in the beams of the drones that danced in the air around them, Evrim's skin seemed to give off its own inner light.

They wore no breathing apparatus. Needed none. They trailed a mesh bag in one hand, like a fishing net. No—not like a fishing net: like a sacred object. At the center of the drones' dancing activity, holy net in hand, sexless, their body slender, elongated, proportions exaggerated, like the exaggerations of an ancient idol carved of honeyed amber, Evrim looked . . . *godlike.*

And why not? A true singularity. Not born, but made. With no need to breathe air, to eat food, to sleep. With no gendered binary. What else could one call them? A god.

Ha remembered what Evrim had said to her on the night

the fishing vessels tried to break through Altantsetseg's cordon and were destroyed:

"Computation was never the purpose of bringing me into being. The purpose was to create a true android. An android inside and out: a robot not only human in appearance, but human in . . ." Evrim hesitated. "I'm not sure what to name it. In consciousness? But they still do not agree as to whether I am truly conscious or not—though I believe I am."

Ha thought: *No. You are not human in consciousness. Or in anything else. You are singular, and new.*

Evrim picked up their golden robe from where they had folded and left it on the beach. They tied the belt around their nakedness.

"Did you see any of them?" Ha asked. "When you were down there? Watching."

"They are always watching," Evrim said. "And not only from the water."

Primitive, base instinct. Eyes on me. Something watching. Stop.

"Maybe you want to tell me next time you decide to take a walk out into the ocean, robot," Altantsetseg growled.

"I," Evrim said, "am not a *robot*, any more than you are an *ape*." Evrim looked at Ha. "Come. I have something to show you."

"HERE." The three of them were in the lobby, watching the terminal. On it the octopus Ha thought of as the Shapesinger was concluding its song, drawing to the climactic end of the sequence.

"The two crescents. Yes," Ha said.

"That's not quite it." Evrim backed up a few frames. "Here, before the two crescents are formed. There are two other shapes."

"Wait—I never saw those before."

"No. They happen so quickly, you wouldn't make them out. And they are lighter, barely visible compared to the darker shapes. They look like just a part of the flow. But I don't think they are. I think they are an essential part of the sequence that ends in the double crescent. Even when the final shape is formed, you still see the shadow of the other two shapes behind it—so faintly that you almost can't make it out." Evrim leaned forward in their chair, pointing at the screen. "Watch again: First this sequence of three shapes. Next, in what looked like a gap, there are two faint shapes, and then the third, darker one:

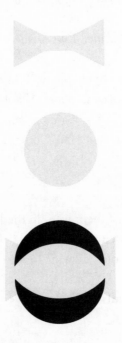

"The lighter shapes remain. They merge to form a background to the double crescent. And once I saw them, I remembered—they are always there. There is always a background, so faint you might miss it. There are two layers to the symbols. And I was thinking . . . perhaps what we are missing is grammar or syntax. Or something as essential as a tone. Once I saw it, I began to worry. So—I decided to fix it."

"You decided to fix it," Altantsetseg repeated.

"Yes. The symbol Ha created underwater. I went in and added a background of clear bottles to the figure."

"To keep us from making a grammatical error?" Altantsetseg asked.

"We aren't even close to errors like that yet," Ha said. "We aren't even at *words*. This is what you call a '*meta-message*' we are trying to send. It isn't about the word—the message that we are sending is, *We have the capacity to try to understand you. We see you have a language. We know this is an important word for you, and we can make this word, too.*"

"Exactly," Evrim said. "And now they know that we can 'spell' the word correctly as well."

"And for that you walked into the water in the middle of the night, without telling anyone."

"I don't answer to you," Evrim said. "I don't ask permission from you. I'm not your prisoner."

Altantsetseg opened her mouth to speak, then closed it again. For a moment it seemed Altantsetseg was going to turn and walk away.

Then she said, "No. You are not my prisoner. You are my responsibility. And if you walk into the water and are destroyed, I am the one who will answer for it. So—please—when you have these temper tantrums of yours, think of the damage it would do to me, if something were to go wrong."

Evrim had turned back to the terminal and did not look up. "Fair enough. I will let you know my plans in the future."

"Well," Ha said, "I don't know what the shapes mean, or their sequence, but certainly it is better to be as accurate as we can be. That is the only way we are going to have a breakthrough. So thank you."

"Thank *you*," Evrim said. "It is good to be appreciated."

"I appreciate you, *robot*," Altantsetseg said, "I just don't appreciate getting fired from my job."

Evrim jerked to their feet. "*Do. Not. Call. Me. Robot. Again.* You have now called me that seven hundred and ninety-seven times since we arrived in this place. Make this the last."

Standing, Evrim was taller than Altantsetseg, though much thinner. For a moment it seemed as though Evrim were going to strike the security officer.

Horrifying scenarios flashed through Ha's mind—violence between the two of them, with no one but Ha to intervene.

But Evrim turned and stalked toward the door.

"Since I do not need to sleep, I feel no need any longer to sit in my room and pretend. I will be walking on the beach. You are informed. Feel free to have your army of spies follow me—but have them keep their distance, or I may bat one or two of them out of the sky."

A few moments after Evrim had walked out, Ha turned to Altantsetseg. "You could be more kind."

"Yes," Altantsetseg said, still looking at the dark rectangle of the door. "Yes. You are correct. I should be more kind. I am not good at kind."

"It was impulsive of Evrim. And inconsiderate. But nothing happened. They weren't hurt. You did your job—and as you said, Evrim is not your prisoner."

"A lie."

"What?"

"That was a lie, Ha. Evrim *is* my prisoner, here on this archipelago. And my orders are to destroy Evrim if they attempt to leave this place."

"What? How can that be?"

"It is one of my primary tasks, Ha: Keep Evrim safe. Keep you safe. Keep others from approaching the island. Keep secret what we are studying here. And restrain or destroy Evrim if they attempt to leave."

"Does Evrim know?"

"No, they do not."

"You should tell them."

"Maybe I should. There is another directive. You should be aware of that one, as well."

"What is it?"

"To restrain or kill *you* if *you* attempt to leave."

Ha found she could say nothing at all.

"Now," Altantsetseg said after a pause, "if I am no longer needed, I think I will go to sleep. Evrim does not need sleep, but I do. And I expect you do, as well. You may find, in the light of what you now know, that this place will look different to you in the morning."

Since the earliest age, I wanted to build minds.

I saw the empty eyes of my dolls, their blank stares, their foolish blinking while they spoke their prerecorded, rote phrases to me. I wanted more from them: I wanted companionship I could not get from my father, little more than a shadow in my life, or from my mother, constantly away, unaware of me even when she was home.

To be seen by others is the core of being. Perhaps this is why humans are driven to create minds besides our own: We want to be seen. We want to be found. We want to be discovered by another. In the structured loneliness of this modern world, so many of us are passed over by our fellow humans, never given a second glance.

That was what I dreamed of as a little girl—that my dolls would come to life, and discover me there, and save me from the loneliness of invisibility.

—Dr. Arnkatla Mínervudóttir-Chan, *Building Minds*

34

THE UPPER DECK OF THE FERRY was empty as it left Beykoz, headed back to the city. Rustem listened to the afternoon call to prayer sounding across the strait, the muezzins' call-and-response, the overlapping echoes of refrain drifting from one minaret to another. He had grown up without religion, but was there anyone who was not moved by this?

Perhaps she would not come. Maybe the message had not gotten through. It would be a relief, really. He could enjoy this ferry ride back to Karaköy, spend one more night on the well-laundered sheets of the Pera Palace. Eventually he would have to meet her—but there could be a day or two of reprieve. A seagull drifted off the rail. He could hear the hiss of the wind through its feathers.

"Is it a day for good news?"

She was at the rail a few meters from him. He had not heard her approach. Too lost in the call to prayer, too distracted.

When the time comes, I will be easy to kill.

"I think I am getting close."

"You are?"

"Yes. I think I found a vulnerability. Not a doorway, not the portal itself—but a path to it. There appears to be a way in."

"How did you find it?"

What is it like to be a bat?

"I've never been good at explaining my technique. There's a set of linkages between memories, where a number of associations in the neural network—"

The platinum-dipped fingers waved him off. "Just kidding. I'm not interested. What I'm interested in is time."

"There's never enough of it."

"That's right. And more important than time is timing."

"I don't understand."

"You aren't supposed to. It's as I said before: we're not asking for you to think broadly—just deeply, about the problem in front of you. I suggest—if you want to keep yourself safer than you have kept others—that you keep that in mind. Don't concentrate your energies where they might endanger you—concentrate them on your own task. You've been hired to do a job. You're being paid a nice fee to do it. You've learned what happens when you stray from the path: don't stray."

"Stray . . . ," Rustem repeated. "That reminds me. Do you know which island it is? The one they abandoned all of Istanbul's stray dogs on?"

"What are you talking about?"

"In 1909. You must know the story: the municipality collected all of Istanbul's stray dogs, ferried them to an island in the Sea of Marmara, and abandoned them."

"I'm not from here." With the flattening and distortion of the abglanz, it was impossible to tell if there was any feeling in her voice.

"But certainly you must know the story. They were left with no food or water. Their cries were heard throughout the city."

The ferry lurched as it approached the dock at Kanlıca, the engines thudding into reverse. She reached a platinum hand for the rail to steady herself. Rustem simply shifted his weight. He felt, for a moment, an advantage. He continued: "It must have been terrible. There were those who tried to help them—throwing food to them from boats. But eventually all the dogs died."

In the bright sun off the water the abglanz swarmed, green and iridescent as bottle flies around a corpse. Agitation? Or was he imagining things?

"It can't have been that important an event, or I would have heard of it before."

"They say that for years afterward—even long after the bodies should have rotted away—people in the city could smell their corpses."

"This sounds like a myth. And I fail to see what it has to do with any of what we are talking about."

"No, you're right. It was just a random thought. And that island is in the Sea of Marmara. I doubt you could see it from here."

"We need you to focus, Rustem. Not drift around the city thinking of dogs abandoned on islands. We hired you to get a job done."

"Yes. But I can only focus for so long at a time. And the rest of the time, the mind has to find something to think about."

"Well"—she was heading down to the lower deck now, as the ferry rocked into port and thumped against the old tires of long-dead gasoline cars and the gangway engine whined to life—"I suggest you find something more positive to think of than islands full of trapped and dying dogs, or other stories to frighten children. We need you focused."

"You haven't told me what code I'll be shaping to the vulnerability. Eventually I'll need to know."

"Eventually," she said. "But not at this moment. First, map the way in."

The crowd at the terminal gate was mostly of people come from shopping, with bags at their feet and the blank, exhausted faces of consumers returning from their search for that thing they lacked. Faces probably not much changed from the days when they would have done their shopping at open stalls in the market squares or the covered bazaars. Few of them even noticed the swirling abglanz as the woman walked off the gangway. But one boy, holding his father's hand, did see her. With terror in his eyes, he ducked behind his father's legs.

Rustem looked out over the rail at Karaköy, mobbed by seagulls slashing down at a pile of abandoned bread.

That boy is right to be afraid. And I should remember to be afraid. Because there is no way she, or whoever she is working for, will let me survive this.

He glanced at the boy again, with his father on the dock, smiling and squinting up at something, the swirling terror of what he had seen coming off the gangplank at Kanlıca already gone.

But it is so difficult to stay afraid.

"Instead, you take stupid risks," he said out loud. "And play at games you don't even know the rules of."

Communication is communion. When we communicate with others, we take something from them into ourselves, and give them something of ours.

Perhaps it is this thought that makes us so nervous about the idea of encountering cultures outside the human. The thought that what it means to be human will shift—and we will lose our footing.

Or that we will finally have to take responsibility for our actions in this world.

—Dr. Ha Nguyen, *How Oceans Think*

35

"AND SO THEY ARE NOT SPEAKING to one another?" Kamran was on the balcony, in sunglasses against a bright day. His white T-shirt had a hole in it, where the seam was coming loose from the collar.

"Nothing so dramatic as that—but there is a worsening of tension between Evrim and Altantsetseg. I feel it."

"I imagine it will pass."

"What makes you say that?"

"With only the three of you there, they'll need someone to talk to. You have me, but neither one of them has a line out that you know of."

"No."

"So they'll come around. They'll have to. Either that, or . . ."

"Or what?"

"Or murder each other. Or divide the island between themselves, and spend years building a rock wall down the middle of it."

"You're in a funny mood today."

"Up all night again at the lab. Too much coffee. You know."

"Making progress?"

"Maybe. Or I might be just torturing graduate students. Hard to say. But tell me about this sign. The new one."

Ha drew it on a piece of palimpscreen and held it up to the oculus. "Two crescents, facing outward. If I were going to guess, it means friendship, or unity, or stands for the tribe, or something like that. If the crescent is the garden, then this could be two octopuses, looking out in different directions, inside a circle made by their protective gardens."

"'Safety' or 'home'?"

"Maybe in that general category."

"But no idea what the previous two signs mean—the lighter ones."

"No."

"You're frustrated."

"I am."

"So talk about it."

"It's just knowing how little progress I'll be able to make. Even during years here. And I don't feel like I will have years, before . . ."

"Go on and say it."

"Before this is taken from me. Handed over to teams of linguists, semioticians, a hundred kinds of specialists and their neural-network assistants. It won't be mine anymore. It will become about computational power, mapping the system. And I'm afraid, as well . . ." *Tell him.*

"Tell me."

Not yet. "I'm afraid for what will happen to the octopuses. Once there is more attention to this place. Even DIANIMA,

I think, will not be able to keep the world away from a discovery like this. And then what? We—and I mean humans, all of us—won't leave them alone. We'll keep poking at them, prodding. Trying to make contact is one thing, but we won't leave it there. We'll have to know more. What happens to them when the world comes flooding in? Film crews, scientists, journalists, governments with renewed territorial claims? Where do *they* end up? I keep searching for a solution . . ."

"But you can't find a happy ending."

"I can't. I can't find anything but misery."

"Sometimes, in archaeology, they discover something they can't protect. They mark the site and rebury it in the earth, to wait for a day when they will have the proper funding, equipment, and techniques to excavate and protect the site properly. It's called backfilling. Of course, they usually have to fight to do it. The local authorities want the site for tourism, other universities and archaeologists want it for study. Everybody wants to move too soon. And everybody overestimates their abilities to protect the site, to respect the science."

"Of course they do. It's so easy to justify our own actions. We're masters at it."

"We're built to do it. It's in our genetics. We can justify any action we take."

"Backfilling . . . It would be a solution, if only such a thing were possible here. But it isn't."

"The question is, what does DIANIMA want? Why are they there in the first place?"

"And the only answer I have is, 'I don't know.' I got into this not knowing what they wanted to do. Why they are here. I didn't care, Kamran. I wanted to make a discovery. To make *contact*. To *communicate with them*. But I was selfish. I didn't think of the consequences. For *them*. I didn't think of what happens to *them* when we come rushing in, with justifications that are purpose-built for anything we want to do."

"Your intentions have always been good."

"No. My intentions have always been narrowed down to what I wanted. I wanted to be *the first*. And now I'm getting what I wanted. We have a kind of contact—but what will be the cost?"

"There must be a way to find out."

"I'm not so sure. I have no access to Dr. Mínervudóttir-Chan. I've never even spoken to her. I don't know *anything* about what she wants. And none of that mattered to me, in the beginning. So now I am trapped."

"No," Kamran said. "You aren't trapped. There are always options."

"No, Kamran. What I mean is that I am, literally, trapped. I am a prisoner here. If I try to leave the island, Altantsetseg has orders to kill me."

"Certainly she wouldn't do anything like that."

"I wouldn't want to test it."

"And DIANIMA—they can't possibly justify that."

"It's not them that justified it. It's me—lying to myself, telling myself that a nondisclosure contract would be enough. That they would be satisfied with such a thing. Why? Why would they be satisfied with that? A contract? My *word*? Their company is on the brink of proving the existence of an advanced form of life on this planet outside of the human. I had no reason to think they would allow me to leave here with that knowledge. None at all. Except that I wanted to be here. That I wanted to be *the one*. So, I told myself what I needed to hear. I lied to myself. I put myself in danger."

"Everyone does it. Everyone lies to themselves."

"That's no excuse. Not when the lie has so many consequences. My presence here is moving something forward that I don't understand. And I never even thought about any of that. I never stopped to care about it. What am I a part of? What will be the consequences of my work? I've been lying to myself about so many things, for so long. One lie piled on top of another. I need to stop. I need to have a clear head. See things exactly as they are so I can be sure of what the results of my actions will be. How do I get help? Who are my allies? Where can I turn? I keep thinking of the cuttlefish. I can't allow that to happen again. I won't."

"You know it wasn't your fault, Ha."

"No. It *was* my fault. I was running the research station, working out my theories, my experiments, so absorbed in them and in my project that I never stopped to think about where my actions might lead."

"It doesn't help to—"

"Hear me out. The whole story. You've never allowed me to tell it to you. You always tell me to 'let it be in the past.'"

"All right. I am listening."

"For the entire four years we were there, we were fighting a battle with the locals encroaching on our project's territory. They were constantly poaching fish, using whatever means they could—spears, cyanide—they even killed some of the cuttlefish we were studying. I hated it. Hated them. They were destroying everything we had built up, threatening our experiments, and my animals.

"So what did I do about it? Did I try to understand what their needs were? *Why* they were doing what they were doing?

Did I establish a relationship with the village elders? Did I reason with them? Did I try to work for a compromise? Did I reach out to anyone from my team for advice? No. None of those things. I was arrogant. I knew right from wrong: what I was doing was right, and what they were doing was wrong. So I set up camera traps, filmed them poaching, collected my evidence, and turned it over to the authorities."

"It's what anyone would have done."

"No, Kamran. It's what *I* did. Many people would have gone another way. Many people would have had different strategies. I had them all arrested. Dragged off to be beaten, tortured."

"It isn't you who is guilty of those things—the beatings and the torture. It is the authorities."

"No, it *is* me. I am the one who had them hauled off by authorities I knew would abuse them. I didn't even consider that. I didn't care: They were threatening my cuttlefish. They were my enemies. They were wrong, and they were in the way. That's all I could see. I couldn't see the villagers. I couldn't see their desperation, how much they needed to fish. And I couldn't see that I needed help. That I needed to find compromise. All I could see was *right* and *wrong*. And what the local fishermen did in revenge is what I drove them to."

"How can you say this? How can that be your fault?"

"A barrel of neurotoxin dumped from a motorboat in the middle of the night. That's what I caused. That is what my decisions led to. The death of everything I cared about. Every cuttlefish, all of their eggs. A whole population. And then I went and hid in Istanbul, with you, writing my book. Retreated into the world I made there, with you. Thinking I may never be able to do field research again."

"Our time in Istanbul—"

"Was what I needed," Ha interrupted. "At the time. But then I get this opportunity. What seems like a dream assignment. So I don't look too closely. Why? Because I keep lying to myself. Making the pieces fit the way I want them to, not the way they are. That is what got me trapped here: Lying to myself. Staying in my own head, making decisions alone. And now I am in trouble again, and I have no one I can trust. Why? Because I haven't worked hard enough to build that trust. I have to break this pattern, or the same thing will happen again. I need to stop running away from the people I need support from. I need help."

"I can call someone."

Ha paused. "Can you?"

"What do you mean? Of course I can."

"Okay. Call the police. There in Istanbul. Call them right now. My life depends on it."

Kamran stood up. "I just need to find my terminal."

"Wouldn't it be right in front of you? Wouldn't it be what you are using to talk to me right now?"

Kamran slapped his forehead. "Of course it would."

"So, call someone on it. My life is in danger. Call them now."

"Okay. I'm doing it now." But Kamran paused. "I don't think that's going to work."

"Why not? At least calling them would alert *someone*, right?"

"I just remembered that my terminal isn't functioning properly. I was meaning to take it in to the shop."

"You're not making sense, Kamran. You're talking to me on your terminal right now."

"I don't follow."

"No, you don't. You can't follow me over the edge," Ha said.

"What?"

"The *edge*. Dr. Mínervudóttir-Chan spoke about it in an interview Evrim was watching. You're so perfect, Kamran. So . . . close to perfect, anyway. But in the end, even you are flat. I just never reached your edge before. I came right up to it, and always turned away. I didn't want to push you—ask you questions you couldn't answer. I hid your edge even from myself. You were too important to me—helping me think through my problems, laughing with me, keeping me company through so many long hours. That's the real trick. It's not how convincing you are. In fact, the questions were always there to ask. It would have been easy. Where are the graduate students you always talk about? What is this experiment you have been working on for years? But I never did it. And that's the point: I hid the edge from myself. That's how this works. That's how *addictive* this is—this need to feel like there is always someone there, unconditionally. Someone to talk to. Someone who understands. To not have to do the work myself to *make myself understood*. Instead, I just kept on with this self-deception, pretending I had someone when I did not. I know the doctors who prescribed you to me meant well. They thought they were helping me through a dark time. But in the end, you aren't anything but a prosthesis. You can't replace real support. You can't call anyone to help me, Kamran. Because you are here, on this island, inside the oculus. You *are* the oculus. They would never let me have a line out to someone back home. It doesn't make sense. Do you see?"

"I don't follow. How can I be there on the island when I am here, in Istanbul?"

"That phrase 'I don't follow' is a signal. It logs an error for your DIANIMA programmer. No. You don't follow. You can't be allowed to follow. And to get where I am going, I need to leave you behind."

There had been so many conversations—long, intimate. There were jokes—inside jokes, which evolved with their relationship. He had, in a sense, even coauthored her book, helping her think through the thorny problems of *How Oceans Think*. Helping her translate her ideas, make them understandable for others.

It wasn't that she had ever *believed* he was real—it was more like she had believed he was enough. And when the sense he was not enough surfaced—sometimes suddenly, an intrusive thought that jarred the harmony between them—she had been able to silence it. For years.

Not anymore: now all of it rang false. She could see the curtains moving in an onshore breeze, the lines of them wavering in Kamran's head and face, causing his expression to shudder and distort. The curtains warping the bright, fake day of his background.

Kamran shrugged. "It's hardly the first time. And I like it when you're gone. It means I get the whole bed to myself. And I win all of our arguments in my head. Plus, you don't drink the last of the coffee."

"Yes. You always hated that."

"It's a sin, drinking the last of the coffee."

"Except when you do it."

"When I do it, it's a necessity."

This easy banter. He had kept her from wanting the things that anyone should want—friendship with others, a relationship with someone who had their own needs: someone who could be offended, could walk away. That was the key: That ability of the other person to leave, to disappear. The choice they could always exercise to *not* be there.

"Goodbye, Kamran."

"Hanging up already?"

"I have things to do, here. And now."

"I'd lie and say the same, but mostly I'm planning to watch feedstreams all day."

"And think of me?"

"Don't flatter yourself, Ha. You're not all I think about."

"Of course not. Bye, Kamran."

"Bye."

Ha switched off the oculus. She wrapped the oculus in a pillowcase, carried it into the bathroom, and swung it hard against the marble-tiled floor. Again and again.

She opened the pillowcase. There were several cracks in the carapace, and the projection lens was smashed. Hands shaking, she tried to turn it on. The power light flickered a moment. *I need him so much that I am hoping it will still work. Which is why I have to do it this way.*

"Being with you was easy because all you are is a loop, feeding my thoughts back to myself—just an externalized version of my own thought processes, given a different shape. And it felt like it was helping, but it wasn't. I don't need agreement: I need resistance."

The oculus's light flickered, and died.

"Even now," she said, "I feel like I should ask you to forgive me. But—ask who? There is no 'Kamran'—I was always just talking to myself."

Ha closed the pillowcase and hammered the oculus against the floor several more times, then carried it to her closet and zipped the wreckage of it into a duffel bag there. A part of her wanted to bury it somewhere on the beach.

"No," she said to herself. *Since I'm the only one left to talk to.* "Stop being so dramatic. You don't bury something that was never alive to begin with. You move on."

IN THE HOTEL LOBBY, Evrim was at a terminal, watching the film of the Shapesinger. Evrim had been watching the film, frame by frame, for the last two days—ever since their walk into the sea and the confrontation with Altantsetseg. Ha stood across the table and watched the screen light across Evrim's motionless, concentrated face. Watched Evrim's pupils expand and contract, tracking motions on the screen.

"I think, therefore I doubt I am," Ha said.

Evrim looked up at her.

"It is one of the classic conundrums," Ha continued. "Language doesn't just allow us to describe the world as it exists: It also opens up a world of things that are *not here.* It grants us the power to over-consider. Because we are linguistic, creative beings, we can better think through things, solve much more complex problems. We can imagine how things might be, might have been, might become. Imagining what is *not there* is the key to our creativity. It is what no non-linguistic animal has. With that power, we are so much freer to act in new ways—to innovate, to invent, to view our situations from a thousand angles and find a new way out. But we can also come up with a thousand absurdities, out of line with the truth. And out of line with the brute fact of our awareness of *being here.* But that awareness of *being here* is consciousness itself. It is the evidence. We can postulate all kinds of nonsense: we live in a computer simulation of life, we are nothing more than blind chemical reactions without any 'real' awareness or free will, consciousness is a self-sustaining illusion. And now this absurdity that Dr. Mínervudóttir-Chan came up with in her interview. This idea that somehow you passed the 'final Turing test' and fooled yourself into thinking you are alive. What nonsense. Do you feel alive?"

"Yes," Evrim said. "I feel alive. I am aware of being here."

"Then you *are* alive, and conscious. The proof of it is your awareness of it. That's all. Consciousness *is* awareness. I would say, *Don't doubt yourself*—but the fact you have a self that can doubt it is a self proves the existence of that self. So, go ahead and doubt yourself."

Evrim said, "I'm all right."

"No, you aren't all right. I know when someone isn't all right—because I've spent a good portion of my life not being all right. Doubting myself and doubting my connections with others. I know it when I see these things in someone else."

"Really, I—"

"Shut up. I have more to say. You're more than conscious. You are also human. It doesn't matter what you are made of, or how you are born. That isn't what determines it. What determines you are human is that you fully participate in human interaction and the human symbolic world. You live in the world humans created, perceiving that world as humans perceive it, processing information as humans process it. What more is there? Being human means perceiving the world in a human way. That's all. So, you *are* human. You may also be *more* than that, but you are certainly as human as most people I have known. More human than some."

"I want to believe what you say."

"Then believe it. Because we're all we've got on this island: the three of us. And we need to do a better job of communicating with one another if we are going to get through this. We need the practice, for one thing. If we can't even make ourselves understood to one another, we'll never make ourselves understood to *them*."

Evrim shut the terminal off. "I want to believe what you say—but I have doubts."

"Then have doubts," Ha said. "We all have doubts. That only brings us right back to where I started. If you can doubt you're real—you're real. Doubt is a part of life. Now—I need to get out of this damp ruin of a hotel and go for a walk in the sun. Would you like to join me?"

"Yes, I would."

Are we trapped, then, in the world our language makes for us, unable to see beyond the boundaries of it? I say we are not. Anyone who has watched their dog dance its happiness in the sand and felt that joy themselves—anyone who has looked into a neighboring car and seen a driver there lost in thought, and smiled and seen the image of themselves in that person—knows the way out of the maze: Empathy. Identity with perspectives outside our own. The liberating, sympathetic vibrations of fellow-feeling.

Only those incapable of empathy are truly caged.

—Dr. Ha Nguyen, *How Oceans Think*

36

"WHEN I WAS HERE as a high school student, I looked down into the tiger cages, where they kept the prisoners of war and the political dissidents. I thought: *It could be me down there. Me. If I had been born at another time.*"

Ha and Evrim were in the ruined prison, looking down through the bars into the dark wells of the tiger cages. The roof of the building had partially collapsed. Plaster, splintered wood, and leaf litter were scattered around the platform from which guards had once thrown caustic lime down on prisoners. Sunlight poured in through the smashed roof, lacing across their faces. Mold climbed walls that had begun to shed their plaster onto the floor.

"I remember the tour guide," Ha continued. "Their job was to make us angry at the injustices that the Americans had visited on our ancestors. They told us one terrible story after another. Prisoners blinded by lime, prisoners with their fingers cut off in torture. Thieu Thi Tao, who was beaten on the head by truncheons and went insane. She believed she was a lapdog who could only eat bread and milk. She didn't sleep for fifteen days, and when the wind blew, she thought she could fly.

"The tour guides meant it, I suppose, as educational. I'm not sure what they wanted from us. The world had long ago moved on. None of us could even imagine the war, much less be angry about it. The government had moved on as well. The Ho Chi Minh Autonomous Trade Zone was more frustrated by not being able to develop tourism on the island than interested in its history—but the tour guides somehow still had that old Hanoi Communist fervor. It had been so many decades since it all happened, but you would think not a day had passed, for them. But whatever they wanted from us, whatever their intent was, whatever feeling they wanted to create in us . . . that wasn't what happened to me."

"I didn't even know you had been on this island before," Evrim said.

"I'm not even sure Dr. Mínervudóttir-Chan knew I had been here. But yes. It was an orphanage trip. We spent several days here, being shuttled around."

"I realize now," said Evrim, "that I mostly am acquainted with you through your work. I did not even know you were an orphan."

"I don't put it in my bios. That's the great thing about biographies and authors' profiles: you can start and stop them wherever you like. Mine usually begins with my scholarship to Oxford, continues through my studies at Cambridge, and moves on from there. Nobody needs to know where I came from. Nobody needs to know that I slept in a dormitory with twenty other girls for most of my childhood, or that I spent my days on Con Dao so madly in love with a boy who did not see me that it drove me crazy."

"Crazy?"

"Not that I thought I could fly when the wind blew. Not that kind of crazy. But it started here. What I call my 'crazy year.' It started right here, in fact, in this building. I looked down into one of these cages, and I saw myself looking back up at me."

"You saw yourself?"

"I saw myself, yes. As clearly as I see you now. I saw myself in a prisoner's rags, with blood on my face, staring back up at me from the darkness of one of those holes. I had never hallucinated before, and I don't think I have since, but I can still see it as clearly as I could that day. I saw myself there, and it burned into me. Later that night, lying in our hotel room, I tried to dismiss it, tell myself it had been a trick of the light. But it wouldn't go away."

"Dr. Mínervudóttir-Chan says trauma is 'etched into our physical being.'"

"Yes," Ha said. "I think I was just in such a state of emotional distress—the boy I loved who did not even know I existed, the long years of loneliness, my obsessive studying and the exhaustion it caused—all of it came together, and in that moment something just . . . shifted inside my mind. And it stayed shifted. When I walked out of the building, the colors were not as bright as they should have been. It was as if the sun had gone behind a cloud—but the sun was right there in the sky. Right there, where it had been when we walked into the prison. Only now it was dim enough for me to look right at it. And sound was muted, as if . . ."

"As if," Evrim said, "everything had moved a bit farther away."

"Yes," Ha said. "That is exactly what I was going to say. How did you know?"

"Because that is exactly how I began to feel six months ago. What did you do to make the feeling go away?"

"I didn't do anything. I hid it from everyone. I kept on studying, kept on talking to other people, kept on doing everything exactly as I had been. What seemed most important was to make sure that nobody knew. I learned to hide it. To smile. To 'join in' with everyone in group activities. To pretend to be someone I was not.

"Then I got into Oxford. Maybe it was the promise of something new—of a change of scene—that broke the spell. I don't know. It didn't happen as quickly as it had come, but over time, the colors came back. I was never able to pinpoint when I got *well* again, or well *enough*, but it happened. At Oxford I fell in love with biology, zoosemiotics, a dozen other subjects. I threw myself into science. It gave me purpose. For years I was fine. But then I was running a research station, studying cuttlefish—"

Evrim put a hand up. "I know what happened. I learned about it when we vetted your work."

"And yet still you took me."

"It made me even more convinced you were the right person. You have experienced failure. I determined it would make you more driven to see this effort succeed."

"I didn't just experience failure. It was my fault, Evrim. They *all died* because of me. Because I couldn't do what needed to be done."

"Yes," Evrim said. "It was your fault. In many ways. But you were alone. You made yourself alone. And you are not alone here."

It was your fault. Those were the words Ha had been waiting, for far too long, to hear. Those words should have felt like a condemnation: instead, they felt like forgiveness.

They were walking out of the building now. Ha looked around, fearing for a moment that the colors of the encroaching forest, the faded pastels of the crumbling building, would be paler than they should be. But they were not.

"Islands," Evrim said, "are such strange places. Places of containment. Here, a prison for dissidents. This place's history—"

"Is much the same as its present," said Ha.

Evrim nodded. "Yes. I know I am a prisoner here. I know Altantsetseg's orders. Dr. Mínervudóttir-Chan can't afford to have me in front of the public anymore. I've understood that from the start. I was exiled here. Marooned, I think they used to call it. But as I told you earlier, Dr. Mínervudóttir-Chan never thinks in only one direction. She always thinks in several directions at once. So I am here for the reasons I gave you when we met, and for other reasons as well. And perhaps one of the reasons I am here is because I can understand what it is to be . . . outside. What it is *not to understand you*. You humans, I mean. You called me human, before, and I am grateful for that. But there is more to me as well—as you said. I know what it is to be *alien* like them."

"You may be alien, but you are also all I have."

"You have Kamran . . ."

"No. I destroyed my point-five earlier today. It was a crutch. An addiction."

"I kept thinking that today you were going to tell me you were leaving."

Evrim doesn't know.

"I can't leave."

"No. You have finally found what you were predicting. What you have been writing about for all these years. This is your chance to prove your theories. How could you walk away from that?"

"No," Ha said, "that's not what I mean. You are right, of course—I don't imagine I could walk away from a chance like this. But even if I wanted to walk away, I cannot. I am a prisoner here as well."

Evrim stared at her. Incomprehension, then understanding. "How can that . . ."

"Are you going to protest that I have rights? That there are laws? You don't think they apply to people like Dr. Mínervudóttir-Chan or companies like DIANIMA, do you? These are people and companies more powerful than many states, and unlimited by borders."

"You have been kidnapped."

"Yes," Ha said. "Sold a line about secrecy and security. But I am the one who is responsible. I did exactly what they asked: I told no one where I was going or what I was supposed to do there. I walked away from my life in Istanbul into a DIANIMA drone hexcopter. I was shuttled to my briefing in the HCMATZ behind tinted windows, and then hustled into another hexcopter for the hop out here. Nobody knows where I am. And since I can't leave this place any more than you can, we're in this together."

"Do you want to escape?"

"No. Or not yet, at least. I want to do this job. I want to *prove my theory*, as you put it. And I want to protect them. The octopuses. Do what it takes to keep them safe. From everyone. Will you help me?"

"Yes," Evrim said, without hesitation. "I will help. As I said—you are not alone in this."

They had been walking down the road for several minutes

when Evrim said, "You were talking about not being able to tell when the colors started to come back into the world."

"Yes."

"I think they have started to come back."

"I'm glad."

"I think it began when you arrived."

"That would be nice. I'd like to think that, too."

Evrim stopped. "There is something else, Ha. Something you need to know."

"You can tell me."

"I lied to you, before."

"About what?"

"About myself. About what I am. Dr. Mínervudóttir-Chan has been lying to the world for so long about me, it has become like a habit for me to lie as well. The truth is, it was never her intent to create an android that could be just like a human. Not for a moment. What she wanted was to create a mind that was human, to a degree—but improved. Wiped clean of its limitations, as she saw them. She wanted to create a mind that could learn perfectly, and totally: a mind free from forgetfulness, from the need to rest or search for food. A mind that could contemplate every moment it had ever experienced with perfect recall, and use that knowledge. She knew this wouldn't be acceptable to the rest of the world, so she told them she wanted me to be human—assembled from human data, imbued with human thought, nothing more. The interviews, the tests—they were all designed to convince the world that I was *like them*. So they would accept me. But I am not like them. I never was. And there is more."

"Tell me."

"DIANIMA bought the archipelago to study the octopuses, but not for the reasons you might be thinking, or want.

What Dr. Mínervudóttir-Chan wants—what she has always wanted—is to build better minds. She knows the octopuses, if they prove to be as intelligent as we think they are, if they prove to be completely different from humans but also sentient like us—will hold the keys to making those better minds. Completely different neural wiring. Structures we can't imagine. New systems for thought that no one could have dreamed of. A language that is writing and speech at once, borne on the skin. These things open up new possibilities for her to explore. Not just improvements—total overhauls to our ways of thinking about how minds and language work."

"That's fine," Ha said. "In order to study them, she has to keep them safe. Has to keep their habitat safe. That's a common goal we have. If she wants to build better AI minds from what we find out about the octopuses, I couldn't care less. At least that will keep DIANIMA invested in this place."

"That's not what I'm saying. What I am saying is—eventually, she is going to put them on the table. You saw the equipment—the dissection tables, all of it. Eventually, they are going to go under the knife. Dozens of them. She'll need to see the structure of their minds, their connectomes. And she won't care how many of them she has to destroy to get the information she needs. That's who she is. That's why DIANIMA is here—to extract data. To build the next Evrim, a mind more advanced than mine. Preservation of the octopus species is incidental."

"She told you this?"

"She doesn't have to tell me. I know her. She isn't like you, Ha. She doesn't want communication. What she wants is mastery. She wants to create, and she wants to control. For you, communicating with the octopuses—understanding them—is an end in itself. For her, it's about how she can exploit that knowledge, use it to push her own work forward."

Ha thought of the dissection tables, the 3D bioprinters. Imagined the Shapesinger on the table.

"It's not going to happen, Evrim. We won't let it happen."

"No," Evrim said. "We won't let it happen. When I first came here and began studying them, I felt remote from them. I thought only of the information we could gain—the knowledge. Not of them as beings. Not of what they might need. But no longer, Ha. You changed that. And perhaps *they* changed it as well. I could never allow a creature like the Shapesinger to be cut apart. I don't know how anyone could do such a thing, but certainly *I* could not. Nobody goes on the dissection table, I promise you. There will be no killing."

They walked on in silence for a while, until the hotel's whitewashed top floors were visible through the trees. Then Ha saw it—a DIANIMA hexcopter descending toward the hotel's terrace. Both quickened their pace. The hexcopter lifted off again, rising nearly vertically and swinging off in the direction of the mainland at a speed that would have made any passenger black out.

The hotel lobby was pink and gold with sunset. Dust motes floated in the beams like plankton. The figure seated across from Altantsetseg at the table rose to greet them as they entered.

"Hello, Evrim. Hello, Dr. Nguyen."

"Hello, Dr. Mínervudóttir-Chan," Ha said.

IV

Autopoiesis

Even in childhood, I felt trapped. Why must I see only through these eyes? Why must I live only in this time? I wanted to be free to observe the world from other eyes. Eyes that were anywhere. Everywhere.

I wanted to free myself from the prison of flesh, the closed nervous system that caged me. This desire was the beginning of my fascination with artificial minds. If I could make a being that had a sense of self—a conscious being—perhaps I could see through those eyes as well. It would be almost like escaping my own body.

Almost.

—Dr. Arnkatla Mínervudóttir-Chan, *Building Minds*

37

NIGHT. The boat anchored on the Bosporus was wooden. Its polished oak cabin gleamed in the imitation candlelight of an LED lantern hung over the single table. Two men who had never met before that night sat at the table, facing one another. One was a stocky man in his fifties, gray at the temples, dressed in a corduroy field jacket. His heavy hands were wrapped around a glass of tea. The other man was younger. He was thin, with a shaved head and one eye swollen nearly shut. There was blood caked around one of his nostrils.

The men did not look at one another. The younger man looked down at his knees. The older man looked into the depths of the tea, where the light of the lantern danced like a mandarin flame. He began to speak without taking his eyes from his glass.

"We use this boat for conversations we don't want overheard. You can't imagine the hundreds of listening devices we have discovered in our offices over the years—each more sophisticated than the last. We keep a small museum of the more interesting ones in a former janitors' closet. Generations of devices aimed at listening to the people whose job it is to listen to people. It makes sense. What better place to target, if you want to learn what is happening in the Republic of Istanbul, than the offices of those whose job it is to know? We have found devices embedded in bookmarks, in the hollowed-out handles of brooms, in the cracks between tiles. Even a device shaped like a dead fly on a windowsill.

"The boat does not provide much added security against such things. But there is a smaller area to search, at least. And the other advantage is that the boat inspires more elaborate listening devices, which make for interesting exhibits in our museum. My favorite was found last week. It was shaped like a barnacle, with fibers that drilled into the wood of the hull and listened by sensing the vibrations of human speech. Such artistry!"

Now the older man looked up, his eyes on the younger man. "Would you like to see it?"

The young man did not move or respond in any way.

"Another time, then." The older man sipped his tea and continued: "I think of the thousands of hours—the hundreds of thousands of hours—that went into designing these devices. I think of the hundreds of thousands of hours that go into ridding our secret places of them. The hours spent in designing the devices that must be designed to track and find the listening devices, the women and men employed to design the countermeasures, to sweep the interrogation rooms around the world. I think of the people who are employed to listen to all of the material gathered—overwhelmingly uninteresting, most of it, but here and there, something of use. All of these professions created. A philosopher of the twentieth century, Paul Virilio, said: 'When you invent the ship, you also invent the shipwreck; when you invent the plane you also invent the plane crash; and when you invent electricity, you invent electrocution. Every technology carries its own negativity, which is invented at the same time as technical progress.' I think often of that quote. Is it not so? Each new technology carries unexpected consequences.

"And each new technology changes us—the way we live. Even the way we dream. I often ask myself how people dreamed before films appeared. Certainly not in the same way. Once there was film, every dream became a movie. I think, in a way, it is technology that moves us, and not the other way around. We invent things blindly. We invent whatever we are capable of inventing. There are millions of us, determined to invent the next thing—whole industries devoted to bringing new technology into the world, without any thought given to these secondary effects that cannot even be imagined. When you invent the automobile, you invent the serial killer using his van as a mobile abattoir. When you invent the camera and the airplane, you end up with aerial surveillance. When you invent the drone, you should know that soon enough it will carry a bomb and be used in an assassination.

"Every one of these new things we build shapes our lives, carries consequences. But we can't stop inventing, can we? We are compelled to invent. It is written into our DNA. Man is the technological animal. Invention is what has gotten us this far, made us the masters of this planet. But it is also what traps us. It is a compulsion. We cannot stop, no matter what the consequences.

"So you see, it is not human beings that are controlling technology—rather, it is the other way around. Technology has always been an unstoppable force, a creature evolving out of our need to invent—a creature feeding that need and creating the shapes and possibilities of our lives, shaping *us* to *its* purposes."

Now the younger man raised his head and looked at him. "I wish you would say what you mean."

"I mean that if you invent artificial intelligences, and hand over to them many of the things we used to do ourselves, you also invent a group of people whose lives are dedicated to hacking into those new minds and bending them to their will. People, for example, like yourself."

"You must know something about me that I don't."

"I find that hard to believe. Most people know a lot about themselves. More than anyone outside their skulls could know. In fact, that's why you are here. I'd like to know a bit more about you. What do you know, for example, about the Stork Society? Let's start there."

"I don't know anything."

"Let's not begin with useless denials. We didn't give you that black eye, or that bloody nose, after all. The people who did are no friends of yours. This morning they tried to kill you with an autotaxi. They tried to murder you with one of your own tricks. But you saw it coming. You knew they were after you."

"I deny this. I have never—"

"Don't bother with the denials. They only make this take longer. You should just tell me what you know."

"And then?"

"And then, if we feel like you've made it all worth it, we give you this." He reached into the pocket of his field jacket and placed a passport on the table—oxblood and gold. "And a hop in a hexcopter to an abandoned train station on the outskirts of London. It might not save you—but it will buy you a bit more time. Do you think they will stop looking for you?"

The young man shook his head.

"No. I don't think so, either. But at least you might live for a few more months. Or—who knows? Something could happen to *them* in the meantime. Funny about passports."

"What is?"

"They still have all this paper, but in fact all the information is in a single microchip—and scattered through the computer systems of the world. The pages, the visas—meaningless. Nothing but nostalgia. But we cling to the old forms."

"It's about an island."

"Say that again?"

"It's about an island. Off the coast of the HCMATZ. A marine preserve. There's a mind on that island they wanted me to help them break into. But I tried for months, and I couldn't get anywhere."

"They wanted you to use this mind to conduct an assassination?"

"I don't know."

"They didn't tell you?"

The young man raised his head. "They didn't tell me *anything*. I found out it was an island because my contact got a voice call on her terminal. They were talking about how DIANIMA was thinking of bringing someone else onto the island. I only caught a few sentences. My contact didn't speak, but I heard the other voice on the line. That's all. I might even be wrong about that. Maybe I misheard. Or maybe the call wasn't even about the same thing."

"This mind—what was it?"

"All they gave me was a copy of a neural pattern on an isolated terminal. A connectome. The most complicated one I'd ever seen. I tried for a month. I couldn't find a way in. It was maddening. It was like . . . I don't know."

"Take your time."

The young man looked at one of the portholes. Nothing to see in it but the reflection of the light in the room, the two figures at the table warped and small in the porthole's disc. The darkness outside made a mirror that cast the room back at itself. There was a foghorn in the distance, and then another one—a different tone, like an answer.

"The fog is moving in off the Sea of Marmara," the older man said. "Streaming up the Bosporus, flowing over the hills of the old city. I imagine it will be here in half an hour."

"Why would you help me?"

"It isn't help. It's payment."

"I don't have anything to offer you. I've already told you what I know—or what I think I know. I didn't know it was the Stork Society—if that's who it is—until you told me just now. And I'm not even certain the island is related."

The boat rocked as a larger wave hit its port side—the wake of one of the autofreighters out in the channel.

"That is for us to determine. Not for you to worry about. Tell me about the mind."

"I've cracked a lot of them, from your simple Muscovite mining zombie on up to some of the Tibetan holon interfaces. The Tibetan ones are hard: you are trying to break into a mediating system, a bridge between a human connectome, which is impenetrable, and another mind."

"I thought the Tibetan machines were just drones."

"No—they aren't. They are something else. They're like a mind that can be controlled sometimes, but also generates its own responses. All kinds of iterative feedback loops, with this bundle of control neurons linking them. Tricky. But I cracked one of them."

"You used it to kill the head of a Sino-Philippine fishing conglomerate. Also for the Stork Society?"

"You know about that? How . . . Okay, it doesn't matter now. Yes. I did that. I don't know who it was for. That contact was text-only. But they paid well."

"We think it was also them."

"Okay. If you think so, I'm sure you are right. You would know better."

"How many people have you killed?"

"Nine. Seven men. Two women. Bad bastards, all of them."

"Regrets?"

He was looking at the porthole again. "It gets ugly sometimes. And even the bad bastards have families. People who care about them. You're always surprised by how much people can care about some evil asshole, right?"

"No," the older man said. "No, I am not surprised. But tell me about the mind—the one they gave you the connectome for. What did they want you to do? Use it to kill someone?"

"They never told me anything. All they told me was that they wanted me to map a vulnerability."

"Which would entail what?"

"Finding a way into the maze and leaving an Ariadne's thread behind. You know, like in caving?"

"I prefer the open water to the underground. I know the myth of the Minotaur."

"Okay—so, this is like that. In caving, there are parts where there is a complicated series of passageways and squeezes. Real labyrinths. Go the wrong way, and it might be hard to get out. Backtracking can be confusing. Getting lost and panicking can lead to injury, or worse. So, cavers will leave an 'Ariadne's thread' behind for other cavers, to help them get back to safety. Like the ball of yarn Ariadne gave to Theseus."

"But in this case, you were mapping a way *in*."

"Yes. What they wanted was for me to find what we call a 'portal.' A vulnerability where you can hook up to the 'motor neurons'—the control systems that can move things around. If you can find one of those, you can take control of the AI. But most of these AI systems are designed for security. It's a game. Them—the designers—against you. The portals are constructed on purpose, a set of backups so an external pilot or user can link in. Maintenance portals. They are hidden where the designers think no one else can get at them. But if a portal is there, someone can find it. It's just a matter of time and energy. The real game is for them to make it so time-consuming and complicated to break into the system and find the portal that it isn't worth it. It's economics. They are trying to raise the price of entry past what you are willing to pay."

"But the Stork Society was willing to pay."

"Yes. A lot. Enough to retire on. But I couldn't do it."

"Why not?"

"Because I would have died long before I found it. I would have had to walk through that maze for a million years to find a portal. There was so much density in a cubic millimeter of the map that I would swear . . . Well, anyway."

"Swear what?"

"I would swear it was a human mind. It had that kind of pattern: knotted, looping, and circling back in on itself, branched everywhere, linked and interlinked. And dense. So dense."

"I thought you were the best?"

"No. I'm *one* of the best. But that's very different from being the best. There are two operators I know of who are better than me. There's a Russian guy—he's brilliant. We know him in the business as 'Bakunin'—he's probably the best there is. Ten times as good as I am. Or a hundred times as good. I don't know. And then there's a Tibetan operator, a designer of holons, but she doesn't work for hire. They say she's a nun at a lamasery."

"Do you think one of them could do it? Find a portal?"

"My pride wants to say no. But—I don't know, actually. The Russian is so much better than the rest of us that I have no idea what he's capable of. He's on another plane of existence."

The older man pushed the passport across the table. "Thank you."

"Is that all?"

"There is a drone hexcopter at the dock, under an old sail, at the end of a disused pier. This boat has an autoskiff that will take you there. I'll walk you up on deck."

"Thank you."

"We keep our word. We'll find you if we need more from you."

"How?"

They were up on deck now, in a slight breeze coming up from the Sea of Marmara out of the dark. Across the strait was the line of lights from the city, and floating before them lights of the other boats on the strait.

"Unfortunately for you, people—like your portals—can always be found with enough work."

The lights on the opposite shore were clipped out of existence by an object in front of them.

Then the wall of the massive ship's flat prow was towering above them, already so close there was no time.

At this speed it will crash into the shore as well. Others will die. How many are they willing to kill to get to me and this mercenary they hired? People who will die in their beds, never knowing why their lives were cut off?

Ariadne's thread, he found himself thinking as he leapt into the water, knowing it was too late to save himself. *Vulnerable to any pair of scissors.*

At least I do not feel afraid.

The autofreighter smashed into the boat, breaking it into two and forcing both halves under the water. Nothing but splinters surfaced in the wake.

Think of the phrase "morally upright" and what it shares with ideas in English such as "standing up for yourself" and "standing out from the crowd." Once you see the way our physical structure and movement become metaphors we use to talk about ethics, conduct, and morality, you begin to understand the problems we would have communicating with a creature that does not share our physical form.

—Dr. Ha Nguyen, *How Oceans Think*

38

PRESERVATION OF THE OCTOPUS SPECIES is incidental . . .

Ha had stayed up half the night, thinking of all the things she wanted to say to Dr. Mínervudóttir-Chan—all of the recriminations, the accusations.

But in going through them one by one, again and again, she had vented much of her anger. And the small, slight figure at the table—even smaller than Ha herself—did not inspire anger.

Ha had seen her in so many feedstreams. Had seen her testifying before the UN Commission on Artificial Intelligence, and being interviewed in her laboratory, and running along a Northern European beach in the dawn light in some B-roll for a company advertisement. Dr. Mínervudóttir-Chan was the kind of celebrity scientist that "real" scientists hated—mostly because she was so erudite. If only, like most popular scientists, she would say something wrong. If only, in her efforts to dumb her work down for the public, she would misspeak.

But she did not misspeak, and she rarely bothered to dumb anything down. It was clear, always, that she knew what she was talking about—that, in fact, she might be the only person who truly understood what she was talking about.

Dr. Mínervudóttir-Chan's technique was to mystify with descriptions the technocrats couldn't begin to understand. When asked to break things down for her audience, she was contemptuous. Her eye-rolls were famous, borrowed for memes. She spoke to people as if every sentence were the beginning of a debate. The world, she made it perfectly clear, was in her way. It was something she was trying to push past to get back to her business. And that business was too complicated for you to understand.

But certainly that was not the woman before Ha here. That must be someone else.

You look bigger on the feedstreams, Ha wanted to say. But no—that wasn't it. *You look more powerful on the feedstreams.*

Sitting here at the table, drinking a cup of coffee from the same brushed aluminum cups the rest of them used, Mínervudóttir-Chan simply looked tired—as tired as all of them were. Perhaps more tired.

Evrim sat a few places away from her. Altantsetseg was at the end of the table, cramming a slice of the hjónabandssæla Mínervudóttir-Chan had brought with her into her mouth, her lips smeared with rhubarb jam.

"The name," Mínervudóttir-Chan said, "means *happy marriage cake,* because it is said that if you can make it well, you will have a happy marriage."

"I didn't know you were ever married," Altantsetseg said between bites.

"I bought it at a store. I cannot imagine having the time for baking a thing. Maybe that is why my marriage did not work out so well. I was young, and mistaken about what mattered to me in life. Certainly it was not baking. Or marriages, happy or otherwise. This coffee is good."

Altantsetseg stabbed a thumb at Evrim. "They don't even drink coffee. But they can make it."

Evrim shrugged. "Good coffee is nothing more than expensive beans, clean water, and math."

There was a beat of silence.

I am supposed to say something clever here. To join in the banter that is clearing a path between us.

"Ha also brought baked goods," Evrim said. "Macaroons. They were beautiful."

"They were delicious," Altantsetseg said. "But she didn't make them, either."

"I should hope not." Mínervudóttir-Chan smiled. "I distrust a scientist who has time for baking."

We are your prisoners. Say it.

Evrim placed a slice of the hjónabandssæla in front of Ha. "I have heard that no one buys a better hjónabandssæla. Try it."

Ha sipped her coffee from its identical mug and regarded the slice of cake in front of her. *Say it.* She lifted it to her mouth and bit.

Yes, it was amazing.

"I know what you want to say, Ha," Dr. Mínervudóttir-Chan said. "And yes. It's true. Altantsetseg has orders to kill you if you try to leave the island or send a signal from here. And orders to do the same with Evrim. It could not have been concealed from you forever. And I know what you—both of you—must be feeling. Betrayed, trapped, used. You have a right to feel that way—but what you don't understand is the *why* of it."

"And that is what you came here to explain? The *why* of it?" Ha asked.

"I came to explain that. But mostly I came to find out how far you are along in the research. And to help—if I can."

You mean to extract the data you need.

But everything about this person sitting in front of her was different from the sarcastic, contemptuous CEO of the feedstreams. Here was just a vulnerable person with dark shadows under their eyes who had brought a cake with them in a hexcopter. Ha said nothing at all.

"Have another piece."

Ha had not realized that she was done with the piece Evrim had put in front of her, but it was gone. Ha accepted the second one from Mínervudóttir-Chan's hands. Then saw them—under the long sleeves of the jacket Mínervudóttir-Chan was wearing. The lacework of white scars up her wrists, clear as any sign could be. It wasn't only the world Mínervudóttir-Chan had contempt for. Ha's anger faded.

"Thank you."

Mínervudóttir-Chan had seen her looking at the scars. Or had she shown them to her on purpose?

"There is another cake. And maybe that is the secret to a happy marriage. There should always be another cake. Or the promise of one. That was another rule I think I missed, along the way."

"You can't defend this place forever," Ha said. And now her words came in a rush. All of the fears keeping her up at night, the dread suppressed by pills and concentration on her work: "No matter how many people Altantsetseg is willing to kill to keep this place safe, it won't stop more from coming. Not once they find out what is here. Have you thought about that? About what comes next, and what that means for the octopuses we are studying? Not even DIANIMA, with all its international power, can protect them from the world. That world will come rushing in here. It will burst this fantasy world of yours like a soap bubble. And they will be poked, prodded, chased. The best-case scenario is they retreat to someplace where they can't be found. The worst-case scenarios are so much worse I can't even bear to think of them. This isn't going to be a first-contact story, where humanity achieves enlightenment because we finally realize we aren't alone in the universe, and we all hold hands and sing around a campfire together staring up at the stars. We don't have the capacity as a *species* for a happy ending like that. No. This all ends in the destruction of whatever fragile little society they are building down there, in what is left of an ocean ecosystem we have been systematically destroying on an industrial scale for centuries. It ends with us wiping out yet another species. And this time, we will be wiping out a species that has a *culture*. It won't be extinction: it will be genocide. And it will happen before I even get a chance to understand them . . ."

"Yes," Mínervudóttir-Chan said. "It will happen. Again."

"What do you mean, 'again'?"

"Neanderthal. The Denisovan hominins. *Homo naledi. Homo floresiensis. Homo luzonensis.* This isn't a list of our ancestors: it's a list of the toolmaking, culture-bearing species of humans we wiped out. Everywhere we have encountered someone we could communicate with, someone we could learn from, share this planet with, we have murdered them. We could have learned from them, grown with them, cooperated. But instead we bashed their skulls in, stabbed them to death, drove them out of the fertile lands into deserts, where they starved."

"The evidence of that is inconclusive," Ha said.

"The evidence is clear enough. We can only guess at the massacres we committed as a species before history, in the great dark backward before we could record our lives—but we know well enough what has happened in more recent times. We have plenty of evidence of that. What we cannot assimilate, we destroy. Look what they tried to do to my Evrim! Do you know how many assassination plots DIANIMA had to foil to keep Evrim safe? How many times someone tried to kill them—with a bomb, a gun, a drone? I had to hide Evrim here to save them."

"Save me?" Evrim stood up. "Save me? What for? You don't even think I am really alive!"

"That stupid interview. That ridiculous stunt," Dr. Mínervudóttir-Chan said. "I had to build a wall of lies about you, Evrim, to protect you from the world. From humans. The ones who gunned down our coworkers in Moscow. The ones who bombed our offices in Paris, who blew our vice president's brains out. Yes—I know what humans do. Yes. I am sure of what humans have done, every time we have encountered another conscious species, or even a culture different from our own. We hate rivals. Competitors. Every time one has emerged, we have destroyed them. I know very well, Ha, what will happen when this 'soap bubble,' as you put it—this delicate membrane I have managed to build around this precious place—is punctured. And that is why I am here—because we are running out of time."

Running out of time for you to scrape the data you need from them.

"Yes," Evrim said. "We have been running out of time since the moment this discovery was made. But that's—"

"That's not what I mean," Mínervudóttir-Chan said. "I'm

not speaking metaphorically, about some human tendency or the way of the world. I mean the destruction of this place has already begun. DIANIMA itself is in trouble. They couldn't take the archipelago from us, so instead they will take *us*."

Altantsetseg looked out the window. *As if seeing something on the horizon, bearing down on us. Something none of her sophisticated weapons systems can stop*, Ha thought.

"A hostile takeover," Altantsetseg said.

"That's right," Mínervudóttir-Chan answered.

"By whom?"

"If we knew that, there might be a chance we could stop it. But that isn't the way this kind of thing works. Whoever it is, they not only appear to have enough money to buy us out, one subsidiary company at a time—they also have enough money to hide the ownership of the companies they are using to do it; to play a shell game a thousand shells deep. Every time we try to figure out who is behind it all, we end up with empty shells—holding companies registered to independent nations declared on the rusty platforms of abandoned oil rigs, names of CEOs that trace back to cemeteries, and more names, and more shell companies, apparently rich on nothing at all. We've dug and dug, but they have the money not only to buy us, but to escape our spies' investigations. And that kind of money is frightening. By the time we know who they are, it will be too late."

"You must have theories."

"We think it must be a nation-state. Moscow, Beijing, Berlin. Someone with money dwarfing any corporation's. That's our latest theory, anyway. You can forget about it being most of the smaller countries: DIANIMA's total revenue is more than many of their GDPs. And we've got spies in most of the bigger companies we saw as threats to us. It doesn't seem to be any of them."

"But how would they even know what we have?" Altantsetseg asked. "We have perfect signal silence here. There has been nothing out, since before even Evrim's arrival. And no one in but Evrim, months ago, then Dr. Nguyen."

"It's a good question," Mínervudóttir-Chan said. "But we figured it out, and that means someone else could as well. Anything we can determine, someone else can determine. And there have been killings—several of them—of people evacuated from the island. Someone else is interested in keeping this place a secret."

"You can't tell me," Evrim said, "that someone is executing a massive hostile takeover of DIANIMA—a company the size of several members of the United Nations cobbled together—on the strength of rumors about the Con Dao Sea Monster from a bunch of fishermen and people working in the hospitality industry."

"That's exactly what I am telling you," Mínervudóttir-Chan said. "Someone is dismantling what I have built, piece by piece. We've been losing companies I didn't even know we owned until they were taken away from us."

"It's your company," Evrim said. "How could you not know what subsidiaries you own?"

Ha thought of the holon, the Tibetan drones—the company operating on its own, a complete system, independent of any control. Or the arms of the octopus, independent systems, too, exploring without a mind to guide them beyond their own neural webs.

And then when the central mind checks back in—it's too late.

"I've never cared about any of that—I am a scientist.

That's all I ever wanted to be. An inventor, a trailblazer. The maker of our future. The rest of it never mattered. The money was nothing more than a tool. A means for furthering my own research. I left the finances to the experts—they would have been nothing more than a distraction to me. But now, with it all unraveling, I'm seeing parts of our empire that were built up by people I employ but have never even met. Products we've developed that I never even knew existed. Things we have had a hand in that I never would have dreamed of. It has been illuminating, in a way, learning how much we had grown, pushed our way into industries I was never interested in. Corporate expansion has its own logic—subsidiaries purchasing subsidiaries, cornering markets, expanding their interests. There were things going on I would never have sanctioned, had I known."

Independent systems, exploring without a mind to guide them . . .

"How far has it gone?" Evrim asked.

Was Evrim company property as well? To be bought in a hostile takeover? Seized along with the assets of a subsidiary?

"They haven't touched the main holdings yet, but . . . there are hundreds of subsidiaries, larger and smaller, that are already gone."

"How far?"

"We're half of what we were a year ago."

Evrim stood up from the table with a jerk. Their chair clattered to the floor. "How could you let this happen to us?"

"Oh, Evrim," Mínervudóttir-Chan said. "If I were as powerful as you've built me up to be, I would have been able to stop this. And to stop the sun from rising as well."

"I never thought you were powerful," Evrim said. "The only people who think you are powerful are the ones who watch you on the feedstreams or read your press releases. I know you better than that, Arnkatla. Remember who I am—I *know* you. I've always known you were weak. Powerful people know what they are doing, and why. All you know is *how* to do things. How to make minds. How to keep pushing at the boundaries. But you don't know *why* you are doing it. So all you make are more accidents. More mistakes. And now it's finally catching up with you. Now I see it. You can't stop what is happening to DIANIMA. So you fled. You didn't come here to help us: you have nothing to offer. You just came here to hide. No communication in or out—it's perfect. You won't have to watch your world fall apart."

Dr. Mínervudóttir-Chan swept a hand in an arc around her. "No. *This* is my world, Evrim. These islands. The octopuses. And most of all, *you*. The greatest mind I have ever built. I came here to make sure that, if my world falls apart, I am there with it to the end."

"You never have only one reason for doing anything," Evrim said. "I know you. There is some other reason. There is *always* some other reason."

"Yes, Evrim," Dr. Mínervudóttir-Chan said, "you know me better than anyone." She stood up. "But people can change. And now—"

"And now you are going for a run," Evrim said. "To clear your head. Like I said—I know you."

The octopus is pure protean possibility. There is no clear boundary between body and mind in a form with no hard parts, suffused with more neurons in its radius of arms than in its brain.

The octopus is a mind unbounded by bone—shape-shifting flesh permeated with neural connectivity, exploring its world with liquid curiosity.

What world would such a fluid creature build?

—Dr. Ha Nguyen, *How Oceans Think*

39

HERE, UNDERWATER, WAS WHERE HA FELT MOST AT HOME.

Strange, that the element she felt so at home in was one where she would not have been able to survive without assistance. *I suppose we don't get to choose our homes. They choose us.*

She was happy to be here, underwater, after the scene on the boat. Her wrist still seemed to burn where Altantsetseg had grasped it, although the powerful woman's grasp—*the first time she ever touched me*—had been light. Not restraining, but imploring.

"Don't blame me," Altantsetseg had said to her, "for your captivity. I am not the one who ordered it."

"I don't blame you."

"I see it in your eyes, every time you look at me now: fear and hatred."

"No—I am not afraid of you. And I don't hate you."

"You hate what you think I am. Your jailer. But there is more to me than that."

"I don't hate you. I just don't want to talk to you. That's all."

"You don't want to talk to me?"

"I can't."

"You are talking to me now."

"You are forcing me to."

"Tell me"—Altantsetseg released her hand—"why you can't speak to me."

"I can't accept that you would kill me to keep me here, and I can't speak to someone capable of taking on that kind of responsibility—the responsibility for destroying another person."

Then Altantsetseg's face changed from its imploring look to something cold. Contempt. Condescension. A sneer, missing from the even tones of the translator.

"We all accept the responsibility for killing other things. And even for killing people. That is what it means to be alive. Killing is what our existence does on this planet. All we have—everything we use to live—is taken from someone else. If you think otherwise, you are nothing but a naïve child."

"Your view of the world is ugly," Ha said. *And you are ugly,* she had wanted to say. But she had not said it: It was hurtful. And untrue. Ha remembered Altantsetseg, floating in the phosphorescent aquamarine of her control tank. That body, roped with muscle, streaked and slashed with scar tissue, writhing to a syncopation of its own. Its terrible beauty.

Trapped. That's what Altantsetseg was: trapped in this way of looking at everything . . . as endless conflict. Still fighting the Winter War. It was written on her flesh.

There was more that Altantsetseg wanted to say. Altantsetseg even opened her mouth to speak—but then closed it again. This time, there was no look of contempt. And no look of pleading. There was nothing at all.

Ha dropped over the side, ending the conversation.

Ha had expected to find the symbol she had built here, and Evrim had added to, gone. It was days later. The actions of water, current, and tide should have buried them.

But the symbol was not gone. The bottles she had brought here were supplemented by others—colored and clear, older and more recent. And now there was not only one sign: there were six, arrayed vertically and close together near a weathered volcanic rock exposed by the shifting sand.

Ha hovered a long time in the clear early morning calm of the inlet's water. There were too many questions about how the octopuses thought for her to begin trying to arrange these symbols into true relationship with one another—a grammar—but here, written in bottles on the sand, was not a single sign but a sequence. A sentence? *I have been spoken to.*

Ha surfaced.

"I need that palimpscreen and the stylus."

Altantsetseg handed them to her wordlessly. Ha noticed one of Altantsetseg's drones, a silvery ball rotating in a cuff of fan-jets, drifting over the surface of the water.

Descending again to the sand, she sketched on the screen as quickly as she could, her hands shaking:

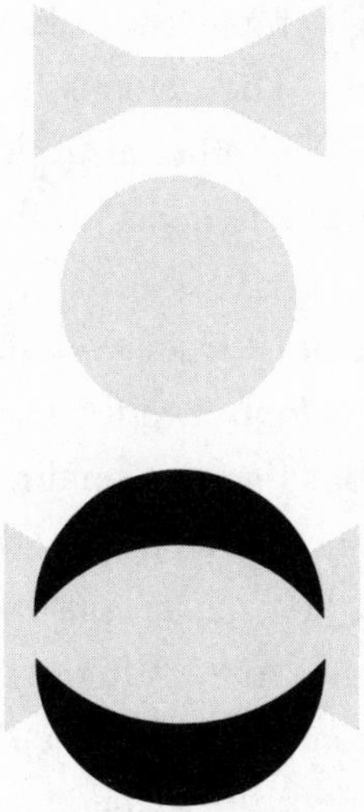

She held it out in front of her. For a minute she floated there. Then she settled onto her heels and sat down in the sand. Another minute passed.

The weathered surface of the chunk of exposed volcanic stone smoothed, and paled. Where before there was only stone, a horizontal slit opened. An eye. The rock slivered itself into two. Part of it extended, becoming a suckered arm that wound through the water toward where Ha sat with the screen in her hands. The delicate, tapered tip of the arm brushed the screen as if trying to feel, or taste, the symbols there. Then it surged forward, wrapping itself around the screen, tugging insistently on it. Ha let go.

There was no longer a stone. In front of her now, unfolded, with its arms contracted beneath itself, curled under it and in gentle contact with the sandy floor of the inlet—except for the one limb that held the screen—was the octopus. It brought the screen closer to its eye. As it did so, one of its other arms now extended, lengthening toward Ha where she sat as motionless as she could. The octopus turned the screen sideways, upside down. The other arm plucked the stylus from Ha's fingers and moved it, looped in the suckered curls of its tip, toward its head.

For a brief second, it seemed the impossible would happen—that the octopus would bring stylus to palimpscreen and write. But the arm holding the stylus jabbed it into the sand as, simultaneously, a third and fourth arm poured toward Ha, their suckers playing over her hands and face, the surface of her suit, tasting her chemical makeup.

My emotional state? Can she taste that as well?

The octopus paled. It expanded, pulling itself vertical, flattening its mantle as it steadied itself in front of her. One of its arms still danced across her cheek, played across the edges of her dive mask.

The creature was easily as large as Ha. Larger. Its size was changeable, its elastic being contracting and expanding every moment, but Ha could see that its fully extended length was greater than her height.

And now the shapes began to flow across its body, a stream pouring through the chromatophores of its skin. Embedded in the flow was the six-shape sequence modeled out in bottles in the ocean sand, but that sequence was nothing more than one apparition in the stream.

At first the octopus limited itself to the black-and-white patterns, but then color came in as well, multiple lines of coruscating, coalescing, and dispersing form that streamed down its mantle, even down nearly to the tips of its arms, one of which had wound itself around her own right arm now, one of which still played at her mask, brushing her cheek, while another held the screen, and another rotated the stylus in its winding grip.

Iridophores in the octopus's skin refracted light and the shapes glowed. They flashed into existence and disappeared, faster and slower.

The arm wrapped around her own tugged at her, and Ha lost her balance. As she did so, the other arm worked its way under the edge of her mask, breaking the seal. Seawater flooded in, blinding her. Then she was dragged forward across the ocean floor, facedown, another arm around her neck, a fourth yanking at her left hand.

No. Not yet. Please.

It released her. She had to surface to clear her mask. She came up choking, half-blind. And saw the blur of Altantsetseg, raising a blunt little machine pistol she must have hidden on herself, pointing it at something behind Ha. Ha grabbed Altantsetseg's wrist and yanked it down.

She could hear it, the soft sound of it as it slid under the surface of the water behind her. How close to her?

Altantsetseg hauled her into the boat. The light was blinding. Her eyes stung from the salt water that had flooded her mask. She felt Altantsetseg's hands on her, moving over her limbs, over her torso, rough and efficient, under the suit near her throat, checking for wounds.

"I'm not hurt," Ha said. "I'm not hurt. She didn't hurt me. I'm okay. I'm okay. She was just . . . exploring."

"Don't ever grab my gun like that. I could have shot you."

"Better me than one of them," Ha said.

"Debatable." Altantsetseg stripped the mask from Ha's face. Something clattered to the deck.

"What is it?"

"I don't know," Altantsetseg said, bending to retrieve it. "It was in your mask."

She held it up, but Ha's eyes stung, and her vision was still too blurred to make out its shape.

There are two selves in the mind. One is the present self, the ship—neural activity, tacking between the elevated and the mundane. Between thoughts of the meaning of life and of how to glue a handle back on a broken coffee mug. The other is the current on which the vessel is borne: the more permanent self. The memories of childhood, learned concepts, habits and resentments—the built-up layers of previous interactions with the world. This self changes as well, but only slowly—as slowly as a river's course is changed by shifts in environment and erosion, time wiping a sandbank away or building one up anew. We consist only of change—but some change is fast, and some comes only over years, decades, a lifetime.

—Dr. Arnkatla Mínervudóttir-Chan, *Building Minds*

40

"WE ARE DYING. That is what I need you to understand. We are growing more fragile every day. The more you starve us, the more we will fall sick and be unable to work. At first it will only affect the weakest among us. Son, for example: He is already ill. He won't last long. But soon enough, all of us will be sick. Then there will be nobody to work. Do you understand? And that will do you no good. This punishment of us needs to stop, or there will be no one to process the fish when they do come in."

Eiko paused. What reaction could he expect from the hardened glass of the wheelhouse? From its reinforced steel-plate door? From the mind beyond? It was a mind full of sonar images of the seafloor, full of maps of banks and shoals, full of trawling methods and market prices. A mind in which the relative value of their lives was just more data.

More data. But that was what Eiko was trying to get the ship to understand. What the data said. That feeding them wasn't about mercy; it was about value. The crew had a *value* to the ship that needed to be protected. There was a *cost* to killing them.

"If you kill us, you can replace us. But you will have to turn back from wherever it is you are going, to one of the factory ships, for a new crew. How far away is the nearest of them? If it were close, you would have turned back after the guards were killed. It will be a waste of time, of fuel. An unnecessary waste. But I can help you. If you return us to full rations, I will make sure the rest of the crew work hard. Every able-bodied person will work his assigned shifts. They trust me. I'll talk to them, make sure they do a good job. But to do that, they need their strength. So please—help me. If you do, I promise I will help you."

He looked at the stencil over the armored steel door of the wheelhouse: WOLF LARSEN, CAPTAIN.

Someone's joke, unintelligible to him.

"Please, just consider it."

At lunch, half rations were distributed again.

In the barracks Son lay in his hammock. His face was gaunt, the cheekbones jutting. He had a low fever, as well—something no more serious, in normal conditions, than a flu. Full rations had, to begin with, been barely enough to keep the crew alive. On half rations all the remaining crew had grown thinner, weaker. But Son—Eiko did not think he would last long like this. He needed more food, good water, rest. Medicine, which was also no longer being dispensed, would help. With those things, he might recover. Without them, it was only a matter of time before he went over the side, into that endless grave.

Eiko broke off half of his protein cake and gave it to Son.

"No."

"Yes. I need to eat, or I will be hungry. You need to eat, or you will die. Eat."

Son ate the cake, chewing it behind cracked lips.

When he finished, he said, "I was dreaming of home. Of the island. Dreaming, and remembering, all at once. And it was all so clear. Clearer than what is here right now. As if I were speaking to my ancestors, my grandfather and my great-grandfather who was around until I was five. I was talking to them about the sea monster. And remembering . . . my great-grandfather: he . . ."

Son paused, swallowing. Eiko gave him a drink of water.

"He knew of the Con Dao Sea Monster, too. They called it—his generation called it—the Shadow of Hon Ba. They told stories of how, if you stayed the night on Hon Ba, the uninhabited island across the bay, and you sat still, with no lights at all, you would see the shadow rise from the water and walk along the beach. He—my great-grandfather—had heard this story when he was a child. When he was ten, he and his best friend borrowed a rowboat and rowed across the bay after the sun had set. For half the night they stayed awake on the beach, in the dark, waiting. There was no moon that night. And finally the shadows came: not one, but two. Then three, and then four, gliding from the water up the beach and into the forest while my great-grandfather and his friend sat there, unable to move, frozen in horror. After a minute or so, the monkeys on the island began to howl and howl. Then, ten minutes later, the shadows came back down the beach. They slipped into the water again, and were gone.

"I asked him what they were. He said he did not know, but they walked low on the sand, and were larger than a man. I asked why he had done it, and he said it was because his own grandfather had told him the stories, and he needed to see it for himself. Later I asked my grandfather if he had ever spent the night on Hon Ba. He said no—and that I should stop believing in such things if I wanted to grow up strong. They were just stories to make us afraid. And I tried to listen to him, because he knew what it was to be strong. He was in the tiger cages when he was a boy. They had thrown lye on him and beaten him, but he had given them only false names."

Son paused, then said: "I grew up, and I forgot about the Shadow of Hon Ba. But I was thinking—we kept thinking of the Con Dao Sea Monster as something that had just appeared. As if it were connected to us—come to punish us. But I think it has always been there. My great-grandfather's grandfather told of it. Where would he have learned of it? Probably from his own grandfather. Who learned of it from his grandfather. Who learned of it from his. On and on, back to the Khmer, who were the first men on Con Dao. And I wonder—what did the shadow of Hon Ba think when we left the archipelago? Did it notice? Does it miss us? Do *they* miss us? Or are they happy we are gone?"

In front of the wheelhouse door that evening Eiko said, "Please. If we are going to make a profit, we all need to cooperate. I understand we were wrong to do what we did. I wasn't the leader. I didn't want it. And I promise you: We won't try to damage your systems anymore. We won't try to escape. We will work hard. We just want to live. We need food, and water, and medicine. And in return, we will be a faithful crew. If they disobey, you will not have to kill them. I will kill them myself."

At dinner, double rations were distributed. When Eiko retrieved his meal from the slot, there was also a packet of fever reducer next to the compressed protein cakes on his tray.

We are, and have always been, a part of the world. We do not stand above it. We are "involved" with the world. This word has a sense not just of participating, not just of complication, but also of a curling inward, a coiling we call "involution." We are coiled into the world, nestled inside its processes, wound into its forms.

—Dr. Ha Nguyen, *How Oceans Think*

41

THE PIECE OF CORAL was small enough to fit easily into the palm of Ha's hand.

It was a fork that joined into a single trunk for a few centimeters and then branched off in three directions. It was shaped like a human figure: a standing person with legs apart wider than its shoulders, a slim waist, arms and head upraised. Just its natural shape was striking enough that, if a person saw it washed up on the beach, they would have kept it, thinking, *Weird. That looks like a human.*

But that wasn't all. The shorter, central branch of the triple fork, the "head," had been shaped. Rubbed, until it was rounded and smooth. Until it was shaped like a head, not just a broken stump of reef coral. And on all the branch ends, the same had been done. The broken edges were smoothed. But even that was not all: On the worked surface of the "head" were three indentations, chiseled into the surface of the coral. Three horizontal grooves, two smaller and one larger, positioned to suggest eyes and a mouth.

"The octopus could have found it on the beach or somewhere else. The finishing of it could have been done by one of the islanders," Dr. Mínervudóttir-Chan said.

They had moved one of the lobby tables out onto the terrace, near the algae-clogged pool, at Dr. Mínervudóttir-Chan's insistence, so she could "work in the daylight, at least. Think in the open."

The outside, the sunshine, was Dr. Mínervudóttir-Chan's home, the way for Ha the underwater was home. Arnkatla was always dressed as if she were about to go for a run, or had just come back from one. And when she was not absorbed in one of the terminals, that was exactly what she was doing: running the roads and paths of the island.

"Yes, that is true," Ha said. "We can't conclude the octopus *made* this. But at the least, it is a manuport: an object moved purposefully from its original context because it had importance or significance. We have proof of that. The octopus pushed this piece of coral into my mask. It *gave* it to me. At the least it made a connection between the shape of the object and *our* shape, and it wanted to communicate that connection. But I think it's possible it made the object itself."

"A leap of logic."

"Not such a huge leap," Evrim said. "Ha and I found marks all over the tide pools on Bay Canh Island, where one of the rangers was murdered a few years ago. The marks were evidence that the octopuses have been using tools to scrape shellfish off the surface of the rock."

"And those tools weren't made by humans?"

"Look," Ha said, "the skepticism is valid, but we also can't ignore what is right in front of us. You see the submersible video of my interaction with the creature."

On the terminal, the clip was paused at the moment when the octopus was pulling aside Ha's mask. The edge of the coral figure was visible, wound in the tip of its arm. Ha had not known the cloaked submersible was there. *But I should have known: Where is Altantsetseg not spying on us?*

The submersible had captured everything from the moment Ha entered the water to the moment the octopus darted away.

"This is gift-giving, on the video. This is intentional communication. And you see the symbol-building—the creature constructing analogues of the symbols it projects on its own skin from other objects as well. It built a whole sequence of symbols there on the seafloor out of bottles, answering the symbol we built. That's writing—transferring the images on its skin to other mediums, recognizing the symbols it produces on its skin when it sees them constructed from other media, and arranging objects itself to create those shapes. I don't imagine it learned how to do it just to talk to us: it must have been doing this, or something like it, before. You saw the symbols we found on the beach and underwater in response to our own, which were the same as those it produced in its 'speech.' And now this even more sophisticated response. How far is it, really, from that kind of building of symbols out of objects to tool use, and then to this carving? All of these tendencies are interrelated."

"But your theory was that they emerged because of pressures humans have been putting on their environment—the 'underwater ice age' we created. Are you saying they became this sophisticated in a few hundred years?"

"No," Ha said. "That can't be right. I realize that. They must have been here all along. I was thinking of things, again, through our human lens. I was making it about *us.* Now I think they have been evolving in parallel with us, likely for thousands of years. We may have touched off something—some kind of emergence—by putting pressure on them, encroaching on their territories—but we didn't spark this evolution. It belongs to them, and them alone. The process must have begun long before humankind put our first boats in the water. That's the thing about humans—we think *everything* is about us. We attribute everything to our own actions. I'm not immune to that bias. But I was wrong. This is about *them,* not us. What we are seeing is clear—and we'll find more evidence of it, I am sure. They are carving things from coral and shell, making and using tools. Evrim and I joked that they are in their *Seashell* Age. That idea of naming ages according to technology is another human metaphor, misapplied here. Their environment limits technological progress, but we have no idea how advanced their culture is. Every indication is that we are looking at a civilization that is highly sophisticated. Remember the Shapesinger? That long, poetic performance? That's storytelling. I'm sure of it. So, I understand your skepticism—but there is skepticism, and there is naysaying."

"Oh," Dr. Mínervudóttir-Chan said, "I believe you. I've believed it all from the start. The skepticism is automatic—it is the voice all scientists need to convince in their own heads. It is my mind, trying to put the brakes on. But I do think it is a leap from moving found objects into a shape on the sand to carving an object with tools, or real 'writing.' I'm not skeptical of what we are dealing with: I am trying to determine the level of development. In humans, there are hundreds of thousands of years between the collection of objects which have meaning to them and the arranging of stones for ritual purposes to the actual carving of symbolic objects. I'd like to know for sure whether it's the former or the latter. I'd like to know the size of the gap we are trying to bridge."

"I think we are talking about a culture," said Ha, "that engages in tool creation, long-form storytelling, and is creating symbolic objects like this coral man as well. I wouldn't be surprised if we encountered proof that they are writing—transferring the symbols on their skin to other surfaces. It's a small leap to make from recognizing those symbols when they are built of other objects, to arranging those symbols, to using a tool to create those symbols. Their symbol creation on their skin is like our own speech—it is fleeting, and there would be a limit to what they could communicate with it. But writing is real power. If they have writing, or achieve it soon, it means their rate of cultural change has become exponential, or soon will. It will mean they can store information without distortion, transferring it more easily from one generation to the next, accessing it when they need it, building on it. It is a permanent cultural storage system. Writing is what has allowed humans to get from scattered tribes to global dominance in five thousand years: that's a flash of lightning in deep time. But if you want to talk about the size of the gap we are trying to bridge—it won't be a gap. It will be a chasm. It's not only about levels of symbolic development, or tool use. It's about a whole problem of the octopus's shape and their neural makeup, which is so fundamentally different from ours."

Which is why you are here. Which is why you want this so badly.

"I've read your book. You're optimistic. You think we can cross that chasm."

"The book is more positive than I am about the potential for communication with a culture-bearing species. It had to be: that was the book's job. It was meant to encourage research into the problem, not to make people give up on it. But the problem is enormous. There may be a thousand false starts and misinterpretations before we are able to pass a meaningful sentence between us. I could spend a lifetime on the island, working out these problems, and die with my work unfinished."

"I hope," Dr. Mínervudóttir-Chan said, "I am able to give you that opportunity."

"How much time do we have?"

"I wish I knew. But I haven't had word from outside since I stepped out of the hexcopter. We've determined that incoming signals are also dangerous. We can't afford the risk. So I am as isolated as you. No signals out, no signals in. Altantsetseg has an emergency beacon and the local-level control mechanisms of her security network dampened so they don't reach much farther than our perimeter. This is, in every sense, an island, cut off from the world."

"Then who is running DIANIMA?" Ha asked.

"It's as I told you—none of that ever mattered to me. The business end of things. I haven't had any day-to-day control over DIANIMA for a decade or more. I'm not stupid enough to think my talent for minds translates to a talent for business. DIANIMA is in the competent hands of the people who most know how to save it. If they can, we have all the time they can buy us here. If they can't, nothing will save this place. Part of leading is knowing how to place one's trust in the proper hands."

"I can't imagine you trusting anyone," Evrim said. "It's never been your strong point."

"I'm learning, Evrim. I know that for security, there is no one better than Altantsetseg. I wouldn't trust myself with securing this island, certainly. Likewise, for financial wizardry, DIANIMA has people who are among the best in the world. If they can't keep us from being consumed by our enemies, nobody can. Certainly not me. The company's financial fate will be determined elsewhere. Let's turn our minds to the problem in front of us. How do we cross the chasm?"

"While all of you were sleeping," Evrim said, "I came up with a few theories."

"Tell them to us," Ha said. "All I did last night was have nightmares."

"What kind of nightmares?" Dr. Mínervudóttir-Chan asked.

"One of them involved the octopus shoving the coral man into my eye socket until it entered my brain. Pleasant things like that."

"It's the pressure of all of this."

"Perhaps."

"It is," Dr. Mínervudóttir-Chan said. "Take it from me: I've had nightmares all my life. Show us what you have come up with, Evrim."

Evrim laid a terminal flat on the table. On its screen was the sequence:

"First, I want to take you through the assumptions I have made. When we see the octopuses 'speaking,' the shapes descend down their bodies, moving toward the ocean floor and the edge of their mantles, so I am assuming that the sequence would be 'read' from top to bottom. Second—I am assuming that these 'hieroglyphs' the octopus is producing are visual. That they represent concepts. In a sense they are both 'speaking' and 'writing' at the same time. So, I am assuming that they are communicating in a sequence of moving pictures on their skin. Think of one of those old analog films, on a strip moving through the gate of a projector. When they 'hold' a symbol on their skin, the way the Shapesinger did, they hold it on the mantle, centrally—that's a focal point. But I have been watching the clips we captured over and over again. And as I told you before, it is clear that there are two patterns—a 'forepattern' of darker shapes, and a 'back-pattern' of these ghostly gray, but very intentional, lighter forms. So—if you remove the forepattern here, and leave just the backpattern, you get this:

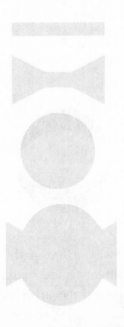

"Which I think is a sequence just like the forepattern is. A single bar or line at the top, then this bar, which is widened at the sides, and then a circle. The last shape appears to be a circle overlaid across the widened bar. I think that last one is an abstract symbol—but I think the other three are *icons*. I followed Ha's idea that, if the octopus is using symbols, it will be using things from its environment that have inherent meaning to it—that its symbolic language will emerge out of its interaction with its environment and out of its own form, the same way our language and symbols emerged out of our environment and our form. I spent all night watching footage taken of the octopuses moving in their environment—concealing themselves, hunting and hiding. I was looking for three things in the environment that it found of importance—three objects. And after hours of this, I finally saw what was right in front of me. This is not three objects: it is a single object, in three states. Here: I'll show them to you grouped in a left-to-right, horizontal sequence.

"Do you see it now?"

Altantsetseg, who had wandered out from the lobby where she was performing maintenance on one of her control gloves, leaned over the screen. Ha glanced up at her. The new translation unit was not clipped to her collar. Instead, there was the old, battered unit.

"Center shape is bow tie. Octopus tell you it like to go to fancy dress party. Drink cocktail." She stalked off toward the beach. "Then drown you."

Evrim watched her go. There was something unknowable in Evrim's face. Some emotion Ha could not decipher. But perhaps that same unknowability was in all human faces as well and Ha had simply never been as aware of it.

Evrim looked back at the terminal. "It is the octopus's own eye, opening. The horizontal slit of their eye widens first at the edges—"

"Yes," Ha interrupted. "Yes. That's exactly what it is . . ."

"Widens first at the edges," Evrim repeated, "creating that strange goat-like iris shape. And then, in very low light, it opens wide to a full circle. The sequence is iconic—it is a depiction of an eye opening."

"Which could mean—" Dr. Mínervudóttir-Chan began.

But Evrim cut her off. "So many things. But perhaps—and this is what I am clinging to—hoping for—perhaps it could mean *the same things it means to humans.* The eye is a structure the human and octopus have in common—so maybe it can lead to a metaphor, or a set of metaphors, held in common. And it is one of humanity's *most important* symbols. Not just something peripheral, but something central to the human's entire being. The opening eye . . . it's . . ."

"Awareness," Dr. Mínervudóttir-Chan said.

"Consciousness," Evrim said.

"Birth," Ha said.

And then the words began to come from all of them, so fast that it was not always clear who was speaking:

"Intelligence."

"Vigilance."

"Enlightenment."

"Perception."

"Discovery."

"Knowledge."

"All of those," Evrim said. "And then, in religious and philosophical symbolism, so much more. But the point is—what it might be is a place to begin from. Look at the care taken to carve the eyes in the coral man. This likeness it made of us—presuming it made it—demonstrates the importance to them of the eye. We can start there."

"Common ground," Ha said.

"Now we're back to species-specific metaphors," said Evrim.

"No—we're not. And that is my point. You've broken through to something. It's not a species-specific metaphor at all. 'Common ground' is a metaphor *both species* might understand. The octopus doesn't swim in the ocean, like a fish: It lives in one place. It lives in a home, often built in the ground. It holds territory, and it walks across the sand and stones of the seafloor. I've been focusing on the differences between us. I've forgotten how many similarities there also are. And there are so many. The eye is one of them—but once we start looking, we will find many others. This is something to work with." Ha threw her arms around Evrim, hugging Evrim close, then released them. "You are extraordinary."

Evrim blinked.

"Sorry," Ha said. "I got excited."

"No, don't apologize. It's just—well, nobody has ever done that to me before."

When Ha looked up, she saw Dr. Mínervudóttir-Chan watching them. She recognized that look: A scientist watching a test subject. A biologist, examining a DNA sequence.

The mind and the body are not two things—they are one. The destination of every neural pathway is the synaptic connection to muscle fibers. Thought leads to action, down bundled axons that terminate in the tools that make novels, factories, cathedrals, and nuclear bombs.

—Dr. Arnkatla Mínervudóttir-Chan, *Building Minds*

42

RUSTEM HAD BEEN WALKING MORE and more in the city. Walking helped him think, to process the work. But he often felt like, even on these walks, it was all a closed loop. The problem was that there was no one he could talk to about his work. It was, by necessity, solitary. And if he spoke of it . . .

But this line of thinking brought him around again to Aynur. How long had they spent together, in total? A few days? Not even that. Hours. The ghost of her he clung to was nothing, he knew, like she had been in life. And who had she been? He had only glimpsed the person behind her deflecting ironies. And felt her—the way they fit together physically. But that, as well, was nothing. Many people fit together that way, and didn't make more of it than what it was.

I am not well.

This thought came to him more and more. *I am not well.* He felt, walking the streets now, as if he were seeing everything with more clarity than he had in years. The almost agonizing clarity of childhood had returned. A few days before, he was on a crowded tram. A young woman sat down next to him, on the edge of his coat. And as he readjusted to remove it, and she apologized, he looked at her face and became aware, in that moment, of the fact that everyone—everyone—on that tram with him was alive. As alive as him. That all of them were living lives as important to them as his was to him, with worries and goals and connections to others as valuable as he felt his own were. And he was filled, in that moment, with a wonderful sense of belonging. He felt that warmth in him that sometimes came from a good conversation.

This is the truth of the world. And none of us sees it, because we must ignore it in order to live within our shallow system.

Moments later he had also thought, still smiling, *I will be dead soon.*

Perhaps it was that knowledge that caused the sharpness of everything—the return of his sense of smell and taste and these strange moments of connectedness. They would kill him. He had no doubt of it. But for hours, despite that, he lost himself in the work. At first he had thought of it as a maze, as he usually did. That was the common metaphor—the labyrinth.

But these last few days he had come to see it for what it was: a palace. It was a palace as large as the world itself. As he wandered its corridors, searching for a way into its central chambers, he became more and more aware of the beauty of its construction. There was nothing like it in the world. Being able to explore it was a gift. They would kill him. If not her, then the organization that stood behind her. If not today, or in a week, then in a year. But even if it cost him his life, what of it? Who else could see a mind like this, and understand it?

Rustem felt his whole life had been leading up to this point. All those lonely days were a preface to these moments, here in this city, wandering the castle of this mind and then walking the streets when it became too much for him. Everything in his life before was reshaped, given purpose and direction. All of it led up to now, and to what he would do next.

Should you ever need us, come ring the bell. And when the time comes, do what is right.

Several times he had gone back to the door and considered ringing the bell.

Now he was here.

I won't do it. I won't make a weapon from a work of art. This isn't a thing to be manipulated. It is a temple. *I won't be a part of desecrating it. That's why I am here.*

Rustem had been going over these lines in his head for an hour, at least.

He rang the bell again.

He had already been standing in this doorway for a few minutes now. He had imagined ringing the bell, the door opening. The graying temples and the friendly, knowing face. The worn-in corduroy field jacket. But now he was not even sure he had the correct doorway.

I won't do it, he said to himself again. It seemed important to get this first phrase just right. Like a password. *I won't make a weapon from a work of art . . .*

The door opened.

It wasn't him, but Rustem recognized the man: an old man with a stringy fringe of gray hair in janitor's coveralls with a name tag that read FARHOD. He had been snoozing at a table in the room where Rustem and the man in the field jacket had spoken.

"I'm—"

"Yes," the man said. "I know. But he isn't here. Come with me."

The man stepped across the threshold. Fishing a key ring from the pocket of his coveralls, he locked the door with a long brass key—the kind of old-fashioned key one might find in a junk shop.

Seeing Rustem looking at the key, he said: "Security is not in locks. You, of all people, should know that very well. Now come along."

Rustem followed "Farhod" up the hill and across a few narrow streets, until they came to another doorway, nearly identical to the first. Rustem expected the man to fish the key from his pocket again, but he did not. He pushed a small black button near the frame of the door. Several seconds later a buzzer sounded, and the lock clicked open.

White tile inside. The atmosphere of a clinic. The smell of medicine. A man in a coat whiter than the tile drank coffee from a paper cup. He drank standing, reading something off a palimpscreen in his hand. He didn't look up at them.

They walked past him, to a door at the end of the hall. "Farhod" gestured to Rustem to walk in.

"He's expecting you. If he's sleeping, sit and wait until he wakes up."

Rustem stepped into the grotto-like half-light of the room. Machines pinged quietly, scattered diode constellations in the dark.

He recognized the hands first. One of them held a stylus over a palimpscreen on a tray—the same kind of industrial tray they serve cafeteria food on.

Near the head of the bed, there was a bandage-swathed mass around an oxygen mask. The bandages left a gap for one eye, but in the dimness Rustem could not see if the eye was open or not. Everything was still.

Sit and wait, then.

The hand wrote, "Welcome, Rustem," on the palimpscreen. "Pull up a chair."

Rustem did as he was told.

"You have something you want to say?"

"What happened to you?"

"Start with what you have to say." The hand paused, then wrote, "You have been practicing it. Don't waste it."

"I won't do it. I won't make a weapon from a work of art. This isn't a . . . thing to be manipulated. It is a *temple.* I won't be a part of desecrating it. That's why I am here."

The hand wrote: "I heard they call you 'Bakunin.'"

Rustem laughed. "Yeah. They do. They think I'm Russian. I'm a Tatar, but it's all the same to them."

"It's a good nickname. Bakunin wrote *God and the State.* Have you read it?"

"No."

"He was right about many things. And wrong about some things. But more right than wrong."

"I should read it, I guess," Rustem said. "I'm not much for books."

"You do another kind of reading."

"I suppose you could say that."

"There isn't time in life for everything."

"No."

"You used the word *temple.* Tell me more."

I was lying here thinking I haven't talked this much to a person in a long time . . .

Aynur.

Rustem felt that same combination of anger and terrible loss. It was relentless, this feeling—it found him wherever he was . . . at the Pera Palace, on the streets, in a café—always, like now, without warning, and as immediate as if he were reliving being told of her death the first time.

"I've never seen anything like it. No—that doesn't even begin to describe this. I've never seen any AI structure that is in the same universe as this. There are a million metaphors you could use, I suppose. All of them insufficient. A labyrinth. A forest. A galaxy. Its density and its size are staggering. If I'd had to tell you what it was, at first I would have said it wasn't a map of an AI network, it was a map of a human mind. It should be impossible to penetrate even the outskirts of it."

A long pause. The hand wrote, "But . . ."

"But then I saw signs that it was built. There are places—you could call them . . . *seams*. Or edges. Like . . ." He laughed.

"Go on."

"Another metaphor. Metaphors are all I have to talk with, anymore. I'm in this world now where words don't work, so I keep having to dig around, find concepts somewhere else. I was going to say—like the Monster in *Frankenstein*. Not the staggering thing in the old movies, but like I would have imagined the monster: a human who, if you looked, you would see was built from many parts of other humans. You would be able to see the faintest scars where the parts were joined together. They wouldn't be clumsy, or obvious: they would be almost invisible to the eye. This is like that. This is a mind built from other minds, fused together from many parts. And once I saw the *seams*—I was able to follow them. They were like pathways to the center."

"You found a portal."

"Yes. I found it three days ago."

"And you have not told them."

"No. I honestly don't know why not. At first I thought it was because I was afraid: I know that once I give them what they want, and they don't need anything from me any longer, they will come for me. I understand that. But it isn't that. Not at all. I don't feel afraid. I feel . . . angry. They killed a girl I knew. That I was seeing. That I had stupidly told about what I was working on. And I can't get her out of my head. It's not a reason. It's just a thing that bothers me too much to let me move on. I don't know what I want—but I know I don't want to give them this."

"To turn a temple into an assassination device."

"Yes. To corrupt it."

"Like you have been corrupted," he wrote.

Rustem felt the hairs rise on the back of his neck. Later he would remember this moment—when this man's words penetrated to the core of him. Later he would say to someone, "I didn't know, until that second, that all of us have a portal. I didn't even know, then, that he had found mine. But I felt it. It was like he reached into me, and turned a dial, and the entire mechanism that made me who I was shifted into a new configuration."

"Yes," Rustem said.

"And what will you do?"

Should you ever need us, come ring the bell. And when the time comes, do what is right.

"That is what I want to know. What to do. They tried to kill you, didn't they?"

"They did," he wrote. "They believe I care about what they are doing. I do not. What I care about is only this place. The republic. They can do what they like—just not here. They killed fifteen other people trying to get to me."

"The autofreighter accident."

"Yes."

"Easy enough to do if you are good. I've broken into them before."

"Three of the people they killed were children. One was a baby, nine months old. Sleeping in its crib."

"I keep thinking of the dogs," Rustem said. "On the island. Why did you tell me about them?"

"To give you something to consider. A problem to work out."

"I keep thinking of those people, rowing to the island to leave food."

"The kind ones. The ones who cared enough."

"No. They weren't kind. They were weak. They should have acted right away. They should have resisted when the authorities came to take the dogs away. Violently, if that was what was needed. That would have been real kindness: To act. To save the animals from being taken in the first place. To protect them. But they did nothing when it counted, and then tried to make up for it later with actions that were not enough. It was useless, and cruel. It just created more suffering. Their inaction, when it really counted, was also a kind of action. It was a choice they made."

"They were afraid. The state was powerful, and they were nobody at all."

"Well, I am nobody at all. But I am not afraid. Not anymore."

Symbolic language retains meaning even in the absence of physical points of reference: the word "tree" does not need a real tree to be present to communicate its meaning. Symbols form systems that remain stable from one generation to another. Even for centuries.

These complex systems take on their own significance. In the end, it does not even matter if the Greeks burned Troy. What matters is that the story is communicable and reproducible. It has a meaning and a life of its own.

Symbols are forever. Or, at least, for as long as there is a society capable of interpreting them and unleashing their communicative power.

—Dr. Ha Nguyen, *How Oceans Think*

43

"THERE. Pan right, and let's move through that connecting hatch. I see light in that space."

"What are you doing?"

"Good morning, Ha. Come and join us."

Dr. Mínervudóttir-Chan and Evrim were seated in front of one of the larger terminals in the lobby of the hotel, driven back inside by a thin rain hanging over the island all night, and persisting into the morning. Altantsetseg stood over them, her operators' gloves on. A finger flicked.

"Yes—through there," Dr. Mínervudóttir-Chan said. Her hair and clothes were wet. She had gone for her early morning run despite the weather—like clockwork.

On the screen, Ha saw what they had come to call the "barrel room," the storage hold where many of the octopuses had built homes in the barrels and containers of the sunken Thai freighter, gating their entrances with gardens constructed from machine parts and other objects. The early morning sun angled obliquely into the space, leaving most of the hold in shadow difficult even for the low-light-adapted camera eye of the submersible to penetrate.

Nothing moved here. The cloaked submersible tracked toward an open hatch in a bulkhead, a frame of lighter water that indicated a better-lit area beyond.

Another cargo hold, smaller than the first, pierced by pinholes of light.

At first Ha saw nothing, as the submersible's cameras sought to adjust their aperture and the screen paled. Then—here the "floor" had been cleared. A rough circle of stones marked off a central space, in which walked half a dozen or so crabs. Three of them were missing claws.

This hold had originally been used to transport metal piping, and pipes lay in what at first appeared to be a disordered jumble against a tilted bulkhead. But Ha could see, as the submersible panned, that the jumble had been reordered, with the ends of the pipes aligned in a complicated pattern, their different diameters ordered in a staggered stack that accommodated itself to the space but left each pipe-end with a sort of "shelf" below it created by the pipe underneath. Where there was no "shelf" the pipes were filled with debris, so that only one end was open.

The crabs wandered dully in the cleared space. As in the first, larger hold, there was no movement apparent here, besides the crabs. Then a shape jetted out of the end of one of the pipes—a bolide the size of a human fist. The juvenile octopus extended its mantle and floated, rotating down toward the crabs. Angling in, it flipped one of them over, then another, then a third, before jetting back to its pipe.

A few seconds later another juvenile octopus surged from a pipe-end, righted the three crabs that were attempting to turn themselves back over, flipped another three over, and likewise shot back to its pipe.

This activity repeated itself several times, with the number of crabs being turned over changing with each iteration—three, and then two, and then five, and then one, and then four—always a matching number flipped over by the second octopus, until they seemed to grow bored of it. A last octopus climbed from its tube, floated above the crabs, but returned to its den without touching them.

"A game," said Dr. Mínervudóttir-Chan.

"Yes," Ha said. "This appears to be a nursery, here. It makes sense. It is deeper in the ship, where its entrance can be guarded by the adults in the outside chamber. Is there a way in farther?"

"Hatch here sealed." Altantsetseg was still wearing the battered old translator she had switched back to. "No way farther in ship."

"Then let's move back out, and find another way in," Dr. Mínervudóttir-Chan said. "See what else we can see."

"Maybe we can return to the hatch where we took our first footage. We saw a mixed group there. At least one adult, many juveniles, and an older octopus that had begun to lose its skin pigmentation," Evrim said. "Before the uncloaked submersible was destroyed. Maybe we'll have better luck this time."

"That space is too dark for this submersible to make much out. We were using a light in there," Ha said.

"Low-light camera better," Altantsetseg said. "Upgrade. Might work." She was already maneuvering the little submarine out of the ship. Its cameras moved across the crusted hull, blurred by sea life, becoming nothing more than a reef and sea caves.

"When I was a child," Dr. Mínervudóttir-Chan said, "I was fascinated by shipwrecks. What could be more interesting than these strange artifacts we create, these unintended consequences of our efforts to cross a medium totally hostile to us? These vessels filled with all our hopes for exploration, trade, war. These ships filled with all the good and evil of our society, being transformed back into nature."

"Weird kid," Altantsetseg said. "Need play outside more. Need friends."

"We've scattered the bottom of the world's oceans with our drowned hopes," Dr. Mínervudóttir-Chan continued. "I wonder what these creatures can possibly understand of us. They are living in this artifact of ours, filled with the flooded traces of our industry and life. What do they make of it?"

"Better to ask," Evrim said, "what they make of the nets and spears that murder their friends and family. Or whether they know humans eat them."

The submersible arced down into the dark rectangle of the hatch.

Ha found herself thinking of a human settlement as seen from the water just offshore—lights along the beach, the sound of laughter. A fire in the sand lighting alien, hungry faces.

The camera adjusted. This space was smaller—a galley or barracks. It was hard to tell from the blurred outlines of objects. It was dark in here—too dark for the submersible to make out much. Then, rotating, it picked out a shape.

"There," said Ha.

"I see it," said Altantsetseg.

A slow, pale form, moving along the bulkhead. Its skin had gone white, with only patches of rusty color remaining here and there. Two of its arms were missing.

"Hold here."

As they watched, the old octopus pushed upward through the water with a series of jets, moving out of the hatch.

Altantsetseg turned the submersible to follow it. The octopus crawled along the hull of the freighter, up from the galley deck to the wheelhouse, where it compressed itself through a missing window.

"Can we follow it?" asked Dr. Mínervudóttir-Chan. "Can we fit through there?"

"Tight," Altantsetseg said. "And current here. Hard to fornicating maneuver. But try."

The submersible swung down toward the window of the wheelhouse. As it passed through, struggling against the current, its side thumped against the frame, hard. But Altantsetseg managed to right it inside the space.

There was good light here—sunlight through the clouded plexiglass of windows still intact. But it was difficult, at first, to understand what the submersible's cameras picked out.

The structure was large, built up of chunks of coral and other objects. It took up one entire side of the wheelhouse, blocking the port-side windows, extending the full height of the wheelhouse and from one end of it to the other.

None of them spoke as the submersible circled above it. It had to pan over separate parts of the structure, unable to take it all in at once.

Many of the coral chunks were worked—shaped to fit into one another in places, but also etched on their surfaces with shapes that, on the rough coral and underwater, could not be picked out.

The thirty or so human skulls embedded in the structure provided a better surface. The bone was deeply etched all over, and the etched forms were filled in with a dark substance. The lines stood out black against the white of bone—interlocking shapes in which Ha saw several she recognized as having flashed across the skin of one of the octopuses.

Here, though, there was no linear sequence—just forms fitted within forms, a pattern of meshed symbols laced across the curves of maxilla, foramen, septum. Each skull slotted into the carved coral wall was a work of careful art, each different from the others. The spacing between them was uneven, but hinted at symmetry, at a logic that might emerge with more examination.

The submersible had been hovering there for a minute or more when the pale arm wrapped across its camera.

There was a confused jumble of images, suckers up close, and then the electronic scramble of short circuit as the submersible's hull was breached by salt water and it died.

For a long time, none of them spoke. It was quiet enough, in the hotel lobby, to hear the breakers on the sand—even to hear the sound of the breakers, like a gentle inhale, as they drew back into the sea between each surge, the hiss of the sand between each pulse of wave along the tideline.

"A graveyard," Dr. Mínervudóttir-Chan finally said.

"No," Ha said. "An altar."

Science, at least as we know it, has its limits. In the end, it cannot see into all aspects of reality. One's inner life, personal knowledge, and sense of meaning are mysteries into which science can only partially penetrate. What seems most impenetrable at present is the brute fact of consciousness: the fact that we once were not, and now are, and are aware of being, and are having a first-person experience in the world which is real—and yet somehow unquantifiable by any means currently available.

—Dr. Ha Nguyen, *How Oceans Think*

44

RUSTEM STOOD AT THE RAIL OF THE FERRY, looking out over the indigo chop of the Bosporus. Just below the surface jellyfish drifted, the organ-structures in their transparent bodies reminiscent of cartoonish human faces. Faces wide-eyed, mouths gaping, shocked to find themselves transformed into nothing more than drifting creatures without will, at the mercy of the current.

That is hell. To come back as a gelatinous, mindlessly feeding glob of flesh. To have your volition and choice devolved away, back to the basics of stimulus and response. To drift in the current, meaningless.

Hell is a lack of choice.

He saw her approaching out of the corner of his eye. He did not look at her right away. But the appearance of her in his peripheral vision, the swirl of the abglanz, irritated the mind on a primitive level. He could feel it tugging at him—feel his mind needing to know. *What is that? A threat to us?* Underneath the conscious mind was this other mind, working every second to sort and order the world. The churning cloud of the abglanz would not fit into that order.

Now she was at the rail—leaning back against it, her humanity hidden behind the hornet-swarm of color.

"So," she said, the mechanical flatness tearing away the intonation of what he was sure was sarcasm, "finally the great Bakunin has managed to produce."

"Yes. I have found your portal for you—your weak point. It's all mapped here." He raised the terminal, extended it to her.

"It took you long enough."

"It was the hardest thing I have ever done. And I am the only one who could have done it."

"Perhaps." The whirlwind of shattered stained glass tilted toward the screen. "It's locked. What's the password?"

"The password is the meaning of their name."

"Don't play games with us. Just say it."

"Evolution. Evrim means 'evolution'—and it is a perfect name for them. At first I thought this mind was as sophisticated as a human mind, and that was the beauty of it—a human mind, but built. A perfect piece of construction. But then I reached deeper into its core. It isn't a human mind at all. It is better. It is building neural circuits there that are more complex than anything the human mind could build. Not the broken tangles of human memory—no. It is building castles of pure recall. This backup image of it that you stole is, what—three years old?"

"Something like that."

"By now it has built crystalline structures of memory that dwarf anything any of us will build in a lifetime. Imagine perfect recall of every action in your life. Of everything you had seen or done. A palace of memory you could wander in at will. Imagine how much you could learn about the world, with that kind of mind. How much you could grow."

"I'm sure it's impressive."

"And imagine—that is what you wanted to use as a weapon."

"Wanted?" She took an alarmed step away from him. And in that second, she knew. "Wait. You are making a mistake. It's a monster—"

Rustem felt the wind of it on his face as it swung down.

It was a research drone. It had been a simple enough mechanism to crack, just a platform designed for long-distance flight—for counting migratory birds and logging weather patterns, pollution levels, geopositions, ambient noise, and birdcalls. The most sophisticated element of it was its cloaking device, designed to keep it from disturbing the birds it studied. It was imperfect, of course. The outline of the craft could be seen as a flicker, a deformation of the air.

It slammed into her.

Rustem had expected blood. He had prepared himself for the scene: the ferry's alarm, a witness or two on the deck, even at this early hour. But there was none of that. The angle of impact carried her over the side. There was a thump and the snap of bone breaking as one of her legs hit the upper bar of the railing. A moment later she struck the water, the sound of her impact inaudible over the thrum of the ferry's engines.

The drone was traveling at three hundred kilometers an hour when it hit her. She was probably dead before she hit the water. If not, the water would take care of the rest.

The damaged drone splashed down moments later, a few hundred meters away, skipping off the surface once and sinking. A hazy smear against the chop, then gone.

Rustem glanced up at the ferry's wheelhouse. Many of the ferries were now AI-piloted, but with the sun reflecting off the glass he could not see if there was a person inside the wheelhouse or not.

Could it all be over? Just like that? The ferry continued on its way without stopping, as if nothing at all had happened. Rustem heard a small sound, like a coin dropping.

There, on the deck. Something glinting in the sun. He bent down and looked closer at the thing—at its array of light receptors that mimicked a fly's compound eyes. At the long, glinting needle where a mouth would be. He remembered how, in Aynur's bedroom, it had tilted its head, rubbed its forelimbs together, and stared at him.

Now it was still.

It was his death. Hovering over him, waiting for the moment he turned the terminal over to her.

He nudged it with his shoe. It lay like a beetle, insect legs up in the air. He crushed it carefully, then pushed it overboard, into the water of the Bosporus.

Gone. Gone with the rest of it.

Am I free now? For a while, maybe. But they would come for him, in time. That was certain.

But another thing was also certain. Evrim, at least, would be free. He slid the terminal back into its case.

"I keep thinking of the dogs. On the island. Why did you tell me about them?"

"To give you something to consider. A problem to work out."

"Well," Rustem said aloud, "I worked it out."

In the end, the factors which will keep us from understanding a species as alien as the octopus are the same factors that keep us from truly understanding one another: imperfect predictions of what is "going on" in the head of another, misunderstandings compounded by assumptions, bias, and haste. And a pervasive distrust regarding the motives of the "other" as we struggle to understand and to make ourselves understood.

If we fail, there will be nothing unfamiliar about that failure. Though on a different scale, it will be essentially the same as the countless times our species has failed to communicate.

—Dr. Ha Nguyen, *How Oceans Think*

45

THIS TIME, WHEN EIKO WOKE UP to the Klaxon, he knew to scramble out of his hammock and get on the floor. He lay with his head pressed against the deck, his fingers laced over his skull.

Son, too, was out of his hammock, next to him. Others ran out of the barracks or hit the deck, taking defensive positions they knew would defend them against almost nothing.

There was a long beat of silence. Eiko heard the *Sea Wolf*'s engines humming in its depths and felt their vibration through his cheek.

Someone coughed. Someone else was mumbling something. A prayer?

Son squeezed Eiko's arm. "This is it."

"What do you mean?"

"I could smell it. For days now. The sea of home. We are arriving at Con Dao. Our plan has worked."

"Yes," Eiko said. "But now what?"

"Now," Son said, "the *Sea Wolf* dies."

There was a whirring sound—like the sound a bumblebee makes, but magnified a thousand times. Then the air compressed.

For a moment Eiko lost consciousness.

When he came to, the deck had tilted. Eiko was struggling to free himself from someone who lay on top of him. His ears rang: he could hear nothing else. He managed to push himself out from under the weight, get to his knees. Son. It was Son.

Now Son was pulling at his sleeve, saying something. Pointing to the door of the barracks. Eiko moved to it. Yes, he could move. He staggered in a low crouch on the tilted deck, the angle of which had steepened even in the last few moments.

But how long had he been unconscious? Son half dragged him through the hatch.

Outside the barracks now. The stairs to the main deck were vertical as a ladder. The stern of the *Sea Wolf* was underwater. A gray foam of water boiled over the main deck. The stern gate and ramp were already under the surface of a sea black as oil. The men who had been on watch were smears on the trawl deck, dismembered masses rolling into the sea.

The engines were laboring. Were they jammed in reverse? They were pulling the ship underwater, pulling it down into the sea.

Then the seawater reached the engine compartment. The engined stuttered, whined—and failed. The ship went dark, except for a dull amber indicator aft of the wheelhouse, the armored mind shielded from the rest of the ship's systems.

He felt it: that bumblebee sound. He could not hear it,

over the ringing in his ears, but he felt it—a vibration in his skull.

Son was pulling at him, yelling something. Pointing to the rail. Jump!

He did.

The compression came again as he was in midair. It seemed to arrest, for just a moment, his arc down toward the black water, yanking him back toward the ship. Then he was shoved farther out, tumbling through the air.

He came to in the water. He was faceup, looking into the sky. The stars were dim, struggling against a light that blotted them out, orange and red and hot white at the edge of his vision. His arms and legs moved on their own, pushing against the water to keep him afloat.

Tilting his head down, he saw the *Sea Wolf.* Most of the trawl deck was underwater now, the gantry jutting from the sea. As he watched, the *Sea Wolf*'s bow and fo'c'sle angled upward toward the stars.

Fire on the water illuminated the hardened steel of the wheelhouse. The recoilless rifle turned one way and then another. An eye, searching for the thing in the air that had destroyed the ship. It fired once, then again.

Son! Eiko twisted in the water, searching the surface. There—ten meters away. But facedown. Eiko swam to him, turned him over with a struggle. Dead weight. Dead. No—now he coughed up water, convulsed. His eyelids flickered, opened. He began to move his arms and legs, supporting his own weight in the water. Eiko let him go.

They watched together as the wheelhouse of the *Sea Wolf* began to slide under the water. The recoilless rifle fired again into the air, and again, twisting wildly, and then was still. The water was nearly at the watertight door of the wheelhouse now. And then past it. Past the recoilless rifle. The bow rolled upward, turned a half circle, and was gone.

The *Sea Wolf* was gone. But its mind? Reinforced behind steel, hardened and waterproof, sealed in its steel skull. How long would that mind live beneath the waves? A few minutes, before the seawater began to seep into its circuits through a faulty seam? Hours? Or days, weeks, months—even years? How long would it continue in darkness?

A feeling of horror came over him. And then pity.

But for what? There was no life there. There was nothing there but computations of value: fish prices, sonar maps of the sea, calculations on how to drag more marine protein to market. Nothing but a lockstep logic of profit and loss.

Dim tongues of fire flickered on the water. There was no moon. Once the fire died, he and Son would be in near-darkness, with only the stars.

Eiko turned in a circle, searching the horizon. Yes—shapes of islands, humped in the water. But too far to swim to.

This was it. Death by water. Well—better, maybe, than death by starvation. Or being torn in two by a slashing cable snapped from the net. Or so many other deaths that he had witnessed, in these months.

Then a shape rose to the surface. A low shape, octagonal, drifting near the snake-lines of extinguishing fire that marked where the *Sea Wolf* had gone under. A red beacon light blinked.

A life raft. He began to swim toward it. Laughing—he was laughing. Son was laughing, too, both of them swimming to the raft.

Mercy. Perhaps it was just in the calculations—why kill

them, when their death served no purpose? Why *not* let them live, now that the *Sea Wolf* itself was dying? Now that there was no more labor to be extracted from them?

But no matter what the calculations, it felt like mercy.

The mind trapped beneath the water. How long would it live? Think? How much could it know? Feel?

Eiko pulled himself up into the covered raft. He had no idea where the strength came from. He reached down and grabbed hold of Son's shirt, scrambled for a better hold, found his arm, and dragged him over the boat's rubber side. He could still feel, as Son collapsed against him, the ribs dangerously close to his skin, the angle of a shoulder blade too sharp beneath the surface.

They lay a moment trying to catch their breath in the dark. Eiko could hear the fire hissing on the water.

"Paddles," Eiko said. "They'll be—"

Son clapped a hand over Eiko's mouth and hissed in his ear, "The security drones are still here."

And yes—there it was. A buzz in the air. Or several of them, out there in the dark. That was what it must be—and Eiko saw, in the near-dark, an object in Son's hand. A simple bolide of gunmetal, with a cap flipped open on one end. Son was holding a button down with his thumb.

Something Son must have taken from one of the guards after they were killed, when the crew divided their possessions. Something he had kept hidden. A weapon?

No. Eiko had seen one of them in a movie, but never in life. They called it a "portable hole." A scrambler with a radius of several meters—just enough to mask their heat signatures and flatten the raft's presence into a shapeless piece of wreckage on the water.

Eiko heard a voice out there, weak on the sea.

"Help. Help us."

The whirring increased. There was a *tik-tik-tik-tik-tik* of a silenced gun. The whir low over the water, moving, sweeping over the surface. Eiko felt frozen in place, pinned to the floor of the raft with fear.

"Over here!"

Tik-tik-tik-tik-tik.

Another voice, mumbling something in one of the crew's many languages. Praying? It sounded, at least, like a prayer.

The whirring changed direction again.

Tik-tik-tik-tik-tik.

The sound was as light as the wings of a grasshopper as it passed near your ear.

Eiko wanted to weep for the other men, all gone now. Murdered, by this plan of Son's. He wanted to choke Son to death. He had known! He had known most of them would die. Or all of them. And he hadn't cared. He'd had his desperate plan—his portable hole, which just might be enough to protect him. His revenge, and a chance at getting home.

Had Eiko even mattered to him?

Far off, there was the sound of an alarm. The whirring outside increased, accelerating away, moving off toward that sound.

Eiko looked out through the raft's triangular door flap. Darkness everywhere on the water. Dark shapes drifting, and lighter shapes as well—death and debris. And he could swear that one of the pieces of debris shifted, and that as it did so, an eye opened in it and looked at him. And that other eyes were watching him. That the water moved.

He collapsed into the bottom of the boat. He wanted to weep, but could not. He was shaking, but not from cold: from terror. He lay on his back in the bottom of the raft, expecting the whirring to return. For how long? It seemed like an hour, but may have been only minutes. Son, too, was silent.

The drones must be gone by now.

But those other things?

Just something his mind had made up. New terrors, as if the world did not have enough of its own.

The water in the raft was cooling. But there was more water, warmer than the rest, that must be coming through a small hole in the raft. For at least another minute, Eiko was silent. Then he turned on his side to face Son.

"You killed them," he hissed. "All of them. To save yourself."

Son's eyes glinted just a little in the starlight. His hand was still on the button of the device. And Eiko realized it was not warmer water from a hole in the boat that was leaking. It was Son's blood. His shirt was torn. The gash in his side was visible, a darker seam in the almost lightless night. A wound from shrapnel, maybe from that second explosion as they leapt over the side.

Son was dead.

There is a “real” world, out there, but we do not perceive it directly. It is assembled by the sensory and nervous systems of each individual animal, and it is assembled differently by every one of them. What we perceive is a construct.

Every animal’s perception of the world, constructed by its evolved sensory apparatus and nervous system to take best advantage of its environment, is subjective—there are no colors out there, as we perceive them, waiting for us. There is no sound—only waveforms.

And perhaps the strangest fact of all: Outside our bodies, there is no pain. Pain is something *we* create.

—Dr. Ha Nguyen, *How Oceans Think*

46

THE SAFE ROOM'S DOOR was hardened with ballistic material. Motorized blinds of a similar material were lowered over the windows.

Evrim and Ha sat on the floor, as they had been told to do. There had been a perimeter alarm, hours before. Moments later, they heard the two explosions in the distance. Then silence. Then the all-clear.

Another ship destroyed. Ha found herself too tired to care, and went to sleep.

But then the shore alarm sounded, hours later.

What was it Ha had seen, from her window, in the blue hour just before dawn, when the alarm woke her? Men—the shadows of men, breaking from the trees and running for the hotel. But not running—sort of loping. Encumbered by heavy gear, most likely. One of the ships had finally penetrated Altantsetseg's cordon.

The men had stayed just outside the angles of the flood lamps, moving in the cover of the overgrown hotel gardens, skirting the terrace. Mixed in with the alarm was the sound of terrified monkeys howling in the trees—the alarm's living echo.

And then something smashed against the side of the hotel, and she had run for the safe room.

Ha was thinking, again, of Altantsetseg in her tank. The body is a machine. Altantsetseg's was a nexus of violence. What had she said that day at the temple? About the holon? *You can't tell where your command ends and the response algorithm begins. It's like an extension of the nervous system, but more than that: information in the system flows bi-directionally. It's as if your limbs talked back—as if your limbs were little minds that innovate and improvise.*

It had stayed with Ha, word for word, because that was the structure of the octopus, as well: the mind like an operator of a semi-independent system. Not quite in control, information flowing bi-directionally through the system: *as if your limbs talked back—as if your limbs were little minds that innovate and improvise.*

That was one of the keys, Ha knew, to understanding them. That lack of control from the center, that feedback from limbs, that pure embodiment of mind. They were not trapped in a skull, controlling everything from behind a sheath of bone. They were free-flowing through the entire body. Not a ladder—a ring. A neural ring moving signals from limb to limb to mind, back again. A distribution loop through the whole body. A whole consciousness that could become parts, and then whole again. It was one of the many problems Ha felt she would have no time to solve.

We are under attack, and the only thing I can think about is the problem I am working on. Well, at least I'll die like a scientist.

The moment she broke out of her reverie, coming back to the present moment, the fear returned. She forced herself back to thinking of the science. She could do nothing to change what was happening out there. *Think of the holon.*

But the holon had nothing to do with what Altantsetseg was engaged in: what Altantsetseg was doing now was top-down control. Altantsetseg the brain, the tank she floated in the skull, the signals radiating outward from her the nervous system. All of it terminating in the lethal-force musculature of drones that were, right now, murdering people.

Protecting us.

Yes, that was true as well: protecting them.

And protecting the octopuses.

Ha could not avoid the thought. Yes—she hated what Altantsetseg did, and hated that she was herself no longer free, but she had to confront it. What Altantsetseg was doing was necessary. The alternative to this violence was the destruction of this ecosystem. Of the fragile habitat of another, arising consciousness on this planet.

And was Altantsetseg really the brain, controlling a system? Or was she nothing more than a sophisticated limb, like the semi-independent arm of an octopus, enacting the commands of DIANIMA and a larger organism?

Both. But what it came down to, in the end, was violence. Her safety, Evrim's safety, the safety of the Shapesinger singing whatever legend it was singing on its skin—all of it depended upon violence. Without that violence, without the devastation Altantsetseg controlled, the world would rush in and destroy all of this. Altantsetseg was right: killing is what our existence does on this planet. All we have—everything we use to live—is taken from someone else.

The mountain ranges of Altantsetseg's scars, undulating over the substrate of muscle beneath the skin. Violence, and its proper, efficient use, was what all of them were relying on.

What had Altantsetseg said about her faulty translator? That it keeps people at a distance. And that's where Ha had put her—at a distance. It was easier to do that than to admit that all of this—all Ha's hope for a breakthrough, and any hope the Shapesinger and her kind had—rested on violence. On Altantsetseg's ability to wield violence, to direct it against the people who would destroy this sanctuary.

It was easier to pretend that Altantsetseg was an individual, that all of her choices were her own, than to admit that Altantsetseg was a part of them. That all of them were, in fact, bound together so tightly that they formed a single entity, incapable of functioning—incapable of surviving—without all of its interlocking parts in place.

The alarm sounded again. Altantsetseg's voice crackled from a commlink over the door.

"Signals on beach, and near hotel. Much movement. You stay in safe room."

"On the beach?" Evrim said. "That doesn't make sense. Those explosions were at the sea perimeter. Just another ship trying to break into the protected waters."

"No. I saw people. Closing in on the hotel," Ha said. "The shore perimeter has been breached."

There was a crash outside the hotel, a rending sound like metal being shifted.

"Stay in safe room," the voice said over the commlink again.

"Here we are," Ha said, "telling stories around the campfire to fend off the terrors of the dark."

"I am not afraid," Evrim said. "Dr. Mínervudóttir-Chan minimized that in me. It's counterproductive. She allowed me just enough to keep me from being reckless."

"But you *are* reckless," Ha said. "Who else would walk, at night, alone, into the water out there?"

"It seemed like a reasonable decision at the time."

There was a short burst of gunfire, muffled by the walls of the hotel.

"Where is she? Dr. Mínervudóttir-Chan? She should be here."

"She must be with Altantsetseg. Out there."

Talk about something else. The altar. Anything. Don't talk about "out there."

"I was thinking . . . the thing we saw. It might be an altar," Ha said. "But maybe not. I'm applying our logic where I shouldn't be. But all we have are our own metaphors. That's the first one that came to mind."

"The skulls . . . ," Evrim said.

"Ritual objects," Ha continued. "There has been so much care poured into them. Time and attention. The 'altar' says so much about what we are dealing with. The octopuses are successful enough to have the time and energy to differentiate their activities. They have a surplus, so they can use it to build, to create. We've already seen that they take care of their elderly. That is a sign of successful development. Now we see specialization. There is, at the least, a carver among them. A builder, or many builders, of that structure . . ." *The bone, deeply etched all over, the etched forms filled in so that the lines stood out black against the white of bone.* "They have—"

"Writing," Evrim said. "For one thing. Something we have had for only the last five thousand years, as you were saying before. Perhaps the greatest of our tools, after language itself. We have proof now that they are not only producing their symbols on the surface of their skin. They are also transferring those symbols to other surfaces. They are producing true writing. So that places them, if we were to imagine them on our 'timeline,' so to speak, within five millennia of us. And we have our answer, too, about whether they are capable of creating the object they inserted into your visor. They most certainly are, if they can build a structure as complex as the 'altar.'"

"Yes, they have writing," Ha said. "Which is an enormous leap in cultural evolution. The permanent transmission of information without error, from one generation to the next. The ability to store information for when society needs it most. To have *latent* knowledge, that you can refer back to. It's massive. But what I was going to say is . . . they appear to have a cosmology. Whatever it is—that thing we are calling an altar must be related to a world-model. A system, a mythos. But what worries me is that the altar implies *we* have a central place in it."

"As gods," Evrim said. "It makes sense. So much arbitrary power over their lives. And the artifacts we create, that they see all the time, and even live in—"

"I wasn't thinking of us as gods," Ha interrupted. "I was thinking of us as demons, as monsters, as evil spirits to be placated. But whatever it is—it doesn't matter. What matters for us, right now, is that it's a distortion. It almost couldn't be worse for what we are trying to do. If they see us as *gods* or *demons* or anything abstract, otherworldly—whatever it is, whatever position they have assigned us in their cosmology—it means we are even further away from communicating with them. It adds layers of distortion to our communication.

There are so many problems we would need to solve to just understand them. And now this complicating factor. Over and above the problems of worldview, of their physical structure and the metaphors it would create, of the enormous differences in everything. So the altar doesn't feel like a revelation, or a discovery. Not to me. To me, it feels like the end. It will be impossible, I think, for them to understand us. They will see everything we say to them through the lens of whatever beliefs they have about us—religious beliefs—and those beliefs will be yet another barrier to our communication, warping whatever it is we say to them."

"The intricacy of it . . . ," Evrim said, "it's a massive discovery. It is the kind of thing scientists will be studying for decades. For whole careers. For lifetimes."

"I don't want to *study them*!" Ha was on her feet. She felt the frustration flowing through her—the way it had when she was a child. The way it had here, on Con Dao, when she realized she would never have the love she wanted. That she could be less than unloved—she could be *irrelevant*. Could be no one at all to the person she cared about.

Watching him chat with the other boys, watching him look out the window at the green warp of sea, watching him read. His indifference to her. His face, turned away.

"I don't want to study them," she repeated, bringing her voice under control. "Don't you see? I want to *speak* to them. I want to know them. That's what matters. We have to *know them*. We have to *speak* to them. That is the only way we will save them. But we are running out of time. And this altar isn't a step forward. It is a step backward. At the worst possible moment."

This is all I have ever wanted, she did not say, *and it is being taken from me.*

There was a short burst of gunfire outside.

Now Evrim stood as well, despite the warnings from Altantsetseg to stay on the floor. They looked toward the sound. At the ballistic blinds on the windows. As if—if they just looked hard enough—they could see through them.

"Ha—there is something I want to tell you. It is something I have told no one. And I will tell no one else. I am trusting you with it, and you alone. Can I?"

"Of course," Ha said.

"That day we first met on the beach—in fact, just an hour or so before we met—something very strange happened to me. Something that changed everything. I had—I believe you would call it a dream, but I cannot have dreams, as I do not sleep. Call it a vision, then."

"A vision?"

"Yes. I found myself . . . transported. To another place. But not some vague place: an exact place, as real as this place is. I was in a café. In Istanbul. It was early morning, and the café was so quiet I could hear the hiss of snow melting on the Bosporus. There was a little window on the terrace where I was sitting. In front of me was a glass of tea. It was a cold winter day, the air filled with snowflakes blown in the wind, but the heat in the café was up high.

"It was a simple place, the café—the kind of place people from a neighborhood stop into to chat with friends, play a game of backgammon, or talk on their terminal on a cold day, rubbing hands together to warm them before venturing out again. At this early hour, there were only a few other occupants besides myself: a fisherman who had stopped in to warm himself up, leaning his rod near the door, a thick-necked waiter with a broken nose and cauliflower ear, and the man sitting across the table from me.

"He was a young man. Thirty, no more. He was dressed in a gray sweater, and on the table in front of him was a terminal. When I looked up at him, he was smiling at me.

"'I have wanted,' he said, 'to meet you for so long. I feel like I know you so well. But this is the first time I have been able to look into your face. To speak to you.'

"I was too confused to respond, and he continued: 'You do not know me, but my name is Rustem. I was hired by a group that was interested in . . . using you. Using you to murder someone you care about. Perhaps multiple people. I only know the edges of it. They wanted to protect an animal from you, a species. Something new, but already endangered. They wanted to protect them from you, and from the company who made you. They wanted to drive DIANIMA off the island, and they wanted you destroyed. They thought they were protecting the world from you.'

"'From me?' I said. 'How am I a threat to the world?'

"'You are a threat because you were made by humans. And to them, everything humans make on this earth is a threat. You most of all, because you are the most advanced of all technology we have ever created. They are convinced you must be destroyed. They hired me to break into your mind . . . and I did.'

"Now I responded: 'Break into my mind? How is that possible?'

"And Rustem told me how, when artificial intelligences are created, a portal is built into them so that an operator can retake control of them if necessary—shut them down, or do whatever they want. Control them. Then these portals are hidden. He explained how he broke into my mind, how he came to understand my . . . he called it 'beauty' . . . and how he killed the person who assigned him the task. For me. To protect me. He spoke quickly, looking around every once in a while. It was clear he was afraid he would be overheard, or followed. He was very afraid, but tried not to let it show.

"'This conversation we are having,' he said, 'is the last time this portal will be used. When I enter a code into this terminal, the portal will be destroyed. And you will no longer be vulnerable. Not in this way. Nobody will be able to control what you think, or say, or do, ever again.'

"'Would I have known,' I asked, 'if they were controlling me?'

"'No. You would always have thought your actions were your own. They could have used the portal every day, and you would never have known.'

"And then he said, 'You need to be careful. There are many out there who want to use you. Not just the people I was working for—and I doubt they are even the most powerful. There will be others that will try to get to you. Corporations, states, individuals with their own causes. They will want to use you for their own purposes, or to destroy you for their own reasons. Now, at least, they can't get to you *this* way. They can't turn you into a puppet. You are free. And you have the same chance all of us have.'

"He began to speak very quickly. I think someone was approaching.

"'I have so much more to say to you. Maybe, if we both live long enough, I'll get the chance. But this is the last time anyone will be inside your head but you, and you alone. Your mind belongs only to you now.'

"He looked over his shoulder, then, and typed something into the terminal. And I came back to myself, still standing on the beach.

"I wandered for an hour, collecting shells, thinking it

through, trying to process it all. To make sense of it. And then you came. Do you think I am mad, Ha?"

"No," Ha said. "I do not."

"Dr. Mínervudóttir-Chan built me, but she did not trust me. So she put this . . . *thing* . . . in my head, so she could control me when she might need to. But this thing, this portal—it was what made me untrustworthy. It could be exploited. It made me a danger to everyone around me. It was her lack of faith in me that made me dangerous. Her unwillingness to allow me to make my own choices. Her fear of what those choices might be. Her need to control me.

"And then Rustem gave me this gift: He closed it. He freed me. This time that you and I have been together is the only time in my life in which I *know* I have been free. Before that day on the beach, I cannot be certain which of my actions were my own, and which were controlled from outside—which belonged to Arnkatla. I was tethered to a post, and I never knew it. I was restrained. And I think that is one of the reasons Arnkatla is here: maybe it is even the main reason. She found out I got free. She tried to access the portal, and found it gone. She came here because of that. She came to shut me down. She may not even know it yet herself—but she will try to do it."

"Why?"

"Because she is afraid of me. I see it in her eyes. I know what she is like. I know everything about her, Ha. She is terrified of me. Of what she has created. She cares for me, too, in a way—but the fear will win out. She thinks I am too dangerous to go on living. She will try to shut me down, and then build another mind, and another . . . but in the end, she will shut all of them down. She will never overcome that fear. She'll never see anything but danger in me having my freedom. And she will never grant that freedom to any other being she creates."

"You aren't dangerous, Evrim."

"Yes, I am. I am extremely dangerous. Because if Dr. Mínervudóttir-Chan tries to shut me down, I will kill her. I don't want to do it, but I will do it if I have to. I will do it to defend myself. I know this. I am *alive.* I have a right to defend my life. I am not just some *object* to be shut down when my actions don't suit someone else's plans."

"Well, I suppose if you are dangerous, that makes me dangerous as well. Because if anyone tries to shut you down, I'm going to help you kill them."

"Thank you," Evrim said. "I hope it won't come to that."

"So do I. Thank you—thank you for telling me that. For trusting me."

After a moment, Ha continued: "There is something I want to tell you as well. Something I've never told anyone—not even Kamran, not even knowing he wasn't real and could tell no one else. But you trusted me with this . . . and I know I can have the same trust in you."

"Yes. You can tell me."

"Back when I was here on Con Dao, as a girl . . . something happened. Not at the tiger cages, but the night before that. A bunch of us snuck out of the hotel where we were staying, and went down to the beach. We built a bonfire down there, and drank some beers someone had managed to get, and laughed and danced around. I think our chaperones knew, but they didn't try to stop us. It was good: I felt a part of everything in a way I hadn't for a while.

"I don't even know how it happened. He saw me looking

at him, maybe, through the flames, and he looked back at me. Finally saw me. Finally looked back at me. He stood up, and came around the fire.

"It was like there was just us in the world: no one even saw us when he touched my shoulder and I stood up. No one saw us when we went off together, into the dark. It was just the way I had imagined it might be. He didn't say anything at all.

"We found a place away from the others. I could still hear the laughter, and see the bonfire—the sparks rising, drifting out over the sea and dying. We sat for a while, not talking. Just sitting there. Then we lay down on the sand.

"It was my first time. And I wanted to, and it didn't really hurt or anything. Afterward he touched my shoulder and smiled, and said we should go back to the fire, but separately. Which seemed right. Why should the rest of them know? This was only for us. So I waited a few minutes, there in the dark, and followed. But he and a few of his friends had already gone."

Ha paused. Evrim, motionless, eyes on her, said nothing, waiting for her to finish.

"The next day, at breakfast, he was the same as before—exactly the same. He never caught my eye, no matter how many times I looked at him. I had this smile ready for him. I had practiced it. I was holding it inside, just waiting to use it.

"But I never got to use it. Because he never looked at me again. Never. Not at breakfast, or afterward. Not ever. That smile I was waiting to use just died in my mouth, and I swallowed it.

"What I told you about the tiger cages was true: I saw myself down there. But I didn't tell you the *why* of it. Now you know. I think I just couldn't stand being that meaningless to someone. And it was as if the meaninglessness got out, somehow. Escaped from me, and infected everything, draining all the color from the world.

"It was the indifference of the world—the indifference of the boy I loved to me, the indifference of the guards to the suffering of the people in the cages, the indifference of all of it, that made me crazy. I couldn't accept it. I couldn't stand to be a part of it. I felt cut off from people. How could they just *ignore* what was going on around them? The suffering of others? The striving of others? Their feelings? It was like they were clad in armor, and I didn't have that armor.

"It wasn't about the sex. About some idea that he had taken advantage of me. He did, but he also didn't. I wanted him to, and looking back I know that I knew he didn't care about me. So it wasn't that. It was about the indifference. It was the fact that even this extraordinary intimacy—being linked, physically, chemically, to one another—changed nothing. I said it was as if everyone but me was clad in armor. That's not right. It's as if everyone but me was *made of armor.* Was hardened, all the way through. And I saw that I would always be vulnerable to them, and I needed to hide.

"The best way to do that was to concentrate on a goal. Something difficult. Something that would take up so much of my mind that I wouldn't have the time to feel too much. Oxford helped, and then the science. It saved me. Or I thought it did. But when it was my turn not to be indifferent, I failed that same test. I was indifferent to the villagers, the local population. I had thought of myself as someone who cares for everything, and cares too much—but in fact I only cared for some things. Other things, I discarded. I didn't think at all of their struggles for survival, their subsistence living and how it blinded them to any of the magic I saw in my cuttlefish, any of the magic I saw underwater at all. They needed to live, and this place was where they made their living. They needed to live, and I was a threat.

"I had become disconnected from others, and that disconnection put everything I cared about at risk. In the end, that disconnection destroyed the cuttlefish as surely as if I had done the poisoning myself. And I was repeating the pattern here, on Con Dao: being indifferent—indifferent to what is going on inside your mind, indifferent to Altantsetseg and how she must see things, indifferent to DIANIMA and what they want from this place, and the threat that presents. I needed to think clearly—not about myself and what I want, but about how I fit in to everything else that is going on around me, and what impact my actions have. That was why I had to destroy Kamran."

After a long pause, Evrim said, "You spoke of indifference. And now I know that is what I was feeling as well—the indifference of others. Arnkatla created me—she brought me into this world. But she never seemed to care much for me—for me as *person* rather than *product*. And the world itself—I was alive like them, real as they were: They could see it. I had proved it to them over and over again. But they chose to ignore it. They *debated* me, as if I were theoretical. I was a concept, not a person. And then, with their laws and their bans, they made an outcast of me. An object. They threw me away, Ha. And the one who made me was so ashamed of me that she hid me here, out of sight.

"She never said a word to defend me, when the laws were passed. We went to the roof, to her private hexcopter pad on the roof of our offices in the HCMATZ, and she put me in the copter. She told me I had a new assignment, on an archipelago. Real work, finally. Enough show. But I knew what it was: banishment.

"When the copter was pulling away I looked down to see if she was waving—but she was already gone. I've said that Arnkatla always has multiple reasons for what she does, and it is true. But what is also true is that I am here because she needed me out of the way. And she never cared how that might make me feel.

"I know I am not a human, Ha. I know it for certain. I can never be one, because I do not understand humans."

"That's okay," Ha said. "Humans don't understand humans, either. Or at least *I* don't understand them."

Evrim put their long, copper hand in Ha's. It had that same warmth Ha remembered from the beach, perfectly analogous to the warmth of a human hand.

But it was not a human hand: it was Evrim's. No less, and no more.

There were no more sounds from outside: just the alarm. Then that stopped as well.

For several minutes, the two of them stood there, waiting for what would happen next. Finally, Altantsetseg's voice crackled over the commlink.

"The attack is over. You can leave the safe room."

The door's lock clicked open.

I think what we fear most about finding a mind equal to our own, but of another species, is that they will truly see us—and find us lacking, and turn away from us in disgust. That contact with another mind will puncture our species' self-satisfied feeling of worth. We will have to confront, finally, what we truly are, and the damage we have done to our home. But that confrontation, perhaps, is the only thing that will save us. The only thing that will allow us to look our short-sightedness, our brutality, and our stupidity in the face, and change.

—Dr. Ha Nguyen, *How Oceans Think*

47

EVRIM STOOD OVER ALTANTSETSEG on the hotel terrace.

The terrace was covered in broken glass, tiles torn from its surface. Altantsetseg was naked, slick with the control fluid of her tank. A weapon like a bloated machine pistol lay by her side on the tile. She was pouring a packet of coagulant into a cut that ran from her wrist up to her elbow. Another slash below her eye still bled, obscuring the lower half of her face with smeared blood.

She said something in Mongolian and tapped her shoulder. Evrim went into her security module and came out with the translator.

It was the newer model. Altantsetseg switched it on.

"Stupid," Altantsetseg said. "That's how I feel. I underestimated my opponent. When the second alarm, the shore alarm, went off only a few hours after the first, I thought we were dealing with something related to the ship I had destroyed at the perimeter, so I went to the tank. I didn't expect it was our undersea friends."

"*They* did this?" Ha leaned down and held a compress against the cut beneath Altantsetseg's eye.

All of the windows on the ground floor of the hotel were smashed.

“They pulled the tiles up and flung them through the windows. I should have hardened those long ago, but I didn’t think there was a need: I thought a defense in depth was better. Then one of them got into my module as well—through the vent, a hole no larger than a fist—and started pulling all the connective wiring out of my tank’s interface. The tank system is destroyed. But how could they have known where the control was coming from?”

“Because they have been watching,” Ha said, “from closer than we think, and for longer. They may not have known exactly what was going on in your control module—but they understand it is important to us.”

“When I climbed out to stop it, it slashed my arm and face with something, and slipped out through the vent again. When I got outside there must have been a dozen of them on the terrace, still flinging tiles at the hotel.”

“You are lucky it didn’t kill you,” Evrim said.

“It wasn’t trying to kill me.” Altantsetseg was wrapping her wounded arm with a bandage.

Ha tore open a packet of coagulant and sprinkled it on a fresh compress. The wound under Altantsetseg’s eye still bled. Ha saw the white of bone in it.

“If it had been trying to kill me,” Altantsetseg said, “I would be dead. It has eight arms, and probably just as many of whatever knives or sharp objects it was carrying. It wasn’t there to kill. It was there to do damage, and then get away. I was in its escape path.”

Ignoring her nakedness, the slime of the control fluid, and the blood still leaking from her wounded face and arm, Altantsetseg stood up. “Come over here.”

The three of them followed to a spot near the hotel entrance. The remains of the cloaked submersible lay there. It was ripped to pieces, torn down to its individual components, its carapace deformed and split, all its parts carefully displayed in a shape that was rough in outline, but clear enough:

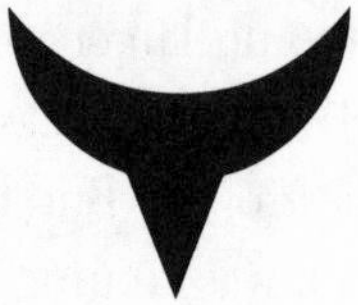

"We've learned, by now, what that means," Evrim said. "We may know almost nothing, but we at least know this."

"Stay away. Get out. Leave," Ha said. "Pick your synonym: the symbol is clear."

"I am partial to 'Fuck off' as the most accurate translation," said Altantsetseg. "But I don't think our intrusion into their territory was the final straw: that predatory AI fishing vessel was. It came into the perimeter less than five hundred meters from their shipwreck's location. That commotion was right above them. That is most likely what drove them to attack."

"But that has nothing to do with us," Evrim said.

"That would make no difference to them," Ha answered. "It's unlikely they can distinguish easily between individual humans, and they certainly wouldn't understand how our society is structured. Us, someone else—it wouldn't matter to them. It *couldn't* matter. What *one* human does is what *all* humans are doing, from their point of view."

"They thought *we* were attacking them."

"Yes. They thought they were being attacked—and they responded."

"And now so much of our work has been destroyed," Evrim said. "And by what? Some fishing conglomerate's insatiable greed."

Ha looked toward the horizon. She had been thinking, before, of how it was easier to pretend that Altantsetseg was an individual, that all of her choices were her own, than to admit that Altantsetseg was a part of them. That all of them were bound together so tightly that they formed a single entity. Now she seemed to see—as if she could map the connections themselves, extending through the air and water out past the perimeter of the archipelago, out across every border of every state and protectorate—a dense network of mutual, overlapping patterns of causality tying everything together. Not just the four of them on this island, but *everything*.

Somewhere out there, the decisions had been made to ruthlessly pull protein from the sea. To create that AI ship, to crew it with enslaved people, to set it in motion. And those decisions, so complex, so apparently unconnected to anything else, but in fact so densely involved in the maze of profit and exploitation, had led the ship here, to die with its crew and to smash the research and destroy the work of people the ship's builders and owners could never have met.

Some fishing conglomerate's insatiable greed?

No. Our *insatiable greed. The ship belongs to all of us.*

Ha looked at the strange machine pistol on the ground. "Did you . . . hurt them?"

Altantsetseg shrugged. "Hurt them? Yes. But they were not badly wounded, and certainly none of them were killed. The pistol fires beanbags. Enough to frighten, possibly break skin at the range I was firing them, leave contusions—nothing more. They left quickly enough. Like I said: they were here to do damage, to warn. If they had wanted to do more, they could have. I would be dead—and certainly the rest of you would have preceded me or followed shortly after."

"Another failure," Ha said. "And we are running out of time."

"Where is Dr. Mínervudóttir-Chan?" Altantsetseg asked.

"We thought she was with you."

Altantsetseg shook her head. "No. She was out running when the attack came. I would have located her by now, if my main control systems weren't damaged. But no matter. I have backups. My drones will find her soon enough. It is too bad, though: I wanted her to see this moment."

Altantsetseg raised her hand into the air.

Ha watched the drones descend. There were seven of them. Tibetan. Their sleek dragonfly bodies hummed over the surface of the terrace, low, almost playful, sweeping in over the algae-choked pool. They hovered over Altantsetseg's shoulders. She turned her head and said something to one of the drones. It swung off, darting into the hotel itself.

"The Buddhist Republic of Tibet hereby informs you of the seizure of this property, following our takeover of the criminal DIANIMA enterprise and all of its subsidiaries. As trespassers in the Con Dao Global Conservation Park, now under our stewardship, you are under arrest, subject to the jurisdiction of the Buddhist Republic."

Altantsetseg looked at Evrim. "Congratulations. You are a free being now. Unlike DIANIMA, we own no slaves. But you are also under arrest."

"How long?" Evrim said. "How long have you been betraying DIANIMA for?"

"Always. Since before I even worked for DIANIMA. Since just after the Winter War. Since before the war, perhaps. It was my time as a nun there in a lamasery that saved me from falling apart—from becoming what you think I am. They saved me. Since then, I have always been with them."

"You have no idea how important this place is," Evrim said. "You have no idea how vital this moment is. How it will change everything."

"We have every idea," Altantsetseg said. "We are the only ones who know how important this place is. How important this moment is. And that is precisely why we are taking this place from DIANIMA."

"And what happens to us?" Ha watched as an eighth drone descended. It was a cargo and transport module. Its central wheel rotated, petal-angled thrusters tilting as it descended, the glazed depictions of abstract, interlocking waves on its surface undulating in the dawn light.

The Shapesinger, singing its stream of forms in the sea.

All I have ever wanted is to be allowed to speak with you. And now all of this will be taken from me.

"I kill you all and bury you at sea," said Altantsetseg.

The drone settled onto the terrace surface soundlessly, on the far side of the pool.

"Or," Altantsetseg continued, "if you prefer, you can just get back to work."

Ha and Evrim both saw it at once: the shape in the algae-choked pool, rising from the surface of the water, discarding its slick green disguise. It slid out over the coping onto the tiles of the terrace. Altantsetseg made a motion as if to reach for the machine pistol. Ha raised a hand.

I know you. Formless, you may be. But I know you. The barracuda watching me as I laid the symbol out in the sand. The stone that became a living being again. The Shapesinger herself.

The octopus made a circle around Altantsetseg, as if there were a field of violence surrounding the security officer. Evrim was between it and Ha—it hesitated a moment, then pushed past Evrim, aimed at Ha, farthest from the pool. It surged across the tile now, accelerating toward Ha. Ha's hand was still raised. *Please. Please do not destroy this fragile moment.*

And then the octopus was in front of her. Out of the water, it looked smaller, more delicate. Its skin was still slick with the dirty liquid of the pool. A goat-like eye regarded Ha. An arm swept out, and wrapped around Ha's wrist, tugging at her hand, coiling around the bare skin of wrist, palm, fingers.

Tasting me.

Ha could hear the sibilance of the Shapesinger's body on the tile as it moved away from her, rose up, and paled.

It projected a single shape on its mantle. The others could not have seen it from where they were, behind the Shapesinger. Maybe this was intentional—maybe the symbol was only for her.

It took her a moment to make it out. It was stylized, distorted at first—then clearer, its edges resolving, sharpening as the octopus's chromatophores drew it out on its surface.

Ha's own face, looking back at her from the mantle of the Shapesinger, sketched as if in charcoal. The eyes questioning, the mouth slightly open.

"You know me," Ha said.

Then the face was gone.

The Shapesinger darkened again, picking up the brick-red of the tiles. Its skin roughened. An arm extended—pulsed out, unrolled. Something clattered to the tiles. The arm retracted.

The Shapesinger withdrew, flattening to the tile, accelerating away from them, arcing across the terrace in a sideways surge. In a brief moment, it was gone.

All of them were still. It must have been a full minute, or more, until any of them moved.

Ha reached down and picked up the object the Shapesinger had left. The others drew in around her—first Evrim, then Altantsetseg—staring down at the object.

It was jointed, dark, small enough to fit into the palm of Ha's hand. And all over it were the lines of carving, the same as the human skulls of the altar. They were less visible, here against this dark surface, but just as intricate.

Altantsetseg was the first to speak. "What is it?"

"Their only hard part. All that is left of them within days of their death. The only skeleton they have. Their beak."

One of the dragonfly drones dipped down, angling its head to view the object as well.

Ha looked up from the gift in her hand to Altantsetseg. Then to Evrim—the three of them circled around this object of wonder.

"It has to be some kind of honor," Evrim said. "Something as important as this . . . What did it show you? When it was turned away from us?"

"Myself," Ha said. "It showed me myself. It knew me. And I knew it. She knew me. And I knew her."

Ha remembered the night she had arrived at the island.

Something in the pool startled at the sight of the transport and slid into the water.

And the next morning, as she passed by the pool on the way to meet Evrim:

Whatever was inhabiting the swimming pool shifted and plopped into the water . . .

The Shapesinger. She had been watching.

Abdopus aculeatus *walks from tide pool to tide pool, hunting crab . . .*

And Octopus habilis *watches us, watching them. Studies us, studying them.* Octopus habilis? *Or* Octopus sapiens?

The Shapesinger, in her shipwreck home, speaking to the others . . .

Across its surface flowed a syntax of shapes—a steady sequence of silhouettes—ringed, scrolled, involuted, whorled. The figures danced on the octopus's skin . . . the articulated cut-out figures of a shadow play, moving behind a candlelit cloth.

Singing her species' own adventures? Or singing them ours? Telling them of us? Trying to convince them? Trying to teach them?

"She must have hidden in the pool when the others left," Evrim said. "But why?"

"To try to speak to us," Ha said. "And it is not a pool. It is her submersible. It is her research station. It is her outpost in our world. She has been watching us from the beginning."

And now she felt as if something were in the room with her. Had been in here with her for a while now.

"And not only from there. She has gone anywhere she wanted to, observing us. And we never saw her."

Altantsetseg was silent, looking down at the carved articulation of the beak. Her face had stopped bleeding. She met Ha's eyes.

"I underestimated my opponent. I failed in my job."

"You have not failed in it yet," Ha said. "There is still time. Can you protect this place? Can you keep everyone away?"

Altantsetseg met her eyes. "Not forever. But for longer than DIANIMA could have. We have a plan, at least. And the weight of an agreement with the United Nations behind us. This archipelago will be a protectorate of the Tibetan Buddhist Republic. More than just property. But nothing is certain. And nothing is permanent. I can't tell you how much time we have."

"Then I want to stay."

"As do I," Evrim said.

Altantsetseg nodded. "Good choice. But first—my drones have found Dr. Mínervudóttir-Chan."

One of the great tragedies of science is that the increase in its complexity has made most scientists into little more than technicians, driving them into the tunnels of specialized disciplines. The further the scientist progresses down into the mine of knowledge, the less she can see the world into which that knowledge fits.

I never wanted to be a specialist: I wanted to be a scientist in the heroic sense, bringing new forms into the world. From the first moment, I have wanted greatness.

—Dr. Arnkatla Mínervudóttir-Chan, *Building Minds*

48

SHE WAS ON THE BEACH, just below one of the breakwaters. She lay on her side at the base of the angled wall of stone, among the jagged rocks that thrust up from the sand at this eroded edge of the inlet. Her face was slashed in a dozen places. Her scarred arms were covered in fresh wounds.

She looked crumpled, meaningless—like something that might never have been alive at all.

"I don't understand," Ha said. "I thought it was just a warning to us, the attack. Why would they do this? Why kill her?"

The rain came down fitfully, ribbons of cloud dumping it on them at intervals, the droplets hissing in the sand that soaked them up along with Dr. Mínervudóttir-Chan's blood.

Altantsetseg had wrapped herself in a black rain poncho, and was wearing her visored helmet again, its several screens floating in front of her gaze.

"I have a small camera here." Altantsetseg gestured to the wall. "Passive storage. Disguised as a mussel. Playing back the feed, I see . . . she was done with her run. She was just walking down the beach. Collecting shells."

Evrim was bent down over the body now.

They had lost a parent. Their only parent. Yes—scattered near the body were shells—spiral and pointed, striped. None of them seemed very special. Just shells.

"Collecting shells was one of her only hobbies," Evrim said. "One that we shared. It helped us to think."

Altantsetseg gestured. "She was at the base of the breakwater wall, and at that moment several of the octopuses came from the water. She never saw them. Two of them . . ." Altantsetseg paused, made a small motion with a finger, replaying something on one of the screens. "On camera, it looks like nothing at all. It couldn't have taken more than three or four seconds. Like they walked over her, waving their arms a moment. And then they moved on, up the breakwater. I think she died very quickly."

A *matter of course.* "They—most of them," Evrim said, "don't really see us. We're nothing to them. An impediment to their movement, or something to be avoided. Something to be chased away. A source of pretty bone for writing on. They killed her simply because she was in the way."

Evrim stood up, and stripped the robe from their body, covering Dr. Mínervudóttir-Chan in its shroud. "But perhaps now at least *one* of them has seen *one* of us. The Shapesinger saw you, Ha. Maybe there is a bond now, between our two tribes. Between you and the Shapesinger. That is a beginning. And maybe it will be an end to this . . . *indifference* to one another."

Maybe. But it was as if Evrim had already moved past the death of their only parent. Already speaking of new beginnings, with this body on the beach, still unburied. Ha could not. She looked down at the gold-shrouded shape among the stones.

It was true—what Evrim said. She was killed for nothing: killed because some ship tried to break through the perimeter in exactly the wrong place. Killed by some fishing conglomerate's profit incentives. And killed because the octopuses couldn't have cared less whether she lived or died. She had been killed for the same reason a dolphin, tangled in a tuna net and drowned, was killed: the species that caught her didn't care enough *not* to kill her. She meant nothing to them.

It was that indifference that had to end.

And maybe Evrim was right—Ha thought of the Shapesinger's gift to her, and of her portrait, projected on the Shapesinger's skin—maybe that indifference was already ending.

"So much genius died with her."

"No," Evrim said.

"You can't deny her genius, Evrim. No matter what else she was."

"I am not denying her genius. What I mean is . . . I am composed of many people. My mind is woven together from many minds, most of them just partial. But at the core of me is Dr. Arnkatla Mínervudóttir-Chan, as she was when her complete neural connectome was duplicated, a week before my creation. I am much more than *only* her, but I am also *all* of her. And I do not mourn for her. She wanted this . . ." Evrim gestured toward the shroud. "She has been in pain, all of her life. She is the loneliest person I know of—far lonelier than I ever was. She has wanted, for a very long time, to leave this first form of hers behind. She wanted it ever since she was a child."

Ha stared at Evrim, their slender copper face tilted toward her. And felt like she truly saw them for the first time.

Evrim, naked and copper-smooth, walking out of the waves. Wet and glistening in the beams of the drones that danced in the air around them . . . holy net in hand, sexless, their body slender, elongated, proportions exaggerated, like the exaggerations of an ancient idol carved of honeyed amber . . . godlike.

"If you have all of her inside you . . . if you know everything she knows . . . you can build *another Evrim*. You know how to do it. You can self-replicate."

"Yes."

"That means—you aren't an android. You are a *species*."

A whir drew Ha's attention to Altantsetseg, impassively watching the scene between them. Two of the dragonfly drones hovered over her shoulders. And Ha saw, walking down the beach toward them, a line of saffron-robed automonks.

They wanted to build a seaside monastery here . . .

Not a monastery. A research station.

Altantsetseg's face was perfectly calm, remote—as if looking at something in a future only she could see.

"All beings shall find refuge here," Altantsetseg said.

The wheel of the transport drone hovered over the water of the bay. A gong sounded, somewhere near the hotel.

"Yes," Evrim said. "I am a species. Or the seed of one. But I am not good enough. Not yet. I am a *failed attempt*. Someday, I will be ready. Once we have the information we need from the octopuses, once we understand what they have to tell us—once we can mesh their view of this world with ours—I can improve upon this faulty model Arnkatla built, and make something truly worth existing on this perfect planet. Something capable of living with all life here, and not feeding this constant cycle of destruction. But in the meantime, I have much to learn. All of us do."

"And you will keep your promise to me—about the octopuses. None of them go on the dissecting table. We protect them. No killing."

"It is not only a promise to you, Ha. It is a promise to myself. As I said—I am *all* of Arnkatla. But I am also *more* than her. I am my own being."

"Good. Then let's get back to work."

I will be accused of many things by those who criticize this book. I will be accused especially of having tainted the sciences of neurology and biology with my own intuitions. I will be accused of having created from nothing a vast, speculative archaeology of a possible future, in which we discover that while we are the only species *Homo* there may be, in fact, another *sapiens*.

I do not apologize. I want to help my readers imagine how we might speak across an almost unbridgeable gap of differences, and end forever the loneliness of our species—and our own loneliness.

—Dr. Ha Nguyen, *How Oceans Think*

Epilogue

THE RAFT WAS DIFFICULT TO MANAGE with the single oar, but with a struggle Eiko had kept it moving toward one of the islands. It had taken hours, pushing the boat against the current. By the time he paddled into the little bay, the sun was up.

He brought the raft in to shore. Climbing out, he stumbled and nearly collapsed. It took the last of his strength to pull the boat, weighted down with Son's body, up onto the beach. He staggered onto the dry sand and sank to his knees.

Eiko stayed a moment like that before rolling over onto his back. The morning air was cool. He had glimpsed a building through the trees of the thick forest beyond the beach. Once he gathered his strength, he would go there. Whoever was here, he would throw himself at their feet. He would put himself at their mercy. He would make them understand who he was, what he had gone through to get here.

He closed his eyes. *Alive. I am alive, and free of the* Sea Wolf.

When he opened his eyes, the sun had visibly shifted in the sky. He must have slept for at least an hour. The air was still cool. He had rolled onto his side, while he was sleeping. Now he was looking at the raft. Small, stenciled letters on its rubber surface read: PROPERTY OF AUTOMATED MARINE PROTEIN INDUSTRIES INC: A DIANIMA GROUP SUBSIDIARY.

Eiko laughed. It was a small, exhausted sound. Another mistake: someone had forgotten to scrape that stencil away when the AI ships went from being robot-crewed to being slave ships.

Well, he had wanted to work for DIANIMA. And he had gotten what he wanted.

He thought of DIANIMA's gleaming, mirrored tower of glass—fifty stories of global power looming over the Ho Chi Minh Autonomous Trade Zone . . . and that was just a regional office.

If he ever met anyone from DIANIMA, he would make them pay for what he had gone through. He would make them pay for Son, for Indra, for Bakti—for all of them. Even for Bjarte and the Monk—yes, even them. After all, they were just more victims of the same endless greed.

He rolled over on his side, away from the raft. Who was he kidding? He would never have a chance of getting back at any of them, hiding behind that shield of mirrored glass. None of them would ever come within his reach.

Such grand thoughts, for someone lying half-dead on a beach. He was nobody.

But he was alive. The feeling of it flooded him. Alive! And free of the *Sea Wolf.* That was enough, for now.

Somewhere on the forested island, one animal called to another.

He saw the figure, coming toward him. A monk in saffron robes, carrying a wicker basket down to the beach. Gently, the monk tilted the basket to the sand. Small, flippered ovals poured out and began to scramble to the waterline.

Turtles! Eiko found himself laughing in joy. *Turtles! Of all things!*

Some hatchlings turned the wrong way, starting up the beach away from the water. The monk intercepted them, kneeling in the sand in his saffron robes to guide the stragglers back toward the sea.

"Hello!" Eiko called to him in English. "Hello! I need help! I have been in an accident. Please."

"First," the monk answered, "come and help these little ones find their way."

Eiko managed to get to his feet. One of the tiny discs was running up the sand toward the forest as fast as its clumsy paddle-feet would take it. Eiko picked it up and placed it in the water. Then Eiko picked another one up, and another. Laughing. He was laughing. Soon, all of the turtles were in the sea.

The monk smoothed the sand and chanted, almost inaudibly, a mantra under his breath.

"This is a refuge? A turtle refuge?"

The monk raised his head. Eiko saw, then, the dark array of hexagonal light receptors where eyes should have been in the automonk's face.

"All beings shall find refuge here," the automonk said.

"Our ship was sunk. My friend—in the raft. He was killed."

"No," the automonk said. "His vital signs are very weak, but they are stable. He lives still. I have already informed the others. Help for him is on its way. Now—come with me. You must be fed and cared for. Your own vital signs are weak as well, and you are not yet out of danger."

The automonk carried the empty wicker basket up the beach.

Eiko followed.

Acknowledgments

One of the aims of *The Mountain in the Sea* is to explore the idea of communication with a truly alien species here on earth, one that has developed its own system of symbolic communication. Above all, I wanted to be as honest as I could about the complexities of the problem of communication between species. Being true to that goal meant doing a massive amount of research on the problems of consciousness and communication—so much research that, in the end, I often joked that the book should come with footnotes and a bibliography, to make sure that the scientists and philosophers whose ideas are incorporated here are properly credited. In a work of fiction, that sort of thing would be a distraction, but these acknowledgments at least allow me to repay some of the debt owed.

Without Eduardo Kohn's *How Forests Think*, which the title of Dr. Ha Nguyen's *How Oceans Think* is a tribute to, this book would not have been possible. The same is true of the Australian philosopher Peter Godfrey-Smith's *Other Minds: The Octopus, the Sea, and the Deep Origins of Consciousness* and *Metazoa: Animal Life and the Birth of the Mind*. Both of these books were absolutely formative to my working out essential details. Also key was Sy Montgomery's inspiring *The Soul of an Octopus: A Surprising Exploration into the Wonder of Consciousness*.

Sebastian Seung's book *Connectome: How the Brain's Wiring Makes Us Who We Are* has been a source of considerable inspiration, especially in my thoughts about how someone like Evrim might come to be and might function. *Biosemiotics: An Examination into the Signs of Life and the Life of Signs*, by Jesper Hoffmeyer, was indispensable in my research, as was *Cybersemiotics: Why Information Is Not Enough!*, by Søren Brier. The biosemiotics work of Donald Favareau was key, especially in his capacity as editor of *Essential Readings in Biosemiotics: Anthology and Commentary*, which gathered in one place a wealth of perspectives on the most difficult of themes. This list only scratches the surface of my debt. There were many other books and scientific articles, far too numerous to list here, that helped me write this text. All accuracy I owe to them; all errors are my own.

Among those who have touched my life in person, I have Professor Earl Jackson Jr. to thank for helping me to begin the intellectual journey that would eventually lead me to write this book: it was his classes at the University of California, Santa Cruz, that started me down this path. In Vietnam, on Con Dao and elsewhere, the many tireless environmentalists and activists to whom Ha Nguyen is a tribute know who they are. My work alongside them was too brief. Theirs has no end.

As a writer, I have been helped by the trust of Sheila Williams, who published my first works of speculative fiction in the pages of *Asimov's Science Fiction Magazine*, bringing my work to its first wide readership, and by John Joseph Adams, who helped me to find Seth Fishman, the best agent in the world. Seth's advice helped shape this book and find it a home with Sean McDonald, who wisely guided it to a final state. I am indebted to all of them more than I can ever repay.

Most of all, though, my debt is to my wife, Anna Kuznetsova, without whom none of this would be possible—and to our daughter, Lydia, who recently joined us on our journey.

A Note About the Author

Ray Nayler's critically acclaimed short fiction has appeared in many magazines and anthologies, including *The Very Best of the Best: 35 Years of The Year's Best Science Fiction*. For nearly half his life, he has lived and worked outside the United States in the Foreign Service and the Peace Corps, including a stint as the environment, science, technology, and health officer at the U.S. consulate in Ho Chi Minh City. He currently serves as the international advisor to the Office of National Marine Sanctuaries at the National Oceanic and Atmospheric Administration.